HYPERBO

Book four of the Veteran of Rome series

By: William Kelso

Visit the author's website **http://www.williamkelso.co.uk/**

William Kelso is the author of:

The Shield of Rome

The Fortune of Carthage

Devotio: The House of Mus

Caledonia – Book One of the Veteran of Rome Series

Hibernia – Book Two of the Veteran of Rome series

Britannia – Book Three of the Veteran of Rome series

Hyperborea – Book Four of the Veteran of Rome series

Germania – Book Five of the Veteran of Rome series

The Dacian War – Book Six of the Veteran of Rome series

Armenia Capta – Book Seven of the Veteran of Rome series

Hyperborea – Veteran of Rome Series

Published in 2016 by FeedARead.com Publishing – Arts Council funded

A CIP catalogue record for this title is available from the British Library.

To: Dimphy and Nick

Chapter One - Homecoming

December AD 103

The snowflakes blanketed the road and the surrounding forest in a whirling white shroud, reducing visibility to a dozen yards. It was dawn but in the dull, grey and bleak sky the sun's light struggled to break through to the frozen earth. Marcus strode on along the forest track, his head bowed into the bitter, moaning wind that was trying to drive him back to the warm tavern he'd just left in Noviomagus Reginorum, Chichester. His long black, Dacian, fur, winter-cloak was covered with snow and a hood was pulled over his head and snow flecks clung to his grey beard. A Gladius, his father's old short sword, hung from his army belt. In his right hand he clutched a spear and with the two remaining fingers on his left hand, he fiddled tensely with the small bronze phallic amulet, that hung from a cord around his neck. A leather pack was slung over his shoulder. He'd not seen a soul since leaving town and around him the forest was deserted. Warily he lifted his head and peered into the thick whirling snow-fall ahead. If he hurried, and the boat's man was where the tavern owner said he would be, he would be able to make the family farm at Brading on the Isle of Vectis by nightfall.

He grunted and muttered something under his breath. His long journey, all the way from the Dacian frontier, was at last coming to an end. Fourteen hundred miles he had walked and ridden, through vast deserted forests, over desolate, lonely mountains and along heavily guarded and populated rivers and finally across the treacherous sea to the port of Londinium. It had taken him three months. But tonight he would finally be home, under the same roof as his family; Kyna, his beautiful Brigantian wife, Fergus his son, Dylis his little sister, Efa his mother and old Quintus and be just in time to celebrate the Saturnalia festivities. It had been seven years since he'd seen any of them. Seven years! He tried to picture Kyna's face. It had been too long, he thought. Fergus would be seventeen, he would be a man. Tensely he squeezed the phallic amulet around his neck and lowered his eyes. The thought of seeing his family again after such a long time should have filled him with joy and excitement, but instead, an unsettled feeling stirred in the pit of his stomach. What would he find at the farm? It had been eighteen months since the last letter from his wife had reached him and anything could have happened since then. They could all be dead. They could have moved away. Disaster came in many forms and life was short and often brutal. He should know. And perhaps they would not welcome him home? He had been away for a long time. He had not been faithful to his wife since the 2nd Batavian Cohort had been transferred to the Danube frontier, to take part in Emperor Trajan's war of conquest against the Dacians. No, there was no way of knowing what awaited him on Vectis.

He trudged on down the deserted, forest track. His heavy, army boots sent the snow blowing away at his feet. At forty, he should have had two or three more years to serve before he would retire from the army, but the wound to his hand, sustained in a skirmish with Dacian cavalry, had forced him into early honourable-discharge and retirement from the 2nd Batavian Cohort. With a solid army record, the Roman authorities had provided him with a full army pension, paid in newly liberated Dacian gold and a bronze diploma granting him full Roman citizenship. His comrades had thrown him a final, wild and drunken farewell party, after which he had been out; a civilian again after twenty-three years service. No, he shook his head, as he peered into the thick, swirling snowfall, not a civilian, a veteran of Rome, just like his father Corbulo had once been. He was a veteran of Rome and serving in the army was by far the best and finest thing he had ever done. He may not have been much of a husband and a father, but no one could say that he had been a bad soldier. No one would ever take away the pride he felt in serving in the 2nd Batavian Cohort.

In the forest to his right he heard a sudden loud crack and instantly he turned in the direction of the noise and raised the point of his spear towards the trees. What was this? Warily he peered into the snow flurries that whirled around the dark tree trunks and leafless branches, but he could see nothing out of the ordinary. Nothing moved. It must have been a branch breaking in the cold. For a long moment his eyes lingered. Then just as he was about to resume his journey he heard it again, another loud crack and this time he saw a furtive movement in amongst the trees. Instinctively he went into a crouch, his good hand clutching his spear ready to impale any attacker who came at him.

"Show yourself," Marcus roared as he stared into the forest, "I know you are out there. What do you want?"

There was no reply from forest. Then as the silence lengthened, Marcus grunted as a figure detached itself from behind a tree, ten paces away. The figure was cloaked and hooded and he could not see the person's face, but from his size Marcus guessed he was a man. But instead of coming towards him, the figure stayed where he was, staring straight at Marcus, his cloak and hood covered in snow.

Marcus growled irritably as he stood his ground. The man wanted him to see him. He was making no effort to hide. No man with legitimate business would be out in this weather. What was he doing out here in the forest? As he stared at the figure Marcus growled again. Did the stranger know that he was carrying his entire army pension in gold with him? The money was worth a small fortune. Had someone in Londinium or the taverns he stayed in, guessed he was a retired veteran on his way home and had they decided to rob him? It had been a worry he'd had to cope with ever since he'd left the protection of 2nd Batavian's camp. In Pannonia it had not been uncommon for a soldier's enemies to tip off the local gangs when a retired soldier was about to set off for home, laden down with his army pension. Marcus wrenched his eyes from the figure and quickly and carefully glanced around him. The man might not be alone. Only a fool would have come alone.

Amongst the trees the stranger did not move. Instead, he seemed to be looking straight at him. Marcus bit his lip. He could attack, charge straight into the forest, but somehow he knew the man would simply vanish into the gusts of whirling snow. In this visibility it would be impossible to find anyone. The silent standoff lengthened and Marcus felt his patience start to run out. If the stranger was indeed here to rob him of his army pension then what was he waiting for?

"Oh fuck off," Marcus cried out with sudden disgust. Then contemptuously he turned away and started on down the forest track and within moments, the figure in the forest was lost amongst the swirling snowflakes.

***

The old grumpy boat-man had at last fallen silent as he slowly dipped the oars into the water and propelled the small, open currach down the narrow channel that led towards the sea. Around them the marshes were frozen and covered in a thick blanket of snow and amongst the myriad of inland waterways, creeks and small islands, nothing moved. There was just enough space for the two of them to fit into the boat. Marcus ran his finger along the animal-hide bound hull as he stared southwards. The straights that separated the Isle of Vectis from the mainland were only a few miles wide and he could just about make out the grey, low lying coastline in the distance. It was noon and the snow fall had finally petered out but in the sky the dull clouds had not gone away.

Marcus sighed as the sight of the island brought on a sudden rush of memories. It had been Corbulo, his father, who had first brought his family to Vectis. Agricola, ex Governor of Britannia, had owned a farm on the island at Brading and, as the family's patron, he'd instructed Corbulo to make it prosper, which his father had accomplished. Marcus muttered a short silent prayer as he peered across the straights at Vectis, unable to look away. Corbulo had been dead for fourteen years now and Agricola for nine, but upon learning of Corbulo's death, Agricola had immediately given the farm and its land to Marcus. It was a noble and generous act Marcus thought, for Agricola had not been short of loyal and land-hungry clients. But there had been some kind of special bond between his father and Agricola. A friendship and respect that had extended to Marcus too. His elevation to second in command of the 2nd Batavian auxiliary cohort, and his subsequent rehabilitation into the Cohort after his court martial for disobeying orders in the fort at Luguvalium, during the Brigantian uprising, had been solely down to the influence that Agricola had brought to bear on the military authorities.

Moodily Marcus scratched his beard and stared out across the sea, as the small currach left the narrow waterway behind and entered the straights. The power of the sea immediately made itself felt and the small flimsy craft was soon being buffeted and thrown around by one remorseless wave after another. Marcus however, hardly noticed the swell or the freezing cold seawater that slapped over the side of the hull. His thoughts were suddenly faraway, back at the auxiliary fort in Luguvalium, Carlisle, fourteen years ago. Those had been his glory days. During the Brigantian uprising, in the eighth year of the reign of Emperor Domitian, he'd disobeyed a direct order from his commanding officer, Cotta, but his actions that day had saved the entire cohort from annihilation and he'd gone on to command the unit. He had led his men into battle and he had accomplished much. But the army had not forgotten his disobedience and once the uprising had been crushed he'd been hauled in front of a court martial. The legate of the Twentieth had demanded the death penalty but through Agricola's tireless work and influence behind the scenes, he'd been overruled and instead of execution, Marcus had been demoted and allowed to rejoin the 2nd Batavians as a simple trooper, a rank he would retain for the rest of his career. The Roman officers had never again allowed him to command men, but it had not bothered him. The Batavian rank and file, to a man, had known who he was and how he had saved the entire cohort and their loyalty, friendship and respect had meant far more to him than the early termination of his career.

A wave slapped into the side of the boat, soaking him in freezing sea-water and as he wiped his face he sighed and his expression grew pained. His war against the rebels in the north of Britannia had come to an abrupt end when his friend and second in command Lucius, had betrayed him. He'd never received an explanation or the closure of looking down at the man's corpse because, before the end of the uprising, Lucius had deserted and vanished. There had been no word or sighting of Lucius in over thirteen years and Marcus had long ago given up hope of ever confronting his former friend.

A sudden movement on the shore caused him to look back, and as he did so, his eyes narrowed. Standing on the shore, some thirty or forty paces away, with his arms folded across his chest, was the hooded man he'd seen in the forest. The figure was staring straight at him and as he peered back at the man, Marcus felt a sudden tremor of unease run down his spine, as if he had just witnessed something unnatural. Who was following him? What did this stranger want from him?

"See that man on the shore?" Marcus growled, turning to the boat-man, "do you know him. Have you seen him before?"

The boat-man tilted his head so that he could see past Marcus. For a moment he studied the distant figure on the shore. Then he shook his head disinterestedly and grunted something that Marcus did not catch. As the boat steadily pulled away Marcus frowned and stared at the stranger. On the shore the silent man did not move.

Wrenching his eyes from the shoreline, Marcus turned to the boat-man. "I will pay you an extra copper coin if you do not ferry that man across the water after you have dropped me on the island," he exclaimed. The old boat's man looked up and one of eyes twitched. "Two coppers," he grunted, "a man like you can afford two coins and I have children to feed."

"Done," Marcus snapped.

***

Stiffly, Marcus heaved himself over the side of the currach and splashed into the surf. He gasped at the brutally cold seawater, as it lapped around his legs. Then he slung his pack over his shoulder, lifted up his spear, and nodded a farewell to the boat-man. The ferryman however did not return the gesture and Marcus turned away to look at the sandy beach, that stretched away along the shore. There was no one about, not a single soul or animal. Further inland the treeless and gently-rolling farmland lay covered in snow and a few miles to the west, along the shoreline, a river mouth emptied into the sea. He was home. For a brief moment he allowed himself a smile. He was home at last. Slowly he waded through the surf and up onto the beach and as he reached dry land, he stooped and with his right hand he scooped up a handful of sand. Studying the earth, he slowly allowed the grains to slip through his fingers. Then abruptly he looked up in the direction of his farm. Another few miles and he would be there. He could scarcely believe it.

He sighed as he stared out across the deserted, white landscape. What sort of welcome awaited him? Kyna had not wanted to leave Britannia when he'd told her the 2nd Batavians were being transferred to Pannonia. She had not wanted to leave her native land and he had decided not to force her and Fergus to go with him. He was not going to make the same mistake, that Corbulo, his father had made when he'd tried to force Marcus's mother to come with him to Italy. Instead he had brought Kyna and Fergus to Vectis, where he'd told them that they would share their home with Efa, Dylis and old Quintus. It was a sensible, practical solution for the whole family would be together, and it seemed to have worked. He may have put his army service before Kyna and Fergus, he may not have been faithful to Kyna, but he had tried to do the right thing for them. He had sent her money whenever he could and now that his army career was over, he was going home to keep a promise he had made to her long ago. He was going home to marry her and make Fergus his legitimate son, for the army forbade its soldiers from officially marrying until their discharge. But now that he was a full Roman citizen, he had the right to officially marry Kyna and by all the gods, above and below, that was what he was going to do. He was not going to treat his woman and son like his father, Corbulo had treated his, upon his retirement. He had never beaten Fergus, not once, nor had he ever laid a hand on Kyna. No, he was not the man, his father had once been, before he'd sought redemption.

The fields were deserted but in the distance, beyond a small dark wood, Marcus could see smoke curling up into the sky and he caught the faint whiff of burning pine wood. As he trudged on down the rutted country lane, he glanced around at the deserted, snow-covered fields but the land seemed alien and unfamiliar. At the borders of the fields, thin lines of trees and tangled brambles and bushes divided the land into endless patches, squares and rectangles. It was getting dark and the temperature was dropping.

As he approached his farm, he came to an abrupt halt and gasped in astonishment at how the simple farm he'd known had changed. The small original wood, daub, wattle and thatched roofed Briton farmhouse, that he had remembered from many years ago, was completely gone and in its place, a brand new, modern, stone and concrete Roman villa, with neat red roof-tiles occupied three sides of an enclosed courtyard. Snow covered part of the roof and the villa seemed to be divided into three sections, of which the western section contained the main house and the southern, an assembly of agricultural buildings, granaries and storerooms. Smoke was rising from a hole in the roof and drifting away to the east. Everything had changed he thought, as he marvelled at the fine construction that surrounded him. Who had done this? Who'd had the vision to create this beautiful villa? Where had they found the money to do this?

As he stared at his villa he caught sight of movement in the large snow-drifts that lined the rutted, frozen country track. There, just beyond the wooden fence demarking his property, a child was playing in the snow. The boy looked around five and he was building a snow man. Marcus frowned as he drew closer and as the child caught sight of Marcus, the little boy paused, staring at him with a mixture of childish curiosity and alarm.

"Boy," he called out in Latin when he was just a half a dozen paces away, "What are you doing out here at this hour. Where are your mother and father?"

The child did not reply at first. For a long moment the boy simply stared at Marcus. Then slowly and proudly he jutted his chin at Marcus.

"My mother is at home," the boy replied in a high pitched childish voice staring at Marcus, "and my father is a soldier. He's not here. He is a very important man in the 2nd Batavian Auxiliary Cohort. He's fighting in the province of Dacia, but my mother says he will come home one day."

Chapter Two – Family

Marcus strode into the courtyard of his farm as the little boy raced ahead of him, calling out to his mother in an excited voice. There was a dark, angry look on Marcus's face. Who was this boy? There had been no such child on his farm when he'd left all those years ago. What the hell was going on? At the boy's cries, two women, clad in long, brown winter cloaks and warm, fur hoods, had appeared in the main doorway to the villa. They were about to reply to the boy when they caught sight of Marcus. Both women stopped in alarm and one of them gasped and raised a hand to her mouth. Marcus too, came to a halt. The courtyard fell silent and at the older woman's side, the boy clutched her hand and turned to stare at Marcus, standing alone, out in the courtyard with the snowflakes falling around him.

"Kyna," Marcus called out, "Is that you?"

The older woman clutching the boy's hand seemed to flinch, as if something had struck her. She looked about thirty-five.

"Marcus," she gasped the shock visible on her face. "You're back."

Marcus did not move as he stared at his wife. On his long journey from the Dacian frontier he'd often thought about what he would do and say to Kyna when he saw her again, but now standing here before her, it was as if he could not speak. Something was holding him back.

Suddenly the younger woman, standing beside his wife cried out and rushed towards him and before he could stop her, she had flung her arms around him. The woman was shaking and there was real warmth in her greeting. As he gently freed himself from her embrace, he looked down at her attractive face. The woman looked in her mid-twenties and there were tears in her eyes.

"Dylis," Marcus stammered, his anger fading, "Sister?"

She nodded, unable to speak and pressed her head against his chest. Marcus wrapped his arm around his younger sister. Of course Dylis had grown up. She was a woman now. He shouldn't have been surprised, but part of him could not forget the young, half wild girl he'd known, who'd refused to be intimidated by their age gap; the girl who'd refused to speak for a month after witnessing her father's death.

"Little sister, it is so good to see you," Marcus said, as he tightened his grip. Across the courtyard at the entrance into the villa, Kyna stood rooted to the ground with the boy clutching her hand and as he stared at his wife, Marcus suddenly knew something had come between them, an invisible yet formidable barrier. He frowned as he tried to understand. Kyna's lower lip was trembling as she stared at him, but she made no effort to come towards him and greet him.

"Who is the boy? Is he your son?" Marcus called out to Kyna, gesturing at the boy.

Kyna did not reply but as he spoke, Dylis broke away from his close embrace and for a brief moment, a look seemed to pass between the two women.

"The boy is called Ahern," Dylis said smoothly, turning to Marcus as she wiped the tears from her cheeks, "and he is my son. I am married now, brother, I have a husband, he is called Jowan. He is a good man and I have four children. They are all healthy and well. We are happy. So much has happened. You have been gone for such a long time."

Marcus was still staring at his wife. There was something unconvincing about the whole scene.

In the doorway Kyna hurriedly bent down to the boy and gave him a little push.

"Go to your mother, Ahern," she said, her face pale, her lower lip trembling.

Confused, the boy looked up at her but, just as he was about to speak, Dylis called out to him and with a silent, resigned and confused look, the boy ambled over to her. Without another word Kyna, came towards Marcus and embraced him.

"Welcome home, husband," she gasped, "We have waited a long time. I was not sure that you would be coming back, but you have, thank the gods."

Marcus said nothing as Dylis and Kyna embraced him burying their faces into his snow covered Dacian cloak and for a long moment the courtyard was silent.

"Is everything alright Dylis? I heard the boy shouting," a man's voice suddenly broke the silence. Marcus turned and saw a short, stout man in his twenties, clad in a rugged fur cloak and clutching a pickaxe, standing a few yards away. The man's long hair was tied back into a ponytail and he eyed Marcus with concern.

Hurriedly Dylis broke free again from Marcus's embrace.

"Jowan, something great has happened!" she cried as she struggled to contain more tears from streaking down her cheeks. "Marcus, my brother has returned. He has come home."

Jowan straightened up as if someone had bitten him in the arse. For a moment he stared at Marcus and his face went pale. Then he swallowed and dipped his head respectfully at Marcus.

"Welcome home Sir," he said in a sincere voice, "I have done my best to look after your villa and lands. We have made some improvements and added some new buildings. You will find the estate in good shape, Sir."

Marcus nodded. "And you have married my sister," he replied.

"I have," Jowan said meeting Marcus's gaze, "She is a good woman Sir and I treat her with the respect she deserves."

Jowan swallowed nervously, but he stood his ground. "I may not be a Roman citizen Sir, but I come from good freeborn stock. My father served Lord Agricola as an interpreter and scout."

"I chose him, Marcus," Dylis said turning to Marcus as her eyes sparkled with emotion, "I chose my man freely, just like father once promised me I would."

Marcus nodded again. "This is good news," he muttered, "This is better news than I could have hoped for," and turning to Jowan, he inclined his head in silent acknowledgement.

"Marcus!" a woman's sharp voice suddenly cried out in joy.

Marcus turned and saw a woman standing in the doorway to the villa. She was old, in her late forties and her hair was completely white. She stood, arm in arm with an even older man with grey thinning hair and a vacant look.

"Efa," Marcus called out as a little colour shot into his cheeks. Marching past Dylis and Kyna, he strode towards her and kissed her on both cheeks. Affectionately Efa smiled and ran her fingers across his cheek, as if she was making sure it was really him. She had aged hugely since Marcus had last seen her, but here eyes were still bright and alert.

"It is so good to have you back with us," Efa said shaking her head in wonderment, as she examined him carefully. "The years have come and gone but not a day has passed when I did not pray that you would return to us. And now you have. The gods have answered; they have granted me my wish. Your father, Corbulo would be so happy to see us all here together now."

Marcus smiled sadly as he grasped her hand.

"I know he would," he muttered, "His spirit watches us even now. We shall make him proud of who we are."

"He already is," Efa's eyes moistened but she retained her composure.

Marcus glanced at the elderly man standing beside Efa. The man had ignored Marcus completely and was staring at something across the snow covered courtyard. He looked to be in his sixties and his left arm kept shaking and a small wooden cross dangled on a cord around his neck.

"Don't you recognise Quintus, ex-centurion of the Twentieth Legion and your father's friend," Efa said with a sad smile.

Marcus gasped as he stared at Quintus but the old warrior seemed oblivious to his presence.

"What's the matter with him?" he said turning to Efa.

Efa shrugged as she tightened her grip protectively on Quintus's arm.

"He is old, he is not the man he used to be," she replied. "He has forgotten many things and he doesn't recognise anyone anymore and when I tell him who I am, he will forget again." Efa sighed, "But he was your father's friend and he was with Corbulo that day when your father came to set me and Dylis free from that awful Caledonian crannog, so this is his home as much as it is mine. We shall look after him until the day he dies, but don't expect any meaningful conversation. Only young Petrus manages to get a few words out of him these days."

Marcus raised his hand and gripped Quintus's arm, but the old man did not look at him and instead seemed locked into a world only he could see.

Then, sharply Marcus turned to look around the courtyard.

"Where is Fergus, my son?" he suddenly exclaimed in an alarmed voice.

Chapter Three - "We're all together at last"

The spacious dining room was filled with children's happy excited laughter, as the fat kitchen slave carefully placed the plates of meat stew on the long brown wooden table. The stew's rich aroma filled the room and along the stone wall, above the fireplace in which a warm welcoming fire was spitting and crackling, stood a shelf containing an array of death masks, statuettes and icons. Marcus sat at the head of the table, flanked by Efa and Jowan. He was silent as he studied the faces of his family around him. Kyna had taken a seat at the other end of the table with Dylis and old Quintus at her side. His wife had refused to touch him again after her initial embrace or to speak to him and whenever he'd sought to make eye contact, she had avoided his gaze. It was as if she was scared of him. The middle of the dinner table was occupied by Dylis's children, twin girls with long curly blond hair, who seemed to ganging up on their younger brother, a boy of around four. Ahern sat to one side and had refused to take part in his sibling's games. The little boy looked pale and frightened, a very different boy to the one Marcus had met, playing in the snow only a few hours ago. None of the children looked older than seven.

Opposite the twins was an empty seat with an empty plate. Marcus frowned as he watched the fat slave leave the plate unattended.

"It's for your father, Corbulo," Efa said quietly as she caught him staring at the plate, "I have put an empty plate out for him every day since he'd died. His spirit will dine with us. He will be happy tonight."

She lifted her head and gave Marcus a little wise smile and, with her neat white hair, aging features but sharp watchful eyes, she suddenly looked very much like a proper family matriarch. Sharply she clapped her hands and around the table, the children obediently fell silent, as all eyes turned to look at Efa.

"Tonight is a special dinner," Efa said quietly as she glanced around the table with twinkling eyes, "Tonight the gods have answered my prayers. Marcus has returned home. We're all together at last. Now raise your cups and welcome Marcus home, for he is has been gone for a very long time."

Around the dining table the family raised their cups of watered-down red wine and drank.

"Marcus, tell us what happened to you in Pannonia and Dacia," Dylis called out as she spooned some stew into her mouth.

Marcus glanced at Kyna but she avoided his gaze. Slowly he cleared his throat and turned to stare at Ahern. The boy was playing with his food, pushing it around the plate.

So he told them what had happened to him during the seven years he'd been away. He told them about the barbarian frontier, the rough and violent army camps, the wars with the Dacians and how he lost three fingers on his left hand and when at last he stopped talking the dinner table remained uncomfortably silent, until a solitary voice broke the silence.

"Why did you come back?" Kyna said, her eyes moist, her face white like snow and a faint accusatory tone to her voice.

Marcus stared at her from across the table. "I came home to marry you," he replied sharply, "I came home to make Fergus legitimate. I am a Roman citizen now and so is Fergus. I made you a promise once, do you not remember? I came home to keep that promise."

Troubled, Kyna silently shook her head and looked away.

"Fergus is well," Efa said smoothly changing the subject as she placed her hand over Marcus's, "You missed him by a few months. He left to join the Twentieth Legion at Deva Victrix as a new recruit. He is going to be a legionary just like his grandfather was. He specifically chose his grandfather's old unit. He said that he wanted to honour Corbulo."

"He has joined the legions?" Marcus blurted out, as he turned to stare at Efa. "How? He needs a father's permission. He needs a letter of recommendation. He needs to be a Roman citizen. I gave no such permission."

"You were not here to give him anything he needed," Kyna snapped with sudden anger. "We had Quintus write and sign a letter. He pretended to be his father. Quintus is a citizen and the Twentieth remember him and his service. That letter got him in. You were not here to be a father to Fergus. We did what we had to do."

Marcus glared across the table at his wife. Then he glanced quickly at Quintus but the old man was slowly eating his food, as if he was unaware of anything that was going on around him.

"We received a letter from him recently, Marcus," Efa said quietly in her calm soothing voice, "He says that he is with his unit in the northern hills, hunting Arvirargus and his band of rebels. He says he is well. He is a soldier just like you now."

"He's what, seventeen, eighteen?" Marcus snapped angrily. "What does he know about being a soldier?"

"Well, what does any young man of that age know?" Efa replied. "You were seventeen when you joined your regiment Marcus. Kyna is right, we did what we had to do. No one was sure that you were coming home. Fergus is doing what he wants. Let it rest with that."

With a displeased grunt, Marcus sat back in his seat. Efa was right but he hated to admit it. He could still remember the toddler who had liked to waddle around the army camp at Luguvalium with a small wooden sword. That his son would one day become a soldier like his father and grandfather had always been likely, but what had annoyed him was that Fergus had decided to join the Twentieth and not his own, old unit, the 2nd Batavians, and he'd done it without his permission.

"Arvirargus!" Marcus growled shaking his head in disbelief, "Have they still not caught that bastard? Is he really still out there? How long ago was it now that his father's rebellion was crushed? Thirteen years...fourteen."

"He lives and prospers," Efa replied lowering her eyes, "The north remains unsettled, Marcus. They say travellers should be wary, especially citizens."

Marcus cleared his throat. "Well Arvirargus and his friends can fuck off. When the snows clear, I shall go north and visit Fergus," he growled. "The boy needs to see his father."

"Let me tell you our news," Dylis called out. Marcus looked up at his sister and for a moment her attractive features and warm welcoming smile seemed to banish his dark mood. Dylis had done well, he thought. She was happy and her happiness seemed to ooze out of her and infect everyone around her and for that he was glad.

"Much has changed," Dylis said in an excited voice. "Tomorrow when it is light, Jowan will take you out to inspect the farm buildings and the land. We have made many improvements to the villa and thanks to my husband the farm is successful and prosperous. We have twenty slaves working in the fields now. Twenty! and Jowan has plans to expand the business."

"With your permission of course," Jowan interrupted as he glanced at Marcus.

Marcus nodded, "How did you find the money to expand the farm? Are we in debt?"

"Not at all," Dylis replied eagerly, "we just made some good investment decisions. Remember brother, when we read out our father's will. He left us everything split three ways, one third to you, one third to me and a third to Efa. Well Efa and I pooled our resources, made the right investments and the result is all around us. We did not have to borrow anything from anyone. We have no debts Marcus."

"Nor do we want any," Jowan added, "our crops and produce are in demand at the moment but the price we receive is never certain. Bad times are never far away. We must be prudent and make the best of our current good fortune."

"That sounds like good advice," Marcus muttered. "We are not short of money then. You have done well, all of you. This is good news."

Efa was just about to say something when a man in his late twenties appeared in the doorway to the hall. He was dark haired and cloaked in a snow-covered hunters' cloak. A bow and quiver were slung over his shoulder. Silently he placed his weapons against the wall, undid his cloak, handed it to the fat slave girl and sat down at the empty seat reserved for Corbulo. Without any acknowledgment of the diners, he called out for the slave to serve him. A large wooden cross dangled on a cord around his neck.

"Petrus," Efa's sharp, scolding voice lashed out, "Where are your manners? That seat and plate are for Corbulo. Get up at once."

The man raised his hand in an irritated gesture as if this was an argument he'd already had many times.

"He's not coming back," Petrus retorted, "His soul is either with god or in hell. The old man is not here. He won't mind me using his seat and plate and I am hungry. I have been out hunting all day."

Petrus was about to say something else when he suddenly caught sight of Marcus.

"Who are you?" he blurted out.

"He is the head of this family. His name is Marcus and he is Corbulo's son and you are sitting at his table," Efa snapped angrily, "So get up and take a seat beside Quintus. He is getting his food all over his clothes."

"Holy shit, you are Marcus," Petrus said as a little colour shot into his cheeks, "You are the old man's son?"

Marcus nodded without saying a word and abruptly Petrus rose and moved over to sit beside Quintus as he warily eyed Marcus.

"Welcome home," Petrus said with an uncertain smile, "Just so that you know. I am a Christian like Quintus here. I hope you don't have a problem with Christians. Your old man was rather hostile."

"Corbulo saved your life. He saved the lives of all those nine Christian children whom we took north from Londinium all those years ago," Efa interrupted angrily, "You will show Marcus respect."

"That he did," Petrus admitted.

"Corbulo was the finest fighting man I ever knew," Quintus suddenly blurted out. The old man's hand shook as he spoke and he was staring vacantly at the wall. The room fell silent. Then tenderly Petrus reached out and laid his hand on the old warrior's shoulder.

"We all know he was, Quintus," Petrus said quietly, "even Efa knows that I know. Come let's drink to the old warrior's health."

Silently the whole family raised their cups and drank with Petrus raising Quintus's cup to his mouth so that the veteran drank.

Marcus placed his cup on the table and his eyes came to rest on Ahern. The boy seemed to cringe as he suddenly became aware of Marcus's gaze. Slowly Marcus raised his hand and pointed a finger straight at Ahern.

"Who is that boy?" he exclaimed. "I do not know that boy. Whose son is he?"

Instantly the dinner table went silent and for a moment, it seemed as if no one dared to move or breath. No one answered.

"Well?" Marcus growled.

With a muffled despairing cry, Kyna rose from her seat and fled into the kitchen. Marcus watched her go, with a smouldering, furious look. Then abruptly he rose from his chair and without saying a word he strode out of the room.

Outside in darkness the night was quiet and freezing. The pickaxe made irritatingly small progress as Marcus slung it repeatedly into the frozen earth. Close by, an ancient oak tree seemed to be only witness to what he was doing. For a moment he paused to wipe the sweat from his brow, and as he did so, he glanced back at the villa, twenty paces away. The oil lamps were still burning in the dining room. With a grunt he lifted the pickaxe and resumed hammering it into the earth. When at last he'd managed to make a sizeable hole in the ground, he dropped the axe and sank down onto his knees in the snow. From inside his thick Dacian cloak, he carefully withdrew a large leather bag and placed it at the bottom of the narrow hole he'd dug. Quickly he glanced around but he could see nothing in the freezing darkness and the only noise was his own laboured breathing. The bag contained his army pension, the whole lot in pure Dacian gold, a small fortune. Swiftly he started to fill in the hole with the clumps of earth he'd excavated. He was stamping down the disturbed earth with his feet when he suddenly noticed two torches bearing down on him, followed moments later by a woman's voice calling out his name.

Stiffly he picked up the pickaxe and strode towards the torches.

"I am here," he snapped as he recognised Efa and Dylis. The two women were clad in their fur winter cloaks and each was holding a flaming torch. They looked concerned.

"What are you doing out here in the dark and cold?" Dylis said. "Come inside Marcus, we need to talk."

"That boy," Marcus growled turning to Dylis, "He is not your son is he? He is Kyna's. Don't lie to me. I am not a fool."

"Yes Marcus," Efa said sharply, "You are right. He is Kyna's son. She did not think that you were going to return from the wars. She was lonely. She made a mistake, but the man who fathered the child is gone. He is not coming back and Ahern is here with us now."

"Kyna is terrified that you are going to harm Ahern," Dylis exclaimed.

"Well, she is damn right to be afraid," Marcus roared, "the boy is not my son. Kyna has brought great dishonour to this family. It is my right to decide whether he lives or dies. A father has the right to accept a child or not."

"He's only five years old," Dylis pleaded, as her face grew pale.

"And one day he will grow up to be a man," Marcus snapped, "a man who is not of my blood, but of some other, some stranger. That boy will never be my son. I will never know who he is. No, he has no right to live here, amongst us."

"Marcus," Dylis squealed, "Don't you dare cast him out. Don't you dare. You will break Kyna's heart. You will break all our hearts if you throw him out. He will die in this weather. None of this is his fault."

"That boy is not of my blood," Marcus roared, pointing a finger at the villa, "Kyna should have thought about that, when she broke her promise to me."

"And how many times were you unfaithful to her," Dylis said, as a bitter tone entered her voice, "Seven years on the frontier. Don't tell me you did not have a woman when you were away."

Marcus growled and muttered something under his breath.

"Marcus," Efa's voice cut through the freezing night air, "You are the head of this family and we all know that you can do what you like with Ahern. To accept him or not as your son is your decision. All I ask is that you think it over until Saturnalia has passed."

Slowly Marcus turned to look at Efa. Then without saying a word he stomped away into the darkness.

Chapter Four - The Memorial Stone

Marcus paused beside the small, ice bound stream and peered at the stepping stones that led to the opposite bank. It was morning and two days had passed since he'd returned home. A fresh layer of snow covered the frozen ground, the tangled undergrowth and the bare branches of the trees that lined the river bank. In the distance he could hear the faint booming of the waves on the beach. At his side Dylis was staring fondly at the stepping stones. Her gaze was distant, as if she was remembering another time.

"He used to take me for walks over those stones," she said, as she gave her brother a sad little smile, "When I was still just a child, we would go all the way to the beach and he would watch me playing in the sea with my dog. He didn't say much, but I think he really enjoyed those walks. That's why we placed his stone on the other side of the creek beside the path we always took." Dylis gripped her brother's arm. "I will leave you alone," she said as she turned and quickly walked away.

Marcus watched his sister go. Then slowly he turned to stare at the frozen water. Efa had erected a stone memorial to Corbulo. They had called it a grave but it was nothing more than a memorial stone, for the family had never been able to properly bury Corbulo's mortal remains. There had never been a body to bury for Emogene, the druid, after murdering Corbulo, had taken his body with her. Marcus lowered his eyes in sudden shame as he remembered. The pain from that terrible day had been dulled by the passage of time but he could still recall every detail. The ancient, crumbling and abandoned Celtic fort, Corbulo's final words, the look on his father's face. His father had sacrificed himself to save him. Faced with an impossible choice of choosing between which of his children to send to their deaths, the old man had offered his own life instead and Emogene had taken it. The fingers on Marcus' hand idly came to rest on the pommel of his gladius. The sword was Corbulo's. He had picked it up after his father had discarded it and during the many years that had followed it had served him well.

With a grunt he stepped out onto the stones and quickly crossed the frozen stream. On the opposite bank he climbed up the embankment and emerged into an open snow covered field. A solitary stone had been erected beside the path that led onwards across the fields towards the distant sea, just like Dylis had said. Marcus stared at it. Then he approached and knelt down beside it and brushed the snow from the stone. An inscription had been chiselled into the memorial.

"Here lies Corbulo, veteran of twenty-five year's service in the XX Legion. This stone was erected by Efa his loving wife and Dylis his daughter."

Marcus sat back on the ground and bowed his head in shame, as he remembered. He had done nothing for his father, whose spirit was still un-avenged. After murdering him, Emogene had taken Corbulo's body with her. He did not know why, nor did he know what she had done with the corpse. She and her men had thrown the body across the back of one of their horses and had vanished off northwards, as the Roman cavalry patrol had advanced to rescue Marcus and the others. Tensely Marcus scratched his forehead, as his cheeks burned with shame. That final glimpse of Emogene and her men riding away, was the last he had ever seen or heard of the woman who had taken Corbulo's life. There had been moments in the weeks and months that had followed, in which he had thought about tracking her down but the task was impossible. The Brigantian and Caledonian tribal rebellion was still ongoing and the north was not safe for any Roman, soldier or civilian. By the time he'd gotten Efa and Dylis to safety, Emogene could have been anywhere, and he would have wasted a lifetime without finding her. So he had concentrated on the survival of his family, the survival of the living over vengeance for the dead, for the living had to come first. Efa and Dylis were both deeply traumatised and exhausted from their ordeal and he also had Kyna and

Fergus to think about. So once he had finally settled them all on the farm on Vectis, he'd sought out Agricola, the family's patron and upon Agricola's advice he had handed himself over to the military authorities who had brought him before a court martial in Londinium.

Slowly Marcus blew the air from his mouth as he stared at the memorial stone. So what would his father do in his situation? Would Corbulo accept another man's son as his own? Wearily he lowered his head. Kyna had given in to her despair and loneliness. But she had known what kind of life she was destined for when she'd agreed to be his woman. If she had not wanted to be a soldier's wife she should have told him. Marcus shook his head. But none of that mattered now. He had a decision to make.

Corbulo had never been a good father or husband. The old man had beaten him and Alene his first wife for the slightest infringement. He'd drunk too much, whored too much and gotten into too many fights. His indiscipline had meant he'd never risen far in the Twentieth Legion. Marcus shook his head in disbelief. And yet at the very end his father had redeemed himself. He had made something of himself. He'd earned the undying love and respect of his family and friends. How the fuck had he managed that? Marcus sighed and turned to stare at the stone and, as he did so, he suddenly knew what he was going to do about Ahern.

Chapter Five – Saturnalia

Marcus could sense the slaves were in an excited mood as he strode into the hall of his villa. It was afternoon and the house was a hive of activity and from the kitchen he could hear the cooks calling out to each other as they prepared the evening feast. The smell of freshly baked bread wafted through the dining hall. It was all because of the festivities later that evening. Saturnalia after all was the one public festival where everything was turned upside down. Where masters served their slaves and where everyone joined in the feast and enjoyed themselves. A slave boy was polishing and re-arranging the household Lares in their alcoves above the hearth. The boy's face went pale as he saw Marcus but Marcus ignored the slave and paused to squint at the Lares. The stone statuettes of the family guardian spirits, who protected the household, seemed to stare back at him and for a brief uncomfortable moment it felt as if they were judging him.

"Boy," Marcus said turning sharply to the slave, "Go and find Efa and Dylis, bring them here. Tell everyone that I wish to see them right away here in the dining room, the slaves too."

The slave boy said nothing as he scampered off towards the kitchen. Marcus muttered something to himself as alone, he paced up and down, his hands clasped behind his back and as he did so he felt strangely nervous. Irritably he inspected the two remaining fingers on his left hand. Kyna was not going to like his decision but she was going to accept it nonetheless. He was the head of family and he had to make the right decisions for all of them and that was that. The honour of the family could not be tarnished. The spirits of the family ancestors would not stand for it.

They entered the room at short intervals, Dylis quiet and tense, wearing a beautiful dress, Jowan straight from the stables, Efa, bedecked in fine jewellery, her appearance calm and immaculate, Kyna gripping Ahern's hand and avoiding his gaze

30

and last of all Petrus, supporting Quintus, as the old warrior shuffled slowly and unsteadily into the room. The slaves and Dylis's children followed one by one in respectful silence. Marcus waited until they were all there watching him.

"Today is Saturnalia," he said clearing his throat, "Tonight we sing, dance and feast but before we do I have something to say." Marcus paused as his eyes slowly passed over each person standing before him as if they were Batavian troopers on parade. "I have been away for a long time and there are certain matters that need attending to," he continued at last. "Decisions need to be made. I came home to keep a promise made long ago. So I am announcing that Kyna and I will be married in three days time. The day is good and there are no bad omens. Fergus will become my legal son, a full Roman citizen like his grandfather was and when I die he will become the head of this family. When the snows clear I will travel north to visit him at Deva." Marcus paused again as he stared at the faces watching him. The dining room remained utterly silent. Kyna's face was white as a sheet and at her side Ahern was trembling with fright. From the corner of his eye Marcus caught Dylis staring at him, her expression tense and cold.

"As for that boy," Marcus said pointing at Ahern, "I have decided to spare him. He will stay here with us but on condition that Jowan adopts him as his son. The boy needs a father and Jowan will raise him."

Marcus turned to Jowan as Kyna gasped and raised a hand to her mouth.

"Well, will you accept this boy as your own?" Marcus asked.

Jowan's cheeks seemed to burn as all eyes turned to look at him. Then without a word he slowly turned to look at Ahern.

"I will do as you ask Sir," Jowan replied, "The boy will be mine. He is a good boy Sir. I will treat him just like my other children."

31

Kyna could not contain herself any longer and with a cry she fled from the room with tears streaking down her face. Marcus watched her go. Then slowly he nodded at Jowan.

"Good, then it is settled. We will have everything made legal in the spring. That will be all."

The gathering began to break up as the slaves dispersed until only Efa and Dylis remained.

"Thank you Marcus, that was a wise decision, worthy of you," Efa said as she came towards him, reached for his hand and kissed it. She was followed moments later by Dylis who also kissed his hand. His sister's expression had softened and she gave him a wry little smile.

"You are a Roman, just like your father," Dylis said, jutting her chin at him, "You soldiers and your sense of honour. But you have forgotten your Celtic mother, Marcus. There was a time once, when the tribes still ruled this land, when women and men had equal say in their own affairs. If you are to marry Kyna you will do well to remember that, for she is no Roman wife, nor will she be ruled like one."

"The time of the free tribes has passed," Marcus replied, "the future belongs to Rome. I will not make the same mistake as Corbulo did. But I will make the decisions that are right for us, as a family."

Efa slipped her arm in between Marcus and Dylis' arms and began to steer them out of the room, "Enough of this," she said quietly, "Marcus's heart is in the right place, Dylis, and that's all that matters."

***

The dining hall was filled with raucous laughter, squeals and loud excited voices. Marcus leaned against the doorway leading into the kitchen as he watched his family and the slaves enjoying the festivities. In his hand he held a cup of wine and on his head he was wearing victory laurels. He had drunk too much, he knew, but tonight was Saturnalia and he didn't care. In the corner surrounded by Dylis' children, who were clutching their new toys, Petrus was playing on a flute, and in the middle of the long, rectangular dining room some of the slaves were dancing. Everyone seemed to be drunk for it was already well after midnight and the wine had been flowing for hours. A couple of slaves were hunched over a board game using nuts as stakes and beside them on the table lay a small discarded wax figurine. Idly Marcus's eyes came to rest on Kyna who was sitting beside Ahern and listening to Petrus playing his flute. She was clad as the huntress, Diane, and in her hand she was holding a child's bow. As he stared at her she seemed to become aware of his gaze and slowly she turned her head to look at him, her face proud, her eyes defiant. Marcus pushed himself away from the wall and came towards her and as he did so, Petrus lowered his flute and the people around him fell silent as everyone turned to look at Marcus. As he reached her Marcus stretched out his hand to Kyna.

"Will you dance with me?" he grunted.

Kyna did not reply as she stared up at him. Then slowly she rose to her feet and took his hand and as she did so, a smile appeared on Petrus' face and he raised the flute once more to his lips. The music sprang forth sweet and unassuming and around him the children cried out in excitement and started to clap their hands. Marcus took Kyna into the centre of the whirling mass of dancers and as Petrus played, Dylis and Efa suddenly raised their voices and began to sing in tune with the flute, their voices rich, strong and confident as if they had done this many times before. Their hauntingly beautiful Celtic song filled the room and soon the children tried to join in. Marcus however did not seem to hear them. He was staring at Kyna as they danced, trying to remember the young woman he'd fallen in love with all those years ago.

"Why did you spare my son?" Kyna said, "Why did you not throw Ahern out of your house? It was your right."

Marcus gazed at her without replying, as around them the music, dancing and singing filled the room.

"If I would have done that I would have lost you too," he said at last, "and the boy should not have to suffer for the mistakes made by his mother."

Kyna blushed and bit her lip.

"I did not think you were coming back," she said, "We heard things, pieces of news, of terrible slaughter along the frontier, of thousands dead through war, starvation and disease. I am sorry Marcus, I truly am. I lost hope of seeing you again."

Marcus leaned his forehead against hers and his expression softened. "What is done is done, it no longer matters," he growled. "We are strong and we will improvise." He paused as a resigned look appeared in his eyes.

"I am tired of war and of violence," he said as they danced, "I have seen enough of death and I wish to see no more. What matters now is us Kyna, this family, Fergus. I came home to keep a promise to you and I intend to keep it. What I have here in this house is the most precious thing I can ever have. I will not let anything threaten that."

Slowly a smile appeared on Kyna's face and affectionately she raised her finger and touched his nose.

"Now I recognise the young soldier I first met at Luguvalium," she said as her eyes grew moist. "He has come home at last, thank the gods."

Marcus nodded and, as they danced, the noise in the room seemed to rise in volume and as he stared at his family, enjoying themselves, together, and the dancing slaves, he felt a sudden happiness flooding into his body like an unstoppable tide, raw, powerful and uplifting.

"We have a lot to talk about," he muttered. "and in the spring I will go and visit Fergus and..."

But Kyna did not seem to be listening. She was pressing her lips against his cheek.

"Kiss me, you fool," she whispered.

Chapter Six – Cunomoltus

Marcus was woken by the sound of a slave calling out his name. Sleepily he raised himself up onto his elbows and looked around the bedroom. It was morning and at his side Kyna muttered to herself but did not open her eyes, as she rolled over and pulled the woollen blanket over her naked body. With an annoyed grunt, Marcus heaved himself off the bed and picked up his discarded clothes lying on the cold stone floor of the house.

"What is it?" he cried, as he heard the slave calling his name again.

"There is someone at the gate," the slave replied from behind the door, "He is asking to see the master of the house. He says its urgent. He is refusing to leave."

Marcus frowned but did not say anything as he quickly dressed himself. What was this? He was not expecting any visitors.

The slave looked anxious as he followed Marcus down the hall and towards the doorway leading into the courtyard. In the dining room the remains of last night's party were still strewn about. A thin layer of fresh snow covered the courtyard and heavy, grey clouds hid the sun from sight. A figure was leaning against the gate that marked the edge of his property. Marcus squinted as he strode towards him, his boots crunching through the snow. The man looked around thirty-five with long, black hair. He was clean shaven, clad in a long, winter cloak with a hood that was lowered and he seemed unarmed, apart from a short knife hanging from his belt. Abruptly Marcus came to a halt and swore as he suddenly recognised the stranger. It was the man who'd been following and watching him in the forest. Softly Marcus swore again as he stared at the stranger. The man had not moved and was watching him with a strange, sad grin.

As Marcus approached the wooden gate he suddenly wished he'd brought his father's old sword with him.

"Go and find Jowan, tell him I need him here," Marcus snapped turning to the slave at his side. The man nodded and giving the visitor a worried glance, he hurried away towards the house.

Warily Marcus studied the stranger and for a long silent moment the two of them peered at each other from across the gate and as he did, Marcus suddenly became aware of an overwhelming sadness, an almost tragic aura that clung to the newcomer, like a persistent and unshakeable smell. Marcus' eyes narrowed suspiciously. The man was fit enough, but he was no soldier, nor did he look like a mercenary or bandit looking for a quick and easy robbery. And yet there was something oddly familiar about his face.

"You were following me in the forest that day, why? What do you want?" Marcus said sternly, his eyes fixed on the stranger.

The man's eyes glinted mysteriously and then his eyes seemed suddenly drawn to the bronze phallic amulet that hung around Marcus's neck.

"You were easy to track," the stranger replied in heavily accented Latin, "I had expected a soldier with your army record, Marcus, to have been more difficult to follow but you left a trail like a hungry hound in a sausage shop. You should have been more carefu,l especially with all that gold you were carrying."

Marcus grunted in shock.

"How do you know my name?" he replied sharply. "Who are you?"

"Oh I know everything about you," the stranger replied with a sad little smile, "I have been following you since you arrived in Londinium, weeks ago. You didn't notice me in those crowded streets, but I was there. Don't worry Marcus, I am not here to rob you, not in that way. I have come to talk. You and I need to talk. It's important and it cannot wait."

Warily Marcus studied the stranger. The man had him at a disadvantage and it unsettled and annoyed him.

"Well if that is all you want to do, then why did you not approach me in the forest," Marcus growled, annoyed, "instead of skulking around like some sort of wild animal. Who follows a man into a blizzard like that?"

Abruptly the stranger turned to stare at the villa behind Marcus. "It's a nice house. You have done well for yourself, Marcus," the man said with an approving nod. "Better than me, anyway."

"What the fuck do you want?"

"I had to be sure," the newcomer said, "I had to be sure that you did indeed own this farm and its land."

From the corner of his eye Marcus noticed Jowan and two male slaves hurrying towards him from across the courtyard. Jowan had his pickaxe slung over his shoulder.

"I am not discussing anything until I know who I am talking to," Marcus said, folding his arms across his chest.

The stranger sighed and turned to look at Marcus and as he did so there was a sudden bitterness in his eyes.

"You really don't know, do you? My name is Cunomoltus," the man said, raising his chin, "Dog handler and breeder; a man on the run, a fuck up and second-born son to Corbulo, retired veteran of the XX Legion, your father..."

Marcus stared at the stranger in stunned silence. Behind him Jowan and the slaves came to a panting halt in the snow.

"What did you just say?" Marcus gasped.

"I am your younger brother," Cunomoltus sneered, "and I am on the run. I have been looking for you for over a year, Marcus. My mother was Cornovii, a local girl, whom our father met whilst he was stationed at Deva."

"What?" Marcus looked confused.

"It's not that difficult," Cunomoltus said with a little mocking shake of his head, "and as your brother I have now come to claim my half of Corbulo's inheritance. I want half of all this," Cunomoltus said gesturing at the house, "the villa, the land, the slaves and the farm income."

Marcus stared at him in stunned, shocked silence. Then slowly he turned to Jowan who had come to stand by his side and who was clutching his pickaxe.

"If this prick," Marcus said, slowly pointing a finger at Cunomoltus, "so much as sets one foot on my property, I want him whipped until he begs for mercy."

Chapter Seven - A Lucky Day

The whole household including the slaves, had gathered in the dining room of the villa, the largest room in the house. It was morning and Marcus and Kyna stood facing each other in solemn silence in the middle of the room. Marcus was clad in his finest tunic and was clean-shaven and opposite him Kyna was dressed in a simple white dress with a red veil covering her head and face. At her side Dylis, her face made up with expensive make-up, could barely contain the tears from streaming down her cheeks. On a table, to one side lay the remains of a slaughtered chicken, its bloody entrails spread out on an earthenware plate and, standing beside the table were the owner of the neighbouring farm and his wife. Both were watching the proceedings with a stern approving look.

"It is time to sign the marriage contract," Jowan said as he carefully placed a parchment with small, neat handwriting onto the table and took a respectful step backwards. Marcus nodded and bent down to sign it. He was followed moments later by Kyna, who slowly and carefully engraved her initials into the document. Marcus watched her and as he did he felt a sudden up swell of emotion. He had kept his promise to her. He had honoured her. After all these years. The gods would be pleased he thought for the gods liked those who kept their word.

Kyna laid the stylus pen, on the table and raised her veiled head to look at Marcus. He could not see the expression on her face but he sensed the emotion and tension in her body. This was her day, the day she had always talked about, the day she had yearned for, the day he had promised her and now the climax of the wedding ceremony was upon them.

Without saying a word Efa stepped forwards and slowly and with infinitive dignity, she took Marcus's right hand and placed it in Kyna's right hand and, as she did so, the assembled household and witnesses gasped and a murmur ran through the gathering. Marcus stood bolt upright as if he was on parade as he gripped his bride's hand in a silent exchange of vows. The room fell silent as the couple clasped each other's hand and then, after what seemed an age, the hall suddenly erupted with cries and cheers. Slowly Kyna lifted her veil and to Marcus's surprise she was smiling. Quickly he bent down and kissed her.

"This is a lucky day, husband," Kyna whispered into his ear as the wedding guests cried out their approval of the newly married couple.

"It is," Marcus replied as the grin on his face widened, "I am only sorry that Corbulo and Fergus are not here to witness this day."

Kyna nodded. "You must go and see Fergus as soon as possible," she whispered, "but it can wait until after the celebrations. I want to keep you to myself for a little longer."

***

The loud, drunken but good natured wedding celebrations were in full swing when Efa came up to Marcus and quietly took his arm and led him to a quieter corner of the room and, as she did so, his expression suddenly darkened as he guessed what she had come to discuss.

"Not now, not today, of all days," Marcus growled in warning.

But Efa shook her head.

"We need to talk about him," she said in a determined voice as she turned to look at the wedding guests enjoying themselves. "He is refusing to leave, Marcus. He has been camped out in the snow just beyond our gates for two days and nights now. He suffers from the shaking sickness and he is going to freeze to death or starve if you don't do something about it."

"Then let him freeze to death," Marcus growled as he took a swig of wine from his cup, "I don't give a flying fuck. The man is not my brother and he is not having half of this farm. How can you trust a man like that? He seems only interested in money. The man's nothing more than a con man trying his luck."

Efa sighed, a long weary sigh. "Dylis and I went out to speak with him yesterday," she said, "He is not going to leave and he insists that he is your brother. He knows things about Corbulo that no man should or could know. He even looks a bit like your father. Please Marcus give the man a chance. He is going to die if he has to stay outside for a few more days. The weather is getting worse."

Angrily Marcus rounded on Efa.

"Do you really believe that he is Corbulo's son" he exclaimed sharply. "He could have learned those things about my father from veterans, men who'd known Corbulo. If he really is my half-brother, then why is he only now showing interest in us, not when we were poor, but when we are finally wealthy and prosperous? He is after our wealth Efa, it's obvious."

"It's possible," Efa said with a little shrug, "But it is also quite possible that he is Corbulo's son. Your father liked the ladies and must have slept with dozens of them. I think I believe him, Marcus, I really do." Efa paused as she searched for the right words, "He lives with this terrible regret and sadness," Efa continued with a frown, "When Dylis and I went to speak to him, he told us that he had wanted to be just like his father. He wanted to have what Corbulo had, to be a proud soldier of the legions, but he never made it, because he was not a citizen, and they did not accept him. He regrets never having been the man that you and your father were and are. So the things he said to you, Marcus, out by the gate; "he said these because I think he is jealous of you, nothing more. Give him a chance to prove himself to you."

"Do you really believe all of this crap?"

"Yes I do. You could call it instinct," Efa replied quickly, "but in these matters I am rarely wrong."

Marcus shook his head in despair.

"I will hear no more about this," he growled, "If he chooses to freeze to death then so be it. I owe that man nothing. He is not my brother. He is an imposter."

Marcus was sipping his wine observing the wedding party when he groaned as he saw Efa, Dylis and Kyna suddenly coming towards him. The three women seemed to anticipate his reaction for silently they spread out, blocking his escape routes. They looked worried as they bore down on him.

"The answer is no," Marcus growled defiantly catching Efa's eye. "I don't trust him."

"Don't be so heartless," Dylis interrupted, "The poor man is freezing and starving. If he was a fraud he would have given up by now, surely."

"The answer is no."

"He told us he wanted to join the army just like you and Dad did," Dylis said, folding her arms across her chest with a stubborn expression, "But the legions wouldn't accept him. He had no proof that he was a citizen. He had no one to vouch for him. Corbulo never helped him. Our father abandoned him, he never showed any interest in helping him. We owe him, Marcus. He is part of our family."

"Are you all insane," Marcus snapped, "Listen to yourselves. Since when is this man part of our family? Two days ago we did not even know he existed. So Corbulo tried to fuck every woman he could, that doesn't mean that, that man out there is my brother. He has bewitched all of you; he is making fools of you."

"Marcus," Kyna said, laying her hand gently on his shoulder, "Please, what harm can it do to at least show him some hospitality and clemency. Efa and Dylis believe that he is speaking the truth."

"Why do you all believe him?" Marcus growled in an exasperated voice.

"Please, Marcus," Kyna said again, "Give him a chance to prove himself. If he is indeed your brother, then the gods will not forgive you, if you let him die out there in the snow. These things, they are placed before us, to test us, the gods make them happen, to test us."

"Marcus," Efa said, her voice strong and filled with sudden purpose, "Kyna is right. The gods are testing us and you have a part to play. If Cunomoltus is indeed one of us, the truth will emerge. That man out there in the snow believes that Corbulo abandoned him and he may be right. Corbulo was not always a good man. Corbulo made many mistakes, and this may be one of them and if it is, then we need to make it right. Corbulo would want us to."

"What can I do?" Marcus exclaimed looking exasperated.

Efa took a step towards him, her face suddenly flush and alive with emotion.

"This is a man who has nowhere to go," she said sharply. "He needs our help and you, Marcus, you can influence him. I know you can. You can turn him into a better person. He is practically asking you to help him. So give him a chance. He is a good man. I know it. Do not let Cunomoltus descend into bitterness and spitefulness. Yes, I know you don't trust him. I know you are suspicious. But Corbulo managed to make something of himself. At the end your father showed us all what a real man is. A real man does not let fear, jealousy or greed sway him, he just does what is right."

A little tear had appeared in Efa's eyes as she spoke.

"Do what is right, Marcus," she whispered, "Be the man your father was and you will honour him. You will honour us all."

Marcus muttered something under his breath as he turned to look at his wife. Then he turned to Dylis and finally to Efa, but all three women seemed united by the same purpose and they met his gaze with calm determination. Marcus took a deep breath and emitted a weary sigh.

"You are mad, all of you. Fine," he snapped, "He can sleep in the barn with the horses. The slaves can bring him some food. I will speak with him tomorrow and I will settle this matter."

***

Marcus sat on the wooden bench just outside the door to his villa and studied the barn across the courtyard with an annoyed expression. It was dawn and the courtyard was covered in a fine layer of powdery snow. In the nearby copse a northern breeze was playing with the branches of the trees and in one of the workshops a slave was repairing a plough. Through the door he could smell the cooks preparing breakfast. Wearily Marcus rapped the two remaining fingers of his left hand on the wooden bench. It was as if his father, Corbulo, had never died. After all the years that had passed the old man still had the ability to remind him of his youth. Here, once again, he was having to deal with his father's legacy. It had been the story of his youth, whether comforting his mother and trying to fix her bruised, battered face or lying to the centurion when the officer came round looking for his money, which Corbulo had lost. He had spent his days as a boy, covering for his father. It was the reason why he had finally run away to join the 2nd Batavian

45

Cohort. Marcus sighed. And now once again, he was being asked to sort out one of the old man's mistakes.

Had his father known he'd had another son? He must have done, but he'd never spoken about it to anyone. Marcus sighed again. It was certainly possible that Corbulo, somewhere in his

drunken, whoring past, had gotten a girl pregnant and abandoned her. Wearily Marcus muttered something to himself and glanced up at the heavens. Maybe Kyna was right. Somewhere his father was watching him and laughing and testing him. And as he stared up at the sky, Marcus slowly rose to his feet with sudden grim determination. Well if his father was watching, he would show him how he should have behaved, he would show him what he should have done, for he was not going to repeat the mistakes Corbulo had made.

The barn was filled with straw and hay and in the dim light it smelt of horse shit. The farm's four horses were standing clustered close together in quiet and calm companionship as Marcus entered. Cunomoltus stood next to one of the animals, tenderly stroking the horse's nose and muttering quietly to the beast in his native Celtic language. He looked up as he heard Marcus come in.

"Thanks, brother," Cunomoltus exclaimed with a grateful smile, "for letting me stay in the barn. I was freezing my balls off in the snow."

Marcus, his right hand resting on the pommel of his father's old sword, said nothing as he strode towards Cunomoltus.

"That was your choice, you did not have to stay," Marcus said at last, speaking in the Briton language he'd learned from his mother.

"Oh but I do," Cunomoltus replied spreading his arms out wide, "I have come home and I am not leaving, not now. Half of this place, half of everything here is mine. Why would I want to leave?"

"Keep talking like that and you will find yourself a shallow grave," Marcus said sharply, pointing a threatening finger at him.

The smile on Cunomoltus's lips slowly faded away. Then he shrugged.

"Then that would make you a murderer," he sighed, "but I don't think you are the kind of man who would kill his own brother."

"Maybe one day I will surprise you," Marcus replied darkly, ""But you know nothing about me. You and I have never met until a few days ago. You may have fooled the women of this family, but you won't do the same with me. So I will be asking the questions and you will be providing answers. That is how this is going to work, so shut the fuck up and listen."

"Yes Sir," Cunomoltus barked giving Marcus a mock salute.

Marcus shook his head in disgust.

"It is easy for a man to claim to be something he's not," Marcus said as his eyes narrowed. "I have met dozens of men like you in my time in the army and all of them are eventually weeded out and exposed. Now, that shit that you told the women the other day, you could have learnt that from any veteran who'd known my father. What proof can you offer, that you are indeed Corbulo's son?"

Cunomoltus looked down at the earthen floor and chuckled.

"You are looking for certainty Marcus, but no one can offer that. The only person who can really prove that to you is my mother and she has been dead for over a year now."

"So is that it? Is that all you have to say?" Marcus barked.

"No," Cunomoltus said with sudden pride, "I also have this," and as he spoke his fingers touched his neck and swiftly exposed a bronze amulet from where it had been hidden under his tunic. "See Marcus," Cunomoltus said, with a glint in his eye, "my amulet is exactly the same as yours. I bet our father carved his initials into yours like he did with mine. Want to find out?"

Marcus said nothing as he stared in shocked silence at the bronze phallic amulet around the man's neck. Cunomoltus was right, it looked exactly like his own. His eyes widened. But how was this possible?

"Corbulo gave it to me when I was still very young," Cunomoltus explained, "He told my mother it would ward off the evil eye, that it would keep me safe. It is the only fucking thing my father ever did for me, but I suppose it worked, for I am still here, just like you brother."

"That proves nothing," Marcus muttered, "You could have picked that up in any trinket shop..."

His voice trailed off.

"Here, have a look at the initials carved into the bronze," Cunomoltus said helpfully undoing the amulet from around his neck and tossing it to Marcus. "My mother told me they are mine, hers and our father's. She also told me that you had three initials carved into yours. She said she saw you once when you were still a boy. She said you liked hunting and that you liked to wander the forests on your own, just like I did."

Marcus caught the phallic amulet and his face suddenly went pale. How could this man possibly know about such a thing? The only people who knew about the initials carved into his amulet were Kyna, Fergus, Efa and Dylis. Quickly he turned the amulet over his fingers and examined it carefully and there

48

carved into the bronze, just as the man had said, were three faded initials, just like the three initials carved into his own amulet. Marcus stared at the letters in shock. Then abruptly he tossed the amulet back to Cunomoltus.

"Who the fuck are you?" Marcus hissed taking a step forwards. "How do you know so much about me?"

"I am telling the truth. I am your brother, your half-brother," Cunomoltus replied in a determined voice, "I haven't spent the past two days and nights freezing my balls off in the snow to lie to you."

"Who the fuck are you?" Marcus roared, taking another threatening step towards Cunomoltus. "Answer me or by the gods I will slice open your throat!"

"I am the son whom our father chose to abandon," Cunomoltus yelled defiantly as he stood his ground, "I am the arsehole of the family, the black sheep, the maimed dog. I am the one Corbulo did not want to accept. I am not an honourable man like you Marcus. I happily lie, cheat and steal. That is who I am."

Marcus stood glaring at Cunomoltus with a furious expression, his hands clenched into fists.

"The arsehole of the family, really," Marcus hissed.

"My mother told me about Corbulo," Cunomoltus cried, looking Marcus straight in the eye, his voice shaking with emotion. "She said she met Corbulo when he was posted to the camp at Deva. They saw each other for a few years. Then one day he came to our home to say goodbye. I don't know why he left. My mother said she never saw him again. But I know this, he didn't give a rat's arse about me or her. He abandoned us. But you? You got everything!"

Abruptly Cunomoltus's body and arms shuddered and jerked uncontrollably and for a few brief seconds, he swayed on his feet and his eyes rolled in their sockets before the fit passed. Alarmed Marcus took a step backwards.

"Sorry," Cunomoltus gasped as he bent forwards and steadied himself, "I suffer from the shaking illness. It strikes without warning but the seizures do not last long. The doctors say that I have been touched by the gods."

"More like cursed by the gods," Marcus growled unsympathetically.

Cunomoltus was silent for a long moment as he collected himself. Then he straightened up and looked at Marcus.

"I was too young to remember Corbulo," he said at last in a calmer voice, "but he gave me this amulet. My mother told me about you. She said that I had a half-brother and that you had an amulet just like mine. She said that I should go and find you one day. She said that I would need you one day."

"So why didn't you?" Marcus snapped.

Cunomoltus shrugged.

"Why should I go looking for an arsehole like you," he replied in a sour voice, "I had better things to do. I wanted to be like my father, a soldier in the legions. That was my dream. That would have been a life that a man could be truly proud of. That would have been a truly worthy life, but they refused to accept me. So instead I became a breeder of hunting and war dogs. It was a good profession I suppose, for it provided me with enough to survive and look after my mother. I sold my dogs to wealthy men and sometimes to the army."

Cunomoltus looked up and glared at Marcus. "But a year ago my mother died and I got into trouble, so I decided to try and find you. It has taken me a year, but now that I am here, I am not going anywhere. You will have to kill me, Marcus, if you want me gone. I belong here. I am your brother and our father owes me."

"What kind of trouble are you in?" Marcus said sharply.

Cunomoltus shrugged and gave Marcus a sheepish look. "It's nothing, forget I mentioned it," he replied. "So," Cunomoltus said quickly changing the subject and taking a deep breath, "after my mother died I went to Camulodunum and Londinium in the hope of finding you. It took me a whole year. I managed to meet some veterans of the XX Legion, who told me that they had heard that my father was dead. They also told me that you were serving in a Batavian regiment. After that it was fairly easy to track you down. From the Batavian diaspora in Londinium I finally learned that you had returned home. So I followed you here to Vectis."

Marcus said nothing and the barn fell silent. His eyes were fixed on Cunomoltus and his right hand had a firm grip on the pommel of his sword. The man's story seemed plausible and the amulet had shocked him, but despite all this he was still not convinced. Could he really trust this man? Was he truly his brother or just some sharp and convincing con man?

"Well," Cunomoltus said raising his eyebrows, "Is that enough proof for you?"

"No," Marcus growled as he slowly raised and pointed a finger at the man, "No it isn't. You will remain in this barn with the horses and until you have proven yourself to be my brother, you will not be setting a foot inside my house."

Chapter Eight – Honour

Marcus stood at the top of the wooden ladder that leant against the wall of his house and carefully watched Jowan, as his brother in law raised his hammer and smashed the defective roof tile into several pieces. Jowan lay on his stomach, stretched out across the snow covered roof, his boots wedged into the gutter. Slowly he pried the broken tile from the roof and threw the pieces down onto the ground, where they smashed into tiny fragments. It was mid-morning and the low, dull, grey clouds covered the sky. Silently Marcus gripped the side of the roof with his left hand as he leaned forwards and handed Jowan the new roof tile.

The shrill, high pitched squeals of Dylis's children caught his attention and he turned to look at them playing in the nearby field. The four of them had built a huge snow man, around which they had started a snow ball fight. A little smile appeared on Marcus' lips as he watched the children screaming in delight and excitement as they ran around hurling snow balls at each other. His smile however rapidly vanished as he suddenly caught sight of Cunomoltus. The man had stepped away from the party of slaves, who were collecting firewood and, as Marcus stared at him, Cunomoltus bent down, gathered some snow into his hands, and sent a snow ball of his own hurtling at the children. His intervention was met by a chorus of excited yells as the children turned their aim on him. Within seconds Cunomoltus was struck by at least three snow balls and with a theatrical swoon, he collapsed into the snow. The children shouted in triumph as they charged towards him, sending another barrage of snow balls at his body. Marcus's face darkened. Cunomoltus did not fool him. He didn't like what the man was trying to do. Two weeks had passed since he'd shown up at his home. Grudgingly he'd allowed him to sleep in the barn with the horses and help out around the farm, but he'd forbidden him from entering the house or sharing food with his family. But it had not stopped the man from trying to wriggle his way into his family's life. Cunomoltus had started by befriending the women and now the children. Marcus's eyes narrowed further in distrust and he muttered something under his breath.

"You," he suddenly bellowed at Cunomoltus, "get back to work. You eat my food so that means you do the work."

The children stopped in their tracks and fell silent as Cunomoltus slowly got to his feet and shook the snow from his clothes. Then with a little wave at the children and a glance in Marcus' direction, he turned away and strode back to where the slaves were gathering the fire wood.

With an angry look Marcus watched him go. He should really kick this imposter off his land but that would only alienate Efa, Dylis and Kyna, and he was not prepared to face an unhappy home with three moody, moaning women. What man would be able to put up with that?

"Sir," a voice called out close by and Marcus turned to see one of the slave boys standing at the bottom of the ladder.

"Sir, there is a carriage waiting at the front gate," the boy gasped, "the man says he has come to see you, Sir. He says his name is Falco. He says he knew your father. He says it's important."

"A carriage," Marcus exclaimed with a frown, as he turned to look in the direction of the front gate, but the roof blocked his view. Only wealthy men travelled by carriage. Gently, Marcus shook his head. Falco, the name sounded familiar. Where had he heard this name before? For a moment he stood on the ladder looking undecided. Then, as he remembered, he grunted in surprise and quickly started to clamber down the ladder.

"Show the way, boy," he said as he reached the ground.

The carriage was a brand new looking Carpentum, a four wheeled, wooden arched rooftop vehicle with a team of two horses. It had come to a halt on the rutted, frozen track, just outside the main gate onto the property. A driver, clutching a whip was standing beside one of the horses and inside the luxury wagon, Marcus could see a small, aged man with a large protruding belly, who looked to be in his late fifties. A warm and cosy looking fur blanket was draped over the man's legs and feet. As he saw Marcus, the man acknowledged him with a little respectful dip of his head.

"I wasn't sure whether you would be here, Marcus," the man called out, as Marcus accompanied by the slave boy approached, "I hope all is well with Efa and Dylis and the children. I heard she has three little ones now."

"She has four," Marcus replied gruffly as he came to a halt in the snow beside the carriage. Steam was rising from the two horses as if they had just completed a fast and energetic journey. "What brings you out here to my farm, Falco?" Marcus continued folding his arms across his chest. "The last time we met was what, fourteen years ago, after my father died?"

"Ah," Falco raised his hand in a little nostalgic gesture, "Well it's partly to come and say goodbye to you and your family. You have been good clients of mine over the years and it would not be proper if I left without seeing you and your family one final time," Falco said giving Marcus a broad smile. "I was on my way to Isca, to sell my home there. The banking business has been good to me, Marcus, and I now have branches in Londinium, Eburacum and Aquae Sulis plus a new one opening up soon in Colonia Agrippina. If you ever need a loan my boys will be more than happy to help you out. Your father made one of the best decisions of his life, when he put me in charge of Agricola's old bank. It was an inspired decision, may his spirit rest easy for that." Falco sighed and a hint of melancholy entered his voice. "But now Marcus, I am an old man and I have decided to retire and head south to Hispania. An old man deserves to spend his twilight retirement years in a warm climate. So I am leaving

Londinium and Britannia. I am leaving the banking profession. I am off to get even fatter, browner and happier than I am now."

Marcus rubbed his cheek as he contemplated the banker in silence.

"That is kind of you," Marcus replied at last, "I will have the cooks prepare some food for you and your driver. You are welcome. But first you should tell me why you have really come here."

"Straight to business then, just like your father," Falco sighed with a gentle nostalgic grin. "Corbulo never did like small talk. Well I am glad you remember me, Marcus. I have come out of my way to see you. Your father was a fine man, an excellent soldier and business partner. There is something important that I need to discuss with you. Something I unfortunately only learned about recently."

"What do we need to discuss?" Marcus exclaimed.

Falco glanced at the slave boy and then turned to look out across the white snow covered fields.

"Do you remember Marcus, when you came to Londinium all those years ago with Efa and Dylis and I handed you my copy of Corbulo's will and last testament? Your father had deposited a copy in the bank for safekeeping and he had instructed me to ensure that his final wishes were properly executed."

"I do," Marcus replied, "That was the last time we met, fourteen years ago."

"Well," Falco nodded, "a few weeks ago, whilst I was going through all my old files, preparing to sell the bank and head south to Hispania, I discovered another copy of your father's will. The date on this version was after the one which I originally gave to you, so making this new copy the more recent and therefore the more valid one." Falco raised his hands in a dramatic gesture. "Now, I am not a lawyer but it seems that your father, Corbulo, changed his will a few months before he died and that this new version is the actual legal copy."

Marcus stood motionless as he stared at the banker. Then a little colour shot into his cheeks.

"My father changed his will?" he exclaimed.

"He did," Falco nodded, "There is no doubt about it. I am sorry that I only discovered this new document so recently."

"So what does it say?" Marcus blurted out.

Falco sucked the air into his lungs in a sign of disgust. "I don't know," he snapped looking mildly offended, "I do not make it a habit of reading my client's wills. This one is protected by your father's mark and the seal is unbroken. No one has ever read this copy, I am certain of that. You have my absolute word. No one has read this will since it was first written down."

"Have you got it with you?" Marcus said staring at Falco.

"Of course," Falco replied, turning to glance at the villa and its out houses, "That is the reason I have come here in person, to give it to you."

"Boy," Marcus said, turning quickly to the slave, "tell everyone to gather in the dining room right away, everyone except Cunomoltus. Go."

The slave scampered off in the direction of the house as Marcus turned back to Falco. "Come and join me and my family in our home. It is proper that everyone should hear the news you have brought. I will have some food brought out to your driver."

Without saying a word Falco got down from his carriage and landed heavily in the snow. The old man suddenly looked very frail as Marcus offered him his arm.

"Thank you," Falco muttered as he grasped hold of Marcus's proffered arm and the two of them started out towards the house. "I am sorry that this news has come as a shock to you, Marcus, but it is my legal obligation that you and Efa should know."

"It's alright," Marcus said, "You did the right thing. I am sure the new version of the will is nothing for us to worry about."

As they slowly made their way through the snow covered courtyard, Marcus felt his heart thumping in his chest and suddenly he realised how nervous and tense he'd become. What did this new copy of his father's will mean? Had the old man gone crazy in his final months? Had he left everything to someone else? Was he about to lose his farm and business, his land? What the fuck was going on?

***

Falco cleared his throat as he stood occupying the middle of the silent room. Marcus stood by his side, staring tensely at the tightly rolled parchment document that lay on the table. Around him the family had gathered, their faces anxious and concerned. From the corner of his eye Marcus caught Efa looking at him, but he refused to meet her gaze. Dylis and Kyna were both staring at the scroll on the table and, in the background Jowan had quietly settled himself into a chair. Quintus, his arm shaking uncontrollably and his chin resting on his chest stood in the doorway with Petrus at his side, steadying him.

"Why would he change his will? Why would he do that?" Dylis exclaimed breaking the silence as she shook her head.

No one answered.

"It is an official document," Falco said turning to Marcus, "You will need a witness to confirm that you have received it, someone who is not part of the family and it can't be me."

Marcus grunted and turned to look around the room.

"What about your man, the driver," he muttered.

Falco nodded. "That will do," he said, "If one of your slaves will go and fetch him, we can then begin."

When at last the driver came in he had a sheepish look on his face and Falco gestured for him to go and stand over by the far wall. Once he'd done so, Falco picked up the scroll and showed the unbroken wax seal to Marcus, who nodded his agreement.

As Falco broke the seal and carefully unrolled the parchment, all eyes turned to stare at him and Petrus nudged Quintus, forcing him to lift his head up. Falco cleared his throat again and then in a clear, steady and well-practised voice he began to read out aloud.

"I swear by all the immortal gods that this is the true and last will and testament of I, Corbulo, Tesserarius in the XX Legion, born in Italia and raised as a citizen, who served faithfully for twenty-five years and was awarded an honourable discharge.

To Efa my strong faithful wife, I leave half my gold and ask her to look after our family, to keep us together for nothing is more precious than family.

To Dylis, my beautiful daughter, I leave the other half of my gold and my wish that she tell her children who their grandfather was.

To Quintus, old comrade in arms, he may live on my property until his days are over and no one shall have the right to kick him out.

To Marcus, my son, I leave him my farm and land on the Island of Vectis and my good name. May he not screw it up. And it is my final wish that my mortal remains should be buried on the battlefield where I fought the Barbarian Queen, beside those of my comrades who fell during the battle, for that was the promise we made to each other that day."

Falco fell silent and looked up at the faces around him.

"That's it," he murmured.

For a long moment the room remained silent. Then Efa stirred and wiped a tear from her eye.

"It sounds just like the will you read out to us fourteen years ago," she muttered.

"No," Marcus interrupted, shaking his head as he turned to look down at the floor, "the last part, the bit about him wanting to be buried on the battlefield where he fought Queen Boudicca, that is new. That was not in the first will."

"Marcus is right," Falco nodded, "I remember it too. He must have added the last part into the new will and forgotten to tell me about it."

"So nothing really changes," Petrus said from the doorway.

"It changes everything," Marcus snapped, raising his voice. He lifted his head, turning to stare at his family and there was a sudden fierce, smouldering shame in his eyes.

"It changes everything," he repeated, lowering his voice, "It is a son's duty to ensure that his father is properly buried, that all the funeral rites are correctly observed. If this is not done, my father's spirit will not be able to find its way to the afterlife. This was my task and I failed. Without a proper burial, Corbulo's spirit is doomed to wander this world in eternal unhappiness."

Across from him Efa muttered a hasty prayer and beside her Kyna raised her hand to her mouth.

"But you never had a body to bury," Dylis cried out, "We erected a memorial stone to him. We honoured him even though we did not have his body. That woman, that druid who murdered him, she took it with her. How can you do your duty when you never had his mortal remains in the first place? It's not fair."

Marcus sighed and gently shook his head.

"It doesn't matter," he replied wearily, "You heard his will. His final wish is to be buried beside his comrades on the battlefield, where he fought against Boudicca. As his son, it is my responsibility to ensure his final wish is carried out. I cannot just ignore that."

An awkward silence descended on the room.

"I too will be buried on the field where we fought the Barbarian Queen," an unsteady, stumbling voice said from the doorway and, as he spoke all eyes turned to stare at Quintus. The old man had raised his head and was staring blankly at the far wall and some spittle was making its way down his chin.

"Marcus is right," Efa said abruptly, her voice suddenly strong and filled with purpose. "Corbulo's will is clear. We need to honour his final wish. I will not rest knowing that we have failed to carry out his final wish, nor will I allow his spirit to wonder this world in unhappiness."

"But what can we do?" Dylis blurted out as a flush appeared in her cheeks, "We have no idea what that druid did with his body. It's an impossible task. Fourteen years have passed. How will we ever know what she did with the body?"

Once again the room fell silent. Then at last Marcus stirred and turned to look at his family and, as he did so, it seemed as if some invisible burden had suddenly fallen from his shoulders.

"It is a matter of honour," he said quietly, "For too long I have carried this shame of not having been able to give my father a proper burial. For too long I have hidden behind the impossibility of the task. But today that shame ends. Nothing is impossible, not when you truly put your mind to it. So I shall try and find out what happened to his body. I will retrieve his mortal remains and I will bury them on the battlefield just like he wants, so that his spirit will find peace, for all eternity. As his son, I will do this."

"How?" Dylis cried, "This is madness. Where do you start? You are going to get into trouble if you head north. I don't want to lose you too..."

"Dylis!" Efa's interrupted sharply in an angry voice, "Be silent! Marcus is right. Something needs to be done. In this house we honour the spirits of our ancestors. We remember them and we love them. Death does not change that, nor are we afraid of doing what is right, even if the task seems impossible."

"Marcus should go," Kyna nodded as she took a deep breath, "He should at least try to find out what happened to Corbulo's body, even if he does not find it. He has a duty. Fergus will have that same duty one day. A father must set an example. He must be the man he was raised to be."

Efa took a step towards Marcus and ran her fingers lightly across his chest as she muttered something under her breath. "It is settled then," she said in a louder voice, "Maybe the news that Falco has brought us is another challenge, sent by the immortals to test us."

For a moment Efa was silent, as a little sad and wise smile appeared on her lips.

"Maybe the gods are wiser than we think," she muttered at last, "They have given you a new purpose Marcus. If you had stayed here on the farm, you would quickly have grown bored and you would make an exceedingly bad farmer. No, maybe this journey is for the best. Maybe this is what the gods wish for you. I have no doubt that you will succeed."

Marcus said nothing as he glanced at Kyna and then at Dylis. Then as Falco handed him the scroll containing his father's will he lifted his head.

"I will not be going alone," he said, "I will be taking Cunomoltus with me. If he truly is my half-brother, as he claims, then I will know it by the journey's end."

Chapter Nine – Fergus

January 104 – The North

"Search the village, I want every house searched," the centurion bellowed at the hundred and sixty legionaries of his battle group. The Roman soldiers, clutching their spears and large oval shields, their boots crunching through the snow, were spread out in a loosely spaced, crescent line and were advancing at a steady walk towards the small cluster of round houses, nestling in the valley beside the mountain stream. Inside the village, Fergus could see the Brigantian inhabitants rushing around in panic. Their alarmed cries rent the peaceful morning as mothers snatched up their babies and hastily ushered their children into the small miserable-looking, thatched, round houses, whilst their men folk rushed to arm themselves.

Tensely Fergus tightened his grip on his pilum and shield as he closed in on the village. The four months of basic training had only finished a couple of weeks ago and already his instructors had decided he was ready for active duty and that was fine with him. He was ready. This was it then, his first engagement in the service of the XX Legion, the legion to which his grandfather Corbulo had once belonged. Fergus steadied his breathing as he felt his heart thumping away. He could not remember his grandfather of course, he'd been too young, but growing up on the island of Vectis, he'd spent his youth listening to Quintus' war stories and the adventures he and Corbulo had been involved in and it had shaped his ambition. There had been just one reason he'd decided to join his grandfather's old regiment and that was to be like his grandfather, Corbulo, a soldier of the legions.

He was well built for his eighteen years and recently the first ginger smattering of a beard had started to appear on his chin. His legionary helmet with the wide cheek- guards and rimmed neck-guard, covered his shortly cut, red hair but could not hide the black eye that had not yet fully healed. Carefully Fergus glanced sideways at Furius, his decanus, corporal, who was in charge of the eight-man tent group to which Fergus had been assigned and who had given him the black eye. The man was a couple of years older than himself and a more experienced soldier, who relished using his authority to violently bully his own men. It had been an unlucky day when Furius had been placed in charge of his eight-man squad, Fergus thought.

Some of the villagers had gathered around their leader, a tall man with a wise, weather beaten face and clad in a black woollen cloak but they did not offer any resistance as the Romans entered the village. Fergus glanced at the hostile and frightened faces of the Britons as the legionaries began to fan out amongst the round houses. The Brigantes with their wild, untrimmed beards were armed with spears, axes and swords but the quality of their weapons looked poor and their clothing, neck-torcs and metal arm bracelets were of simpler and more savage design than the tribal communities Fergus had known in the south.

"We are looking for the fugitive Arvirargus and his war band," Titus the centurion shouted in the Briton language, as he and his men approached the group of villagers. "Has anyone here seen this man or given him shelter or supplies?"

The centurion's question was met with a wall of silence from the Brigantes. Impatiently the Centurion slapped his vine staff against his thigh and glared at the villagers.

"You know the punishment for harbouring and aiding fugitives from Roman justice," he roared, "If any man here knows of Arvirargus's whereabouts it is his duty to report this to the Roman authorities. He is a wanted man and an enemy of Rome. Failure to do so is punishable by death. Now for the last time, has anyone seen or heard anything of this man?"

The villagers remained silent and with an annoyed shake of his head Titus, the veteran officer in command of the battle group turned to the legionaries standing behind him.

"Take a few of the women," he growled in Latin, "separate them and interrogate them, but don't kill them or harm them. I want to know everything there is to know and I want it done without having to fight the whole village. There is to be no repeat of what happened in the last settlement, understood."

"Fergus!" Furius shouted, "Stop dawdling and search that hut over there."

Quickly Fergus turned and hastened across the snowy ground towards the small thatched round house to which his decanus was pointing and, as he did so, he caught the disapproving angry glare on Furius's face. "You're a prick, you're a prick, you're a prick," Fergus thought as he hurried past Furius. The decanus had given him the black eye because Fergus had been the only man in his squad who'd dared stand up to the bullying that was being meted out.

The round house was small, with a thatched roof, and its walls were made of tightly woven wicker wood. Fergus flung aside the heavy woollen blanket that covered the doorway into the Brigantian home and lowered his spear as he ducked inside. In the gloom he could make out a circular room. Animal skins were strewn across the earthen floor and the place stank like the latrines he'd had to clean at the legionary base at Deva. From somewhere in the gloom he heard a pig squeal and, as his eyes adjusted to the light, he caught sight of a woman cowering against the far wall, shielding two young children with her arms. She stared at him with frightened eyes as Fergus took a step forwards and lowered his shield to the ground.

Awkwardly Fergus glanced around him, unsure about what to do. The home was poor and there were few possessions, just a metal cooking pot on top of a circle of blackened stones and a dead fire, a few earthenware pots, a hunting bow and quiver and a fresh sheep's skin hanging out to dry from a hook in the roof. The pig, which seemed to share the house with its human occupants, was rooting in the ground. He took a hesitant step

towards the woman but, as he did so, a loud commotion suddenly erupted from outside the hut. Fergus raised his shield and hastily turned to the exit, blinking as he emerged into the daylight outside. In the village the legionaries were shouting to each other in excited voices and, as Fergus came round the side of the round house, he saw a figure scurrying and limping up the steep bare mountain side. A group of legionaries were closing in on him from three sides. At last, seeing his way of escape cut off the man came to a halt and cried out something Fergus did not catch.

"What's going on?" Fergus called out to one of the new legionary recruits.

The soldier, slightly older than Fergus, gestured at the cornered man on the mountain slope.

"They've caught one of Arvirargus's men. Arsehole made a run for it."

Excited, Fergus turned to stare at the figure. The legionaries were approaching him warily and suddenly Fergus noticed the sword in the man's hand. So this was the enemy they had been sent to hunt down. Would he fight? When they had been preparing to leave the camp at Deva and his company centurion had first briefed them on the mission, Fergus had relished the challenge of finding and capturing Arvirargus and his fugitive war band, for Arvirargus was famous throughout the province of Britannia. He and his men had been the only Brigantian war band who had refused to make peace with Rome when, starving, decimated and demoralised, the northern rebellion of Brigantian and Caledonian tribes had collapsed some fourteen years ago. Despite their hopeless situation, Arvirargus and his men had continued the rebellion, harassing and attacking Roman interests across the vast wild mountains of the north. But now, as he stared at the lonely figure trapped on the hillside the enemy looked surprisingly ordinary, Fergus thought.

***

It was dark and the Roman battle group had made their camp in a forest. Amongst the pine trees and bare, snow covered ground, the men huddled around their small camp-fires, which provided some welcome warmth from the rapidly falling temperature. There had been no time to prepare any defences and the ground had been too hard for the men to erect a palisade. The pause was only for a few hours anyway for Titus, their commanding officer, had made it clear he wished to reach the legionary base at Deva as soon as possible. Standing beside a large oak in the centre of the camp, Fergus stamped his feet on the ground as he tried to keep warm. A coarse army cloak was wrapped around his shoulders and in his hand he clutched his spear. The fugitive, whom the legionaries had captured on the mountain was sitting on the ground, his back resting against the oak, his ankles and wrists securely fastened together with iron slavers chains. The man had his eyes closed and seemed to be asleep and down the side of his shin, his tunic was stained with dried blood.

Wearily Fergus touched his bruised eye. The task of guarding the prisoner had been given to Furius' squad and of course the decanus had given him the shittiest watch. Close by, Furius and the rest of the squad were sleeping, curled up around the small crackling fire, wrapped in their grey army blankets with their shields and weapons within easy reach. A blackened and well used metal cooking pot stood to one side. Bored, Fergus yawned and kicked at a clump of snow. Then he turned to stare at his sleeping companions. Vittius, Aledus and Catinius were alright. They were about his age and they had all come through basic training together and had been accepted into the legion as newly trained Munifex, privates, like himself. The three older men however were Furius' friends and for most of the time they pretended that he did not exist. Fergus sighed. Aledus came from Londinium and Vittius and Catinius were both from Gaul and worshipped Mithras, but none of them had come to his aid when he'd stood up to Furius' bullying and had been punched in the face for his efforts.

Fergus turned away from the fire and peered into the forest. The Roman camp fires were burning low and the night was quiet. But he had done the right thing in standing up for himself he thought. Corbulo would have done the same. He was sure of it. During basic training he'd never given his instructors reason for complaint. He had never fallen behind on the brutal route marches, or during the swimming and daily routine of physical exercises or the weapons training. He had done everything they had asked him to do and he had done it well. Some of his fellow recruits had quickly dropped out, unable to cope with the harsh unrelenting training routine and Fergus had been glad they did, for as his instructors had repeated again and again, once in the legion, a legionary must be able to completely trust the man standing beside him. And sometimes when he'd lain in his barracks bunk at night, he'd thought about how it would be if he and Corbulo had stood together in the line, facing the enemy. What a day that would have been.

His watch dragged on and after a while Fergus noticed that it had begun to snow. Slowly the snowflakes came drifting down through the branches of the trees covering the ground in a fresh layer of snow. For a while he stared at the flakes, watching them tumble into oblivion on the ground. Then he turned sharply to look at the prisoner. The man had his eyes closed and he seemed to be asleep. He wasn't going anywhere in those chains. Fergus raised his hand to his mouth and blew some hot air onto his fingers. With a bit of luck they would be back in Deva within two days and he would be able to visit the Lucky Legionary tavern again. The Lucky was a popular and favourite tavern for many of the soldiers based at Deva but Fergus had a special reason to want to visit. The inn owner's daughter was called Galena and she was the most beautiful girl he'd ever seen. A little colour shot into Fergus's cheeks as he wondered what she would be like without any clothes on.

Fergus was just about to kick Vittius awake and tell him that his watch had started, when a sudden cry rang out from the edge of the camp. Startled, Fergus spun round in the direction from

which the noise had come. For a moment all was silent as he squinted at the trees. Then the night erupted with shouts and cries of panic and alarm. Fergus raised his shield and his eyes widened in horror as three horsemen came thundering towards him, swerving and weaving expertly through the forest. The riders were clutching burning torches and they were heading straight towards him.

"What's the fuck," Fergus cried out, stumbling backwards. There was no time to see whether his comrades were awake. Instinctively he raised his large oval shield and lowered his spear. Then the riders were upon him. A large black horse reared up in front of him and he caught a glimpse of its rider. The man was clad in a white cloak, his head covered by a hood and he was clutching a spear. From the corner of his eye, Fergus caught movement to his left and instinctively he ducked as an axe came whistling through the air, narrowly missing him before embedding itself into a tree. Another horseman appeared from the gloom, as around the camp fire, Fergus' comrades were shouting, stumbling to their feet and reaching for their weapons in a mix of confusion and horror.

Fergus stood rooted to the ground, unable to move. As he stared at the horsemen milling around in the snow, one of Furius' friends staggered backwards and collapsed onto the ground with an axe sticking out of his back. The man dropped his sword, opened his mouth and screamed, spitting blood onto the fine white snow.

Close by, someone else was shouting and Fergus heard the rattle and chink of chains. Wide-eyed he whipped round to see that the prisoner was wide awake and on his feet and stumbling towards the horsemen and as he saw the man shuffling towards the riders, with his arm stretched out to them, Fergus suddenly understood what was happening. The riders had come to rescue their comrade. With a savage roar, Fergus lowered his head like a bull and charged forwards, his shield covering his body and his spear aimed at the prisoner. The force of his charge sent his spear straight through the man's back and out through his chest and, as they collided, both of them tumbled to the ground in a confused mass of legs and arms. Fergus lost his grip on his shield and hit the solid rock hard earth with a painful thud. At his side the impaled prisoner lay moaning and groaning on the ground with Fergus's spear sticking from his back, as the snow around him started to turn dark red. A horse whinnied and a pair of hooves slammed into the ground inches from Fergus's head. Terrified he rolled away and onto his back and stared up at the horseman looming high above him. The man was staring at the prisoner on the ground, his mouth twisting and working on a furious and silent curse. Shaking, Fergus reached for his Gladius, short sword, but before he could draw it from its scabbard the horsemen were crying out to each other and were streaming away into the wood, leaving behind the screams of the wounded and the shouts of the shocked and enraged legionaries.

***

Fergus stood stiffly to attention in the blood soaked snow, staring rigidly into space as Furius slowly circled the body of the prisoner, which still lay where it had fallen. The decanus was shaking his head in disbelief and was running his hand across his forehead in an agitated manner. Clustered around the fire, Vittius, Aledus, Catinius and the others were watching their commanding officer in silence. Catinius had a blood stained bandage wrapped around his neck and was grimacing with pain and one of the older men was squatting beside their wounded comrade, who was lying on the ground, wrapped in a blanket.

The man's eyes were closed. Wherever he lived or not was in the hands of the gods now, the doctor had muttered.

"Do you realise how annoyed and angry Titus is?" Furius hissed as he rounded on Fergus, his face contorted in rage. "We were tasked with guarding the prisoner. It was our job to keep that fucker alive so that the boys on the legate's staff could interrogate him and find out where these rebels are holed up. But instead you go and kill him." Furius's finger jabbed painfully into Fergus' chest. "You had to fucking well kill him didn't you, so now we have no prisoner and no intelligence and the commander has just given me an earful of shit. Don't expect he will grant us any favours anytime soon."

"I prevented him from escaping Sir," Fergus replied clearing his throat. "The riders came to rescue him."

"I know that," Furius roared bringing his face right up against Fergus', "But he is still dead and it is your fault that he is. You ran him through with your spear!"

"So what was I supposed to have done Sir," Fergus said struggling to remain calm.

"You were on guard duty," Furius bellowed, "You should have sounded the alarm and woken us. We could have saved our prisoner if you had done that, you fucking brainless fool."

"There was no time Sir," Fergus muttered, "They were upon us before I could act. They must have been watching us for a while because those horsemen knew exactly where the prisoner was being held."

"Are you trying to be smart with me?" Furius roared.

"No Sir," Fergus replied lowering his eyes, "Just pointing out that these Britons should not be underestimated. Arvirargus has been on the run for a long time. He will not be so easily caught. We should have posted a stronger guard."

For a moment Furius stared at Fergus in silence. Then he shook his head in despair.

"Where the fuck did they find you Fergus" he growled, as frustrated, he turned and gave the corpse a savage kick.

Chapter Ten – The Run

Fergus sat on the freezing, cold, stone floor of the cramped barrack room grinding the grain into a fine flour with a small portable stone hand mill. It was dawn and beside him Catinius, a blood stained bandage wrapped around his neck, was quietly repairing a tear in his tunic. The only other occupants of the eight man, Contubernium, barrack room, Vittius and Aledus were lounging on their bunks hungrily watching Fergus preparing breakfast. The men's equipment, armour, swords, spears and shields lay neatly stacked against the far wall of the stone room and a small glowing hearth provided some warmth. A single night had passed since Fergus and his company had returned to their barracks at the legionary fortress of Deva Victrix.

"Porridge or pancakes boys?" Fergus called out as he finished grinding the grain and carefully scooped the fine flour into a bowl.

"Pancakes," Catinius growled, "the water is rotten around here, just like the bloody weather and women."

Fergus raised his eyebrows but said nothing. Catinius was a born pessimist, grumbler and liked to complain about everything when he got the chance. As a boy he'd witnessed his family being butchered by Germanic tribesmen, who had crossed the Rhine to raid Roman territory and the experience had left him with a fierce hatred of any non-Roman people.

"Should we not wait until Furius is back?" Vittius replied guardedly. "He should be back soon, best let him decide."

Fergus glanced cautiously at the doorway. The decanus had gone to collect the day's orders from the company Centurion, Titus, and would be back soon, together with the others, and when he returned there was going to be hell to pay, Fergus thought, for he was certain to get the shittiest job going that day.

The decanus was not about to let him forget about the embarrassment he'd caused him.

"Fuck that," Fergus muttered, as he stiffly rose to his feet. "Pancakes it is."

"Yeah screw him," Aledus said elbowing Vittius in his ribs, "Fergus is right. I am tired of that arsehole's bullying and I am not going to pay him anything either. Do you see how the others bribe him in exchange for the easy jobs?"

"All I am saying is he's in charge," Vittius exclaimed giving Aledus a shove, "You should be careful, he can make things a lot worse for you."

"So why are you not one of his friends then?" Aledus sneered, "Or do you secretly suck his cock at night and rat on us during the day?"

Vittius shook his head in disgust but refused to rise to the bait. Instead he ran his fingers over the little amulet to Mithras that hung around his neck. He was by nature a serious young man and very religious, never ever missing his three daily prayer's to the sun god at sunrise, noon and sunset.

"Leave him alone Aledus," Fergus said, "Of course Vittius is one of us and I for one, am happy to have him standing beside me in the line."

"Do you think he is going to make it?" Catinius said abruptly changing the subject.

Fergus said nothing as he carried on preparing breakfast and for a long moment the barracks room was silent as the men's thoughts turned to their wounded mess mate, who'd been transferred to the camp's hospital.

"He's not going to make it. He's as good as dead. That wound looked pretty bad," Catinius muttered at last.

"I bet you," Aledus exclaimed raising a finger in the air, "that he lives. I have heard that those doctors over at the hospital are pretty good. One denarii says that he will live."

Fergus shook his head and Catinius frowned. Aledus, a native of Londinium was a cocky, confident spirit and his good looks and natural charm had, he'd boasted, gotten him more girls, than the years he'd lived.

But before any of them could answer the door, was flung open and Furius stomped into the barracks room.

"I've got the company orders for the day," the decanus snapped as he pushed his way through towards the fire to warm his hands. "The day's password is Trajan. The company is to help unload the grain wagons that are arriving from the supply depot." Furius paused and turned to glare at Fergus, and for a split moment, Fergus thought he detected a hint of satisfaction on Furius's face. "Everyone except you four." Furius continued pointing his finger at the men. "You have another task. Due to the recent disgrace you have brought to the company, Titus has ordered you to run ten laps around the camp. And if any of you fails to complete the run you will all repeat it again tomorrow. The centurion has detailed one of his men to make sure you complete the exercise. So get yourself ready, breakfast can wait."

The barracks room went silent. Ten laps around the perimeter of the legionary fortress, that was nearly twelve miles, Fergus thought. He glanced at his mess mates and saw the same gloomy resigned look on their faces but none of mates uttered a word of protest.

"Sir, if the centurion wishes to punish us," Fergus said at last slowly rising to his feet, "It should only be me. I was the one who killed the prisoner. The others were asleep. It was not their fault. It was mine alone."

"No Fergus," Furius replied sharply, "Titus has ordered that all four of you are to do the run and if you speak out again, I will make you all run naked."

"But Sir," Aledus said carefully, "What about the others? Will they join us on the run? Fergus is right, we were all tasked with guarding the prisoner. It's not fair."

"What the fuck did I just say," Furius growled, swinging round to stare at Aledus. "The centurion has ordered that it be just you four. Now move it. Titus wants you out their sweating within the hour."

***

The flurry of snow balls came flying towards the four jogging men as they neared the main gates into the vast legionary fortress. Fergus ducked just in time but ahead of him Catinius was hit on the shoulder and from the gates the legionaries on guard duty raised a triumphant cheer which ended in laughter and a few shouted insults. Fergus and his three mess mates however ignored the guards as they ran on towards the watch tower marking the far corner of the playing card shaped camp. The four of them were clad in their hobnailed army boots and simple white tunics with short sleeves and despite the cold, their faces and backs were covered in sweat. It was the third time they had been pelted by their bored comrades. Fergus raised his head and glanced quickly at Catinius who was leading. The bandage around his mess mate's neck was stained dark red with fresh blood and Fergus could hear his friend's laboured breathing.

"That's lap four boys," Fergus cried out, "We're nearly half way. Come on we can do this."

The others said nothing.

Fergus lowered his head and clenched his hands into fists as he stared at the snow covered ground moving beneath his feet. However hard they had made his army training he was not going to give up. He was going to succeed. He was not going to quit. He was going to take everything they threw at him. He would suffer the harsh, relentless physical exercise, the training swims in freezing cold water and the hours of boring guard duty and latrine cleaning duties handed out to new recruits. He was going to be a legionary for somewhere his grandfather, Corbulo, was watching him, judging him, and he would be damned if he was not going to make his grandfather proud. He was going to make Corbulo proud. For that was all that really mattered and no punishment run, nor a bully like Furius was going to change that.

As they started down the side of the fortress a few civilians paused to stare at them. Fergus raised his head again and glanced at Catinius. His mess mate was starting to flag and slow. He should never have been forced onto a punishment run, not with his neck wound, he thought.

"Aledus," Fergus gasped, "Take over the lead from Catinius, we'll each lead for one lap, change when we reach the gates."

Aledus said nothing as he silently moved to the front and began to set the pace and as Catinius drifted back, Fergus gave him a nudge with his elbow.

"You alright mate?"

Catinius replied by shaking his head. His face was lathered in sweat and one of his eyes was twitching uncontrollably. He looked exhausted.

"You are doing well," Fergus gasped, "You are doing well. Not far now."

"What do you mean?" Vittius exclaimed with a red face, "We're not even fucking half way yet."

"Shut up," Fergus hissed, giving Vittius a furious glance.

"I get it, I really do," Vittius snapped, "If one of us fails to complete the run we all do it again tomorrow. But I am telling you, we're not even half way yet."

"We're going to make it," Fergus said with sudden conviction in his voice, "Don't any of you dare doubt that. I am not going to face Furius and the centurion and report that we failed to complete this task. Fuck that! Don't any of you dare give up. Don't you even think about it!"

Vittius did not reply and Fergus turned to look at Catinius.

"We're going to do this," Fergus gasped, "We're going to complete this run together. We are going to show that piece of shit, Furius, who we really are."

**

"Final lap, final lap," Fergus cried out excitedly as he led his mess mates around the corner of the fortress walls and they once again started to head towards the gates leading into the legionary camp. Behind him Aledus and Vittius were supporting Catinius, who was stumbling along leaning heavily on his mess mates for support. Their gasps, groans and panting seemed to be the only noise. Fergus stared at the gates expecting the usual flurry of snowballs and insults from the guards but none came and suddenly he noticed that the ramparts of the fort were lined with off-duty legionaries. He blinked in disbelief and as he did so a great roaring cheer rose up from the walls, a roar of encouragement and as he heard it, a hot flush of pride appeared on Fergus's face.

"Come on," he cried out turning to his fellow runners, "We're nearly there."

"Take over from me," Vittius gasped closing his eyes in utter exhaustion. "I am done."

Fergus slowed his pace and grasping Catinius's left arm he slung it over his shoulder. Catinius's eyes were closed and his head was lolling about as if he was sleeping and the back of his tunic was filthy and stained with sweat and fresh blood.

"Listen to those cries," Fergus roared, somehow finding the strength to raise his voice. "We are going to do this. Don't give up, not now. Don't you dare."

No one replied as they stumbled past the gateway and onwards towards the watch tower marking the north western corner of the fortress. Grimly Fergus bit his lip as they slowly turned and began to make their way down the side of the camp. The stone walls and deep V shaped ditch looked formidable and intimidating. At his side Catinius grunted but did not open his eyes. Spittle was trying to escape from his mouth but his body was too dehydrated to allow it and instead it clung to his chin in a hopeless embrace.

Fergus lowered his head. His legs felt heavy and his breath was coming in ragged gasps and his mouth was bone dry, so dry he could barely swallow. Not far to go now he thought.

As the four of them wearily turned the corner for the final stretch, Fergus raised his head and blinked, trying to focus on the finish line. As he drew closer he saw two men standing beside the gate watching them approach. It was Furius and Titus the company centurion clasping his vine stick. Furius shook his head in silent disapproval as Fergus and his mess mates came to a stumbling, groaning halt before him. Aledus let go of Catinius who instantly collapsed onto his knees and then onto his side. With a sudden rush of energy Fergus straightened up, turned to face the officers and saluted.

"I report Sir, that we have completed our task, Sir", he gasped as his chest heaved with exertion. "And I will not kill any prisoners again without permission, Sir."

A little bemused smile appeared on the veteran centurion's face as he stared at Fergus for a moment before turning to gaze at the gasping, exhausted men lying on the ground. Then gently Titus tapped his vine stick against his thigh and turned to Furius. "These men are to receive a pass to leave the camp tonight. They have earned themselves a drink; make sure they do," the centurion said again, and with a final glance at Fergus, he strode away.

Furius watched the centurion walk away. Then slowly he turned to face his men with a sour look.

"I hope you have learned your lesson today," Furius snarled. "Now get yourselves back to the barracks and cleaned up. When you are done we are going to the hospital to visit our comrade. The doctors say he's going to live." Furius paused and then turned towards Fergus. "All of us except you Fergus. I have another task for you."

Chapter Eleven – Fergus decides

Fergus plunged his face into the barrel of ice cold water and rapidly withdrew it, sending water droplets flying in every direction. The water was instantly refreshing and just what he needed. Around him the rows of identical, single-storey stone barracks blocks stretched nearly all the way to the fort's outer walls. It was late in the afternoon and it was already growing dark. The temperature too was dropping. Snow covered the tiled roofs and close by a few legionaries, clad in their winter cloaks were warming their hands over a small open fire. For a moment Fergus stared at the men. Then abruptly he rubbed his face with both of his hands and ran his fingers through his hair before cautiously turning to glance at the door leading to his barracks room.

What did Furius want with him now? Was the decanus preparing yet another humiliation for him? The others had already gone to visit their wounded comrade in the camp hospital but Furius had told him to wait.

"Fergus," Furius suddenly called out from within the barracks room.

Fergus stooped, picked up his leather army belt from which hung his sheathed gladius and quickly fixed it around his waist. Then he strode into the barrack's room. Furius was sitting on a wooden stool beside the table. The decanus was furiously scratching something onto a small wooden tablet with an iron tipped stylus. His writing however was confident, neat and precise.

"Sir," Fergus muttered coming to a halt and clasping his hands behind his back.

Furius did not look up and continued his furious writing and for a moment the only sound in the barracks room was the scratching of the iron pen on the soft wood. Then with a flourish Furius finished and laid down his stylus and studied the neat sentences inscribed on the small wooden tablet.

"Take this to the quartermaster's office," the decanus growled at last, holding up the wooden letter. "Ask for a man called Janus. It is important that this letter is delivered to him and him alone. Do you understand?"

Carefully Fergus took the letter and nodded. "Yes Sir," he said stiffly.

Furius rose from his seat, placed his hands on his hips and gave Fergus a strange look.

"This is important Fergus," Furius said quietly.

"Yes," Fergus replied. Then quickly he turned and walked out of the barracks room and as he strode away in the direction of the camp granaries he had the uncomfortable feeling that Furius was watching him.

Most of the off duty soldiers were inside their barracks rooms and, as Fergus turned a corner and made his way across the frozen mud between the barracks blocks, he looked down at the wooden letter in his hand. What was the decanus doing writing letters to the quartermaster's office? Unable to resist any longer he came to a halt and held the letter up into the fading day light. Whatever else he was, Furius knew how to write Fergus thought, for he had no difficulty in reading the neat, elegant sentences.

Furius, decanus, 2nd company, 2nd Cohort to Janus, quartermaster general's office.

My brother, Lucanius has written to me saying he has in excess of 100 high quality hides in his store houses which he is willing to sell to the quartermaster of the 20th Legion at the previously agreed price.

The hides are at Isca but he is willing to transport them immediately upon confirmation of the order and pay for their transport. My brother writes that he will contribute a donation to the society of the rightful veterans of the Twentieth Legion should the contract be agreed. Please advise me of your reply at the soonest possible occasion and please greet your sister Julia from me.

Your faithful friend and business partner

Fergus frowned and lowered the letter as he trudged on towards the camp granaries and the quartermaster's offices. What was this? The letter had surprised him. What was Furius doing, arranging army supply contracts for his brother? He'd had no idea that such things were possible. As he approached the large warehouses containing the legion's supply of grain, Fergus came to a halt as he suddenly had an uneasy thought. Quickly he raised the letter to the light and read it once again and as he did a little colour shot into his cheeks.

My brother writes that he will contribute a donation to the society of the rightful veterans of the Twentieth Legion should the contract be agreed.

"The Society of Rightful Veterans of the Twentieth Legion," Fergus muttered to himself. He'd never heard of such a society nor had he heard any of his fellow soldiers talk about it. Was this a way of bribing the quartermaster's office into agreeing the supply contract? He lowered the letter and raised his hand and gently stroked his chin. But if it was a bribe why had Furius sent him to deliver the letter? Why was the decanus deliberately showing him his business dealings? It didn't make sense. If the senior officers found out about this; if they suspected corruption in the quartermaster's office; it would surely mean punishment for all those involved. Why had Furius chosen him to deliver the letter? He could have done that himself. The flush on Fergus's cheeks deepened. Was he being set up? But that didn't make sense for Furius had clearly marked the letter as coming from himself. Bewildered Fergus gently shook his head. What was going on?

There were no guards outside the building containing the quartermaster's staff and as Fergus entered, he was met by the welcoming warmth of a roaring and well fed fire. A couple of clerks were gathered around the hearth. They gave Fergus a brief, disinterested glance and quickly turned back to their conversation.

Fergus paused by the door and glanced around the office. Against the far wall stood a wooden table upon which lay stack upon stack of neatly organised, wooden letters similar to the one he was clutching in his hand.

"I am looking for Janus," Fergus said turning to the clerks.

The men's conversation ceased and one of the clerks looked up and, as he caught sight of the letter in Fergus's hand, a glint of interest appeared in his eyes. For a moment the office remained silent.

"He's in the back room," the clerk replied, staring at Fergus.

Fergus said nothing as he quickly strode across the office and through the doorway into the back room. Inside an older man of around thirty, with black hair was sitting at a table reading a parchment scroll. Startled he looked up as Fergus saluted.

"Are you Janus?" Fergus said.

"I am, and who are you?" Janus growled, clearly displeased at the intrusion.

In reply Fergus proffered the letter. "I was told to give this to you."

With a grunt Janus took the letter and read it and as he did so he grunted again.

"Sir," Fergus said as he watched Janus read, "What is the Society of Rightful Veterans of the Twentieth Legion? I have never heard of that before."

Abruptly Janus lowered the letter and turned to stare at Fergus with an incredulous look.

"What are you, stupid?" Janus hissed. "Get the fuck out of my office."

***

The others had not yet returned from the hospital as Fergus strode back into his quarters. Furius was reclining on the only chair with his feet up on the small table. He gave Fergus a careful searching look.

"Did you deliver the letter to Janus?" he growled.

Fergus nodded and moved over to his bunk and awkwardly began re-arranging his thick woollen blanket.

"Good," Furius replied, "Here, this is for you," he said as he chucked a small leather bag at Fergus, who caught it with one hand. "Buy the boys a drink tonight in the tavern or spend it on that woman of yours. The barmaid at the Lucky. Everyone knows how much you like her."

Fergus stared at the small bag of coins in his hand. What was this? Why was Furius being nice to him? Why was he rewarding him for a simple errand?

"That's kind of you, but she is not my woman," Fergus muttered as he slipped the money pouch into a pocket. "I don't even think she likes me."

"Whatever," Furius said, waving his hand dismissively in the air, "But you should listen to the advice from a man who knows a bit more about women than you do. Women like a man with money, a man who can buy them pretty things." Furius shrugged. "Army pay is good but you can always do with some extra cash on the side, right?"

Suddenly Furius was staring at Fergus with a calculating look.

"There is more where that money came from," he said silkily, "I know how it works. So are you in Fergus? This is your opportunity. Can I count on you?"

Fergus turned away so that Furius could not see his face. So that was what the business with the letter to Janus was all about. Furius was trying to get him involved in his business, his money making schemes on the side.

Without saying a word Fergus strode out of the barracks block. It was nearly dark and up on the stone ramparts of the fortress the sentries were shouting to each other as the guard was being changed. Burning beacons lined the walls at intervals and the smell of charcoal was in the air. Without a purpose Fergus started out towards the centre of the camp where the senior legionary officers were quartered and as he did so he touched his bruised eye. So that was why Furius was being nice to him. The decanus was trying to get him involved in his money-making schemes and if he agreed he would forever be in the man's pocket. Angrily his hand clenched into a fist. Furius was trying to bribe him. Furius could fuck off. He should really report this whole affair to Titus, the company centurion. Surely the army did not tolerate its soldiers running private businesses, bribing the quartermasters for supply contracts?

Fergus came to a halt as if he had just run into a brick wall. But what if Titus too was involved? What if the senior officers were doing the same? In the gloom no one noticed the sudden blush that spread across his cheeks. Slowly Fergus turned round and stared in the direction from which he'd just come. He had a choice to make. A big choice. Was this how the army worked? He was not high born, he had no powerful and influential friends and for a man like that, if he wanted to rise up the army hierarchy, then the only way, surely, was to play this game. If he wanted to gain promotion and become someone, then he would have to do this, but on the other hand he would be indebted to Furius for the rest of his career and being indebted to that arsehole was something he really, really didn't want.

Irritated he kicked at a clump of frozen mud and sent it flying against a barracks wall. No, he thought furiously, he needed to remain calm and think this through carefully. He needed to be smart. Wearily he closed his eyes and ran his fingers across his face. What would Corbulo, his grandfather, have done in this situation? Slowly Fergus opened his eyes as a smile appeared on his lips. Corbulo would have told Furius to fuck off and eat his own shit. As he thought about his grandfather's reaction his smile grew. According to Quintus, Corbulo had always said exactly what he was thinking and because of that he had never risen very high in the ranks. Fergus sighed and started out again towards the Principia at the centre of the camp. He had to decide.

As he neared the central square where the senior officers and their families had their quarters, he came to an abrupt halt. In the fading and dying light a small procession of white-robed priests was coming towards him and, in between them, strode the Legion's Aquilifer, proudly holding up the Eagle standard of the Twentieth Legion. Fergus's eyes widened in awe and he hastily took a step backwards as he stared at the golden, sacred eagle as it swept past, and as he did so, Fergus swore that the Eagle's eyes twinkled and looked at him. A legion's Eagle was a God, Quintus had explained to him, on the many evenings he'd spent talking to the old veteran, when he was still a boy growing up on the island of Vectis. And if the Eagle looks at you it is a sign, the old man had muttered, a sign that the gods have taken an interest in you.

Hastily Fergus started off in the opposite direction and as he did so he sensed a new resolve. He would accept Furius' offer, whether he liked it or not, he would have to play the political game. He would make friends with the people who would decide on his promotion prospects. He would do this even if he hated it. Once long ago, Quintus had told him something about Corbulo. He had said that Corbulo had regretted not making anything of himself and that he had spent his whole retirement trying to put things right. And in the end he had sacrificed his life to protect his children. He had pursued his ambition to the end. Yes, Fergus nodded as his resolve grew, he would do this because at the end of the day his grandfather would want him to make something of himself. Corbulo would be the first to applaud him. Corbulo would understand and, if his granddad approved, then he would be able to handle anything.

Chapter Twelve – The Barmaid of the Lucky

The Lucky Legionary tavern was packed with off-duty Legionaries. The soldiers sat drinking wine, beer and mead from long wooden benches beside tables and the noise and mood was loud and boisterous. Against the far wall a cracking and roaring fire was blasting heat into the large room. It was being attended to by a slave who was feeding logs into the greedy flames. Fergus and his mess mates sat together at the end of one of the tables, squeezed in between other groups. The men were clasping their cups to their chests and talking in animated, slightly tipsy voices. Fergus however was silent, and as he listened to his comrades, his attention started to slip and he turned cautiously to look in the direction of the long rectangular bar, with its large circular holes cut into the wood, to allow for easier and quicker access to the drink stored beneath it. Galena and her father, the tavern owner, were busy serving the thirsty men and, as he stared at Galena, a flush appeared on Fergus's cheeks. The tavern owner's daughter was sixteen, with long blond hair which she'd tied back in a ponytail and she was wearing a leather apron over her chest and to Fergus she was the most beautiful woman he'd ever seen. He had noticed her the moment he had first come to the Lucky tavern in the civilian settlement that had grown up around the legionary fortress. But after all these weeks, he'd still not had the courage to get up and talk to her. As he stared at her, she suddenly looked up and with uncanny instinct she seemed to pick him out from the crowd and for a brief moment their eyes made contact. Hastily Fergus turned away, his eyes widening and the flush on his cheeks deepened.

A hand slapped into Fergus's back nearly forcing him to spill his wine.

"I think Fergus has spotted something he likes," Aledus cried out as a smirk appeared on his lips. "Heh lads, how about we all chip in, so that our young friend here can lose his virginity tonight with the barmaid."

Aledus' cry was met with a chorus of encouraging cheers from the others and even Furius looked bemused.

"Shut up!" Fergus snapped as he shrugged himself free from Aledus's arm. "She is no common tavern whore."

"Ooh I think he really likes her," Aledus replied as the grin on his face grew. "Well if you like her so much, why don't you go over there and talk to her?"

"Just shut up will you," Fergus replied moodily as he raised his cup to his lips.

"I think he's afraid of her father," Catinius said, giving Fergus a wink, "He looks like the kind of man who doesn't take kindly to Romans poking around his daughter. They say that he fought against Rome during the Brigantian rebellion. Look at the bastard, he's built like a tree trunk."

"Yes and now he runs a tavern serving the deserving men of the Twentieth," Furius interrupted, "So who won that fight? Not the fucking Brigantes, eh."

No one replied and idly Fergus turned to glance again in the direction of the bar. Galena's father, the tavern owner, was indeed a huge, towering hulk of a man who looked like he knew how to handle himself in a fight, although his grey beard and large belly betrayed his age. The man's forehead glistened with sweat as he went about handing out cups of wine and taking coin in return. He looked around forty.

"Fergus, wasn't your father involved in putting down that rebellion?" Vittius said, carefully wiping his chin with the back of his hand.

Fergus glanced at Vittius and wearily shook his head. He did not know or remember his father, Marcus, at all. The man had left with his Batavian cohort for the Dacian frontier when he'd still been too young to remember. He could not even picture what his father looked like and his mother, Kyna, had never really wanted to talk about him.

"He was with the 2nd Batavian cohort in the fort up at Luguvalium," Fergus muttered, "They say he saved his entire unit from annihilation and that he fought well during the uprising, but that he disobeyed orders and got disgraced and demoted. That's all I know about him. I haven't seen him in thirteen years and I don't expect he will return from Dacia."

The others were silent for a moment, as they pondered what had been said. Then slowly the conversation turned to other matters and, as it did Fergus stiffly rose from his seat and stumbled towards the door. Outside it was dark and quiet and a multitude of stars twinkled in the night sky. Fergus shivered as the coldness hit him and he hastily turned into the dark alley that ran alongside the tavern. In the darkness he fumbled with his tunic and sighed as he sent a satisfying stream of steaming piss arching into the snow. As he emerged from the alley however and turned towards the tavern door, he came to an abrupt halt. A young woman was waiting for him just outside the tavern. In the flickering torchlight he saw that it was Galena. She was staring at him.

"I am no whore," Galena said in good Latin, "If you want me to be your woman, it has to be only me and it has to be for eternity. So if you can't make that promise then I suggest you start staring at some other woman's tits."

And without another word she abruptly turned around and marched back into the tavern leaving Fergus staring in stunned silence at the door as it slammed shut in his face.

***

As he re-entered the tavern Fergus saw that Galena was back behind the bar serving customers. She was talking to her father as she handed out cups of wine but the noise inside the room made it impossible to hear what she was saying. Was she

telling her father about him? Wearily Fergus shook his head. He was such a coward when it came to women. With a sigh he turned back to his comrades and, as he did he immediately noticed that something was wrong. His mess mates had fallen silent and were staring tensely at a group of legionaries, sitting at the next table. Aledus seemed to be having an argument with one of the men.

"What's going on?" Fergus muttered nudging Vittius as he squeezed into his place on the bench.

"They're from the 6th Cohort," Vittius replied in a tense voice," One of those arseholes just insulted Aledus, called him a cocksucker. Aledus is not about to let it go."

"Oh shit," Fergus grunted as he turned to stare at the men seated at the next table. They seemed to be a large group of around twenty. The bad blood between the 2nd Cohort and the 6th was well-known for the 6th prided itself as being one of the finest cohorts in the Legion and its legionaries had a habit of looking down on the 2nd, who were by tradition made up of the newest and youngest recruits.

"And what are you going to do about it, little man?" the soldier with whom Aledus was arguing suddenly sneered. "You and your friends want to take this outside?"

Aledus's face darkened as he rose to his feet and aggressively thrust his head forwards and as he did so, half a dozen men on the opposing table rose to their feet, their faces hard and cold. The soldiers from the 6th all looked like seasoned veterans, men in their prime.

"Aledus, sit down, for fuck's sake," Furius hissed, trying to tug Aledus back down into his seat, but Aledus would not budge. He was staring furiously at the man who had insulted him and there was a murderous glint in his eyes.

"Say what you just said again," Aledus said slowly raising his finger and pointing at the man, "and I will slit your throat."

On the opposite table one of the soldiers from the 6th suddenly slammed the sharp point of a Pugio, knife, into the wooden table.

"Oi, show some respect," Fergus suddenly shouted as he rose to his feet and stared at the large group of men from the 6th Cohort, his face suddenly flush with emotion, and, as he did, the whole tavern fell silent and all eyes turned in his direction.

"Show some respect," Fergus roared again, as a powerful unstoppable emotion surged through him, "My grandfather, Corbulo served for twenty-five years in the Twentieth. He was with the legion when it stormed the druidic stronghold of Mona Insulis. He fought in the battle against the Barbarian Queen. He was with the expedition that was sent to conquer Tara in Hibernia, and when the commander was killed, it was he who was placed in command, and it was he, who brought the survivors home. The Sixth Cohort formed part of that expedition. He led you all back home, so show some fucking respect!"

Fergus was trembling as he stood glaring at the legionaries and for a long moment no one spoke and the only noise in the room was the crackle and roar of the flames in the hearth.

Then, at the back of the room a soldier stood up and folded his arms across his chest. The legionary looked older than the others.

"I was with the battle group that was sent to Hibernia and I knew Corbulo," the man declared, as he stared calmly at Fergus. "But any man can claim to be his grandson."

Fergus turned to look at the man who'd spoken out.

"I am his grandson," Fergus retorted, "My grandfather was a great man. He died during the Brigantian uprising trying to escape with his family. He and my family were surrounded inside an old hill fort by a druidess called Emogene, who forced my grandfather to choose between which of his children would live and which would die. Corbulo sacrificed himself to protect his children, my father and aunt. He died so that they may live. That's the kind of man he was."

The tavern remained silent as Fergus refused to sit down and as the silence lengthened the tension in the room started to fade.

"We're all men of the Twentieth!" a voice from the crowd growled at last. A few others who raised their voices in agreement supported the man.

Slowly the Legionaries started to turn back to their conversations and as they did Fergus noticed that his mess mates were staring at him.

"This isn't over," the legionary who had insulted Aledus hissed as he scowled at Fergus, "You boys had better watch your backs, we're going to find you and I don't give a shit who your grandfather was."

And with that the man contemptuously turned his back on them. "Catinius, swap places with Aledus," Fergus said as he turned to his mess mate, "Keep those two apart, there isn't going to be any more trouble tonight."

Catinius glanced at Aledus and then silently the two of them rose and swapped places along the table.

Slowly Fergus eased himself back down into his seat as around him the noise in the tavern started to pick up. The surge of emotion had gone and suddenly he blushed as he realised what he'd just done. Under the table his legs were trembling. Then,

as he glanced towards the bar he groaned. Galena had her back turned to him but her father was standing motionless, staring straight at him with a strange intensity, his face, dark, brooding and unhappy. Gods, Fergus thought as he looked down at the table, if her father didn't approve of him, how was he ever going to convince Galena to be his woman.

Chapter Thirteen – An Amphora of Wine

Furius seemed in a hurry as he came charging back into the barracks room. There was an excited look on his face.

"Today's password is Legion," he announced, as Fergus and the rest of the mess mates turned to look at him. "Now get moving. We have been given a job to do. There is a ship down in the port with a consignment of wine from Hispania. We're to help unload her and escort the cargo to the officer's quarters in the Principia."

"But it's not even dawn yet," Catinius exclaimed as he tightened a fresh white bandage around his neck. "What's the hurry?"

"Shut up and do as you are told," Furius snapped as he glared at the men in the barracks room, "And for fuck's sake someone wake Aledus. What's that dick still doing asleep. I want to be down at the river side by dawn."

Fergus raised his eyebrows at his comrades and then reached out to the top bunk and slapped Aledus on the cheek. The slap was met with an angry and startled cry.

"Get up mate, we've got a job to do," Fergus said as Aledus raised himself up onto his elbows and glared at him.

Furius gave Fergus a little appreciative glance. Then he was reaching for his leather army belt from which hung his short sword.

"Wine from Hispania, nice," Catinius muttered as he pulled on his heavy, winter cloak and stooped to retrieve his army helmet.

"Nice, if you are an officer," Vittius replied sourly. "The rest of us get the left over shit from the German frontier."

Fergus fastened his belt around his waist and drew his gladius from its scabbard. The blade felt cool, hard and sharp. Satisfied he slid the sword back into place and stepped out through the doorway and into the darkness outside. To the east the sky was a dark blue and close by, a single torch, attached to the side of a barracks block, flickered and spat, as it cast a dying reddish glow on the snow covered ground. Dawn was not far away. Quickly he turned to look around but there was no one about. A week had passed since their encounter with the men from the 6th Cohort in the Lucky Legionary tavern and although there had been no more trouble the incident had put Fergus on guard. It was not unknown for legionaries to suddenly go missing or turn up in a ditch with their throats sliced open.

He turned as he heard a sudden noise behind him. Furius emerged into the gloom, his breath visible in the freezing cold air. He turned towards the east and muttered something under his breath that Fergus didn't catch. For a moment the two of them were silent as they waited for the others.

"It's Tiberius's last week with the company," Furius said at last, keeping his voice low as he spoke. "The old man is finally retiring from the army. He's a good man, Tiberius; he may even have known your grandfather. He's going to give us a farewell party in the Lucky, tomorrow night. Should be a good one."

Fergus did not reply as he peered at the eastern sky.

Furius was silent as he too turned to stare eastwards at the approaching dawn.

"With Tiberius retiring, the centurion will be needing a new company Tesserarius," Furius said in a thoughtful voice, "It's a good position for the man who can get it. More pay, more authority, third in command of the company."

"What's the problem?" Fergus replied glancing in Furius' direction.

Furius sighed. "There is competition for the position. More than one man is interested in becoming the next Tesserarius."

"Who?"

"Fronto, the decanus of that barracks room over there," Furius muttered gesturing at one of the barracks rooms across from them. "Watch out for him today Fergus. He and his boys have been assigned to patrol the civilian settlement. They wanted our job, but I made sure they didn't get it."

"Why would they want our job?" Fergus frowned.

A little smile appeared on Furius' lips. "Gods, you have got a lot to learn haven't you Fergus, and for your sake I hope you do so fast." Furius said as he turned and stepped back into the barracks room, giving Fergus a pat on the shoulder. "Keep your wits about you today lad, this is going to be a big day for both of us," Furius muttered as he disappeared inside.

***

The civilian settlement that had grown up around the legionary fortress was large and prosperous. The streets were lined on both sides with Roman style terraces, long and thin, stone-strip houses, with tiled roofs and alleys that separated each city block. The shops occupied the front rooms of the houses and inside the merchants were already doing a brisk trade with the early morning shoppers, as Furius hastily led his men down the street towards the river that protected the fortress on it southern and western side. The advertising cries of the merchants mingled with the creaking rumble of heavily laden wagons, barking dogs and the thud of the soldiers hobnailed boots on the paving stones. From the alleys the stink of rotting garbage and stale urine seeped out into the main street and in places graffiti covered the walls of the buildings. Fergus however did not seem to notice the civilians around him. What had Furius meant when he'd said that this was going to be a big day for him? Anxiously he kept an eye open for trouble but the streets were calm and orderly and there were few legionaries about.

The river harbour was a hive of activity. A dozen ships ranging in size, lay moored and tied up to the stone embankment and sailors and civilians were swarming over them, loading and unloading their cargoes and amongst them Fergus noticed men with dark skin and strange oriental-looking clothes. Furius led them towards the last galley and, as they approached, Fergus could see it was an ocean going ship, an old battered looking grain carrier. A two-wheeled wagon and a single patient ox stood waiting beside it along the river side.

"Captain," Furius cried out as they approached, "I have been ordered to escort your cargo of wine into the camp."

On the deck of the grain carrier the captain, a tall man with a grey beard and a weather beaten face paused and then raised his hand in greeting.

"We'll be ready soon," the captain cried. "We had a rough crossing. Some of the cargo is damaged."

Furius shook his head, turned and idly lent back against the side of the empty wagon and folded his arms across his chest.

"Aren't we going to help them unload the wine, Sir?" Vittius said looking at the couple of sailors who were visible on the deck.

"Fuck that," Furius growled, "Let them unload the wine themselves. We'll just escort it into camp and see that it is delivered correctly."

At Fergus's side Aledus sniggered and abruptly sat down on the ground and the others quickly followed his example. Fergus however remained standing. Slowly he turned to look at the harbour and, as he did so he grunted. This was the place where, eighteen years ago, Corbulo and Marcus had embarked for Hibernia. And here he was, standing where his grandfather had once stood, wishing he had been there on that day, at his grandfather's side. Slowly he exhaled and, as he stared at the

ships, he imagined what it must have been like to see the heavily armoured and armed legionaries boarding their ships for the invasion of Hibernia. What a sight that must have been. What a day that must have been.

"Fergus, with me," Furius said sharply.

The decanus was boarding the ship via the wooden gang plank that had been laid between the embankment and the galley. Quickly Fergus followed him onto the ship and as he jumped down onto the wooden deck, he narrowly missed landing on a stack of amphorae. The sailors said nothing as they clambered up and down a ladder that led into the belly of the ship, bringing up the cargo of precious amphorae and placing them on the deck. Fergus stared at the sealed ceramic pottery that contained the wine. Each amphora had been neatly stamped with its owner's name. As he looked up towards the bow he saw that Furius was talking to the captain in a quiet, conspiratorial voice. The conversation ended with the captain nodding in agreement. Furius left the sailor and came towards Fergus.

"Take one of the amphora and bring it to Titus' quarters," Furius said bringing his face close to Fergus. "Pick one of the men to help you. You are to hand it to Titus personally, do you understand?"

"Yes Sir," Fergus replied stiffly.

"And Fergus," Furius said, as a faint smile appeared on his lips, "Make sure that Titus knows that this gift comes from me and me alone."

***

"Aledus, come with me," Fergus said as he gingerly stepped back onto land clutching a small two-handled amphora under his arm.

His mess mate gave him a perplexed look, but when Fergus gestured at him he rose to his feet and joined his friend as the two of them hastened away along the harbour front.

"What's going on?" Aledus muttered staring at the amphorae. "What are you doing with that wine?"

Fergus kept his eyes firmly on the path ahead. "Furius wants us to bring this one to the centurion. It's a gift," he replied.

"Fuck," Aledus blurted out, as a grin appeared on his handsome face, "Isn't this consignment destined for the senior officers in the Principia. We're stealing the Legate's wine, Fergus!"

"I know what we are doing," Fergus hissed, as he started to climb the slope that led towards the legionary camp, "And I know why we are doing it too."

"What's in it for me?" Aledus said quickly, as he increased his pace to keep up with Fergus. "Come on, what do I get out of this?"

"You get to shut your mouth," Fergus replied, "And if things go as planned, I will owe you a favour. That's what you get out of this."

"Can't we at least have a taste of the wine?" Aledus said still grinning from ear to ear.

"No."

For a long moment the two of them were silent as they strode up the street leading to the fortress gates.

"Well you are going to owe me a big favour," Aledus said at last, as he shook his head. "And I am not going to let you forget it. I am going to remind you every morning."

Abruptly Fergus came to a halt in the road and his face went pale. "Oh shit," he muttered, as he stared up the street. Coming towards them, clad in their gleaming helmets, full body armour and clasping their legionary spears and shields was Fronto and his seven-man patrol. There was no time to turn around or dart out of view down an alley. Fronto had already spotted them. At his side Aledus took a deep breath.

"This doesn't look good," he muttered.

Fergus hastily glanced around him. To his right was a narrow alley but he couldn't see where it led or whether it was a dead end. He was about to turn round and begin to retrace his steps, when Fronto called out. He was a large, powerfully built man in his mid-twenties with a mouth that was missing his front two teeth.

"You there, stop. I recognise you. Aren't you Furius' mess mates? What are you doing here? You lot are supposed to be down at the harbour."

Fergus straightened up and looked Fronto straight in the eye. "We are," he replied. "Our decanus has sent us on a special errand. Sorry but we don't have time for a chat, orders Sir."

Fergus lowered his head and started towards Fronto as if he was just going to push his way passed the patrol.

"What's that you are carrying?" Fronto's snapped, his voice cutting through the air like the swish of a whip.

"Run," Fergus hissed at Aledus, as he suddenly swayed to his right and dashed into the alley. He nearly slid on some ice and his elbow scraped painfully against the stone wall. Then he was pounding down the alley, in desperate flight clutching the amphora under his arm. Behind him he heard gasping and panting and, as he risked a quick look over his shoulder, he saw that Aledus was close behind him, his face flush with excitement.

"Stop them," Fronto roared, as he and his men came charging down the alley in pursuit.

Desperately Fergus turned to peer down the alley as he ran. He was rapidly approaching a solid looking wall and, as he saw the dead end ahead, he groaned in terror. He was trapped. He had made the wrong decision. But just as he was about to come to a despairing halt, he noticed another alley leading away from the river.

"Aledus, in here," Fergus cried out as he swerved and shot into the entrance of the alley. Up ahead the path ended in a doorway into one of the long thin strip houses and Fergus's heart sank again. He snatched a glance over his shoulder. Fronto and his men were right behind them. If the door ahead was barred, then the patrol would be upon him in an instant.

The weight of the amphora under his arm was slowing him down, but some instinct stopped him from discarding it. With a savage snarl, he launched himself at the door and with a crash he went straight through and instantly collided with a woman. The force of his collision sent the woman screaming and crashing into the far wall and Fergus nearly lost his balance, but managed to recover just in time. Wildly he stared around him, as the woman's high-pitched screams filled the room. A split moment later Aledus came charging into the house, his chest heaving with exertion.

"Hold them at that the door," Fergus roared at Aledus, "I can't out-run them lugging this thing with me."

And without waiting for a reply he was into the central room of the house scattering chairs out of his way. There was no time to see whether Aledus had done as he'd asked. A man, holding a shoe in his hand, was staring at him in open mouthed astonishment as Fergus barged through his workshop and shot out into the street. As he stormed up the street, he risked a quick glance over his shoulder. Aledus had not followed him out of the house and Fergus groaned with sudden guilt. Poor loyal Aledus would be able to hold his pursuers at the door for a while, but not forever and when they got him, he was most likely going to get the shit kicked out of him. Grimly, Fergus forced himself to look away as he headed up the street towards the camp gates, clutching the precious amphora of wine under his arm.

***

It was late in the afternoon when Furius and the others finally returned. As he stood in the doorway of his barracks room watching them approach, with one hand on the pommel of his sword, Fergus saw that Titus, their company centurion was accompanying them. Furius was beaming as he came towards the barracks block and Fergus's eyes narrowed. He had never seen the decanus look so pleased before. But, as he glanced at the faces of the others, he saw only worried, tense eyes, that refused to meet his.

"Fergus, get out here," Titus said in his easy familiar manner. The officer was wearing his magnificent plumed helmet and his vine staff was stuffed into his belt. He gave Fergus a quick examination as Fergus stepped forwards and saluted.

"You've heard that Tiberius will be leaving us at the end of the week," the centurion said. "He's retiring. So there are going to be some organisational changes around here. Furius, here, is taking over as my new Tesserarius. A company cannot do without a dutiful watch commander. But that leaves me short of a decanus. So effectively today I want you to take over as decanus for this tent group. Congratulations on your promotion.

Report to me tomorrow at dawn to receive your day's work schedule."

And with a little nod the centurion turned and strode away.

Fergus watched the officer walk away and then slowly he turned to look at Furius. The new watch commander of the 2nd company of the 2nd Cohort was studying him with a sly, knowing smile.

"We'll be seeing each other again," Furius said, as he gave Fergus a pat on the shoulder and vanished into the barracks room to collect his belongings.

Fergus said nothing, as he turned to look at the four legionaries who stood staring at him waiting for him to speak. He was in charge of them now. He now had the same rank as Fronto and, as the full realisation of his promotion sank in, it brought a little colour to his cheeks.

"Boys, I've got some bad news," Fergus said as he cleared his throat and addressed the men, "Aledus is in hospital. He was beaten half to death in an alley, but the doctor says he's going to pull through. He's a tough lad. But it may be a month or so before he returns to active duty."

"What happened to him?" Catinius growled as he stood a step towards Fergus.

"It was Fronto and his men," Fergus replied sharply, "And one day we are going to pay them back for what they did to Aledus, but only when I deem the moment right. So you are all going to be patient until that day comes."

Chapter Fourteen – The Revelation

The ten company section leaders had gathered in a semi-circle around their centurion as they silently listened to Titus explaining the company's work schedule for the day. The centurion was speaking in his familiar, easy going manner, but Fergus had long ago learnt that this was no invitation for cheekiness or insolence, for Titus was a strict disciplinarian, who did not tolerate the slightest disrespect or hesitate to mercilessly flog any man who disobeyed his orders. No, Fergus thought, you did not fuck with Titus; on that the whole company could agree. It was just after dawn and he stood amongst his peers, watching Furius, the new Tesserarius, who was standing behind Titus, with his arms folded across his chest. Furius however seemed oblivious to everything in the room, as he stared resolutely into space. Slowly Fergus shifted his gaze until it settled on Fronto. This was his first time as a decanus that he had attended the company's morning briefing and it should have been a proud moment, except he could not stop thinking about Aledus, lying on his hospital bed, his eyes so badly swollen that he could barely see. As he noticed Fergus staring at him, Fronto's face darkened contemptuously.

"Quintus, roof repair work, get your tools from the workshop and report to the Optio," Titus said, as he started handing out the day's jobs. "Fronto, guard duty on the eastern gate. Marcus, the first centurion needs some men to help cut wood outside the camp. Report to his quarters for instructions. Fergus, latrine cleaning. Sabinus, weapons training with the new recruits…"

Fergus groaned inwardly as Titus continued to rattle down his list of tasks. Cleaning the latrines was the very worst job in the camp. Was this Titus's way of bringing him back down to earth after the high of being promoted? The centurion sure had not complained when he'd delivered the amphora of wine the other day.

"That's all," Titus concluded as he looked around at his men. "Don't forget to tell your men the day's password. And boys, Tiberius is giving his farewell feast in the Lucky tonight. Make sure the old bastard gets a fitting farewell."

As the gathering broke up and the men turned to leave the Centurion's quarters, Fronto barged past Fergus catching him with his shoulder as he pushed him aside.

"Wanker," Fronto hissed under his breath as he stepped out through the doorway.

Fergus did not react and he emerged into the early morning light. Despite his anger he needed to be careful in how he handled Fronto. The man was no fool. He would be expecting Fergus to do something. No, Fergus thought, biting his lip, he would pay Fronto back for what he'd done to Aledus, there was no doubt about that, but it was going to happen when that dick head was least expecting it.

As he approached his barracks block the sun suddenly emerged from above the eastern ramparts of the fort and as it did, he caught sight of Vittius standing beside the door to their barracks room. The man stood motionless and straight, facing the sun, his arms hanging limply at his side. The Legionary's eyes were closed and his face and head were inclined in the direction of the rising sun.

"Hail to thee, eternal spirit of the sun..." Vittius muttered as Fergus strode past and entered their barracks room.

"So what is it?" Catinius growled, as he looked up at Fergus as he entered the room.

"Cleaning the latrines," Fergus replied.

"Shit," Catinius replied shaking his head in disgust. "That's the second time this week. What does Titus think he's doing?"

"Go on, get yourselves ready," Fergus said turning to the others, "When we're done in the latrines, we will pay our comrades a visit in hospital. Today's password is Barbarian."

"Only an arsehole would come up with such a shit password," Catinius snapped as he turned back to grinding the wheat into flour with the small, hand-held mill stone.

***

It was late in the afternoon when Fergus and his men ambled up to where Aledus was lying on his hospital bed. The hospital ward was a large and spacious building and long rows of camp beds lined the walls upon which lay the legion's wounded and sick. The room was filled with occasional groan and cough and the smell of vinegar hung heavy in the air. Aledus seemed to be asleep as Fergus and the others gathered around his bed. His face was covered in dark purple bruises and his eyes were puffed up so that he was barely recognisable. A fresh bandage was wrapped around his forehead and a woollen army blanket hid the injuries to his body from view.

"Fronto is going to pay for this," Catinius muttered under his breath. "Look at what they did to him."

"Shut up, all of you," Fergus murmured in warning as he noticed one of the legion's doctor's approaching.

The surgeon, an older man with a bald head and clad in a blood-stained white apron, paused to give Aledus a quick practiced glance before he straightened up and nodded a greeting at Fergus.

"You are the man who brought him in," the doctor said. "I thought I recognised you. I was hoping to have a word with you."

"Is he going to be alright?" Vittius interrupted, tapping the doctor on his shoulder.

"I think so," the surgeon sighed, "The bruises will heal and he is lucky to have not lost an eye, but if there is damage to the organs inside his body...well, only time will tell. I would prefer that his fate is determined by my skill but it may be that it is up to the gods to make that decision. Still I am hopeful. What he needs now is rest."

"Do the best you can for him doctor," Fergus muttered looking down at Aledus.

"We always do," the doctor replied, fixing his eyes firmly on Fergus, "But I was hoping to talk to you about something. I need to report all such incidents like this to my commanding officer. Cohort strength reports, you understand." The doctor turned to look down at Aledus and, as he did so, he folded his arms across his chest. "The army spends a huge amount of time and resources training and recruiting you men and it doesn't like it when it's soldiers end up half beaten to death, for no apparent reason. So can you tell me who did this to him? You brought him in. You must know what happened? We can't have our legionaries being assaulted on a daily basis."

Fergus did not immediately reply. Instead he stood staring down at Aledus. Then at last he blinked.

"Did you not ask him?" he muttered gesturing at Aledus.

"I did," the doctor sighed in frustration "And he refused to tell me. He told me some bullshit story about how he had stumbled and hit his head against a wall." The doctor paused and studied Aledus for a moment. "But if you can give me names, tell me what happened and why, maybe I can do something about this, maybe I can stop the violence?"

"Names?" Fergus said turning to look at the doctor with a confused look, "Maybe it was just an accident, just like he said?" For a long moment the doctor studied Fergus in silence. Then he shook his head in disgust.

"You cocky bastards, you are all the same," the doctor snapped in an irritated voice, as he turned and started to walk away, "You don't think I know what's going on, but I do. I see these injuries on a daily basis and the fucking legion isn't even on campaign. I am going to get the Legate to put an end to this."

Fergus watched the doctor stride away. Then his attention was drawn back to the hospital bed, as in it, Aledus groaned and stirred.

"Oh it's you lot," Aledus murmured softly, as he gingerly moved his head from side to side. "What are you bastards doing here?" Fergus leaned forwards over the bed.

"I owe you mate," he muttered. "And I promise you this. When the moment is right we're going to make Fronto pay for what he did to you."

A little smile appeared on Aledus' lips as he recognised Fergus and slowly he raised his hand above the blanket and grasped hold of Fergus' arm.

"And I am going to remind you, you bastard" Aledus whispered as the grin widened on his hideously distorted and smashed up face.

***

Fergus sat watching his mess mate from across the table, as Vittius continued to scratch words onto the soft wooden tablet with his iron tipped stylus. The two of them were squeezed onto a bench inside the Lucky, which as usual was packed. The noise of a hundred-plus legionaries, chatting, shouting and singing was deafening, but Vittius ignored it all as he concentrated on his writing. Slowly Fergus raised his cup to his mouth and took a sip of wine. Vittius had been the only one who had decided to join him in attending Tiberius' farewell party and he was proving to be poor company, Fergus thought. Bored, Fergus turned to glance at Tiberius, who was sitting a few tables away amidst a crowd of men from the 2nd Company. The old

warrior was singing in a loud voice, drunk as a fart, just like the majority of the men in the pub, who'd come to celebrate the retirement. A little smile appeared on Fergus's face as someone threw a shoe at Tiberius and missed. The old veteran did not even seem to notice as he continued belting out one of his favourite songs.

In the hearth the roaring fire blasted heat into the room and across the bar Galena and her father was doing a brisk trade. Fergus sighed. The camp authorities had banned all legionaries from taking weapons beyond the camp gates and the men inside the tavern were without exception unarmed. A couple of centurion's and the duty watch company had made sure of that. The legion's senior officers must finally have become concerned about the violence in the tavern's, Fergus thought, as he took another sip of wine.

"Vittius, who the fuck are you writing to?" Fergus exclaimed in an exasperated voice, as he leaned towards his mess mate. "You've been writing since we got here. Have you forgotten where we are?"

Vittius looked up with a startled expression.

"Sorry Fergus," he muttered as he gave Fergus a wry smile, "It's a letter to my mother. I promised her I would write. She worries." "So do I," Fergus snapped shaking his head.

"Anyway," Vittius said, "I thought you might take the opportunity to talk to the barmaid. Go on Fergus, now would be a good time. The boys are not going to let it go until you bed her."

Fergus muttered something under his breath as he cast a furtive glance at the bar.

"I don't think her father approves of me," he replied.

"Stop being such a chicken shit," Vittius said calmly, "We're men of the Twentieth. We fear nothing."

"Oi, remember who you are talking to," Fergus replied in mock outrage, "I am the decanus here. You can't talk to me like that."

With a good natured little wave, Vittius raised his hand in the air and turned back to studying his letter and, as he did so, Fergus glanced again at the bar. Galena was busy dipping cups into the large circular holes in the bar and scooping up quantities of wine, which she was handing to her thirsty customers and for a long moment he watched her. Vittius was right, he thought at last. He was being a coward. He should get up and go and talk to her. Maybe he had a chance after all. She wouldn't have bothered to say, what she'd said to him the other night, if she wasn't at least a bit interested.

With a grunt Fergus placed his cup onto the table, rose to his feet and turned towards the bar. But just as he was about to cross the short space between the table and the bar, someone shouted his name. It was Fronto. The decanus was pointing a finger at Fergus as he swayed lightly on his feet.

"Heh you," Fronto roared angrily slurring his speech, "You little shit cost me my promotion. You and that fucker we put into hospital. I know what you did. I know what you and Furius were up to."

Fergus's face darkened, but in the noisy tavern no one seemed to notice the exchange.

"Fuck off Fronto," Fergus retorted, "You are lucky we did not report you to Titus."

"You wouldn't dare, you little weasel," Fronto bellowed, "You don't deserve to be a decanus. You are just a boy. You will never be my equal."

Fergus shook his head and, ignoring Fronto, he turned back to his seat. Vittius was watching him.

"What are we going to do about him?" Vittius muttered.

Fergus ran his fingers thoughtfully across his cheek. "We bide our time," he replied, "but when we finally teach him some respect, it's going to be a lesson he is going to remember for the rest of his life."

Vittis nodded in agreement. Then he picked up his letter and stood up.

"Going for a piss, the next round is on me," Vittius said with a grin. "Don't get into any trouble, Sir."

Fergus watched Vittius stride out of the door and vanish into the freezing night. He was about to take another sip of wine, when a chair came flying through the air and smashed into Tiberius sending the veteran tumbling and crashing backwards into the mass of tightly packed legionaries. In an instant the whole tavern was in uproar. A legionary clambered up onto the table and launched himself at the men sitting around Tiberius, catching one of them in the face with his boot. A howl of outrage, yelling and cursing erupted as within seconds the tavern descended into a mass brawl. Fergus was shoved backwards and tumbled to the floor and, before he could recover from his surprise the table was flung aside sending cups of wine and beer flying through the air.

"Kick the shit out of them boys," a voice yelled, rising above the uproar. "No one insults the honour of the 6th."

Fergus rolled away just in time and managed to get up as two men landed on the ground at his feet, locked into a snarling, vicious, wrestling match. Shocked, Fergus staggered backwards and turned to stare at the tavern. The whole room had become a seething, drunken, howling and chaotic mass of desperately

fighting men who were trying to beat and kick the shit out of each other. As he stared at the scene, a man came at him. Fergus ducked under the legionary's clumsy swinging fist and rammed his own fist into the man's nose, sending him staggering backwards into the mass of brawling soldiers. Fergus's eyes widened in alarm. No one could possibly know to which company anyone belonged. No, he thought savagely, the men just wanted to have a fight.

"Fergus, die" a man's enraged voice suddenly roared from close by. It was Fronto. There was a wild, crazy and drunken look on the decanus' face as he came at Fergus and too late Fergus caught the little metallic glint of a knife in Fronto's hand.

But just as Fronto raised his arm and was about to thrust his knife at Fergus, a man swiftly stepped in between them, clasped hold of Fronto's arm and smashed his forehead into that of the decanus, in a sickening crunching, head butt. Fronto staggered backwards with a howl, as blood streamed down his face, but before he could recover his assailant stepped up and sent the decanus flying backwards onto the ground with a powerful and beautifully placed kick.

"Get behind the bar," Galena's father, the tavern owner hissed, turning urgently to Fergus and gesturing at the bar.

Without hesitating, Fergus flung himself at the wooden construction, slid across the smooth surface of the bar, before dropping painfully to the ground behind it. As he landed on the floor behind the bar, he was suddenly aware of someone else already crouching there. It was Galena. She gave him a startled look. In her hand she was clutching a small stone millstone which she immediately raised in a threatening manner.

"No, it's me," Fergus cried out raising his hand, as the girl was about to hit him with the stone.

Galena paused and before she could say anything, another body came sliding across the bar to land with a heavy thud on the ground beside them. It was her father and he was bleeding from a cut to his forehead.

"Into the cellar, now," the man snapped at his daughter.

Galena needed no urging. With calm, practiced fingers she reached for something set into the floor, found it and to Fergus' astonishment she yanked open a trap door.

"Get in Roman," the tavern owner hissed in Latin, as Galena lowered her legs into the hole and silently disappeared into the darkness below.

Fergus scrambled across the floor and dropped down into the void. The drop was not far and he landed painfully on his arse. The floor of the cellar was cold and rock solid and for a moment he was completely disorientated. Then hastily he moved aside as Galena's father's legs came shooting down towards him. The man grunted as he hit the ground and within seconds the trap door above their heads slammed shut, plunging the cellar into utter and absolute darkness.

"It's locked, father," Galena's said from the darkness without any hint of fear.

"Good," her father replied, breathing heavily. "We'll stay down here until they have finished their brawl."

For a moment the cellar was silent as the three of them listened to the noise of the continuing mass brawl above them. Then slowly Fergus raised his hand above his head and his fingers brushed against the wooden ceiling.

"Roman," Galena's father said suddenly," You should stay down here. That man with the knife. He was not just trying to scare you. He was going to kill you."

"I know," Fergus muttered, "Thank you."

"We keep the wine and other supplies down here," the tavern owner growled, "We'll be safe here. It's not the first time there has been a fight like this. My name is Taran, my daughter here is called Galena."

"I know who he is," Galena said sourly from the darkness. "He's the one who keeps looking at me."

"My name is Fergus," Fergus replied as he steadied his breathing, his thoughts still reeling from the realisation that Fronto had just tried to murder him.

For a moment, no one spoke in the darkness. Then slowly Fergus frowned and turned to look at the spot where he thought Taran was sitting.

"Why did you intervene?" he said carefully, "Why did you come to my aid? You didn't have to do this, why?"

From the darkness there was no immediate reply and, for a while Fergus could only hear the noise of breathing and the pandemonium of thuds, splintering furniture and yelling men above them.

"You mentioned a name," Taran said at last, his face invisible in the darkness, "Corbulo. You claimed to be his grandson."

Fergus blinked in surprise. What was this?

"I am his grandson," he replied.

"I knew him," Taran said quickly, "Well, when I say I knew him. I was there when he died. It happened exactly as you described it."

Fergus froze as he peered into the darkness. Was the tavern owner playing some sick joke on him?

"I was young then," Taran shrugged, "the Brigantes were in open rebellion and I had chosen the war band of a druid. Emogene was her name. She had come down from the north and she was afraid of nothing. I was with her when we caught up with your grandfather and his family in that deserted hill fort. I saw your grandfather die. He was a brave man, one of the bravest I have seen."

"You saw him die?" Fergus exclaimed in an incredulous disbelieving voice.

"I did," Taran muttered, "Emogene sliced open his throat. It was quick. Afterwards we took his body with us, because Emogene said that she had something special in mind for your grandfather."

Taran sighed wearily and for a moment he said nothing.

"So later that day we defiled his corpse and burned his body," he continued, "and Emogene took his ashes and placed them in a small sealed canister around her neck. The druids use these canisters to imprison the spirits of their enemies. She told us that she was going to keep your grandfather's spirit close to her, forever as her prisoner. She really hated him. And she turned his skull into a drinking cup."

Fergus's mouth opened in horror.

"She did what?" Fergus stammered.

"She kept his ashes around her neck in a little canister and she and the others used his skull to drink from," Taran replied. "I left her war band shortly afterwards. I have no quarrel with the druids, but what she did to your grandfather was not right. What she did, offended the gods and the laws of man. Your grandfather sacrificed himself for his children. It was a noble, worthy act. He deserved to have been buried in the proper manner, so that his spirit would find peace. What we did with his body was not right and it shames me to this day. So when I heard you raise his name in my tavern and start talking about your grandfather, I knew that the gods were asking me to do something. And now I have, Roman."

In the cellar, Fergus was staring into the darkness in stunned silence. Then slowly he opened his mouth, his eyes and thoughts suddenly faraway.

"Do you know where I can find the woman who did this?" he murmured.

"No," Taran replied firmly, "I have not spoken to or seen Emogene since I left her war band fourteen years ago. But," the tavern owner added, "I saw her husband, Meryn is his name, in Londinium, less than four months ago."

118

Chapter Fifteen – The Temple of Apollo

Marcus sat on his horse, gazing at the magnificent circle of white standing stones that stood, proud, graceful and ageless, dominating the rolling green fields. The stones were huge and were roofed together in a perfect circle by more stones, creating an outer ring of gleaming, connected columns. Within the outer circle stood an inner unfinished ring of stones with a gap facing towards the north east and the snow covered causeway. It was noon and the sun was riding high in a clear blue sky. At Marcus's side Cunomoltus too, was staring at the ancient monument, his eyes betraying a proud excitement.

"And still they stand," Cunomoltus sighed, shaking his head in wonder. "They say that these stones have stood for over a hundred and fifty generations. The ancient's built them to worship the sun and moon. There is nothing that can compare to this. Nothing at all. When our bones have turned to dust, Marcus, and all memory of whom we were, has long been forgotten, these stones shall still stand. They will remember all of us. There is power in those stones, druid magic."

Marcus was silent as he gazed at Stonehenge, and his unshaven rugged face betrayed no emotion. Two days had passed since he and Cunomoltus had left the villa on the Isle of Vectis and had headed north towards the spa town of Aquae Sulis and during that whole time, Marcus had not said a word to the man who claimed to be his brother.

On his horse, Cunomoltus sighed again.

"You know," he said, in a sudden weary tone, "You are going to have to speak to me at some point. You can't be silent forever. Not even a great warrior like you can do that and I am getting rather bored of listening to my own voice."

Marcus did not move as he stared at the standing stones. Then slowly he glanced up at the sun.

"The Romans call this place the temple of Apollo," Marcus muttered. "It is a holy place, home to powerful spirits. We should take a closer look at the stones."

And with that, he urged his horse forwards across the snow-covered fields towards the ditch and low embankment, that completely surrounded the stone circles.

"Finally," Cunomoltus exclaimed triumphantly, as a broad smile appeared on his lips, "So you do listen after all. This is progress."

Then he was urging his horse after Marcus.

"You know," Cunomoltus called out, as he caught up with Marcus, "I have been thinking about this journey. I get it. We're looking for Corbulo's body so that we can give the old man a proper burial. It is an honourable quest, Marcus, even if it's unlikely that we will ever find out what happened to his remains. But I do like it. The sons of Corbulo ride out together, to honour their father. The old man would like that. It is a good story."

Marcus did not reply and Cunomoltus did not see the grim, unhappy expression that briefly flitted across his face.

As his horse surged up the side of the steep perimeter ditch, Marcus slowed the beast's pace and began to walk the animal towards the ancient temple. There was no one about and the place looked deserted. From close by, the massive standing stones were even taller and more impressive than seen from a distance. Marcus drew closer and, as he did so, the stones dazzled him, gleaming in the bright sunlight, and seemed to close ranks as if they had sensed his purpose and were trying to force him back, away from the action, which he knew he must take.

At the edge of the stone circle Marcus came to a halt and dismounted. His horse promptly took the opportunity to lower its head to the ground and nose around in the snow looking for food. Marcus turned to look around, searching for something in the open ground that surrounded the stone temple. At his side, Cunomoltus dismounted, giving Marcus a curious glance.

"What are you looking for?" Cunomoltus asked.

Without replying Marcus took a few steps forwards and knelt down and began to clear away the snow until he had revealed a circular hole in the frozen ground.

"What's that?" Cunomoltus muttered, as he crouched beside Marcus in the snow.

Marcus said nothing as he cleared the loose earth from the hole revealing a couple of bronze Roman coins and a fine antler bone at the bottom. Quickly he pulled the bone out of the hole and studied it before carefully and respectfully placing it back in the ground.

"I get it," Cunomoltus said suddenly in a hushed voice, as he crouched at his side, "That's why we came here, to this place. You wish to make an offering to the gods. An offering to the successful conclusion of our quest. Am I right?"

Marcus paused, as he stared down into the dark hole in the ground. For a long moment he was silent as the tension within him started to rise.

"Yes," he said at last, as he raised his eyes to look at Cunomoltus with a strange gleam. "We have come here to make an offering to the gods. I am going to need all their help and good will if I am to find my father's mortal remains. The gods are going to demand a most special sacrifice for such a favour."

The colour on Cunomoltus's face slowly drained away as he stared at Marcus. Then before he could react, Marcus launched himself at Cunomoltus, bowling him helplessly over onto his back and into the snow. In an instant Marcus was on top of him, the sharp point of a knife pushing into Cunomoltus' exposed throat.

"It is time to stop pretending that you are my brother," Marcus hissed, "You think you can fool everyone, but you won't deceive me nor will you fool the gods when you go to meet them. Now be silent and try to show some dignity in your last few moments in this world."

Cunomoltus cried out in shock as he stared up at Marcus.

"What the fuck?" he screeched, "What are you doing? I am your brother. It's the truth. I swear it."

"Shut up," Marcus hissed as the point of his knife drew a little blood.

Cunomoltus' eyes widened. "What, I am to be your sacrifice," he cried out, "Is that what you are planning? The gods will never accept it. The Romans. They have forbidden human sacrifice. You will be breaking their law. It will offend the gods. It is forbidden."

"Not good enough," Marcus growled, as his knife drew a little more blood. "I am beyond caring. No one is going to mourn for you. No one is going to know what happened to you. I will just tell them that you vanished. I can tell them whatever I like. Your name will soon be forgotten."

Cunomoltus was staring up at Marcus in growing horror. Then suddenly his expression changed.

"Yes Marcus, you could do that, you could kill me," Cunomoltus said with sudden confidence, "but you won't, because underneath that rugged, tough skin you are a good, honourable man. If you kill me, you will forever know in your heart, that you murdered your brother and that is not the kind of man you are."

Marcus said nothing as he stared down at Cunomoltus, the tip of his knife pressing into the man's throat. One gentle thrust and it would be over. All he had to do was slice open the man's throat and end it. But as he glared down at the man lying in the snow his fingers started to tremble and he suddenly knew he could not do it. With an abrupt frustrated cry Marcus lifted the knife away from Cunomoltus' throat and punched the man hard in the face with his fist.

"Take your horse and go," Marcus roared as he got to his feet, "And if you dare come back I will kill you! I don't ever want to see you again. Now fuck off!"

On the ground Cunomoltus groaned, as he painfully rubbed his cheek with his hand. Then slowly he sat up and gave Marcus a defiant, bruised look.

"No," he muttered holding his hand to his jaw bone. "I am not going anywhere and you are not going to kill me. You cannot stop me from following you."

An exasperated look had appeared on Marcus's face.

"What do you want?" he snarled, "How much is it going to cost me to get rid of you?"

Cunomoltus however shook his head. "I am your brother," he retorted, "I am Corbulo's son, just like you are. I may be the arsehole of the family but now that I have finally found my family, I am not going anywhere. I am here to stay. You are just going to have to accept that."

Marcus did not move as he stood glaring at Cunomoltus, his chest heaving with fury. Then with a frustrated snarl, he turned away and strode towards his horse.

"I hear voices in my head," Cunomoltus yelled with sudden shrill defiance. "I hear them when I have my fits. The gods tell me things. You and I, Marcus, we are bound by blood and destiny. The voices say that I was meant to come with you on this journey."

Chapter Sixteen – The Starting Point

It was late in the day when Marcus, clad in his thick Dacian winter cloak, his face half covered by a woollen scarf, raised his two fingered hand in the air. Behind him on the narrow forest path, Cunomoltus came to a halt and for a moment the two riders sat motionless and silent in the midst of the forest. It was snowing and bitterly cold but there was no wind and the forest was quiet. With an experienced eye, Marcus peered at the farm house and out-houses. The buildings were just visible through the dense, green fir trees and tumbling snowflakes. Yes, the place fitted the description that Efa had given him perfectly. For a moment, Marcus was transported back to the damp, cold dungeon in the Caledonian village, where for a few days, as a young trooper under Agricola's command, he'd been held captive together with Emogene, before Corbulo had eventually come to his rescue. He could not remember much about her, except her bitterness and anger. Something bad had happened to the druid, something that was slowly driving her mad. Thoughtfully Marcus stroked his chin with his fingers, as he expertly searched the trees for movement, but there was no one about and in the forest; nothing moved. A single day had passed since they had left the temple of Apollo.

Suddenly Cunomoltus flung back his head and sneezed. The loud trumpeting sneeze was rapidly followed by another and then another and as the noise finally died away, Marcus shifted to look back at his companion with an annoyed, irritated expression.

"What?" Cunomoltus sniffed, with puffed up, fluey-looking eyes as he wiped his red nose with the back of his hand. "You never had a cold before?"

Marcus shook his head in disgust and turned back to stare at the farm.

"Anyway," Cunomoltus exclaimed, "You never did tell me why we are heading for Aquae Sulis. So now that we are about to enter the town, can you tell me what you are hoping to find there?"

"No, not the town, this is the place," Marcus muttered, "That farm over there is why we have come."

Silently Cunomoltus urged his horse alongside Marcus and for a long curious moment he peered at the buildings, just visible through the trees.

"I don't understand," he murmured at last.

"This is where we start," Marcus said in an impatient voice. "That farm over there once belonged to Emogene, the druid who murdered my father. We are looking for her because that evil bitch knows what happened to my father's body."

Marcus's face darkened.

"There is history between my family and this druid," he growled. "In Caledonia, she and her dogs chased my father and I for days. We were lucky to escape. Then years later she caught up with me, during the northern rebellion and forced my father to choose between which of his children should live and die. My father had done nothing to her," Marcus said, as a bitter tone crept into his voice, "but that woman is possessed by evil spirits; demons. Corbulo was just in the wrong place at the wrong time and he paid the price."

Marcus turned to look away, so that Cunomoltus did not see his face.

"Anyway," he muttered, "Emogene's husband was a slaver and ran his business from this place," he continued, "and many years ago during the Brigantian uprising, Efa and Dylis were brought here as slaves. Efa described the place to me. This is it. I am sure."

"And you think she may still be living here?" Cunomoltus said, as a hint of excitement crept into his voice.

Marcus shrugged. "It was many years ago, before I left for the Dacian frontier," he muttered. "Chances are that they moved on long ago. But maybe the new owners will know something. Maybe they can point us in the right direction. Maybe there are clues as to where the bitch and her husband have gone."

"You think so?" Cunomoltus replied, raising his eyebrows.

"Yes," Marcus snapped in an annoyed voice, as he rounded on Cunomoltus. "It's a starting point. Sorry, but I can't think of a better plan right now."

Cunomoltus sniffed and held his hand up to his nose.

"I admire your determination brother," he said, "I really do, but have you ever considered that this woman, this druid, may be dead. I mean, you are trying to find someone whom you last saw fifteen years ago. That's a long time Marcus. Anything could have happened during that time. The chances of discovering what happened to Corbulo's body are slim at best. You are facing the kind of odds that seasoned gamblers would gladly avoid."

"So you are saying that we should give up?" Marcus growled, "Are you saying we should leave my father's spirit to wander eternity in unhappiness? You are a dick. I am not giving up. I owe that man everything, he saved my life twice. Once in Caledonia and then again on the day he died. I am not turning back and I did not ask you to come with me on this journey."

"No, you didn't give me much choice about that," Cunomoltus retorted. "But I am still here, aren't I?"

"You just don't believe we will succeed," Marcus snapped. "Your mouth says one thing but your heart believes in something else."

"Yes," Cunomoltus nodded, "If you must know the truth. This whole idea of finding our father's body after all this time and giving him the burial he wanted, is an honourable quest but also just plain stupid. An impossible task. It would have been far easier and more comfortable if we had stayed at home."

"Then why are you still here?"

Cunomoltus took a deep breath and looked away with a sudden, troubled expression and for a long moment he did not speak.

"Since I was young, I have had these fits; seizures. They do not last long but when I have them I sometimes hear voices in my head," he murmured, "They speak to me. Sometimes the gods also speak to me when I sleep. They tell me all kinds of shit. One day they told me to go out and find you and now they are telling me that I should follow you. I do not know why, but it is the truth. The voices are always right. I have no doubt about that."

"So you are fucking crazy," Marcus said, tapping his finger against his head in disgust. "They should have locked you in a mental hospital."

"I am not crazy," Cunomoltus replied in an offended voice.

"Listen," Marcus snapped, pointing a finger at his companion, "Crazy or not. As long as you are here, you are going to do exactly what I tell you. I don't give a shit if you think this quest is madness, but if I hear you *say* it one more time, I am going to ram my fist into that fucking red nose of yours. Got that, brother."

Cunomoltus sighed and turned to stare at the farm buildings and for a while the two of them did not speak.

"Well what are we waiting for," Cunomoltus exclaimed as he started out, urging his horse down the path towards the farm. "There is only one way of finding out."

The buildings looked deserted and in poor condition as the two riders approached and in the outhouses there was no sign of any farm animals or recent activity. The whole place looked like it had been abandoned. Slowly Marcus dismounted and, handing his horse's reins to Cunomoltus, he approached the front door and banged on the wood with his fist, whilst his other hand came to rest on the pommel of his sword.

For a moment both men stood waiting in silence but the farm remained quiet and the door did not open.

"Where are their dogs?" Cunomoltus said looking around him, "A place like this would have dogs. Why are they not barking?"

Marcus did not reply, as he took a few steps backwards and then, with a charge he launched himself at the door. With a painful grunt, his shoulder made contact with the wood and with a loud splintering crack he was through and into the building, leaving the door swinging, half torn from its wall mountings. Without a word, Marcus vanished into the house leaving Cunomoltus waiting outside. A few moments later he re-appeared rubbing his shoulder, a disappointed expression on his grim, unshaven face.

"The place has been abandoned," he said darkly, "No one has been here in years. It's a complete mess inside."

Cunomoltus sighed. "So now what?" he muttered.

Marcus paused in the doorway and glanced at the out-houses. For a moment he did not reply. Then he snatched his horse's reins from Cunomoltus' fingers and without giving the farm a second glance, he started back the way they'd just come, leading his horse on foot.

"We'll head into town," Marcus growled, "A settlement the size of Aquae Sulis should have an administrative office where all the land records are kept. Maybe we will find something useful there."

Chapter Seventeen – Three Times

The Roman town of Aquae Sulis looked a prosperous and proud settlement. As he led his horse into town, Marcus could see it in the quality of the doors, in the fine brickwork of the buildings and in the clean and well-maintained streets. The gutters were free of debris and even the alleys between the tightly-packed terraces seemed to be free of the usual stink and garbage. In the small vestibules that adorned the long, narrow strip-houses, he could see a dozen, beautifully-crafted statuettes to different deities, proud statements of their owner's faith, that this was a town that enjoyed the protection of powerful gods. Marcus grunted as he looked around. This place would have made a good retirement town, he thought, if he hadn't already had the villa on Vectis. It was getting dark but the shops were still open and people hurried past him without giving him or Cunomoltus a second glance. At the end of the street the great stone temple to Minerva towered over the town, its massive red- tiled roof easily the finest in the city. Curiously Marcus glanced up at the magnificent temple. He had never been to Aquae Sulis before, but the natural hot springs that gushed forth from the earth beneath the temple were famous. It was said that the waters had healing powers and that the temple was the gateway into the spirit world. That must be why the town was so prosperous, Marcus thought, with sudden insight. The thermal baths beneath the temple and their reputation must attract travellers from all over the province, who came here to communicate with their gods.

"Friend," Marcus called, out as he caught hold of a passer-by. "We're looking for the Prefect's office. Can you tell me where it is?"

"No such place here," the man muttered, as he tried to move on, but Marcus' firm hand on his shoulder prevented that.

"Well then, where are the land and census records kept?" Marcus growled.

"What," the passer-by said, as he gave Marcus an annoyed, quizzical look. "The building containing them burnt down three years ago. If you are looking for information, try the priests in the temple, they know everything, but they will charge you. They are greedy men."

Marcus muttered something to himself as he watched the passer-by hurry away. Then at his side Cunomoltus burst into another loud, trumpeting sneezing fit.

"Looks like we have hit another dead end," Cunomoltus said at last in a weary, resigned voice as he closed his eyes and held his hand up to his nose.

"Maybe we should ask those voices in your head for help?" Marcus snapped irritably as he looked around him.

"You are not very funny," Cunomoltus retorted, "I bet in the army no one ever laughed at your jokes."

"Shut up," Marcus growled as he looked up the street towards the temple complex that occupied the centre of the town. Then suddenly he grunted in surprise, as his gaze came to rest upon a gaily coloured sign, hanging outside one of the shops that lined the street on both sides.

"Maybe our luck is about to change," Marcus muttered. "See that sign over there. That's Falco's sign. He's a banker. He was my father's business partner. I forgot that he told me that his bank has a branch in this town. I am going inside to see whether they have any information that we can use. You will stay here and look after the horses."

"Yes Sir. You are the boss," Cunomoltus sighed, raising his eyebrows.

Marcus handed over the reins of his horse and, as he took them Cunomoltus failed to see the careful, crafty look that Marcus gave him.

"Wait here, I won't be long," Marcus said, as he headed off across the street towards the bank, narrowly missing being run over by an ox drawn wagon.

When he finally returned Marcus was carrying a small sturdy looking, iron-rimmed strong box. Cunomoltus gave him a questioning glance as he approached.

"Well?" he exclaimed.

Marcus shook his head. "Nothing," he replied. "They know nothing about Emogene or her husband. It's another dead end."

"So what is in the box?" Cunomoltus frowned gesturing at the small strong box.

"Money," Marcus said, giving the box a little jingling shake before casting a careful glance around him, "A lot of money. We're going to need it on this journey."

"That makes sense," Cunomoltus replied in relief, as he glanced up at the sky, "It's getting late, Marcus. We should find ourselves a tavern for the night. I am getting tired of sleeping out in the open. It has given me this fucking cold. If we've got the money, then let's spend it!"

Marcus said nothing as he took the reins of his horse and started up the street towards the temple complex. He had however, not gone more than fifty paces when his path was suddenly blocked by three unfriendly looking young men with shaven heads and brown tunics. One of them had a knife on display, casually tucked into his belt.

"What's this?" Marcus growled as his face darkened.

A passer-by had paused to stare at the confrontation in the middle of the street and one of the young men calmly gave the pedestrian a rough shove sending him hurrying on his way.

"You are not from around here, are you," the man with the knife said, as he took a confident step towards Marcus. "For if you were, you would know, to be more careful when you entered that bank. The box, give it to me. Hand it over and we'll let you live."

Marcus stood his ground and calmly looked around him. He was standing in the middle of the street, in daylight, but none of the pedestrians and shoppers hurrying past seemed willing to interfere in the confrontation. The people kept their faces to the ground and no one uttered a word of protest. Slowly Marcus's hand dropped to the pommel of his sword.

"No fucking way," Marcus snarled. "Now fuck off. You don't want to fight me. You are going to lose."

"You," the leader of the gang cried, pointing a finger at Cunomoltus, "Get the fuck out of here. This doesn't concern you. We just want the money."

But Cunomoltus did not move as he stood holding his horse's reins a few steps behind Marcus.

"What, are you, stupid?" one of the muggers yelled at Cunomoltus as he took a threatening step towards him. "Get out of here."

"Give us the money, now" the man with the knife roared at Marcus.

"No," Marcus replied.

One of the men cried out and came at Marcus swinging a fist at his face. Marcus stumbled and managed to grasp hold of the man's arm as the two of them crashed backwards onto the paving stones. There was no time to draw his sword. The man with the knife was coming to his comrade's aid but, as he did so Cunomoltus opened his mouth and howled with sudden rage. As Marcus grappled with his assailant, who was trying to prize the strong box from him grasp, Cunomoltus charged forwards, catching the second man in a perfect, low tackle that sent both men tumbling onto the snow covered, paving stones. Cunomoltus however, was the quickest to recover and with a furious yell he smashed his knee into the mugger's face, knocking him straight onto his back. The third assailant stood staring at the scene, rooted to the ground with indecision. There was no stopping Cunomoltus. Viciously he pummelled his helpless attacker's face with his fist, breaking the man's nose. Then he was up on his feet, a ball of howling human aggression, as he charged the third man. For the mugger however, it was too much and swiftly the man turned and fled down the street. He was followed moments later by his two companions, one of whom left a trail of blood in the snow.

"What the fuck!" Cunomoltus roared as he stood in the midst of the street, his hands clenched into fists. "Is that all you got. Go on then, run, you fucking cowards, because if I ever see you again, I am going to gut you and feed you to my dogs!"

Stiffly, Marcus got to his feet and stared at the fleeing men. In his hand he was still clutching the small strong box. A number of pedestrians and shoppers were staring at them in shocked silence. Then Marcus turned and swore. In the melée his horse had bolted.

"You alright?" Marcus muttered, turning to look at Cunomoltus with a little appreciative glance.

Cunomoltus nodded silently, his face flushed with rage.

"Here, look after this for a while," Marcus said thrusting the money box into Cunomoltus's hands, "I am going to find my horse. I will meet you back at the bank. Keep an eye open for those arseholes; they may be back."

"Sure," Cunomoltus snapped with a surprised glance, as he looked down at the box in his hands.

When Marcus finally returned, leading his horse, Cunomoltus was waiting for him outside the bank, just like he'd asked him to and, as he approached on foot, Marcus muttered something under his breath.

"Everything alright?" Marcus said addressing Cunomoltus in a louder voice and casting a quick glance at the strong box that his companion was clutching.

"They didn't come back," Cunomoltus replied with a sniff, as he handed back the small box. "I don't like this town, Marcus. Did you see how no one did anything to help us? This place seems to tolerate people being mugged in the middle of the street. It's a disgrace."

Marcus looked down at the box in silence. Then he sighed and glanced up at the sky.

"It's nearly dark," he said, "We should find a tavern for the night and get some warm food into us. I think I saw a place when I was looking for my horse."

***

The ground floor of "the Eagle" tavern was a large, open, cosy and welcoming place. One side of the room was taken up by a wooden bar with circular holes cut into it, behind which sat a bored looking, elderly man. Opposite him, set into the brick wall, was a roaring, cracking fire that bathed the room in heat and a reddish flickering glow. At the back of the tavern, a ladder led up to the rooms on the second floor. A little boy of no more than six or seven sat on the bottom rung, collecting payment from the few travellers who had chosen to stay the night. At their small wooden table, Marcus leaned forwards in his chair and poured another measure of wine into Cunomoltus' cup. The two of them were sitting close to the fire with the small money box in the middle of the table and Marcus's thick, Dacian winter cloak draped over the back of his chair.

"Drink," Marcus muttered, as he raised his own cup to his lips, "The wine will do you good. I have even added some honey for your cold."

Cunomoltus said nothing, as he downed his cup in one go. Then he burped and wiped his mouth with his hand as he looked down at the table. His puffed up, flue infested eyes looked tired and his cheeks had gone red in the heat.

Marcus studied Cunomoltus carefully and for a while the two of them were silent. In the tavern around them, the few travellers and late night drinkers kept themselves to themselves, chatting quietly to each other, over a cup of wine or beer.

"I was in the army for over twenty years," Marcus said at last, glancing at the fire, "and when you have served as long as I have, you get to know why men sign up. There are three types of men in the army. The first are those who follow their father's footsteps, who do their duty, who don't run and who fight for their friends and their standards. They are honourable men. Then you have the ones who do it for the money and advancement and then finally you have the third group, the one to which you belong, the ones who join up because they are running away from something."

Slowly Cunomoltus raised his head to look at Marcus.

"Who are you really?" Marcus said leaning forwards, "Come on, no more lies. Who are you? It is time that you spoke the truth. I won't hold it against you."

"You think I am running from something?" Cunomoltus muttered, as he reached for the jug of wine and poured some into his cup.

"Yes I think you are running away from something. I think you are scared."

Cunomoltus took a sip of wine and slowly placed his cup back onto the table. Then sharply, he looked up at Marcus and there was a sudden smile on his lips.

"Do you know what I think?" Cunomoltus said in a changed, sober voice, "I think you have been testing me all day."

Cunomoltus leaned back in his chair and stared at Marcus, waiving his finger playfully in the air. "There were three tests. The mugging in the street, did you arrange that to see how I would react? Then there was the money box. You handed it to me to when you went to look for your horse. Was that another test to see whether I would ride away with all your money? And now, right here, you are trying to get me drunk to see if I will tell you what you want to hear. I have been watching you. You have hardly touched your own cup all evening. So, am I right?"

Marcus said nothing as he calmly studied Cunomoltus. Then he lowered his eyes.

"The muggers, they weren't real," he replied, "In the bank, I arranged for them to pretend to rob us and yes I gave you the money box to test your loyalty."

Cunomoltus gave a satisfied nod as he looked down at the strong box on the table.

"I bet there isn't even any real money inside it," he growled.

"Scrap metal, completely worthless," Marcus said. "If you had run, you wouldn't have been a very wealthy man. Do you think I would actually entrust you with real coins?"

"And I suppose you already knew that there was a bank here and that the records office had burned down," Cunomoltus said quickly.

"I knew about the bank yes, but I didn't about the destruction of the records," Marcus replied taking a sip from his cup.

Cunomoltus observed him for a moment from across the table. Then slowly he shook his head with an amused smile.

"You are one sly dog, Marcus," he muttered. "So, did I pass your tests?"

"You did," Marcus replied as he straightened up and turned to look at his companion with a solemn, serious expression. "But I still think you are running from something. On the first day that you arrived at my villa, you said you were on the run. Or did the voices in your head tell you to say that as well?"

Cunomoltus exhaled loudly and reached for his cup.

"Well you have been honest with me for once, so I suppose good manners dictate that I do the same. It is true. Before I left to find you, I made some enemies, powerful men. It's about an unpaid debt, money that I had borrowed from them and could not repay and..," Cunomoltus sighed wearily. "Then there are some related women issues. It's all a bit awkward, but the short of it is that these men are still after me. If they find me they are going to slice me into strips of meat if I can't repay them, which I certainly can't."

"You could have ridden away with the money in the box, why didn't you? You could have repaid these men."

Cunomoltus looked mildly offended as he raised his cup in the air in salute.

"Fuck them," he growled, "I am not paying them back. Let them do their worst and I will do my best. They don't deserve anything."

Wearily Marcus rubbed his fingers across his forehead and closed his eyes.

"It seems," he said, "that you have inherited all of your father's faults and none of his virtues. Don't expect me to do anything about your problems. If these men find you then you are on your own."

Cunomoltus' eyes sparkled with sudden delight as he raised his mug in the air.

"The arsehole of the family," he exclaimed. "Thank you Marcus. That's the first time that you have accepted me as something like a brother."

"Don't get used to it," Marcus growled.

"So what do we do now?" Cunomoltus said, changing the subject. "The trail has gone cold. We still don't know the whereabouts of this Emogene and her husband. So far we have learned absolutely nothing."

"Tomorrow," Marcus said with a confident nod, "I will go to the temple baths and speak to the priests. They may know something."

"Good idea," Cunomoltus replied, "and I will come with you."

"No," Marcus said sharply, "You will stay here and wait until I return. No one is going to want to speak to me if I show up in the baths accompanied by a halfwit, with a streaming cold."

Chapter Eighteen – An Old Acquaintance

Around the temple and baths complex, a warren of alleys and brand new stone workshops, maintenance sheds, shops, homes and store houses, had risen that seemed to surround the Temple to Sulis Minerva in a tight protective embrace. The buildings looked brand new, smart, solid, ordered and undeniably Roman; a clear statement to any newcomer that this was a proud, new Roman town. And rising above it all, loomed the magnificent, red tiled roof of the Temple itself standing directly over the source of the hot springs. Marcus gazed up at it as he joined the queue to enter the Temple. The Province of Britannia was growing wealthier and more prosperous he thought. He had first noticed it in Londinium, when he had returned from the Dacian frontier, and had marvelled at how the city had changed and grown. People might complain about how they had lost their freedom but they could not deny that the long Roman peace had brought benefits too. Only in the north had they not forgotten the ancient ways and freedoms enjoyed by their forefathers.

It was morning and the dull, grey sky was overcast and it was cold. At the entrance to the Temple a few armed temple-guards stood clustered together, gossiping around an open fire as they warmed their hands. A beggar, with a hood pulled over his head and holding out a hand, was sitting on the ground, beside the wall that surrounded the Temple. A little way off, a temple prostitute was plying her trade with a group of newly arrived and excited pilgrims. When it was his turn, Marcus handed a slave a couple of bronze coins and in return received a small pewter vessel. Then he was through the gate and into the complex. The large, colonnaded Temple towered over him, stern and forbidding, and in the courtyard below the solid stone columns, a group of pilgrims had gathered around an altar and were placing their offerings at it's base. The pilgrims were all men. There were no women about. Idly Marcus looked around him, searching for one of the priests. The priests claim to serve the Goddess, Falco had once told him. But in truth they served their own selfish commercial interests and money lending was one of them; the banker had added disapprovingly. That and prostitution; selling worthless trinkets and acting as a safe depository for anything valuable. Marcus grunted. Falco didn't like the priests because the temples competed directly with the banks for business. But the temples were powerful, respected, well connected and prosperous and if a man had a problem or needed advice it was not a bad place to start.

"Sir," Marcus called out, raising his hand as he caught sight of a priest, who had just emerged from the main entrance into the baths.

"Sir, a moment of your time, please," Marcus said, as he swiftly ascended the steps leading into the temple and blocked the man's path.

The priest, clad in a simple white tunic, paused and gave Marcus a quizzical look.

"I am looking for some information," Marcus said quickly, "I am looking for a woman who used to live in a farm house just outside this town. She was called Emogene. She and her husband ran a slave exporting business. They must have visited the baths from time to time. Maybe you know them? Maybe you know what became of them?"

The priest frowned. "No, can't say I know them," he replied.

"I can pay," Marcus said lowering his voice and opening his hand to show the man a silver coin.

For a moment the priest stared at the silver coin. Then abruptly he looked up.

"The priests of Sulis Minerva do not accept coins for their advice," the priest replied in an offended voice, "If you think I can be bought with a piece of silver, then you are gravely mistaken."

Crestfallen, Marcus watched the priest walk away. That was just his luck he thought, when he really needed a break, he had to meet an incorruptible priest.

Wearily, he turned to look at the entrance to the baths. If he didn't find a lead soon the whole quest would be doomed and he would be forced to return to Vectis and the humiliation that awaited him there. Stubbornly he strode up the steps and entered the baths building. The warm, humid heat from the baths was a welcome change to the cold, winter weather and Marcus quickly took off his scarf and cloak and folded them across his arm. Inside the building, the rectangular pool of steaming, dark green water was surrounded by a large crowd of silent, respectful pilgrims and bathers. Incense hung heavy in the air. Marcus took a hesitant step towards the edge of the pool. Above him, the vaulted roof blocked out the daylight and he could not see the bottom of the pool. As he stared at the still, green waters Marcus muttered a silent prayer. He needed a break. He needed a bit of luck. He really did.

"Need a curse tablet, ointment for muscle ache, potion for head pains," a slave said coming up to him, holding a tray filled with a curious looking selection of little pewter sheets and small pots. "Two for one today only. Pay the man at the entrance. No credit given."

Marcus shook his head and the seller moved off to try his luck with another group. Marcus scratched his cheeks as he looked around him. The baths were certainly impressive but that didn't help him much. He was just about to head towards the changing rooms, when a voice suddenly boomed out from across the rectangular basin, shattering the respectful tranquillity of the temple.

"Thunder and lashing rain, so Wodan commeth!"

Marcus stopped dead in his tracks as he felt the hair on his neck stand up. Then abruptly he turned in the direction from which the man had shouted. The crowd of pilgrims too, had stopped what they were doing and were staring in surprise at a bare chested man, as he strode confidently and purposefully around the edge of the pool towards Marcus.

"Thunder and lashing rain, so Wodan commeth," the man roared again oblivious to the consternation he was causing, "Is that really you, commander, is that really you Marcus?"

And as the man approached, Marcus suddenly gasped. It was Hedwig, one of the Batavian officers who had served under him during the great northern rebellion. Hedwig grinned in delight as he came towards Marcus. His right arm had been severed just below the shoulder and was now just a stump.

Hedwig was speaking as he came towards Marcus, his eyes shining with sudden fervour and excitement.

"So trust in the man beside you and do your duty for in the coming days I want our enemy to cry out in alarm as they see our approach; I want to hear them shout: Ah shit! Here come those damned Batavians again."

"That Sir is the speech you gave to us in the fort at Luguvalium after Cotta was killed and we were surrounded by rebel tribesmen," Hedwig cried, "I remember every word. That speech has become a legend in the Cohort. Did you know they are teaching it to the new recruits? Fuck, it's good to see you again Sir."

And with that, Hedwig clasped hold of Marcus in a fierce embrace.

"Hedwig, you old arse," Marcus muttered, shaking his head in wonder, "Of all the places, this is where I find you. Today is a good day, after all."

Hedwig released him and took a step back to study Marcus with a broad grin.

"I live here now. How long has   it been Sir?"

Marcus grinned as he stared at his old comrade in arms. "You lost that arm in the rebellion and you didn't come with us to Pannonia and the Dacian frontier, so I guess it must have been fourteen years or so. The last time I saw you was when I returned to the Cohort to face my court martial. They had just operated on your arm and you wanted to drink yourself to death, because the army was about to discharge you and you didn't want to go."

"That long ago," Hedwig muttered, "Well it doesn't matter. I live well here in this town but the winters are boring as hell. Come Sir, you must tell me about everything that happened to you and the boys out there on the frontier. I want to know everything."

Marcus smiled sadly. "Just another army camp and another enemy, who wanted to rip your guts from your belly. I don't think you missed anything."

Hedwig gave Marcus a little shake of the head.

"I am glad those pricks allowed you to stay in the cohort," he said as his face grew serious, "You saved the entire unit during the rebellion."

"Agricola put in a good word for me," Marcus replied stiffly. "So instead of the death penalty which Cotta had in mind, they demoted me. I was never allowed to command again. But it doesn't matter. I was faithful to the oath that I made on the day of my enlistment."

"Yes, so was I," Hedwig muttered as he looked down at the floor. "When they come to erect my head stone it shall say, here lies Hedwig, a Batavian soldier, Decurion in the 2nd Batavian Cohort, faithful to his oath. That is all the honour that a soldier needs."

Marcus nodded in silent agreement.

"There is a large contingent of retired Batavian veterans in Londinium," Marcus said, "You should go and see them. The older ones will remember us. They like to meet at a tavern called Cum Mula Peperit II. It's the same old tavern where my father liked to drink, just under new management. The veterans look after each other, they pass on messages and they are in contact with our comrades on the Dacian frontier. I used them to send letters to my wife here in Britannia."

Hedwig grinned in delight, "I like the sound of that Marcus. So you are officially married now. This is good news. A man without a good woman is a horse without a rider. And Fergus, your son? He is well?"

"I think he is well," Marcus replied, "I haven't seen him in fifteen years. He has signed up with the Twentieth Legion, the same Legion my father served in. I hope to see him soon."

"Good," Hedwig nodded happily, "I remember Fergus running around the muddy parade ground back in the fort at Luguvalium, waving around that little wooden sword you made for him. How old was he then, three?"

Marcus nodded and allowed himself a little nostalgic smile.

Suddenly Hedwig's expression changed and his eyes widened in sudden realisation.

"Fuck me," he gasped, "I nearly forgot. Did you know that our old comrade Lucius is still alive? I saw him the other day in the market. He goes by the name of Aelianus now and he's changed his appearance but it was definitely him. I swear it. He betrayed you during the battle in the mountains. I found out that he has a home not far from here, close to the Charterhouse lead mines."

Chapter Nineteen – VEBriacum

The Mendip hills stretched away westwards to the horizon and their low summits and ridges were covered in small woodlands and empty, snow covered fields. Marcus and Cunomoltus rode in single file down the narrow, rutted track. It was late in the morning and a day had passed since the unexpected meeting with Hedwig. There was a dark and grim expression on Marcus' face as he led the way up the gentle hillside. His thick, Dacian cloak was covered in snow flakes and his face was half hidden beneath his scarf and Corbulo's old sword, sheathed in its protective, brown- leather scabbard, dangled from his belt. Behind him Cunomoltus followed, his hand clutching his nose, his face pale, tense and unhappy and now and then he broke out into a loud sneezing fit. He had been strangely reluctant to come along that morning and his unhappiness was clearly visible.

Marcus gripped his horse's reins tightly as he struggled to control the surging violent anger that threatened to make him start to gallop. Lucius. Lucius. Lucius. He had thought he had put the pain and anger of that man's betrayal behind him after so many years, but the meeting with Hedwig had only rekindled it and now that he knew where the traitor and deserter was hiding, it drove him on. His former friend would answer for what he had done. He would have to explain why he had left Marcus and his men to die on that bleak northern hillside all those years ago. And as he picked his way up the track, Marcus became aware of something else, something he had buried deep inside him and had tried to forget. Sorrow, the sorrow of having lost a good friend, a fellow officer who had been there at his side at Mons Graupius and during the great northern rebellion.

As he reached the crest of the hill, Marcus paused and stared down into the valley beyond. The country, even in winter, looked beautiful, a picturesque view of a happy, prosperous and peaceful land. Cunomoltus urged his horse alongside Marcus and for a moment the two of them were silent, as they looked down at the small mining town of Vebriacum. The small settlement was nothing more than a cluster of Celtic round houses with thatched roofs. Smoke was rising from somewhere in the settlement and there were no walls or ditches protecting the village. This then, was how the vast bulk of the population of the province of Britannia still lived, not in the smart, modern Roman towns but in small, scattered villages, just like their ancestors had always done.

"We should not have come to this district," Cunomoltus snapped unhappily. "But you are so stubborn, you just don't listen, do you."

"Why?" Marcus retorted. "Why are you so eager to avoid these hills?"

But Cunomoltus shook his head in a little dismissive gesture and remained silent.

"Will we find him down there?" Cunomoltus muttered at last, gesturing at the village down in the valley.

"I hope so," Marcus snapped, "The man goes by the name of Aelianus now and he has changed his appearance, but I will recognise him."

Cunomoltus nodded tensely. "And when you do, Marcus, what will you do? What are you going to do with this man? Are you going to kill him?"

Marcus said nothing as he stared at the settlement.

"I thought we were out here looking for Corbulo's old bones," Cunomoltus exclaimed in annoyed voice, "You have become distracted Marcus. I didn't agree to come along so that you can go off to settle some feud that happened years ago. We should be trying to find out what happened to our father. Not this."

Slowly Marcus turned to stare at his companion. "I have unfinished business with this man," he hissed, "If you don't like it, then fuck off. No one is forcing you to come along. But I am doing this and I am doing it today."

"This is such a waste of time," Cunomoltus glared at him with sudden irritation, "We should not have come here and I am really getting fed up with this fucking head cold."

Marcus snorted in disgust and without another word, he turned and urged his horse down the track that led to the village.

The village of a dozen or so free standing, round houses looked nearly deserted as Marcus approached. From behind one of the houses a dog had started to bark and a couple of women looked up at him from the edge of a stream, where they were collecting water. Slowly Marcus walked his horse towards the centre of the settlement, glancing around him as he did so, but there was no sign of Lucius. Behind him, Cunomoltus was muttering to himself and had raised his scarf over his face so that only his eyes were showing. Marcus came to a halt beside a house, from where inside he could hear the dull metallic hammering of a blacksmith at work. Close by, a young boy was staring at him curiously, as he stood guarding a flock of cackling geese, who were cooped up in a wooden pen.

"Where is everyone?" Marcus said, turning to the boy.

In response the boy immediately raised his arm and pointed southwards towards the hills. "They are over there, working in the mines," he replied, in a high pitched childish voice.

Marcus grunted and was about to ask another question when the blacksmith appeared in the doorway to his home. The big, brawny man had a thick, blackened- leather apron draped over his tunic and he was clutching a hammer.

"What do you want?" the blacksmith growled, sizing up Marcus and Cunomoltus with a suspicious glance.

"I am looking for a man called Aelianus. I was told we could find him here in Vebriacum," Marcus replied.

The blacksmith studied Marcus in silence. Then he turned to stare at Cunomoltus.

"It's like the boy said," the blacksmith replied, "He's over at the Charterhouse lead mines. He owns and works a plot on the hill. You will find him there. It's just a couple of miles away."

Marcus nodded and began to turn away.

"Say, do I know you?" the blacksmith exclaimed as he peered at Cunomoltus. "You look familiar. Aren't you the man who used to come around buying our dogs?"

"I am sorry, you are mistaken, that's not me," Cunomoltus muttered hastily as he averted his face and quickly trotted away.

Marcus frowned as he caught up with him.

"What was that all about?" Marcus inquired glancing back at the blacksmith who was still standing in his doorway watching them.

"It's nothing," Cunomoltus snapped, "I told you that we should not have come to this district, but you didn't want to listen."

"What is it that you are not telling me?" Marcus growled.

Cunomoltus forced his horse to a halt and glanced around him at the houses but there was no one about. Tensely he turned on Marcus.

"Listen," he hissed, "I used to buy and sell my dogs in the villages and towns around here. This is the district where I grew up. People around here know me. I did a lot of travelling. My face is known to many and when they realise that I am back, how long do you think it will be, before my creditors will be on my trail. But you don't give a shit about that, do you, because like you said, if they catch up with me, then I am on my own, right. The arsehole of the family. The son no one gives a shit about."

"Why didn't you tell me this earlier?" Marcus retorted.

"I fucking well tried," Cunomoltus nearly shouted, "But you were so consumed in your desire for revenge that you didn't want to listen."

Darkly, Marcus muttered something to himself and glanced back at the blacksmith's workshop. The blacksmith had not moved and was still watching them.

"Stop being such a pussy," Marcus growled at last, "We will be long gone by the time your creditors find out."

"Fine," Cunomoltus snapped unhappily, "But as we are here now, I may as well find a treatment for this head cold. It's really beginning to annoy me. The stuff is running out of my nose like a river."

"Yes, it's beginning to annoy me too," Marcus said shaking his head.

Expertly. Marcus wheeled his horse around and trotted over towards the stream where the two women he'd seen earlier were coming towards him, carrying their jugs of water.

"We are looking for a healer, someone who can prepare a potion for this arsehole here," Marcus called out, "My companion has a severe head cold. We are willing to pay."

The women paused as they looked up at Marcus. Then one of them pointed in the direction of a round house on the outskirts of the village.

"You can try the woman who lives there," the woman replied. "She likes to collect plants and herbs. She will be able to help your friend."

Marcus nodded his thanks and without waiting for Cunomoltus, he started out towards the thatched, round house. The building looked in a poor state and the roof had partially collapsed. Marcus slid from his horse and calmly tied the reins around a nearby tree. Then he turned towards the entrance. Close to the heavy woollen blanket that covered the doorway, the remains of a fire had left a blackened scorch mark in the fresh snow and a solitary goat stood tied to a wooden post, watching him nervously. Marcus paused as Cunomoltus dismounted.

"Can you help us?" Marcus cried out in loud voice, "My friend needs a mint potion to heal his cold. We were told that you could help. We can pay."

From inside the hut there was no immediate reply. Then slowly and cautiously the heavy blanket was drawn aside and a girl's face peered out at them. The girl looked no older than twelve. She examined Marcus and Cunomoltus warily.

"It will cost you, three copper coins," she said.

Marcus nodded in agreement and glancing at Cunomoltus he stepped forwards and entered the house. Inside the single space was dimly lit. Straw covered the floor and a blackened stone circle with a small fire burning in it marked the centre of the hut. A pair of beautifully crafted, iron fire dogs stood over the fire holding up an iron pot. The smell of wood smoke hung thick in the air. As his eyes adjusted to the light, Marcus suddenly noticed a boy of no more than seven years old sitting beside the fire. The boy was staring at him with large, fearful eyes.

"Where are you mother and father?" Marcus said as he looked around at the few possessions.

"My mother is outside in the ground beside the oak tree," the girl replied, as she calmly reached for a leather bag that hung from a hook in one of the roof beams. "She died giving birth to my brother over there. And my father is out working in the mines.

Everyone around here works the mines. You are not from around here are you?"

Marcus grunted. The girl was sharp. He remained silent as Cunomoltus stepped inside and glanced around.

"They call me the herb girl," the girl said, as she selected some plants from her bag, "I heal people. That is what I do and I am very good. People come a long way to buy my potions. One day my name will be known throughout the whole province. One day I will have a practice in Londinium or Isca."

"Just make sure you get this one right, darling" Cunomoltus sniffed irritably as he peered at the girl, as she prepared her ingredients.

Marcus folded his arms across his chest as he waited for the girl to finish her preparations. The boy beside the fire was staring up at him in mesmerized silence. Then, as he glanced around, Marcus suddenly swore in surprise. There, hanging from a hook on a roof beam, was a Batavian cavalryman's helmet. The distinctive helmet looked in pristine condition.

"Where did you get that?" Marcus's hand shot forwards as he pointed at the helmet.

The girl turned to look in the direction in which he was pointing.

"That belongs to my father," she replied, "His name is Aelianus. He is over at the mines, working his plot."

Chapter Twenty – Vengeance

"What are you going to do to him?" Cunomoltus said, as he and Marcus trotted across the snow-covered field. "Are you going to kill him? You have that right Marcus. He was your friend, your comrade and he betrayed you and left you and your men to die. A man deserves death for such treachery. But if you kill him Marcus, you will be turning those children into orphans."

Marcus's eyes were firmly fixed on the hills a mile away.

"I haven't decided," Marcus replied in a grim, unhappy voice.

Cunomoltus gave him a quick, concerned look.

"Maybe it would have been better to wait for him to come home," he said, "We could have held his children hostage and forced him to surrender. Who knows what it's going to be like in the mines. The man may have friends there, who will come to his aid, who will protect him? It would have been easier if we had stayed in Vebriacum."

"No," Marcus said with a resolute shake of his head, "This is between me and Lucius. His children are not my concern and if he has friends, then they had better not get in my way."

"I knew we should never have come here," Cunomoltus muttered. "This looks like it's going to have an unhappy ending every way you look at it."

"If you are scared then turn back now, I do not need cowards at my side."

Cunomoltus shook his head. "I am not scared," he muttered, "But like you said, this is your fight. I shouldn't be here. I have my own enemies to worry about."

Swiftly Cunomoltus raised his finger in the air.

"But before you tell me to fuck off for the hundredth time," he continued, "I want you to know that if it gets ugly, I will have your back. They may have not accepted me into the army, but I still know how to handle myself in a fight, brother, and I fight dirty. I don't give a shit. I don't have any rules. I just want to win."

"That's good to know," Marcus muttered darkly. "For here I was thinking that all you could do was whine, lie and sneeze."

***

The Charterhouse lead mines were an ugly scar on the valley. As they approached, Marcus could see the compact, industrial mining works stretching out in all directions across the once pristine, barren, high-plateau. There were no defences, no wall, ditch or embankment, but at its western edge the place was protected by a small Roman fort with an attendant amphitheatre. As they rode towards the site, Marcus grunted in surprise. He had been expecting a deep mine, like the gold mines he'd seen in Dacia, but this lead mine was open-cast; the miners were digging up the lead from the surface. Cautiously he reined in his horse. The whole place was alive with activity. Smoke was billowing up into the sky from the forges and in the mineral extraction areas men, women, children, carrying pickaxes, shovels and hammers, their faces and clothes stained and smeared in dirt and earth, were crawling over the rectangular and square pits and platforms like ants. Wooden scaffolding had been erected in some of the pits and ox-drawn wagons loaded with raw ore were moving slowly down the rutted and snow-covered tracks towards the core of the settlement, with its lines of terraced, industrial workshops, yards, furnaces, storage facilities, shops and facilities.

"Keep your eyes open," Marcus muttered, as he turned to Cunomoltus. "And let me do the talking."

The miners did not give the two newcomers a second glance as Marcus and Cunomoltus slowly rode up the frozen, rutted track towards the centre of the sprawling mining complex. The traffic was heavy and the place filled with shouts, barking dogs, creaking wagons, bellowing oxen and the crash of raw ore, as it was dumped into the crushing yards. Marcus glanced around at the faces but no one seemed to want to make eye contact and Lucius was nowhere to be seen. Idly he stared at the crushing yards where the men, whose job it was to wash and crush the raw ore, were picking their way through the mounds. Someone, somewhere though would know where he was.

Beside a food stall with a large collection of amphorae Marcus halted and dismounted. Across the busy track from him, smoke was billowing up from a smelter's workshop and two slaves were unloading a fresh supply of wood from a wagon. Cautiously Marcus looked around. Then his gaze settled on a terraced building next to the furnace, which had a solitary, auxiliary soldier, clutching a shield and spear, standing guard outside the entrance. Gesturing silently at Cunomoltus, he handed his companion the reins to his horse and started out towards the building.

"I am looking for a man called Aelianus? Do you know where I can find him. I was told he works here in the mine." Marcus asked, as the soldier blocked his path.

"No, don't know him," the soldier replied.

"Why are you posted here?" Marcus said curiously, as he tried to get a glimpse of what was going on inside the building behind the guard.

"None of your fucking business, now move on."

Marcus nodded and was about to turn away when two slaves appeared carrying a plank on which lay several ingots of newly moulded lead bullion. The grey lead gleamed in the sunlight and stamped into the ingots were the proud letters IMP TRAJANUS AVG, BRIT EX ARG VEB.

"I see that you have taken an interest in our bullion," a sharp voice said suddenly from the doorway of the moulding factory.

Marcus looked up as a well-dressed man with a smart, neatly trimmed beard came towards him. "My company run this mine, I am the owner. I think you are looking for me?"

"No," Marcus said frowning, "I am looking for a man called Aelianus. He is one of your miners."

For a brief moment the mine owner looked confused. Then he smiled and glanced at the slaves as they loaded the lead bullion onto a wagon.

"I am sorry, I thought you were someone else," the man said apologetically, "I am expecting an important official from the Governor's staff. My mistake." The mine owner took a deep breath. "Those fucking Spaniards from Rio Tinto have petitioned the Emperor again, to force us to cut our lead production. They can't compete with us on quality or quantity, that why. It's going to cost us jobs and people are not going to be happy if we can't change the Emperor's mind. Anyway, my company runs this mine, but we use a franchise system. Each miner works their own individual plot and they sell what they mine to me. Aelianus has a plot over there, by the wagon repair shop. But you won't find him there, not today anyway. He headed down to the river this morning to supervise the loading of some bullion onto the ships. He's a good worker, been with me for a long time. You a friend of his?"

"I was once," Marcus replied, nodding his thanks as he turned away. "But his real name is Lucius and he's an army deserter, so maybe you didn't know him as well as you thought."

***

The Cheddar Yeo river was a narrow strip of quiet, still water, no more than three yards wide and surrounded by tall, frozen reeds and empty, snow-covered fields. It was mid-afternoon and

Marcus and Cunomoltus sat on their horses hidden in the small wood as they observed the small riverside wharf and harbour at Rackley. The river seemed to be free of ice and wide enough to allow the narrow, Roman craft to moor up to the bank whilst it was being loaded and unloaded. Several wagons, filled with lead ingots, were waiting alongside the bank for their cargo to be loaded onto the boats for transport westwards and the sea beyond. Beside the carts a sea captain and several armed men were loitering around a woman, who seemed to be selling them something. Marcus's eyes however were fixed on Lucius. He was standing on the river bank watching the slaves loading the precious cargo of lead ingots into the boat. He'd aged a lot and his fat stomach now protruded over his belt and his grey hair had gone pure white, but the tall, clean-shaven immaculately dressed man standing on the bank was definitely Lucius. There was no mistake and as he watched him, Marcus's face darkened. For a moment he was back on that barren northern hillside, fourteen years ago, with the cold, mountain stream tumbling down the valley and the vicious, screaming battle between his Batavian troopers and rebel tribesmen. Lucius had disobeyed his orders. He was supposed to have come to Marcus' aid like they had planned, but Lucius had done no such thing. He had deliberately allowed Marcus and his men to be slaughtered.

"So what are you going to do?" Cunomoltus muttered, as he stared at the harbour from the cover of the trees.

Marcus wrenched his eyes away from Lucius and glanced towards the armed men beside the wagons.

"We'll take him when he sets out to return home," he muttered.

"That could be a while," Cunomoltus replied as he turned to look at the sky, "And it will be dark soon. We may lose him in the dark."

Marcus said nothing as he stared at the figure standing on the river bank.

"You don't have to kill him, you know," Cunomoltus said in a resigned voice, "We could just kick the shit out of him and rob him of everything of value."

"It's easy for you to say that," Marcus retorted, "But you were not there. You were not the one who was left to die. No, Lucius will pay for what he has done. He will pay."

***

It was growing dark when at last the three, empty, ox drawn wagons started up the track in the direction of the Charterhouse mine. Carefully Marcus watched their progress from his hiding place in the wood. The carts each had a single, slave-driver and Lucius, on foot, was leading them up the path. Quickly Marcus glanced back at the small river port. The heavily-laden boat was leaving, drifting gently downstream with its captain and armed men aboard. Quickly Marcus hissed at Cunomoltus and gestured at the small, slow moving convoy.

"Alright, let's go," he muttered.

The two of them burst from the forest and were upon Lucius and his wagons before anyone could react. Marcus wheeled his horse around in the midst of the track, blocking the convoy's path as Cunomoltus went riding down alongside the wagons, with a drawn sword, screaming at the slaves to get lost.

In the middle of the track, Lucius had come to a stunned, shocked halt. Then as he recognised Marcus his face grew pale and his mouth opened in silent horror.

"Hello friend," Marcus cried out as he looked down at his former army comrade. "Remember me, remember my name?"

"Marcus," Lucius muttered, as he stared up at Marcus with growing horror.

Behind him in the wagons, the unarmed slaves were scrambling down onto the ground and were making a run for it, as

Cunomoltus rode up and down shouting abuse at them and swinging his sword in the air.

"The last time that I saw you, first centurion," Marcus cried, "was when I gave you orders to attack the enemy upon hearing my signal. But you disobeyed those orders didn't you. You left me and my men to die on that hillside. Do you remember that? Do you remember that day?"

Lucius shook his head in stunned, silent dismay.

"Well I do," Marcus shouted his face flushed with anger, "I can still see the faces of my dead men. I can still see their bodies scattered across that valley. Fridwald, do you remember him? He is dead because of you. I too, should have been dead and all because you decided to avenge that worthless brother of yours. Tell me Lucius, how do you sleep at night, knowing what you did?"

Lucius tried to speak but no words came out of his mouth.

"Your brother Bestia was an arsehole," Marcus roared with growing fury, "Gods know how much we all suffered from his bullying. He tried to kill my father but Corbulo killed him instead. Bestia had it coming. You knew this. You knew what kind of a man he was and still you decided to avenge him. But now you are going to pay for what you did. Get down on your knees."

And as he spoke, Marcus slid from his horse and drew his sword and came towards Lucius.

On the track, Lucius raised his hand as if to ward off a blow.

"Get down on your knees," Marcus roared.

Slowly Lucius got down on his knees in the snow. His face was completely pale and his breathing was coming in quick rapid gasps.

"I am sorry Marcus," Lucius said as he tried to collect himself, "I am sorry for the good men we lost that day but as you know, good men die every day in training accidents, or from following stupid orders; hell - from just bad luck. What happened that day in the mountains was no different."

"You can tell that to them, when you meet them again in the next world," Marcus growled as he stood over the kneeling man in the snow.

"Bestia was my brother," Lucius said looking up at Marcus with a sudden hint of defiance, "He was of my blood. Your father murdered him. I could not just let his death go unavenged. Such things are offensive to the gods. Honour dictated that I have my revenge, so when I go to meet Bestia in the next world, he will know what I did, and he will welcome me as a brother."

As he stared up at Marcus, Lucius' defiance seemed to grow.

"And if I had to do it all again, Marcus, I would, so if you are here to kill me, then get on with it. I am not afraid of you."

Marcus struck Lucius hard across the head, sending him tumbling sideways into the snow.

"You are a deserter," Marcus cried, "Just like your brother was. But I am not here to kill you Lucius. I am going to take you to Deva and hand you over to the military authorities of the Twentieth Legion and let them judge and punish you. Desertion is a capital crime, but maybe you can convince them to be lenient."

In the snow Lucius slowly sat up, nursing his face with his hand.

"The army will execute me," Lucius muttered, looking up at Marcus. "You know how they are in such cases. There is no tolerance, no leniency."

"Maybe," Marcus nodded, "but you need to answer for what you did."

Slowly Lucius nodded, as a resigned expression appeared on his face. Then he looked up at Marcus and there was a deep sadness in his voice as he spoke.

"I do not regret what I did, but you are right," he murmured, "we must all answer for what we have done eventually, so it may as well be now. But I must ask you for one favour, Marcus."

Marcus sighed and turned to look away. He knew what was coming and he didn't like it, for it was something he was really trying to avoid.

"I really don't want to go to Deva and face an army court martial," Lucius said, with a little smile, "So you are going to have to wield the blade, for I am not going anywhere, old comrade."

Marcus refused to look at Lucius and for a long moment he said nothing. Beside the wagons, Cunomoltus was watching him from his horse.

"Alright, I will do it," Marcus snapped as he turned to look Lucius in the eye and stepped up to him with his sword raised. The man in the snow nodded gratefully and looked up at the sky and gasped with sudden emotion.

"Please, look after my children, Marcus," Lucius said, as he gasped again. "They have no one to look after them when I am gone."

Without saying a word, Marcus drove his sword deep down into Lucius's neck killing him instantly.

Chapter Twenty-One – A Good Heart, a Stupid Head

It was dawn and the grey overcast skies were filled with tumbling snowflakes. Marcus and Cunomoltus rode slowly, side by side, along the path, their scarfs wrapped around their faces, as they braised themselves against the icy, cold wind. Lucius's frozen corpse lay slumped across the back of Marcus's horse, his arms and legs dangling into space. Around them the bleak, snow-covered fields were deserted except for a group of sheep, who were huddling together in the shelter of a hollow in the ground. As they approached the village, Marcus raised his head to look ahead at Vebriacum, nestling along the valley floor.

"What are we doing here?" Cunomoltus exclaimed irritably. "I told you that my face is known in these parts. We have got what we came for, Marcus. Now can we please get the hell out of here."

Marcus said nothing and his grim, rugged and unshaven face remained unreadable. Then Cunomoltus groaned as he saw where they were heading. The round house at the edge of the village, with the partially collapsed roof looked abandoned, as Marcus slowly rode towards it. As they reached the home, Marcus dismounted and carefully tied his horse to a nearby tree as Cunomoltus remained sitting on his horse, gently shaking his head.

"Come out, both of you, your father has come home," Marcus said, raising his voice as he turned to face the doorway.

For a moment nothing happened. Then the heavy, woollen-blanket covering the doorway was pulled aside and the girl appeared. She stared at Marcus in silence, then her gaze shifted to the frozen corpse slumped across the horse.

"Both of you, come on out here," Marcus said with a stern voice. The girl was staring at her father's corpse in stoic silence. Then quickly she turned and called out to someone inside the hut and a moment later she stepped outside, followed by her younger brother. The two children took a few hesitant steps forwards as they stared in silence at the corpse on the horse, their faces betraying no emotion.

"Where did you bury your mother" Marcus said addressing the girl.

The girl slowly wrenched her gaze from the corpse and pointed at an oak tree a dozen yards away.

"She is over there, beside the tree," the girl replied, in a strong, emotionless voice as her hand slowly reached out to take her brother's hand.

Marcus nodded and abruptly turned towards Cunomoltus, "Get down from your horse and help me dig this grave," he growled.

And with that, Marcus strode towards his horse and lifted Lucius's body up and started to walk with it towards the oak.

The earth was hard and frozen and it took him and Cunomoltus a while before they had managed to create a shallow grave. As he straightened up, Marcus glanced at the two children and sighed. The girl and her young brother stood holding hands as they watched him.

"Did you kill him?" the girl said suddenly.

Marcus looked down at the frozen corpse. Then he gestured for Cunomoltus to pick up his legs and together they laid the body into the grave.

"Come here, both of you," Marcus growled as he knelt down on one knee beside the disturbed earth.

Hesitantly, the two children came up to the side of the grave.

Marcus fished around in a pocket and then handed the girl a silver coin.

"Place it in his mouth and say goodbye to your father, both of you," he said, "Do it now."

The girl looked down at the coin in her hand. Then she looked down at her father's corpse and quickly stooped and placed the coin in the body's mouth.

For a moment all was silent, except for the gentle moaning of the wind in the branches of the tree. Then at last Marcus rose and gestured for Cunomoltus to start covering the body with earth.

"The coin will pay for his journey into the next world," he said turning to the children, "And one day you will see him again together with your mother. But now you have a choice to make. You can either stay here in this village or you can come with me. I own a house; it's on an island. It is a good place. There are children there who are the same age as you." Slowly Marcus folded his arms across his chest. "So what will it be?"

The girl was watching Cunomoltus covering the grave with earth. Then she turned to look at her young brother and for a long moment the children said nothing.

Impatiently, Marcus loosened his arms and tapped his two fingers against his thigh.

"Your father and I were old friends," he said sharply. "He asked me to look after you. But I am going to need your answer now."

A little colour shot into the girl's cheeks. Then she looked up at Marcus and nodded.

"He said that this day may come," she said quietly, "He said that if anything ever happened to him that I should look after my brother. We will come with you, if you promise that I and my brother will never be separated."

Marcus nodded solemnly. "I can make that promise. What's your name?" he replied.

"Elsa," the girl replied, "and my brother is called Armin."

"Good," Marcus said, glancing at Cunomoltus who had nearly finished covering the grave, "Now go and collect your belongings. We are leaving and we have a long journey ahead."

As the two children silently turned and trooped back into the round house Cunomoltus caught hold of Marcus' arm. He looked worried.

"Are you sure this is wise?" Cunomoltus hissed. "How long do you think it will be before they know that it was you who killed their father? And that boy, when he grows up to be a man, he will take revenge for what you did. Maybe we should just cut their throats and have it done with. At least then you won't spend all your time looking over your shoulder waiting for them to plunge an assassin's knife into your back. You know that I am speaking sense Marcus."

"The cycle of revenge must stop somewhere," Marcus growled as he firmly removed Cunomoltus's hand from his arm. "I know the risks."

Cunomoltus shook his head in disbelief. "You soldiers and your sense of loyalty to each other. You spend all your time tracking down one man and eventually killing him and then you decide to look after his children. It's madness, it just doesn't make sense."

"I don't expect you to understand," Marcus replied, as he stood waiting, watching the doorway into the hut. "But those children are not to be harmed, I have given them my word."

"You have a good heart, but a stupid head," Cunomoltus said unhappily. "Keeping those children alive is just storing up trouble for the future."

Cunomoltus took a deep frustrated-breath and turned to look around him. "So now what" he snapped. "Can we finally get the hell out of here?"

"Alright," Marcus nodded. "As we can't seem to find anything on Emogene we're going to head north, to the legionary fortress at Deva. It's time that I saw Fergus, my son."

Cunomoltus nodded in relief and tiredly rubbed his forehead, "Well at least the girl knows how to make an effective potion against a head cold," he muttered.

Suddenly Marcus stiffened, as he caught sight of three men coming towards them across the empty, snow covered field. Quickly he nudged Cunomoltus.

"Looks like trouble," he growled in warning, "Do you know them?"

Cunomoltus turned around to look at the approaching men. For a moment he studied them. Then a little colour appeared in his cheeks and he groaned.

"I borrowed money from four brothers," Cunomoltus said in a tight voice. "They are called the Vindici brothers. They are money lenders who chose the winning side during the northern rebellion. They made their money from slaves. The one on the right," Cunomoltus gestured tensely, "he's the youngest brother. His name is Todd, he's the clever one, his three older brothers are the brute force, but I don't see them with him. The two men with Todd could be his cousins. It's a big, fucked up family if you know what I mean."

Calmly Marcus watched the men, as they silently and purposefully closed in on the house. The men were all in their prime and swords hung from their belts. Behind him, Marcus suddenly heard the blanket covering the doorway to the roundhouse being pulled back.

"Stay inside," he said sharply, without turning round.

Cunomoltus was muttering to himself. He looked tense and unhappy and his hand had dropped to rest on the pommel of his sword.

When they were five yards away, the three men came to a halt. The man Cunomoltus had called Todd was shorter than his two companions but there was a cunning gleam in his eyes as he pointed at Cunomoltus.

"Hello arsehole," Todd said, as a cold smile appeared on his lips, "We heard that you had returned to the district. Didn't think you would be that stupid, but anyway here you are. Have you come back to repay the money plus interest, that you owe us? I hope so, because I am not going to be able to let you leave if you haven't."

"The only thing you are going to get from me," Cunomoltus sneered, "Is my boot in your face. You are not getting anything from me."

"We'll see about that," Todd replied in a confident voice.

"How much does he owe?" Marcus said, as he took a step forwards.

"Who the fuck is this?" Todd snapped, giving Marcus a quick glance before turning his attention back to Cunomoltus.

"I am his brother," Marcus replied, "And I asked you a question."

Slowly Todd wrenched his eyes away from Cunomoltus and turned to stare at Marcus, sizing him up with his clever, cunning eyes.

"Two hundred Denarii," Todd replied at last, raising his chin, "Plus a year's interest at eight percent."

Marcus nodded, "We'll pay you the money," he growled, "But you must give us some time. I can get you the silver by the start of spring."

Todd said nothing as he studied Marcus. Then a little pained expression appeared on his face. "Yes, that all sounds fine, it's just, that I don't really believe you. You see we have heard these promises before and in my experience our debtors very rarely do what they say they will. I can't take that risk."

"I just told you that we will get the money and pay you," Marcus snapped.

Todd sighed and raised his eyebrows and glanced at his two companions with a weary, bored expression, as if to say that he had heard it all before.

"Here is what we are going to do," Todd said sharply, "We are going to take Cunomoltus over there as a slave, in lieu of the debts he owes us. We have that right, by law, and we are going to do it now and I really advise you not to get involved. This has nothing to do with you, so why don't you just quietly fuck off."

Marcus's face darkened. "I can't let you do that I'm afraid," he said, "Like I said, he is my brother. You will be taking no one as a slave today."

"Then we have a problem," Todd growled in a menacing voice.

Marcus took another step forwards and calmly looked Todd in the eye. "You don't want to fight me," he said in a quiet, dangerous voice, "No one has to die here, but it's your choice. So accept my terms or get the fuck out of here."

Todd grunted in surprise as he stared at Marcus and, as the silence lengthened the tension started to rapidly grow.

"Well, what's it going to be?" Marcus suddenly roared.

The man on Todd's right suddenly lunged at Marcus, clasping a knife in his hand but Marcus dodged the blow. A split second later his attacker howled in pain and staggered backwards as Marcus' Pugio army knife sliced a bloody line across the man's chest. At the same time the second man came charging at him

169

with a wild yell but before he could tackle him, Cunomoltus tripped him up, sending him tumbling into the snow and as he landed, Cunomoltus was upon him in an instant, like an enraged wild cat, a screaming, violent ball-of-teeth, nails, punches and kicks. Swiftly Marcus turned towards Todd. The small man stood rooted to the ground, stunned by the speed of events and horrified by his companion's fate. Then, as Marcus came towards him clutching his bloodied knife, Todd turned and started to run. Marcus watched him go with grim contempt. The man whose chest he'd sliced open had dropped his knife and was hobbling away across the snow, his hands clutching his chest, as he left a trail of blood in the fresh snow. Quickly Marcus turned and moved towards where Cunomoltus was trying to sever his opponent's jugular with his teeth. With a powerful grip Marcus caught hold of Cunomoltus and pulled him off his attacker. On the ground the man's face was covered in blood and one of his ears had nearly been ripped from his head, leaving a row of deep teeth marks. He was screaming in agony.

"Get out of here," Marcus shouted giving the man a kick.

"Why did you let them go?" Cunomoltus roared, with a wild, crazy look in his eyes, as the man joined his companions, fleeing unsteadily across the field. Marcus slapped Cunomoltus hard across his face. He looked hard and angry but firmly in control of himself.

"Get a grip," Marcus hissed, "They are gone. Now get your act together. We're leaving before they can come back with reinforcements."

Cunomoltus raised a hand to his burning cheek and glared furiously at Marcus but the slap seemed to have worked, for he seemed to control himself. Marcus took a deep breath as he watched the three men stumbling away across the field. Then he turned to Cunomoltus.

"I don't know who you really are," Marcus said staring at him with disapproval, "and I don't really like you. You could be my brother, maybe you are not, but I am never going to find out am I. So I am going to give you a chance, be my friend, win my trust, be good to my people on Vectis and I will accept you into my family."

Chapter Twenty-Two – Handing Over the Torch

The gates of the legionary fortress of Deva Victrix looked as imposing and formidable as Marcus remembered them to be. He stood waiting a few yards outside the fortress. It was morning and the legionaries on guard duty looked bored as they kept an eye on the continuous stream of people that came and went. Tensely, Marcus ground the toes of his army boot into the snow as he waited. It had been fifteen years since he'd last seen his son. But now the time had finally come. The slave, whom he had sent to summon Fergus had been gone for a long time. Stoically Marcus turned to gaze at the armed legionaries, trying to calm his nerves as he realised that he knew nothing about Fergus. He had not been there to see the boy grow up. It had been the price he'd had to pay for staying in the army and today the burden of that regret weighed heavy.

Suddenly, through the open gateway he caught sight of the slave. The man was accompanied by a young soldier, clad in a white tunic with a brown leather belt from which hung a sheathed gladius. As Marcus caught sight of the slave the man pointed at him and turned away. Marcus took a deep breath as the young legionary slowly came towards him. The soldier had red hair just like himself, with the dark outline of a beard, and he looked muscular and fit. Fergus had become a man. He was no longer the four-year-old child who had liked to run around waving his little wooden sword about. Tensely, Marcus stood his ground, as the young man approached with a quizzical look on his face.

"Who are you?" Fergus asked, as he came to stop before Marcus.

Marcus stood for a moment unable to speak, as he examined the young soldier. Then he sighed with sudden emotion.

"I am your father."

Fergus's face grew pale as he stared at Marcus. Then quickly he looked away and awkwardly raised his hand to scratch his cheek.

Marcus took a step forwards, meaning to embrace his son, but Fergus avoided the embrace by quickly moving backwards.

An awkward, embarrassed silence followed.

"Well, how are you then, son?" Marcus muttered.

"I am fine," Fergus replied as he kept his eyes averted, "I have to be back in the barracks when they change the guard so I don't have long."

"I understand," Marcus nodded quickly. "And the army is treating you well? Any problems? Fights, bullying, debts. Did you get any girls pregnant?"

"Nothing like that," Fergus replied stiffly. "The army was a good choice. I belong here. I really do. They even promoted me to decanus."

"Thunder and lashing rain," Marcus muttered with a surprised look, "Already a decanus at your age. That is a swift promotion. What did you do? Pay the centurion's bar bill?"

The joke however seemed lost on Fergus who glanced at his father with a serious expression, studying him cautiously.

"So you are back from the Dacian frontier then?"

Marcus nodded again as his face grew serious. "Yes. I came home a couple of months ago. I have retired from the army. I am a veteran of Rome now. The Dacians cut three fingers from my hand here," he said raising his left hand. Then he grunted. "Efa and Dylis and the family are doing well. I headed north to see you as soon as I could son. I am staying in one of the taverns in the civilian town."

"Is it the Lucky Legionary?"

Marcus shook his head and for a brief moment he stared at Fergus, lost in a sea of fond memories that threatened to swamp him.

"So then you will know my reasons for joining the Twentieth Legion," Fergus said raising his chin defiantly, "The legions are the best. They are the elite; they are the true soldiers of Rome and of Jupiter. My grandfather served this legion. Corbulo was a great man, a great legionary and I will be like him one day."

For a moment Marcus did not reply.

"I am your father, Fergus," he said in a stern voice. "I may not always have been here for you, but I am still your father. You should have written to me asking for my permission. And if you had done so, I would have granted your wish. Now I am sure that your grandfather will be proud of you, as am I, as are we all."

"I hope so," Fergus replied in a defiant voice.

"When you next get leave you should come south and visit us," Marcus said, "It would be good for your mother to see you again. She says that your letters home are becoming less and less frequent."

"We shall see," Fergus said looking away. "The legion is busy. I don't know when I can get the leave. There is a lot to do."

It was Marcus's turn to look away in disappointment. Then, as the awkward silence between them grew, he turned to look down at his sword. Slowly he undid the sheathed gladius from his belt and held it up for Fergus to see.

"This sword once belonged to Corbulo, my father and your grandfather," Marcus said quietly. "Here, I want you to take it. And exchange, your sword for this one. The army won't care and I have no more need for   it."

Fergus's face lit up with sudden excitement and his eyes widened, as he stared at the sheathed, short sword. Gingerly he took it and turned it over, examining the worn leather sheath in awe struck silence.

"Is this really his?" Fergus said at last looking up.

"It is," Marcus replied. "and now it is your turn to carry it."

"Thank you," Fergus muttered, as he quickly handed his own sword to Marcus.

Marcus allowed himself a little wry smile.

"Come," he said gently, "Let's go for a walk. There is something that I would like to show you."

***

The two of them strode down the paved street between the long and narrow, Roman strip houses and, as they did so Marcus marvelled at how the civilian settlement had expanded and prospered since he'd grown up here, as a boy beside the Dee river. The town was filled with noise and the bustle of civilians and soldiers, citizens and locals alike, but no one paid them any attention. In the doorways of the shops the merchants and prostitutes tried to attract his attention with bawdy, humorous cries but Marcus ignored them. Soon they had left the civilian settlement behind and were heading out along a snow covered track towards the riverbank. The houses rapidly dwindled until they were in the midst of an abandoned, construction site interspersed with a few old, Celtic huts, little more than holes in the ground, roughly covered with branches and thatch. As they approached the river bank, Marcus paused and sighed. Then he pointed at one of the miserable looking subterranean hovels.

"That is where I grew up," he muttered. "That is where your grandmother and I lived whilst your grandfather was stationed at the fortress."

175

Fergus was staring at the hovel in silence.

"This is where I grew up to be a man," Marcus continued, looking around him, "This is where I learned to hunt. This is where your grandmother taught me the ways of our forefathers. She was a good woman, a loving mother. This is the place too where your grandfather taught me how to survive. And it is here, in that hut, that one day I came home to find my mother had cut her own throat. She killed herself because Corbulo, your grandfather, had broken her heart one too many times."

Fergus said nothing. Then at last he stirred.

"Why are you telling me this?" he murmured.

"Because you need to know who you are," Marcus snapped, "Because you need to know where you come from, boy. Because you need to know who your ancestors really were."

A little colour shot into Fergus's cheeks as he turned to stare at the hut beside the river. Without another word, Marcus started off towards a small copse of trees a couple of hundred yards further along the river bank. Fergus followed in silence. The two of them said nothing, as in amongst the trees, Fergus watched his father, as for a while Marcus searched for something in the tangle of bushes. Then Marcus paused and silently beckoned for Fergus to join him. Fergus frowned as he looked down at the simple, white altar-stone, that had been purposefully placed into the earth. The stone looked like it had been there for a while and it was surrounded by weeds and covered in snow and mud. Carefully Marcus got down on his knees and cleared the snow and dirt from the stone until the inscription chiselled into it became visible, and as it did, Fergus gasped.

"To the guardian spirit of the Twentieth Legion, Corbulo fulfilled his vow."

"Your grandfather had this erected the day after he retired from the army," Marcus said, looking up at his son.

"I never knew," Fergus said, as his cheeks burned.

Marcus turned to look at the altar stone. Then he fumbled for something in his tunic and held up a single large golden coin.

"Pure Dacian gold," he said, "We shall bury it here beside his stone, an offering to his spirit, from you and I."

Hastily, Fergus got down on his knees beside his father and with his hands he started to scrape away at the frozen earth. His fingers were sore and covered in dirt when at last Marcus placed the gold coin in the shallow hole beside the stone and gently covered it up with the excavated earth. For a while the two of them were silent as they stared at the altar stone and the only noise was the murmur of the river and the gentle moaning of the wind in the trees.

"Corbulo was a great man," Fergus said, at last raising his eyes to look up at the sky. "I wish he was still here with us."

"You did not know him," Marcus replied sharply, "The man I knew when I was a boy, was a violent, cheating, drunken bastard who used to beat me and your grandmother. There were days when we lived in absolute terror of him."

"And yet he saved your life twice," Fergus retorted with sudden feeling in his voice, "He went into the trackless wastes of Caledonia to rescue you and then he did it again on the day he died."

"He drove your grandmother to suicide," Marcus growled in annoyed voice.

Fergus shook his head. "No, he was a great man," he said, "Quintus told me that he was always loyal to the legionary Eagle and to his comrades."

Marcus's face remained unreadable. Then he turned to his son with a weary, resigned look.

"There is another reason I came north," he said. "You should know that a new copy of Corbulo's will has recently surfaced and in it the old man says that he wants to be buried on the battlefield where he fought against the Barbarian Queen. I made a vow to carry out his final instruction but the task is proving difficult." Marcus sighed and looked down at the ground. "So difficult in fact, that I am thinking about abandoning the quest. Efa and Kyna need me on the farm and Emogene's trail has gone cold. The druid took his body. But I don't know where to start looking for her. Maybe Dylis was right and it is indeed a hopeless search."

Fergus looked away.

"I must get back to the barracks," he said, as he got to his feet. Marcus rose with him and nodded. But just as his son was about to walk away, Marcus laid a hand on the young man's shoulder.

"Allow a father to give his son some advice," Marcus said as his fingers tightened their grip. "Always be your own man, Fergus. Do not become someone else's fool."

And as he spoke there was a sudden warmth and pride in Marcus's voice and eyes.

"Do your duty, honour your family and the gods and you will be a man, son. If you can do that, you have nothing to fear in this life or the next. Look after yourself and remember that one day you will inherit the farm and our land on Vectis and that you will be responsible for all our people there."

Fergus lowered his eyes as Marcus fell silent. Then he stepped forwards and father and son embraced each other.

"You should not give up, father," Fergus said as they parted, "I too, have some news for you. I know where you can find Emogene's husband and I know what she did with Corbulo's body."

Chapter Twenty-Three – The Batavian Diaspora –

Spring AD 104

The river Fleet was high and threatening to burst its banks, filled with melting snow- water, as Marcus and Cunomoltus walked their horses towards the sturdy, pile bridge that spanned the river. Spring had finally come and in the trees that lined the road, the cheerful birds had returned and in the verges beyond the drainage ditches, bright colourful, spring flowers were shooting up everywhere. Beyond the Fleet, the city of Londinium gleamed and bathed in the strong and warm, noon sun; a true metropolis of fine stone houses, warehouses, shops, public buildings and home to twenty thousand people. Here and there along the riverside, the inhabitants had laid sand bags at the entrances to their homes to protect themselves from the flood waters. A hundred yards to the south, through a gap in the waterside storehouses, mills and factories, Marcus could see the Fleet merging into mighty Thames, which was more than two hundred yards wide.

As they clattered across the wooden bridge that led straight towards Ludgate, a small craft laden with a cargo of amphorae passed underneath them. Upstream, on the heavily-revetted western bank, the grave-stones of the city cemetery came right up to the water's edge and on the eastern bank the creaking, splashing wheels of a water mill were turning at full speed. There was no wall or watch towers to enclose the city and instead a low, earthen embankment marked the city's boundary. Marcus kept his eyes on the road ahead; his face a stoic mask of quiet endurance.

Efa and Kyna had promised to look after Lucius's two children. They had understood why he had brought them back home to the farm on Vectis. They had not questioned him and for that he was glad. The only comment Efa had made was to say that he was just like Corbulo, collecting strays from all corners of the land, which he'd taken to be a reference to the nine Christian children his father had once saved from a bloody and violent pogrom. But Lucius's children had chosen wisely. They would have a chance on his farm. On Vectis the children would be safe from the clutches of the slavers and perverts who would otherwise have taken them. Suddenly he looked weary. The return home and the stay with his family had been welcome but it had not lasted very long. The devastating news that Fergus had given him in Deva had weighed heavily, shocking his family into silence. Soon after their return, he'd told Cunomoltus that they would be heading for Londinium to investigate the sighting of Emogene's husband. Fergus was right. He could not give up now. Emogene had purposefully defiled Corbulo's body. Fergus has told him that she was keeping his ashes in a sealed canister around her neck preventing his spirit from finding a final resting place and she had turned his skull into a drinking cup. It was abhorrent, utterly terrifying and it had made him more determined. This insult would not stand. It was his father's final instruction that he be buried beside his comrades on the battlefield, where he'd faced the Barbarian Queen and that was what was going to happen.

The street leading towards the Forum and the centre of Londinium was crowded with people going about their business and the noise was tremendous. Marcus gestured at Cunomoltus to keep an eye on his purse, as on foot, he led his horse through the multitude of pedestrians and wagons that crowded the paved street. The smell of raw sewage, charcoal, smoke, fish and garum filled the street and the usual phalanx of merchants and shop-owners stood on the pavement, trying to attract his attention with their loud advertising cries and sales pitches. Londinium was growing ever more prosperous Marcus thought, as he pushed his way through the crowds. The streets were lined with terraced, strip houses which all seemed to be made of stone with smart, red Roman roof tiles, proper gutters, drains, doors and small vestibules, just like Corbulo had once predicted they would be. The inhabitants of the city looked well fed and dressed, boisterous and confident. As he headed for the Forum, Marcus became aware of the foreign accents and foreign languages and, in between the native Celtic population, he glimpsed the occasional Roman citizen, dressed in his fine white toga; dark skinned Africans; and sailors, soldiers and merchants who looked like they'd come from the Syrian provinces or Egypt.

As he crossed the narrow Wallbrook stream that divided the city into its western and eastern sections, Marcus paused as he caught sight of a man sitting on the pavement with his back against a wall. The man was missing a leg and he was begging, holding up his hand to the passers-by. The faded letters LEG XX had been tattooed onto his forehead.

"It's a scandal," Marcus muttered darkly to no one in particular as he crossed the street and dropped a couple of coins into the man's outstretched hand. "Why are you allowing a veteran to beg like this in your city," Marcus cried out in a loud angry voice, as he rounded on the pedestrians thronging the pavement and the street. "Show some respect for the men who keep this province safe and prosperous! What is the matter with you all!"

In the street a few people had paused to stare at him but no one said anything.

The sign advertising the Cum Mula Peperit II tavern hung from an iron rod above the doorway and it looked brand new. The smart looking inn was located a stone's throw from the Forum. A faint expectant smile appeared on Marcus' lips as he headed towards the building. It was here that he had first come on his return from the Dacian frontier, for the tavern was the centre of the local Batavian diaspora, the place where retired Batavian veterans and their families came together to meet old friends, swap news and pass on letters and requests. The network of Batavian veterans had functioned as a safety net, for the community had looked after their own and also maintained contact with the men serving in the various Batavian cohorts in the north and on the far flung imperial frontiers. Whilst he'd still been a soldier it was through the Batavian diaspora that he'd managed to send and receive letters from Kyna and his family. As they approached the tavern however, Cunomoltus came to a halt in the middle of the street and cast a doubtful look at the inn.

"What?" Marcus growled, as he noticed his companion's hesitation.

With a pensive expression Cunomoltus took a few steps towards Marcus, grasping his horse's reins in one hand.

"You should know," he said taking a deep breath, "that I spent a lot of time in Londinium when I was looking for you. I know this tavern. Do we really have to stay here? There are others in the city, cheaper ones."

"We're staying here," Marcus replied frowning, "If anyone knows anything about the whereabouts of Emogene and her husband, we will find out here. Besides I know the people who run this place."

"Well then, before we continue, you should know something," Cunomoltus said in a serious voice. "I told you that I was on the run. Well one of the Vindici brothers, my creditors, he lives here in Londinium. His name is Nectovelius and he is what I call the brute force in that family." Cunomoltus's lips curled in contempt. "He has a brain the size of an ant and an even smaller cock, but he's well connected and you won't want to fight him man to man. He'll crush you. Anyway, to cut a long story short, I shagged his wife in one of the upstairs rooms of the Mule over there. Nectovelius was beating her up and treating her like dirt and she wanted to leave him. He doesn't know about this of course," Cunomoltus exclaimed, "but just in case we run into him or his wife, I thought you should know. That way you will be prepared."

Marcus sighed and shook his head in disbelief.

"I forgot that you are the arsehole of the family," he muttered. "Maybe you are Corbulo's son after all. You certainly act like him sometimes. He also left a trail of problems behind him wherever he went. There is probably a whole string of pregnant women and bad debts in every town that you have visited. So come on, what else should I know?"

"Well now that you ask," Cunomoltus said sheepishly, "I didn't pay my bills in several taverns and I was chased down the street by a baker once for stealing his bread. I also once sold a dog to a city merchant. The man wanted a dog to guard his premises. He wasn't too happy afterwards."

"Why not?"

"Dog couldn't bark."

"You are a fucking disgrace," Marcus growled as he turned to look away.

***

The tavern was packed, as Marcus followed by Cunomoltus stepped through the doorway. The large, ground floor room was alive with voices, laughter, boisterous cries and every table was occupied. Against the far wall the bar ran the length of the wall and behind it two women and a man were busy serving customers. The smell of wine and beer filled the air and in a corner a ladder led up to the rooms on the second floor. Marcus paused in the doorway as he looked around the inn. The place looked brand new, and the redecoration he'd heard about, when he'd been here a few months earlier, seemed complete. The solid stone walls, held together by wet- looking concrete, were decorated with a host of battle trophies; a captured Brigantian battle axe and shield; a beautifully crafted Hibernian Carnyx; a battle trumpet, Batavian helmets, swords, spears and a single gleaming white skull.

As he stood in the doorway glancing around, a voice suddenly cried out across the tavern.

"Look boys, look, who it is."

Two score of heads turned to stare at Marcus and abruptly the tavern fell silent.

Then an excited voice suddenly yelled out, raising his cup triumphantly in the air.

"So trust in the man beside you and do your duty for in the coming days I want our enemy to cry out in alarm as they see our approach; I want to hear them shout: Ah shit! Here come those damned Batavians again."

For a second the tavern remained silent. Then it erupted with yells and shouts and some of the veterans rose and surged towards Marcus with broad welcoming grins, excitedly slapping him on the back and thrusting a cup of wine into his hand. Marcus's face cracked into a wide smile as the men started to chant.

"Thunder and lashing rain, so Wodan commeth. Thunder and lashing rain, so Wodan commeth."

As he was surrounded by a dozen eager hands reaching out to slap him on his back, his head and to grip his arms, Marcus caught the eye of the bar owner. The man gave him a little welcoming nod.

It took him a while before he could reach the bar but when at last he did, Marcus reached out to grip the owner's arm in greeting. The tavern owner was a huge hulk of a man, a full head taller than Marcus. He looked around forty.

"Good to see you again Marcus," the owner said with a little welcoming smile. "Was not expecting to see you so soon though. I presume you have come back for the anniversary parade?"

"The parade?" Marcus frowned.

"To celebrate the sixtieth anniversary of the founding of Londinium," the tavern owner replied. "Surely you have not forgotten? The parade takes place tomorrow afternoon. The whole garrison is taking part. That's why all the boys are in town."

"Of course," Marcus nodded.

"So do you like what I have done with the tavern?" the innkeeper said.

Fondly Marcus turned to look around, as the crowd inside the inn settled back down. "My father would be horrified," he said jokingly. "He used to drink here, before you bought the place."

"This a Batavian tavern now," the owner said sharply, "No legionaries in here. No beggars and no thieves neither."

"Quite right," Marcus said, nodding in agreement, as he took a sip of beer from a cup that had been thrust into his hand.

For a moment he said nothing as he stared at the boisterous crowd. Then he turned to the bar owner and his face grew serious.

"I found Lucius," he said. "He's dead. I was going to hand him over to the authorities but he preferred death."

The tavern owner's face darkened as he looked down at the wooden bar. Then he nodded.

"I am glad. He had it coming," the owner growled. "Him and his wretched brother Bestia. What Lucius did during that rebellion was unforgivable. How did you find him?"

"I met Hedwig," Marcus said. "He's living in Aquae Sulis. He said he'd seen Lucius and I followed the trail to the lead mines."

"Then Fridwald and the others have been avenged," the owner said quickly pouring himself a large helping of wine and downing it in one go. "Here is to all those, whom we have had to leave behind."

Marcus raised his cup in a salute and for a moment the two of them were silent.

"I am afraid I am not here for the parade," Marcus said at last. "I am looking for someone and I need your help. I need to find a woman called Emogene. She is a druid. I have been told that her husband may live in Londinium. His name is Meryn. He's a Caledonian and he used to be a slaver. He must be around a forty-five and he has got tattoos across his chest and shoulders."

The tavern owner grimaced as he paused to think. Then he shook his head.

"No, can't say I know them," he replied, "But if you are looking for information Marcus, then you should speak to Honorius. He's a retired official from the harbour master's office. He knows everything that is going on in this town. Maybe he can help you."

Chapter Twenty-four – Nothing is what it seems

As he strode down the street leading towards the bridge that spanned the Thames, Marcus could not help but be impressed by the sheer scale of the city around him. Londinium was huge, noisy and growing; alive with activity; people thronged its streets and wooden scaffolding was everywhere. Along the water front, cranes were hoisting cargoes from the bellies of sea-going ships and, facing the street the long, narrow strip houses lined the road in endless rows. And rising behind him Marcus could hear the stone masons at work on the largest Forum north of the Alps. The huge, magnificent, brand-new stone market square that dominated the skyline, rose above the city, several storeys high, as it neared completion, and in places the fine red, roof tiles had already been set in place.

A squad of soldiers from the city garrison were on duty at the entrance to the bridge as Marcus and Cunomoltus joined the queue to cross. A column of wagons, laden with amphorae and newly felled tree trunks, was trundling into the city from the south and out on the river, Marcus could see that the tide was in. More ships, their sails stowed, rode at anchor in the middle of the river, whilst a constant procession of smaller craft plied between them and the harbour, transporting their valuable cargoes to and fro.

"There he is," Cunomoltus muttered as he and Marcus started out across the bridge, heading towards the south bank. "That's look like him."

Marcus said nothing as he caught sight of the old man with grey hair, who was leaning against the side of the wooden bridge, staring at the ships on the river. A boy of no more than eight was lounging at his side.

"Are you Honorius?" Marcus called out as he approached.

The old man slowly turned to gaze at Marcus and Marcus saw that he was blind in one eye. For a moment the retired harbour official studied Marcus carefully.

"I am," he replied at last, "who wants to know?"

"The Batavians in the Mule told me where I could find you," Marcus replied, as he stopped beside Honorius and turned to gaze eastwards across the river. "I was told that you are the man who knows everything that goes on in this town."

Honorius gave a dismissive shrug. "Maybe, maybe not," he grumbled.

"I will make it worth your time," Marcus said, as he opened his hand to reveal a couple of silver coins. "I am looking for a woman. A druid. Her name is Emogene. Also her husband. His name is Meryn. He's a Caledonian, about forty-five and he's got tattoos across his chest and shoulders. Do you know where I can find them?"

Honorius glanced down at the coins in Marcus's hand. Then he turned to look at Cunomoltus before his attention drifted back to the traffic on the water.

"Not many druids around these days," he muttered. "You boys slaughtered them all."

"Can you help or not?" Marcus growled impatiently.

"Well go on, take the coins, boy," the retired harbour official snapped at the boy standing at his side. Marcus frowned as the boy reached out and swiftly snatched the coins from his hand and slipped them into his pocket. The boy looked up at him with a fearless, confident and innocent expression and Marcus was suddenly reminded of the gangs of children, who spent their days as pickpockets in the crowded streets and shops.

"You are either brave or foolish," Honorius muttered, as he stared out across the river, "I do not know any woman claiming to be a druid who goes by the name of Emogene. However, there are three criminal gangs who control Londinium. One of them controls the harbour, one of them runs the traffic on this bridge and the third owns the territory around the Forum. The man you seek is the leader of the gang that runs the harbour front over there. His gang are called the Reds."

Honorius gestured at the cranes. "A word of warning, Batavian," Honorius continued quickly. "These gangs are dangerous. They are constantly fighting each other for territory and they don't like people prying into their affairs. Every day the authorities fish a body from the river or find them dumped down some alley. Anyone whom dares cross these men, they just disappear, so be careful. These criminals have no respect for rank or status, rich or poor."

"Thank you," Marcus said. "So where can I find Meryn?"

"He likes to hang out in the Gay Crab," Honorius replied, "The tavern is over there amongst the harbour warehouses. He uses it as his base. His gang take a cut from every sea captain that wants to ship out or land their goods in the city. Any captain who refuses will soon find his cargo floating away on the tide, if you know what I mean."

Marcus nodded his thanks as he turned to stare at the jumble of buildings and alleys that lined the river front. Then, gesturing to Cunomoltus, he started back the way he had come.

On the bridge Honorius watched them walk away. Then slowly he turned to the boy.

"Go and warn Meryn that someone is looking for him," he growled.

***

The Gay Crab stood squashed in between two large warehouses only a dozen paces from the water's edge. The bawdy sign above the entrance looked like it had seen better days and from his vantage point under the bridge, Marcus could see the two armed gang members, loitering outside the doorway. Marcus tightened his grip on the solid, wooden beam that held up the bridge and which had been driven into the soft riverbed. The piles, upon which London bridge rested, became exposed when the tide was out. Marcus bit his lip impatiently. There had been no sign of Meryn and he'd already identified six gang members. They seemed to relieve each other every hour. But time was not on his side. Soon the tide would start to come back in and then he would be forced from his vantage point. Where was Emogene's husband? Where was the bastard?

It was morning and over his head Marcus could hear the rattle and creak of wagons, the thud of horse's hooves and voices. Out in the river, a battered old sea-going craft was being unloaded and the stinking smell of rotting fish-sauce, garum, filled his nostrils. Wearily Marcus wrenched his eyes from the tavern and gazed out across the placid river. At full tide the Thames became a giant, half a mile wide and along its southern bank the sand banks, creeks, waterways and mud flats were covered by reeds and swarms of migrating birds. Only the higher land directly opposite the bridge, Southwark, seemed to contain buildings. As he stared at the traffic on the river, a dripping wet, river rat scuttled past him.

At the door to the Gay Crab there was sudden movement. A man had appeared and was speaking to the two gang members. He had his back turned to Marcus but there was no mistaking the blue tattoos that snaked down both his arms. Marcus muttered something to himself. Then the man turned to stare at a ship that lay at anchor in the river and, as he did, Marcus caught a glimpse of his face. It was Meryn. The man looked exactly as Fergus had described him. With a final word to the gangsters, Meryn started to walk away along the harbour front. Marcus took a deep breath and emerged from his hiding place. Keeping a respectable distance between himself and Meryn, he started to follow him. The gang master seemed in no hurry as he wove a path along the quays, pausing here and there to speak to the merchants, workers and slaves. As he passed a fast-food shack selling roasted chicken legs, Meryn was beset by a group of children whom he fended off with a laugh and a wave. In an alley the gang master paused to have a word with a prostitute, affectionately running his fingers down her face. Marcus grunted as he pretended to inspect the food in the shack. The way Meryn was treating the prostitute suggested that he'd not seen his wife for a long time.

When Meryn reached the end of the harbour, he paused and turned to glance idly in Marcus's direction before suddenly ducking into an alley and vanishing from sight. Marcus frowned as he closed in on the entrance to the alley. Carefully, he glanced around but no one seemed to be paying him any attention. Quickly he turned and snatched a look down the alley. It was deserted except for a pile of discarded building material and it seemed to end in a solid stone wall. Where the hell had Meryn gone? Marcus leaned back against the wall as he pondered what to do. Then boldly he stepped into the alley.

The dank passageway was just wide enough to allow a single person through at a time and the stone walls stank of stale piss and here and there graffiti had been scratched into the stones. Swiftly Marcus advanced down the alley until he reached the stone wall. There were no doors anywhere but close by, the stone wall bulged outwards, forming a narrow ledge a yard or so from the ground. How could Meryn have just disappeared? What was going on? Confused Marcus turned around and touched the cold stones. Then he looked up. A small window loomed right above him but it was too high for him to climb up to, even if he had ten fingers. Marcus squinted. The window however seemed large enough for a man to clamber through but how had he got up there? A sudden pang of unease made itself felt. Had he walked into a trap? Hesitantly Marcus turned and started back the way he'd come but it was too late. A figure had appeared at the entrance to the alley. He was quickly followed by another and then another. As the men came towards him Marcus swore. It was Meryn. The gang master was smiling broadly but there was nothing friendly about the way he was staring at Marcus.

"That's far enough," Marcus growled in warning as his fingers came to rest on the pommel of his sword.

Meryn caught the movement and paused. He was a big man and although older than Marcus, he still looked agile and formidable. Behind him were four, unfriendly looking men, armed with swords, clubs and knives.

"Did you really think that I wouldn't notice you following me along the harbour front," Meryn snapped. "Who are you? What are you doing here?"

"I am looking for Emogene, your wife."

The gang master's eyes narrowed and his face darkened.

"My wife?" he growled raising his eyebrows in surprise, "What do you want with her? Who the fuck are you?" he cried, as he took a step forwards and angrily yanked a knife from his belt.

Marcus drew his sword and pushed his left leg forwards and raised his sword arm. "One more step and I will gut you," he said in a calm, dangerous voice.

Meryn hesitated.

"No one comes into my part of town without showing me their respect," he hissed. "So I will ask you one final time. Who are you?"

"I have business with your wife," Marcus growled, "And if you tell me where she is I will let you live."

Meryn shook his head in mock confusion. "What," he cried out, "You think you are going to kill me, you piece of useless, pig shit. Have you forgotten where you are? Look around man, it is you who is trapped, not me. It is you who is not going to leave this alley alive."

Marcus flung the stone he'd picked up from the ground straight at Meryn, striking him squarely in the face and forcing him backwards with a howl and as he did, Marcus, leapt onto the narrow ledge of the protruding stone wall and with a mighty effort flung himself across the narrow alley against the far wall. Desperately his hands and elbows grasped hold of the top of the wall and he heaved himself upwards and over the top, losing his sword in the process. The force of his lunge was just enough however and with a cry he went tumbling over the side of the wall and into space. He landed heavily and for a stunned moment, he lay on his back staring up at the sky. Blood was oozing out of a wound to his head but he felt no pain. On the other side of the wall, men were shouting, cursing and yelling. Grimly Marcus forced himself up onto his feet and hastily looked around. He'd lost his sword and there was no question of making a stand now. Hastily he yanked his Pugio army knife from his belt. He was in a small courtyard filled with wooden barrels and a single doorway. Without hesitation he launched himself at the door and crashed through it into a long, dark hallway. A stark-naked woman was coming towards him. As she caught sight of him clutching his knife, she screamed. Marcus pushed her out of the way as he stumbled on down the hall, searching for the exit. As he fled down the passageway one of the door's ahead opened and a naked man appeared, followed moments later by a woman. Marcus shoved the man back into the room as he blundered onwards. Behind him, he heard someone shouting and ahead someone opened a door, caught sight of Marcus and quickly closed it again.

The corridor ended in a reception hall with large erotic paintings adorning the walls and Marcus suddenly realised he was in a whorehouse. A fat madam and a younger man had risen from where they had been sitting behind a table. They looked at Marcus in alarm and the man was reaching for a club.

"No," Marcus shouted at the man as he ran towards the entrance door, "No, you will not."

And the force and tone in his voice made the man hesitate. Marcus flung open the door and poked his head out. The harbour was as if nothing had happened and there was no sign of Meryn and his men. With a grunt, Marcus forced himself out through the door and quickly melted away into the crowd.

Chapter Twenty-Five - Cunomoltus' Woman

The crowds lining both sides of Watling street were in an excited mood as they craned their heads to get a glimpse of the military parade coming towards them. Further down the street, just out of sight, the noise of the roaring, yelling and clapping crowd was steadily drawing closer to where Marcus and Cunomoltus stood hidden amongst the throng of expectant spectators. Marcus, the hood of his cloak pulled over his head, looked annoyed.

"They will be watching the Mule by now," he hissed turning to Cunomoltus, "Meryn knew I was coming. Someone warned him."

"I bet it was that prick on the bridge," Cunomoltus muttered, "I didn't like the look of him or that boy with him."

"I should had seen that coming," Marcus snapped angrily, "Now the task has just got a whole lot harder. Meryn will be on his guard. He will be well protected and he will probably know who we are by now. How long will it be before he either finds us or leaves the city?"

"Marcus, I have an idea," Cunomoltus said suddenly, but just as he was about to explain, the crowd around them suddenly broke into a loud cheering roar.

Coming towards them down the empty street was a lone Imaginifer, standard bearer, his helmet and armour covered by a bear skin. The soldier came on at a steady walk, proudly clutching a small, round shield and in his other hand holding up the Imago standard, a wooden pole bearing the image of Emperor Trajan. He was swiftly followed by three Vexillari, legionaries with wolf skins covering their helmets and armour and holding aloft the Vexillum standards of the Twentieth Valeria Victrix, Ninth Hispana and Second Augusta Legions. As they approached the spot where Marcus and Cunomoltus were standing, some in the crowd broke out into loud ecstatic cries, as they flung small garlands   into the path of the soldiers.

"Hail to the divine Emperor Trajan. Hail to our brave, conquering legions. Hail to the gods who protect us!"

The standard bearers were followed by a column of cavalrymen walking their horses down the street, three abreast, with the riders' faces completely covered by their beautiful yet sinister-looking ceremonial, cavalry masks.

The cavalrymen were followed by the stern-looking Governor of Britannia, riding on horseback and accompanied by his staff and, as they clattered down the street, Marcus suddenly heard the unmistakable sound of hissing from some within the crowd. And close by, a bold spirit dared to shout a curse. The Governor however, did not seem to have heard and kept his eyes fixed firmly on the street ahead.

The rear of the military parade was brought up by the infantry sections from the multitude of different units that had been seconded and assigned to garrison Londinium. It was a long column of marching legionaries and auxiliaries, divided up into their unit groups and all proudly wearing their distinctive armour and clutching their large shields and spears. And as they came marching past, the men were in full deep throated song, a bawdy, humorous and rude song about the Governor that made Marcus smile, as if they were part of a triumphant march into Rome itself, he thought.

As the last of the soldiers marched away down Watling Street, the crowd rushed into the street behind them and started to follow. Marcus watched the eager, excited people streaming away towards the Forum where an altar would have been set up to receive an offering to the gods; a plea for the immortals to maintain the safety and the prosperity and greatness of Londinium.

As the last of the spectators slipped away Marcus turned to Cunomoltus.

"So what's this idea of yours?"

Cunomoltus exhaled and rubbed his eye with his finger.

"We need help, brother," he muttered, "And I know someone who may be able to help us. Remember that woman I was telling you about. Nectovelius's wife, you know, the one I shagged in the Mule. Well she had a sweet spot for me and she knows some important people in this town. Let me go and speak to her."

Marcus frowned. "Are you sure that is wise? What happens if her husband sees you? He won't have forgotten that you owe him a large unpaid debt and he'll kill you if he knows what you did with his wife."

"Don't worry. He won't see me, he never does," Cunomoltus replied, in a confident voice, giving Marcus a wink, "I will be in and out, before he knows it, just like in the old days."

***

Marcus stood looking down at the street from the small window of the second floor room of the Mule tavern. It was growing dark and in the pub, he could hear the murmur of voices and the sound of a soft, mournful harp and from the kitchens the smell of beer and wood smoke was seeping through the floorboards. The tavern owner had brought the harp player into his establishment to celebrate Londinium's sixtieth anniversary, as the city geared up to host the numerous, evening festivities that were now breaking out across town. Marcus however, was not paying any attention. There was still no sign of Cunomoltus. The man had been gone for over two hours now. Impatiently he scratched at his beard. How long could he wait?

The boy came striding down the street with a confident gait and Marcus's eyes narrowed suspiciously, as he watched the boy head straight for the door to the tavern, before vanishing from sight. With a grunt, he turned away from the window, strode into the hallway and started to clamber down the ladder. As he reached the ground floor he caught sight of the boy standing

197

beside the bar with the tavern owner towering over him. The innkeeper, noticing Marcus, beckoned him over.

"The boy says he has a message for you," the tavern owner growled.

The child turned to look up at Marcus with a confident, cheeky expression.

"Are you Marcus?" he said.

Marcus nodded.

"I have a message for you," the boy said, "If you want to see your brother again, you will come to Senovara's office in the Forum before midnight, bringing with you all the money that your brother owes."

And with that, the boy turned and started out towards the door but Marcus caught him by his arm before he could reach it.

"What happened? Who has my brother?" Marcus said in an alarmed voice.

The boy however just shrugged.

"The blues," he replied. "That's all I know. I was just told to give you this message. Now let go of my arm."

Bewildered, Marcus let go, and without another word the boy left through the doorway and vanished into the gathering darkness. Marcus watched him go. Then he groaned and wearily ran his fingers down his face. What had happened? How had Cunomoltus managed to get himself into such trouble?

"Bad news?" the tavern owner said, as Marcus came up to the bar.

Marcus nodded. "What do you know about the blues?"

"The blues," the tavern owner exclaimed with a frown. "The blues are the criminals who own the Forum. Their gang runs the pickpockets and extortionists who operate amongst the banks, lawyers and merchants. Be careful, Marcus. That gang has no respect for anyone and they are ruthless."

Marcus nodded as he allowed the words to sink in. Then he turned to the tavern owner. "I am going to need to borrow a sword," he growled.

***

The Basilica and Forum of Londinium were the largest buildings Marcus had ever seen. The square construction, with its line of grand, solid and haughty stone- columns supporting a sloping roof, rose above the surrounding houses, utterly dominating the heart of the city. Wooden scaffolding rose up against the walls and here and there sections of the roof had not yet been completed. Marcus headed straight for the main gateway that led into the open, central-market square beyond. A solitary soldier on fire-watch duty was loitering outside the fine, arched entrance and from inside the Forum Marcus could hear music, laughter and clapping, coming from one of the celebratory parties. The soldier gave him a casual glance but said nothing as Marcus strode through the gateway and into the Forum. Burning torches had been placed at intervals along the inside of the vast building and in their flickering light, he could see a large group of drunken men and women, dancing and staggering around with cups in their hands.

For a moment he paused on the gravel covered courtyard and turned to look around. The boy had told him to come to Senovara's office. He had no idea where that was but the name sounded like it belonged to a banker, lawyer or merchant, who were known to have their offices and shops inside the Forum. From the corner of his eye, Marcus suddenly caught sight of an armed man, as he appeared from the gloom and slowly lent back against the wall, folding his arms across his chest. The man was looking straight at   him.

Marcus studied the man and as he did, his fingers tapped the sheathed sword hanging from his belt. Then he started towards him. As he approached, the man pushed himself off the wall, and started walking towards a darkened doorway that led into the building. He turned briefly to check whether Marcus was following before ducking inside and vanishing.

At the doorway Marcus paused to listen but the only noise came from the party on the other side of the market square. Boldly, he stepped through the doorway and into the darkness beyond. He found himself in a long, narrow corridor. The hall was deserted except for a dim light that was coming from a room at the very end. Slowly Marcus started down the cool passageway and, as he approached the flickering light he thought he caught the noise of someone groaning. At the entrance to the room he paused. From their fixtures along the walls, small oil lamps were burning, bathing the room in an eerie glow, and in the middle of the chamber was a large, oak table upon which stood an iron cage and inside it, like some wild animal, a stark naked man lay rolled up in the foetal position. It was Cunomoltus. He was groaning and his face was badly bruised and dried blood was plastered across his shoulder and forehead.

Silently Marcus stepped into the room and gazed at the six, calm, confident strangers leaning idly against the far wall. The man he'd spotted out in the Forum was standing beside two others in a corner and all three had knives on display, tucked into their belts. Directly behind the iron cage, a huge hulk of a man, one of the biggest men Marcus had ever encountered, was staring at him with an aggressive, explosive look and at his side was a pretty woman of around thirty, clad in a simple, white woolen tunic. She was clutching the big man's arm and her right hand was covered by a Caestus, a leather and metal boxing glove.

"I thought you said she had a sweet spot for you?" Marcus muttered, glancing at Cunomoltus as he took a step towards the table.

From within his cage, Cunomoltus' only reply was a groan.

"So you came, Batavian," a voice said suddenly. Marcus straightened up, as a small slender man, his head, cheeks and neck covered by a blue tattoo of a snake, came towards him. The man looked in his mid-thirties and there was a cunning, clever gleam in his eyes. "Your brother squealed like a pig when we beat him," the man continued, "but he was adamant that you would come to his rescue and so it appears you have."

"Who are you?" Marcus muttered, sizing the man up.

"I am king of the blues, my friend," the small man replied smoothly, "That's all you need to know. Nectovelius works for me, as does his wife. Your brother should have been more careful in choosing his friends. Now I hope that you have brought me the money. I don't see you carrying it on you."

Slowly Marcus shook his head.

"I don't have the money," he replied. "There is just me."

The gang leader raised his eyebrows in surprise and for a moment he looked confused.

"So what good is that to me?" he hissed. "Your brother owes us a large debt. You are not leaving here tonight until we have collected."

Marcus glanced across the oak table at the big man. Nectovelius looked like a starving dog, that could see and smell a juicy hunk of meat that was just out of reach but there was a slow, unintelligent dullness in his eyes.

"So you are the brute force," Marcus growled at the big man, "Just so that you know. I met your brother Todd and he is lucky to still be alive. I offered to repay my brother's debts but he wouldn't listen. I hope you will be smarter than your brother but somehow I doubt it."

"You have a lot of balls, coming in here Batavian, all alone against all of us," Nectovelius retorted. "I could crush your neck with one hand if I wanted to."

Marcus's eyes slid across to the woman. She was staring at him with a defiant look but her lower lip was trembling.

"Did you beat my brother?" he asked gesturing at Cunomoltus in his cage.

"He got what he deserved," she hissed. "He is no man. He means less than the dirt on my shoes."

"You fucking bitch," Cunomoltus suddenly roared from inside his cage, as in vain he tried to break free, "You set me up. You betrayed me. After everything I did for you. You wanted to run away with me, you told me so yourself. It's the truth and you know it. So stop lying and pretending."

"He lies," the woman cried out, as she took a step towards the cage and rammed her boxing glove against the iron bars. "He will say anything to save his worthless neck."

"My brother told me about you," Marcus interrupted looking at the woman, "He may have a worthless neck but he did trust you, so I am surprised to see you here holding hands with that arsehole you call a husband. A man who beats his wife is no man at all, even if he looks like Hercules."

Nectovelius made a whining noise and took a threatening step towards Marcus, as a furious blush appeared on his wife's face.

"What are you saying, Batavian," the big man blurted out. "Are you saying that my wife was planning to run away with that little prick over there?"

"You should ask your wife," Marcus replied.

"Enough," the gang leader suddenly barked, "I don't think you have come here to just trade insults, Batavian. So here's how things are going to be. You will pay us the money and until then, we will keep your brother. I am going to give you three days to collect what you owe. If you don't deliver by then, you will find your brother floating down the Thames without his head."

"No," Marcus retorted, turning on the gang leader, "I have a better idea. You will release my brother, unharmed and alive and in exchange I will give you the harbour and all its related business."

The room fell silent. The blues gang leader was staring at Marcus in confusion.

"You will give me what" the small man with the blue snake tattoo exclaimed.

"I will give you the harbour of Londinium," Marcus growled, "You know how profitable the business can be along the water front. The money that you can make down there will far exceed the debts that my brother owes."

"The harbour belongs to the reds," Nectovelius blurted out.

"So it does," Marcus replied, "And I am saying that, soon it will belong to the blues."

"How?" the gang master exclaimed, staring at Marcus with sudden interest, "How would you drive Meryn and his men from the harbour? They won't go easily and they know how to fight. Believe me, we have tried."

"Don't you worry about that," Marcus said grimly, "Just keep to your side of the deal."

Chapter Twenty-Six – Whispers of Hyperborea

"Listen, all of you," Marcus said, clearing his throat as he addressed the assembled men whom packed the Mule tavern. "Don't get isolated, don't take any unnecessary risk for me. I appreciate what you are you doing, I really do, but what we are about to do is not worth getting yourself killed over."

The packed assembly of grim, faced Batavian veterans remained silent. The men were armed to the teeth with swords, knives, spears, clubs and axes and some had even polished off their old helmets and chain mail armour. It was morning and a full day had passed since his late night encounter in the Forum.

"Don't worry about the boys, Marcus" the tavern owner growled in a menacing voice. "We're going to go through the harbour like a storm of shit through a laundry. There won't be any of those red bastards left once we're done with them. No one touches one of our own and gets away with it."

Marcus nodded. "Remember I want Meryn alive. I need him alive."

"We'll do our best," the inn keeper of the Mule muttered darkly.

"Good," Marcus said his face darkening, as he raised his borrowed axe in the air, "Then follow me."

***

Along the water front of the harbour the slaves were hard at work, loading and unloading cargoes, whilst the sea captains and merchants conglomerated in small groups as they discussed contracts, prices and cargoes. The smell of fish was in the air and high above the activity on the ground, the screeching sea gulls were circling looking for an easy meal. Marcus led the tight group of silent, Batavians straight towards the Gay Crab and as they strode on through the harbour,r people, stopped what they were doing and turned to stare at the band of grim-faced men, bristling with weapons and intent.

The two hapless gang members posted to guard the entrance of the tavern were the first to see the Batavians bearing down on them. For an instant they did not react. Then one of them yelled a loud warning and drew a knife from his belt. His mate tried to make a run for it but he was set upon by three Batavians, one of whom thrust a knife into the man's neck, sending a fountain of blood arching up into the air. The other gangster screamed and lunged at Marcus but before he could make contact, Marcus's axe thudded into his chest and as he collapsed backwards against the tavern wall, a Batavian stepped forwards and sliced open his throat. At the entrance, the inn keeper of the Mule launched himself at the door of the Gay Crab and with a splintering crash he was through.

"I want Meryn alive," Marcus roared as the Batavians surged into the tavern. Inside, the inn had descended into screaming, yelling chaos. As the Batavians ran riot, a few men and women, holding up their hands and screaming for mercy, were pinned down into a corner behind a jumble of upturned tables and chairs. A knot of armed and determined gang members had however formed at the base of a ladder, leading up to the second floor and amongst them, Marcus suddenly caught sight of Meryn. The gangsters were yelling and shouting as they frantically and desperately tried to defend their boss.

"You," Marcus roared, pointing straight at Meryn as he kicked a broken chair out of his path, "You belong to me now."

As he caught sight of Marcus, Meryn's face went pale.

"I belong to no man," Meryn roared with sudden defiance. "Come over here and try and take me if you think you can."

With a savage cry, Marcus stormed forwards, darted under the wild blow of a gang member and slammed his axe into Meryn's exposed leg. The gang master screamed and made an ineffectual lunge at Marcus, before staggering backwards and slithering to the ground with a groan. Moments later the Batavians overwhelmed the remaining gang members and, as Marcus stumbled backwards, a spray of blood flew through the air and the horrific screams of men. being hacked to pieces filled the tavern. Meryn, bleeding heavily from the wound to his leg, was trying to crawl away under a table as Marcus advanced towards him with his raised, bloodied axe. With a kick, Marcus sent the table tumbling away and as he did so Meryn froze.

"It's over," Marcus cried.

At the base of the ladder, leading up to the second floor, a body came hurtling down onto the ground, landing with a violent, sickening thud. It was followed moments later by a high-pitched female scream. Marcus placed a boot on Meryn's back as he stared around at the carnage. The Batavians had been true to their word and the tavern was a complete mess. Several bodies lay scattered across the floor or slumped over upturned furniture and blood was everywhere, staining the floor, the men's tunic's, faces and walls. On the second floor, the woman continued her screaming and in a tavern, one of the badly wounded gang members was groaning. The Batavian veterans meanwhile had fanned out across the inn, their faces dark and ruthless, chests heaving from the exertion, as they poked around amongst the dead and dying.

"Is this all of them?" Marcus shouted at the blues gang member, who had accompanied them into the Gay Crab and who now stood beside the doorway staring at the carnage in awe.

The man peered at the broken bodies scattered across the floor. Then he nodded.

"That looks about right," he replied, "there are maybe two or three men who aren't here. But you got the bulk of them."

Marcus muttered something to himself as he turned to look down at Meryn. The boss was groaning softly, bleeding from his leg wound, as he lay on the ground with Marcus's boot pressing down on him. Upstairs the woman's screaming came to an abrupt end and suddenly a strange silence descended on the wrecked pub, punctuated by the noise of someone snoring.

"No one up here apart from a couple of women and a sleeping man," the innkeeper of the Mule cried out, poking his head through the hole in the ceiling at the top of the ladder.

"Who is snoring up there?" Marcus shouted.

The tavern owner shrugged. "I don't know. He is still asleep. I can't wake him up. The women insist that they are just guests staying in the tavern. They claim that they have nothing to do with the Reds."

Marcus turned to stare at the small cluster of terrified civilians pressed into the corner. The survivors were sobbing and trembling in terror and shock.

"Get out of here," he roared gesturing at them with his axe.

The terrified people needed no further encouragement and en masse they rushed towards the doorway, stumbling over each other in their panic to get away. Marcus took a deep, relieved breath and turned to look down at Meryn.

"We could have avoided all of this if you had just told me where Emogene, your wife is," he growled, lowering the blade of his axe until it was touching Meryn's neck.

"Go and screw yourself," Meryn muttered in a strained voice.

"It's over. Your time here is finished," Marcus snapped, "But you shall live if you tell me where I can find Emogene, your wife."

For a moment, Meryn was quiet. Then, despite the deep wound to his leg, he began to laugh, his body shaking with the effort.

"So all this death and carnage," he called out, "All of this is because of Emogene? She must have really gotten to you Batavian. She always did know how to make enemies."

Marcus increased the pressure on Meryn's back and the man's laughter ended in a painful rattling groan.

"She murdered my father," Marcus snapped. "His name was Corbulo and I am here to avenge him."

Meryn moaned in pain and closed his eyes as the blood continued to seep from his wound, staining the floor in a growing pool.

"I don't give a shit about injustice," he groaned in a defiant voice, "We all face injustice, it is the way of the world; deal with it Batavian."

"Tell me where I can find Emogene and you shall live," Marcus retorted.

Meryn remained silent as he seemed to consider the offer. Then he groaned.

"Your father was unlucky," Meryn croaked, as he slowly turned over onto his back and stared up at Marcus, "Just like I was. Emogene my wife, she was a damaged woman, not in a physical way, but in her mind. During the Roman invasion of our land she lost her first husband. She was caught, raped, tortured and forced to kill one of her own kin. The experiences slowly drove her insane. She went mad, Batavian. My wife went mad."

"Where can I find her?"

Meryn reached down to touch his wounded leg.

"She drove her own father from her village," Meryn said, his eyes widening, "She drowned her own dog and she burned your father's body and kept his ashes in a canister around her neck, so that his spirit would belong to her forever. She turned his skull into a drinking cup. When she started to grow violent with my children, I sent them away to live with my family. Then one day, a few years ago, she was gone, she left me."

"Where did she go?"

Meryn closed his eyes and was silent for a moment. Then he shook his head.

"I can't tell you."

"Yes you can and you will," Marcus snapped.

"I am sworn to keep it secret, I will tell you nothing."

But Marcus shook his head, his eyes filled with smouldering fury. "If you do not tell me the truth, I will find your children and burn them alive. Then I will go after every member of your family until none remain alive and your name will be forgotten for all eternity," he snarled in a savage voice.

"Alright, alright," Meryn cried out in alarm, "Fuck it. I will tell you what I know. Please, do not harm my children. They are innocent."

"So talk," Marcus said glaring down at Meryn.

"Only to you," Meryn groaned in a miserable voice, "I will whisper what I know."

Marcus muttered to himself as he carefully knelt down beside Meryn and placed his axe against the man's neck.

"Closer, come closer," Meryn muttered weakly.

Marcus lowered his head and waited for Meryn to speak. The gang master took his time, as he grimaced and groaned in pain.

"The druids will kill me," he whispered in a voice so faint that Marcus had difficulty in hearing it, "if they know that I am telling you this. Promise me that you will not harm my children. Promise this on your honour as a soldier."

"Alright, I will," Marcus said gruffly.

The answer seemed to satisfy Meryn.

"After she left me, Emogene crossed the ocean. Just like her father did," Meryn whispered. "She went north, across the sea to the druid trading post amongst the people of the Rocky River. The druids call them the Penawapskewi. No Roman has ever set foot there before. The druids keep the knowledge of the land beyond the ocean a closely guarded secret but I know about it, although I have never been there."

"A land beyond the ocean," Marcus muttered in a quiet voice.

"Yes, there is land out there," Meryn whispered with a feverish nod, "To the north and to the west. Many weeks sail across an endless sea. That is all I know. The druids have known about this place for a long time. They trade with the natives and a few of them have made the crossing for good. They will not be coming back. My wife is one of them."

"Hyperborea," Marcus whispered. "You are talking about Hyperborea, the land beyond the north wind. But that's just a legend, a myth. Why should I believe you?"

Slowly Meryn shook his head as he looked up at Marcus.

"Call it what you like and believe what you like," he whispered with a little forced smile appeared on his lips, "but I am telling you the truth. Emogene has crossed the ocean; she has slipped beyond your grasp forever. Like I said, Batavian, the world is filled with injustice."

Chapter Twenty-Seven – The Myth, the Drunk and the Man with Balls

Abruptly Marcus stood up and looked down at Meryn in astonishment. It was only slowly that he became aware of a man calling out his name.

"Holy Jupiter's cock, what have you done to the place," a voice said from the doorway.

Marcus turned, to see the blues gang boss standing in the doorway. The small man with the blue snake tattooed across his face and neck, was flanked by Nectovelius and his wife. All three looked shocked as they stared at the bloody carnage inside the Gay Crab.

"We did what I said we would do," Marcus growled, "This place, the harbour, they are yours now. The debt has been repaid in full. Now give me back my brother and for your sake I hope that you have not harmed him. These men," Marcus said gesturing at the Batavians, "are veterans and once their blood is up there is no stopping them."

In response the blues gang master half turned and snapped his fingers at someone outside the doorway and a moment later Cunomoltus, clad in his own clothes, was thrust forwards and into the room. He looked dreadful. His face was covered in dark bruises and one of his eyes was shut. He stumbled forwards and grasped hold of an up turned table leg to steady himself.

"You alright?" Marcus said examining him.

Cunomoltus nodded with a silent, embarrassed expression.

"Then we are done here," Marcus called out to the Batavians who were standing spread out in the room. "Let's go."

"Uh not so fast," the blues boss said, raising a finger in the air, "Meryn belongs to me. He will   be staying here."

Marcus glanced at the wounded man, lying on the ground.

"I gave him my word that he would live," Marcus said turning back to the boss of the blues. Then he lifted his foot from Meryn's back, and gesturing at the Batavians to follow him, he grasped hold of Cunomoltus' arm and headed for the doorway. As he passed the blue gang master, the small man sniggered contemptuously.

"Hello Meryn," the blue's boss said in a loud friendly voice as he strode towards him, "and goodbye arsehole," he added, as with a single thrust he buried his knife into Meryn's neck.

"I gave him my word that he would live," Marcus cried angrily.

"But I did not," the blues boss retorted, "We're done here. Now fuck off."

***

The upstairs room in the Mule was small and it had only one bed. Cunomoltus sat on the straw mattress, moodily leaning against the wall, his fingers playing with a knife whilst Marcus stood leaning against the far wall, staring pensively out of the small window at the street below. It was evening and outside it was raining.

"What's on your mind?" Cunomoltus muttered as he studied the knife in his hands. "I have seen that look on your face before. You are trying to decide what to do?"

Marcus muttered something to himself. Then he turned sharply to look at his brother and there was a strange gleam in his eyes.

"Hyperborea," he growled, "This country that Meryn was talking about. The place where he says Emogene has fled to, the land beyond the north wind. I have heard the stories they tell about this place. They are myths and legends. Some people say they are just Greek nonsense. Still, here we are. Meryn believed what he was telling me. I   could see it in his eyes."

"The man was a criminal, how can you trust such a prick," Cunomoltus exclaimed.

Slowly Marcus shook his head.

"I remember," he said with a frown, "my father telling me about the strange things he'd seen out on the outer ocean when we were in Hibernia. Of strange men, the likes he'd never seen before, with feathers in their hair and of inedible fruit that had never grown in this province."

"You don't seriously believe that there is land out there to the north and west," Cunomoltus said, looking up at Marcus. "The further north you go, the colder and darker it gets. That's a fact. How could something grow in those conditions? How could men survive? No, all this talk of a land beyond the north wind that is rich in honey and grain is just complete and utter bullshit. It's just not scientifically possible."

"Nevertheless," Marcus said, turning to look at Cunomoltus with sudden determination, "I am going to find out. I am going to cross the ocean. I am going to find Emogene."

Cunomoltus dropped his knife and stared at Marcus with a startled expression. Then rapidly he scrambled to his feet. "Ooooohh no," he exclaimed raising his hand in the air as he shook his head, "No Marcus, you've got balls but that is going too far. The outer ocean is not meant to be crossed."

"And yet I am doing it," Marcus growled.

"Are you fucking insane," Cunomoltus cried, raising his hand to touch his battered and bruised face. "Don't you hear what I am saying? The outer ocean is not meant to be crossed. There is nothing out there but endless water, demons and monsters the likes we can only guess at. And beyond lies the realm of the gods. They will not let us mortals enter their domain. They will forbid it. It's common sense. Everyone knows you don't attempt to cross the ocean. You are going to die and when you do, your spirit will never find a final resting place. You will be doomed to wander this world, lost, wet and alone for all eternity."

"The druids managed it," Marcus said stubbornly.

"Ah, the fucking druids," Cunomoltus exclaimed, raising his eyes to the ceiling in sudden exasperation, "The druids. What do they know? They are the past. They have no place in the future. They are just a club of superstitious wankers. The future belongs to the men of proper science."

"If your decision is to stay here, then so be it," Marcus said sharply, "But I am going. What else is there for me to do? This is who I am. What should I tell Corbulo when I go to meet him in the next world? That I gave up because I was scared? My father travelled to the end of the world for me. He did not abandon me. So you can say what the fuck you like, but I am not giving up now."

Cunomoltus ran his fingers across his head in exasperation.

"Even if this land exists, how are you going to find this trading post? How are you going to know in which way to sail? All Meryn gave you was the name of a tribe and a vague description of the place."

"We will find it," Marcus nodded confidently.

"Ah shit Marcus," Cunomoltus cried out, as he angrily snatched up his knife and flung it into a corner. "Don't do this to me. You fucking arsehole."

"You are scared," Marcus replied, "But that is alright. Fear keeps you alive, it's natural. Just don't let it take complete control."

"Damned right I am scared," Cunomoltus cried, as he rounded on Marcus. "I am fucking terrified and so should you be."

"Then stay here."

Cunomoltus groaned and turned away from Marcus, so that he could not see his face and for a long moment he was silent. "I can't; that's the problem," he hissed at last. "The voices in my head. They are telling me that I must stay with you. They are telling me that I must not leave your side. They are telling me that you are going to need me before the end."

Marcus said nothing as he returned to his position beside the window and for a long while there was silence in the room, before Marcus spoke again.

"We're going to need to find a captain and a crew willing to make the crossing," Marcus muttered as he stared out at the rain.

***

It was late in the evening and Marcus and Cunomoltus were sitting at a small table beside the roaring fire, as they ate a late supper, when the door to the tavern opened and a figure clad in a long, dark cloak and hood entered. The person's cloak was dripping wet. The newcomer turned to look around the tavern and catching sight of Marcus and Cunomoltus approached. And, as the stranger lowered the hood Marcus choked on his food and Cunomoltus swiftly rose to his feet, sending his cup crashing onto the floor.

"What's this?" Cunomoltus cried. "You have got a lot of balls coming here."

"Hardly," Nectovelius's wife said, as she glared at Cunomoltus examining his face with a hint of glee. "I think I prefer the way you look now. You deserved everything you got, you bastard. Gods, what a mistake I made with you."

Cunomoltus's clenched his hands into fists but he did not move.

"We've had enough of you and your company for one day," Marcus said sharply, "What do you want?"

215

"Likewise," the woman snapped. "But believe it or not I have come here to warn you. This whole bloody business is not over. The Blues are happy but my husband is not. He is trying to hire an assassin to get rid of old pretty face over there."

Marcus frowned. "I don't understand," he muttered, "You betray my brother, you beat the shit out of him and now you have come to warn us that your husband wants him dead? It doesn't make sense. Or is this another one of your tricks?"

The woman shook her head.

"I am doing this for myself," she said, lowering her voice, "I made a mistake with your brother, a big one. My husband is not the brightest spark but he is a violent man and a jealous man. He will kill me if he ever found out about us. So, in exchange for warning you, I want your brother out of this city as fast as possible, and after that I don't ever want to see him again. I want him gone, as far away from me as possible. You should leave tonight before it is too late."

Marcus glanced at Cunomoltus. His brother was staring at the woman with a face that was torn between rage and sorrow.

"Cunomoltus said that you had a sweet spot for him once," Marcus muttered thoughtfully. "He said that you were prepared to run away with him. So why didn't you?"

"He told you that, did he?" the woman said, glancing quickly at Cunomoltus, "Did this faithless idiot also tell you that I was ready to leave with him, but when the appointed hour came, he never showed up. He abandoned me and that was the last I heard from him, until you two showed up a few days ago."

Marcus slowly turned to look at his brother. Cunomoltus was suddenly blushing with embarrassment.

"It wasn't really like that…" Cunomoltus murmured but Marcus cut him off.

"He may not be a very trustworthy man, my brother," Marcus said sharply, looking the woman straight in the eye, "But that is your problem. So what's stopping me from going to your husband right now and telling him everything about your affair? He won't be happy with you, that's for sure."

It was the woman's turn to blush and for a moment she seemed lost for words.

"I came here to warn you," she hissed as her cheeks burned, "How dare you try and threaten me."

"I am not threatening you," Marcus replied, coldly fixing his eyes on her. "But I do need your help. If you want Cunomoltus to leave this city, you are going to have to do something for us."

"What?" the word shot from the woman's voice.

"We need to find a sea captain and a crew for a long voyage north," Marcus replied. "Know any captains with a ship who are willing to go a bit beyond the normal trade routes?"

The woman frowned in confusion. Then her eyes widened.

"Actually I do know someone looking for work," she said lowering her voice, "He's perfect for both of you. His name is Alexandros. He spent years on the Alexandria to Rome grain convoys but now he just likes to drink until he passes out."

"Where can we find this Alexandros? Does he have a ship?" Marcus said quickly.

"Promise that you will leave as soon as possible, both of you," the woman said.

"We make that promise," Marcus growled gesturing at Cunomoltus to remain silent, "On the honour of the 2nd Batavian Cohort."

"Good," the woman muttered, looking satisfied, "Yes he owns the Hermes. You will find the ship moored in the river and you will find Alexandros and his family at the Gay Crab. They are staying in one of the upstairs rooms. Apparently he was so drunk that he did not wake up, even when you and your Batavians butchered the Reds in the tavern below."

Chapter Twenty-Eight – The Hermes

"Is that the ship?" Cunomoltus exclaimed in a doubtful voice.

"Yes, I think so," Marcus replied.

The two of them stood on the quayside looking out across the busy river. The tide was in and before them, the broad Thames stretched away, in places half a mile wide, as out on the water, numerous ships bobbed up and down. It was morning, a fresh, warm breeze was blowing, and in the dull, grey skies, there was a hint of rain. Above them in the breeze, sea gulls were circling, emitting their high-pitched screeches, as they searched for their next meal. The Hermes rode at anchor about thirty yards from the waterfront. The small, eighty-ton merchant ship looked battered and old. Her round, wooden hull rose towards the stern, where it ended in a carved swan's neck, with the two massive steering oars dipping into the water on either side of the poop deck. A small, windowless cabin with a ladder leading up to the helmsman's position on its roof, occupied the rest of the stern. In the centre of the twenty-yard long boat, was a single mast and towards the bow, another smaller mast angled forwards like a spear. A pennant bearing the proud face of Hermes, messenger of the gods, fluttered in the gentle breeze. The sails however had been stowed and there was no sign of life on board.

"Where are the oars? I can't see any holes in the hull for the oars?" Cunomoltus muttered unhappily.

"It's a merchant ship, they don't have oars," Marcus replied. "There would be no space for the cargo if they had banks of oars. The only thing that moves the ship is the sail. The good news is that it means we won't need a large crew."

"Great," Cunomoltus replied in an unconvincing voice, as he gazed at the vessel out on the water.

"Look," Marcus growled, pointing at the prow of the ship, "there on the prow; see the figurehead sticking out at the front. That will be the face of Hermes. These sailors are a superstitious lot, so let me do the talking. I don't want them hearing about the voices in your bloody head."

"It doesn't look like anyone is on board," Cunomoltus replied sulkily.

Marcus said nothing as he raised his arm and beckoned to one of the small boats that was plying between the moored ships, in the river and the harbour.

"Just don't speak," Marcus snapped tensely, as one of the little boats turned and headed towards where they were standing. "You are a much better person when you don't say anything."

Marcus and Cunomoltus were silent as the boat-man ferried them across the water to the Hermes and, as they drew closer, Marcus could see a black cat perched on a wooden yardarm, high up the mast. The animal was watching them with confident, curious, yellow eyes. Just below and around the waterline, the solid looking hull of the ship was covered in places with barnacles, algae and slime. Towards the bow section of the hull, a large, faded blue-eye had been painted onto the side, whose purpose Marcus guessed, was to safeguard the ship and fend off evil, supernatural forces.

As the small lighter came alongside the Hermes, Marcus grabbed hold of the rope netting that hung over the side and heaved himself up the high hull and, after a few awkward moments, he finally clambered over the side and onto the deck. The ship's superstructure was smaller than he had been expecting and the vessel was only five or six yards wide at its widest point. A couple of closed hatches, leading down into the hold, had been set into the deck just in front of the main mast. The square hatches had been battened down and secured by a heavy, iron chain and the deck of the ship was covered with discarded rubbish, mud and bird shit. As Marcus looked around, he heard Cunomoltus behind him, swearing as he clambered up the netting.

"Who are you? What are you doing on my ship?" a deep, voice suddenly boomed from the doorway of the small cabin.

Marcus turned to see a big tanned man of around forty-five with a black beard and a reddish nose standing in the doorway clutching a hammer. The man looked annoyed at the intrusion and one of his eyes was bloodshot.

"My name is Marcus. Are you Alexandros?"

"I am," the captain replied, sizing Marcus up with a practised eye, "what are you doing on my ship? I did not give you permission to come on board."

At Marcus' side, Cunomoltus had finally managed to clamber up the hull, and with a dull groan, he rolled onto the deck.

"I was told that you are looking for work," Marcus said, gazing at the captain. "They told me that you are the most fearless captain in Londinium. I am interested in hiring you, your crew and your ship for a long journey."

Alexandros reached up to stroke his beard with a thoughtful look, as he turned to gaze at Cunomoltus, who was still lying on his back on the deck.

"Who told you this?"

"It doesn't matter. Are you, your crew, and your ship for hire?"

"What's the cargo and the destination?" Alexandros snapped, as Cunomoltus slowly got up onto his feet.

"No cargo, just us, passengers. The destination is north, it will be a long journey," Marcus replied smoothly.

"What, no cargo?" Alexandros frowned and took a step towards Marcus, slapping the hammer into his empty hand. "What is this, a joke? You are either very rich or very stupid."

"I am willing to pay," Marcus said.

"What, just the two of you, no cargo and a destination in the north. It will cost you three hundred Denarii plus expenses and insurance costs."

"What is there to insure, I said there was no cargo," Marcus snapped.

"Yes well," Alexandros said sizing Marcus up, "I figure a man like you has the money and you seem desperate to go, so why not? If something happens to my ship I want her insured."

"Fine," Marcus muttered, "Three hundred it is, half now and half when we reach our destination."

"Which is?"

Marcus paused and glanced at Cunomoltus, who was studying the captain.

"North," Marcus said quietly, "Then out west across the ocean until we reach land. We are heading for the druid trading post in the land of the people of the Rocky River. The druids call them the Penawapskewi. The place I want to go to is called Hyperborea."

The deck of the Hermes fell silent and for a long moment, the only noise was the creaking of ropes, the screeching sea gulls and the gentle slap of the waves against the side of the hull.

"You are not joking are you," Alexandros exclaimed at last, as he stared at Marcus in surprise. "You are really willing to head out into the ocean. You actually mean what you say."

"Well, do you have the balls to make the journey or should I be looking for another captain and crew," Marcus said.

"Hyperborea," Alexandros muttered to himself, as he allowed himself a little shake of his head. "I have been sailing the sea since I was ten years old, but I don't know where Hyperborea is. Some say it does not exist. But you seem certain about this. I can see it in your eyes."

"Are you, or are you not, willing to go there?" Cunomoltus interrupted, in an irritated voice. "I really don't want to be wasting my precious time."

"The druid trading post exists," Marcus said, "The journey is possible. The druids have been making the crossing for many years and if they can do it, then so can we. Think about the fame and fortune you will have when you return."

"Such a crossing of the outer ocean will take weeks, maybe months," Alexandros replied, as an excited gleam appeared in his eyes, "It will be dangerous and the gods only know what we will find out there on the endless sea. The western ocean is not meant to be crossed, but if you are willing to pay for it, then I am your captain. Gods, you have no idea how much I have wanted to do something crazy like this before I become too old. There is just one problem. I don't have a crew."

Marcus nodded. "How many men do you need to handle this ship?" he said.

Alexandros shrugged, "four or five able bodied men should do it. My wife and daughter will be coming with us, but that still leaves us short of two. It is going to be difficult to get sailors to agree to come with us. Most men that I've known are full of courage on land, but piss themselves when they encounter their first storm. And certainly none of them are going to agree to a voyage that means setting out west across the ocean. I can't set sail without the extra hands."

"We'll find them," Marcus replied, with a confident little nod. "Give me a day or two to raise the money and I will meet you back here on board. In the meantime, you will get us the provisions and supplies that we need and you will clean up this shit on deck and get the ship ready to sail. I want to leave as soon as possible."

"Alright," the captain said, extending his right hand towards Marcus. Marcus clasped hold of Alexandros's hand, gripping it tightly with his own, right hand.

"And one more thing," he growled, "As long as you are employed by me, there will be no drunkenness on board. That goes for both of you," he added turning to look at Cunomoltus.

Chapter Twenty-Nine – The Crew

Marcus, his face a stoic mask, sat in the lighter as the boatman ferried them across the water to the Hermes. A sheathed gladius hung from his belt and in his lap he was clutching a leather bag and a larger sack lay at his feet. Cunomoltus sat beside him looking moody and jittery. Two spears leaned against his shoulder and the bruises and cuts on his face were healing. It was morning and three days had passed since they had spoken to Alexandros. Falco's bankers in the Forum had needed time to gather the money and Marcus and Cunomoltus had spent the time waiting in the Mule tavern and keeping off the streets. Marcus had taken the time to write a letter to Kyna, which he had sealed and left in the care of Falco's bankers, to be given to her, only if he failed to return within a year. The unexpected journey would be hard on the women back on the farm on Vectis, but he had consoled himself with the thought that they had known what they were signing up to, when they had married into a military family.

In the river, the Hermes rode at anchor and Marcus could see a couple of figures standing on her deck. Another lighter lay alongside the ship and a man was standing up and handing amphorae up to another person, who was leaning over the side of the hull. As they came alongside Marcus grasped hold of the netting, and handing the leather pouch to his brother, he grasped hold of the rope and pulled himself up and over the side of the ship. As he regained his footing, Cunomoltus tossed the pouch and the larger sack up onto the deck and started to clamber up the netting, awkwardly clutching the two spears. On the deck towards the bow of the vessel, a young woman of around sixteen was on her knees scrubbing the wooden planks with a brush and, as he looked around, Marcus could see that the Hermes had been cleaned up. A cluster of amphorae, sacks, bales of cloth, stacks of wooden planks and two large sealed barrels stood waiting to be lowered into the hull through one of the opened hatchways.

"Have you got the money?" Alexandros called out, as he came up to Marcus from where he'd been supervising the loading of the supplies.

In response Marcus tossed him the small pouch. Alexandros caught it and swiftly undid the leather thongs and peered inside. Then a broad smile appeared on his lips and he turned to look at someone inside the small cabin at the stern of the ship.

"Cora, we're rich," Alexandros boomed happily in his deep voice. "I told you that he would deliver."

From the doorway to the cabin on the superstructure, a woman of around forty appeared. Her jet-black hair was tied back in a ponytail and her face looked every inch as weather beaten and tough as Alexandros's. For a moment she said nothing as she studied Marcus and Cunomoltus.

"If they touch Calista," she said sharply, turning to Alexandros, "I will cut their throats. Make sure that they understand."

And with that she vanished back into the cabin.

Alexandros turned to look down at the bag of gold coins in his hand. Then he looked up at Marcus and shrugged.

"That's my wife, Cora," he said sheepishly, "and that over there is my daughter, Calista. So you heard my wife. This ship is no whorehouse, so I hope for your sake that you have done all your shagging in town. There is going to be none on this ship, none for you at any rate."

And with that Alexandros threw back his head and boomed with laughter.

"We will be no trouble," Marcus said glancing at Cunomoltus. "Just take us where we want to go and you will get the other half of the payment once we get there, like we agreed."

"Like we agreed," Alexandros   nodded.

For a moment the three of them were silent as they watched the boatmen heaving the supplies up onto the deck. On the roof of the deck house, the black, ship's cat was sprawled out in the sun, licking itself.

"The talk in the harbour," Alexandros said at last in a careful voice, "is all about Meryn's execution and the slaughter of the Reds. I was asleep upstairs in the Gay Crab when it happened." Alexandros raised his thick eyebrows. "I slept right through it, but luckily my wife and daughter stopped those Batavians from murdering me. The Blues are in control now but nothing much has changed. A ship's captain still has to pay them if he wants anything done." Alexandros paused and glanced cautiously at Marcus. "You wouldn't happen to have anything to do with all of that, would you?"

"Maybe, maybe not," Marcus said, "Would it bother you if I did?"

"No, not at all," Alexandros said hastily, as he tied together the cords of the leather pouch and slipped it into a pocket.

"Is it not bad luck to have women on board a ship?" Cunomoltus murmured unhappily.

Alexandros turned to look at him with a little contemptuous smile.

"Cora is the daughter of a sailor," he replied, "and she has been with me on every voyage that I have made. She knows the sea better than anyone and she is not afraid like you are. And as for my daughter, she was born at sea on this very ship. Don't worry about my women, they are hardened sea dogs and they know how to cook too."

"So how come you have no work?" Cunomoltus replied with a voice that bristled with wounded pride. "You have a ship and yet you laze about here in the river. You have been a captain for how many years? They told us that you are drunk most of the time."

"Be quiet, brother," Marcus snapped as he angrily rounded on Cunomoltus but Alexandros held up his hand and shook his head.

"No let him speak, he has a fair point," the Captain replied, eyeing Cunomoltus with a sudden gleam. "If you really want to know, I have a dream, but no one believes me or wants to support me when I explain it to them. They call me crazy, a fool, they dismiss me as a dreamer, but what do they know? No one has the balls anymore. No one is curious anymore. People no longer have any grand vision." Alexandros raised his hand and pointed a finger at Cunomoltus. "You won't believe how frustrating it is to be surrounded by such ignorance, fear and disbelief. So yes, I like to have a drink now and then. If I didn't, I would go insane."

"A dream?" Cunomoltus sneered, looking doubtful.

Alexandros took a deep breath and, with a frustrated look, he glanced around at the supplies piling up on the deck.

"Listen," he said lowering his voice conspiratorially as he moved closer to Marcus and Cunomoltus, "This is the best business proposal you are ever going to hear about. In Rome, capital of the world, you won't believe how many rich ladies there are, and what do all these women want?"

Alexandros fell silent as he switched his eager gaze from Cunomoltus to Marcus, but when they didn't answer he sighed. "What all these women desire is silk from the land of the Chin far to the east," he snapped. "The silk worm from which they get the cloth, is only found there and it's expensive, very expensive. Now since the Persians have closed off the overland silk road, the price of silk has risen and risen and the good ladies of Rome are becoming increasingly desperate to get their hands on the stuff."

Alexandros paused and gave Marcus an excited nod.

"So my dream is to open a new trade route," he exclaimed triumphantly, "Not by going east, but by sailing west across the ocean. If I can find a way of reaching the land of the Chin by sailing west across the ocean, I will become the wealthiest and most famous sea captain the world has ever known. That would be a true legacy to leave to my daughter, don't you agree?"

"You are crazy, utterly mad," Cunomoltus said swiftly as he shook his head in despair.

Alexandros shrugged and turned to look at Marcus.

"But you don't think I am," he said with a sudden grin, "I can see it in your eyes. You are willing to go. You are not afraid of crossing the ocean and for that I thank you. At last there is someone who doesn't think me crazy."

Marcus had been studying Alexandros, with a thoughtful expression.

"This ship is going in search of the druid trading post in Hyperborea," Marcus said quietly, "That's where I want to go. We are not going on some random journey to find a new sea route to the land of the Chin."

"Of course," Alexandros said, lowering his gaze, "You are the man with the gold. I am just pleased to have met a man who is not afraid of the endless sea."

Marcus nodded.

"What about a crew?" he said, "Last time we spoke you said that you needed an extra pair of hands to crew the ship?"

"Actually I found them," Alexandros replied, "They are down below in the hull, sleeping. They are keen, very keen. A father and son. They are not true sailors," Alexandros shrugged, "more like passengers, who will work for their passage across the ocean. But they were the only ones to show any interest and they seem fit enough. No one else wanted to go, even at double rates. So it seems that I am going to be the only proper sailor on board. Woe to the ship if anything were to happen to me, eh?" Alexandros grinned as moments later his deep, booming laughter shook the boat.

"What do you mean; they are passengers?" Marcus frowned as he ignored the Captain's laughter. "You are not paying them? Are you saying that they actually want to go to Hyperborea? How can this be so? What business do they have there?"

Alexandros's laughter petered out and he glanced at the square hatch in the deck that led down into the hold.

"They didn't say," he muttered, "They were rather secretive and yes, they didn't want to be paid." The captain paused and then turned to look at Marcus with a thoughtful expression. "I think they want to go to the same place as you do. They also brought a locked, iron box on board. By the care they took in looking after it, it must contain something important, something valuable to them."

"Who are they" Marcus growled, as he turned to stare at the opened hatch in the deck.

"A father and son, like I said," Alexandros said as a hint of alarm edged into his voice, "From the north I think. We are lucky to have found them. There are no sailors in the whole of Londinium who are willing to make the journey and believe me, I went looking. And there is something else," Alexandros said abruptly.

"What" Marcus snapped.

"They claim to know the way to the trading post that you mentioned," Alexandros replied, raising his eyebrows.

***

The interior of the ship was dark, damp and in the stale air below, Marcus caught a whiff of vinegar as he, followed by

Alexandros and Cunomoltus, descended the ladder into the cargo hold. As he reached the bottom, Marcus turned to look around. The wooden planking of the hull, held together by hundreds of simple but strong mortise and tenon joints gracefully curved inwards into a deep, solid and narrow keel. Wedged at the very bottom were a few amphorae, coils of rope, a long and narrow raft and a wooden compartment, that contained drinking water and which was lined with waterproof canvas and sealed with pitch. A small iron cage hung from a hook in the ceiling and inside were three black ravens. The hold was divided into two by a sturdy looking wooden bulkhead, that went right down the length of the keel and beside the base of the mast, someone had placed a small rectangular iron box on the floor. Two men, who had been sleeping on the floor, hastily scrambled to their feet as they heard Marcus coming down the ladder.

"My name is Marcus," Marcus said, as he stared at the two men, "I am the one who has hired and commissioned this ship and its crew. I am paying for this voyage. Now I understand from the captain here, that you are willing to help sail her across the ocean. If that is so, then you are working for me and under my command and you will do what I tell you to do. Is that clear?"

"That's clear Roman," the elder of the two replied in accented Latin. "We ask for nothing apart from passage to the druid trading post in Hyperborea across the ocean. My son and I are prepared to crew the ship in return."

Marcus frowned, as he leaned forwards and peered at the older man in the gloom. The man looked around the same age as himself but, his clothes were typical of those worn by the northern Briton tribesmen and he was completely bald. In his hand he was clutching a gnarled, oak stick and there was a calm and unsettling authority about him. At his side, the man's son was staring at Marcus with a bold, confident, fearless look. The young man looked around sixteen or seventeen and a knife hung from his belt.

"Who are you" Marcus exclaimed, as a tinge of unease suddenly made itself felt. "No one apart from the druids knows about this trading post beyond the ocean. So how do you know so much about it?"

"My name is Caradoc," the older man replied, "this here is Jodoc and the reason for our crossing does not concern you. We will do as you ask, but do not pry into our affairs and reasons for making this journey. If you can do that, then we will all get along just fine, Roman."

Surprised, Marcus gave Alexandros and Cunomoltus a quick glance, as for a moment, he seemed taken aback by the man's calm, confident reply.

"Alexandros says that you know the way to the place where the druids have their trading post. How can this be so" Marcus said in a patient voice. "The only way you can know this, is if you have been there before? But until a few days ago I didn't even know about it. Very few know that the place where we are heading, actually exists. The druids seem to have kept its existence a closely, guarded secret."

"Oh, it exists alright," Caradoc replied in a confident voice, "and I know the way, more or less. But a more important question is why are you making this journey? Why is a Roman spending so much gold on a dangerous voyage into the unknown? It is not every day that I meet a man prepared to do this."

"I will ask the questions," Marcus snapped, in an irritated voice.

"We will crew this ship," Caradoc said firmly, "but the reason why we are here, is our own and will remain so. It is none of your business."

"What's in the box?" Cunomoltus suddenly blurted out.

"My father just said it was none of your business," Jodoc snapped aggressively, as he took a step forwards to protect the iron chest. "Are you deaf, stupid or both?"

Marcus held up his hand in warning, as Cunomoltus' face darkened and he took a threatening step towards the young man.

"Enough," he glared, "I have seen enough. Alexandros, we will set sail as soon as everything is on board and stowed away."

Without another word, Marcus turned and started to climb back up the ladder. As Cunomoltus clambered up out of the hold, Marcus was staring at him grim faced, his eyes gleaming with sudden passion.

"I know who they are," Marcus hissed in a bitter voice, "They're druids. That's why they know so much about Hyperborea."

Chapter Thirty – North

Alexandros and Marcus stood together on the roof of the deck house, at the stern, as the Hermes sailed down the Thames and directly into the rising sun. The ebbing tide was drawing them out towards the sea. Alexandros was clutching the tiller bar that controlled the two, huge steering oars and was explaining how the levers worked. From the roof of the cabin Marcus, had a good view of the bow of the ship as it cut through the water. A large, red square sail billowed in the westerly wind and further forwards, the smaller foresail, the supparum, was at full stretch. The ship groaned and creaked as it sped along at a respectable four knots and, above them in the sky, the screeching sea gulls, that had followed them down the river, circled, swooped and rose on the air currents. Cunomoltus was standing on the deck below, clutching the side of the hull, as he looked back in the direction of Londinium with a moody expression. The city had already vanished from view and along the northern and southern river banks there was nothing to see, apart from forest, swamps, tall river reeds and small creeks and inland waterways.

"I am going to need someone who is capable of steering the ship," Alexandros said as he clutched the tiller. "And that person should be you. The role of the helmsman is by far the most important one on board. The ship needs to be steered at all times. Don't ever forget that. Handling the tiller requires more skill than strength. So we will take it in shifts. I will do dawn till noon, you shall be in control until sunset. During the night we will anchor close to the shore."

Marcus nodded, as he studied the tiller and the cables that connected it to the two, huge, steering-oars either side of the poop deck.

"What happens when we reach the open ocean and there is no land," he muttered.

"Then the shifts will become day and night," Alexandros replied quickly. "My wife and daughter are in charge of cooking and the ships supplies. Your brother, Caradoc and Jodoc will need to help raise and set the sails when necessary. They will also need to help with repairs and act as lookouts. The ship's cat is in charge of catching mice and rats. So you see," Alexandros said with a sudden grin, "Everyone has a job to do and we will only survive this if all of us work as a team." Alexandros paused, as he adjusted the tiller with an experienced hand. "I have already explained it to the others," he continued, "but in these calm waters, it may be useful if we did some practice and training."

Marcus nodded again.

"You have been out on the ocean," he said turning to Alexandros, "You have sailed beyond the sight of land? What was it like?"

Alexandros turned to look towards the north. "You will be frightened at first," he muttered, "Some inexperienced sailors panic but the fear does not last. You get used to it after a while. You've served in the army, I can tell. So you know what I am talking about. That's why you are going to be in charge of discipline."

Alexandros gestured at Cunomoltus standing on the deck below. "He is afraid," he murmured, "I can smell it on him. We are all anxious, but he thinks he is going to die and maybe he will, but if, out there on the endless sea, he starts to panic, then the best remedy will be to knock him unconscious. Panic is infectious and it will lead to disaster. I have seen it happen. It must not happen on this ship."

"There will be no trouble with my brother or the crew," Marcus growled. "But how are you going to navigate on the open ocean? How are you going to know which way to go?"

Alexandros shrugged. "There are a few ways. During the day we watch the sun, at night the stars, a good captain watches everything, the waves, the birds." Alexandros shrugged again. "Don't worry I have a few tricks to play against the spirits of the sea. We have three months of supplies but we will need to replenish our fresh water supply before then."

"Caradoc claims to know the way," Marcus said carefully, "That can only mean that he has been to Hyperborea before."

Alexandros shot him a glance. "You don't like them do you," he muttered.

"They are druids," Marcus replied in an angry, bitter voice, "There is nothing good about them. They are enemies of Rome and I have seen what they like to do to captured soldiers. The druids murdered my father. So no, I don't like them. I hate them."

Alexandros looked grim. "They seem as keen as us to reach Hyperborea," he replied. "I don't think they will trouble you, as long as they are on board. They know they need us to get there."

"Maybe," Marcus nodded, with an unhappy look.

"I have studied the charts," Alexandros continued, "and even purchased a copy of Pytheas' account of his travels on the ocean, from four hundred years ago, but no one is certain where Hyperborea is, if it exists at all," he growled. "All I know is that the world ends at the very tip of the north coast of Britannia. Beyond that, there is just endless sea, the terrors of the deep and the home of the gods."

"Caradoc told me that there are uninhabited islands to the north," Marcus replied, "and that when we reach the land of fire and ice, we should head north west and then south west when we first see mountains of floating ice in the sea. He thinks the journey will take us two months."

"Maybe, who knows," Alexandros growled, "But I will be damned if I am going to place the fate of this ship in the hands of a man who claims to know the way. No, we are going to do this my way."

"Good," Marcus replied with an approving look, "I seem to have chosen a good captain. Hermes, messenger of the gods, it is a good name for a ship that is sailing towards the land of the gods."

"I have been a sailor for over thirty years," Alexandros muttered with a hint of pride, as he turned to stare at the river with a faraway gaze. "I am a Greek, born and raised in the great Greek city of Alexandria. That's in Egypt, if you didn't know, and for most of my time at sea, I and the Hermes were part of the Roman grain fleet, ferrying grain from Egypt to the hungry masses in Rome. The Hermes was designed to carry ten thousand modii of grain, the minimum legal requirement, which allowed her to join the Egyptian grain fleet. She is tiny compared to the big grain carriers. It was steady work, reasonably profitable but boring as hell." Alexandros sighed. "Once you have done the journey a few times you can do it in your sleep. So, after a few years I decided to take a gamble and I journeyed across the desert to the Red Sea port of Berenice. The port is where the ships destined for India, set sail. The Indian trade is one of the most lucrative there is, but it is also one of the most dangerous. The Indians desire our gold and silver and in return we bring back all kinds of exotic spices and animals. But the route is plagued by Arab pirates and many trading ships never return."

For a while Alexandros remained silent, as he guided the Hermes down the Thames.

"But the gods favoured me," he suddenly exclaimed with a short booming laugh. "And I made a fortune on that trade route, enough to allow me, after a few years, to return to Alexandria and buy the Hermes. She is a good ship, a bit old, but she has never let me down yet."

"So what brought you here to   Londinum?" Marcus replied.

"Oh, Londinium is well known amongst sailors," Alexandros said with a nod. "The city is growing in importance, but I have already told you. I came here with the hope of opening up a new trading route to the west." Alexandros paused to glance at the small stone altar that stood behind him. "Maybe the gods sent you to me," he continued in a quieter voice, "Maybe you are my reward for all those times that I have prayed and begged the gods for a chance to fulfil my dream."

Alexandros turned to look at Marcus with a sudden gleam in his eyes.

"You have told me where you want to go," he muttered, "But you have never said why? What are you hoping to find at this druid trading post in Hyperborea?"

"I am looking for someone," Marcus replied. "Someone who means a lot to me."

Marcus remained silent as Alexandros waited for him to continue. Then as the silence lengthened, Alexandros abruptly looked away.

"I like you Batavian," Alexandros said, "You are simple, uncomplicated. A man knows where he stands with you. And you are not afraid of the ocean. That is a rare quality."

"You are wrong, I am afraid," Marcus replied, "but the trick is not to let fear govern what you do. I am my own master. I choose my own destiny. The gods may weigh the odds for or against me, but I do not answer to them."

***

It was late in the morning when, with Marcus at the tiller, the Hermes sailed into the wide Thames estuary, where the river ran into the German sea. The westerly wind seemed to have picked up and the swells had grown and the ship pitched through the waves sending white, salty spray flying up into the air. At the bow of the ship Alexandros turned and gestured at Marcus.

"North, turn her north. We will follow the coast, keep her a mile from the land," he boomed in his deep voice, pointing to the north. Then he turned and yelled at Caradoc and Jodoc to start adjusting the sails.

Unsteadily Marcus moved the tiller, just like Alexandros had explained he should and, as the druids hastily adjusted the sails under Alexandros' guidance, he felt the Hermes respond. The sense of control was intoxicating and Marcus growled in satisfaction, as the vessel started to change course and head northwards. The strong, salty sea wind felt refreshing and calmed his troubled stomach and suddenly Marcus knew that he was going to enjoy sailing. On the starboard side of the estuary, the shoreline seemed to recede away into the grey and choppy German sea and to port, the coastline stretched away northwards towards the horizon. And high up in the masthead, the pennant of the Hermes fluttered madly in the wind and below it, slanting at a crazy angle, the red, square sail bulged in the wind.

On the deck below, Caradoc and Jodoc had come to stand beside Alexandros near the bow. They seemed to be talking, but he was too far away to hear what they were saying. There was no sign of Cora or Calista and he presumed they were either in the hold or the cook house below his feet. The black, ships cat however was perched on the edge of the roof, close to where he was standing, huddled into a protective ball of black fur, as it calmly looked out across the ship and the grey sea.

"Marcus, I need to talk to you," a voice close by said, as a few moments later Cunomoltus appeared, clambering up the ladder onto the roof.

"I have all the time in the world, what is it?"

Cunomoltus looked pale and his lower lip trembled as if he had just been sick.

"It's about the druids," he muttered darkly, holding his hand up to his mouth as he steadied himself with his other. "I have a plan. If you can distract the druids, I will be able to slip into the hold and open that iron box they brought on board. Then we will know why they are really here. What do you say?"

For a moment Marcus did not answer as he stared out to sea. Then slowly he shook his head. "No," he said sharply, "Whatever secrets they have, I am sure we will learn about them before the end. I am the last man to be sympathetic to the druids but on this voyage, we are going to face greater dangers than them and we are going to need to stick together. We need to face these challenges together. Old hatreds and feuds will have to wait."

Cunomoltus did not look happy with the reply he'd received. Annoyed he turned and a stream of swear words spewed from his mouth.

"You should never have agreed to let those two on board," Cunomoltus hissed at last, "They are going to cause trouble. I know it. The voices in my head are warning me about the druids. It was a mistake to bring them with us."

"I don't like them either," Marcus snapped, "but we had no choice. We need a crew and they were the only men who volunteered. It's not ideal but for now, we must make it work and that means, no fighting, no drinking, no touching the captain's daughter, no disputes and no prying into their affairs. We have bigger problems to worry about."

Chapter Thirty-One – Into the Unknown

The Hermes lay at anchor, half a mile off the bleak rocky coast. Along the shoreline the snow-capped, treeless mountains rose steeply from the glens and sea lochs and a strong, biting, north westerly wind was blowing, whipping up the waves. It was a cold, spring day, but at least it wasn't raining Marcus thought, as he steadied himself on the pitching and rolling deck and watched Alexandros and Cora. They were negotiating with the two men in their small log boat that lay alongside the Hermes, bobbing up and down in the green waves. Twelve days had passed since they had left the Thames estuary and had turned north, keeping the coast in view during the daylight hours and anchoring close to shore during the night. The journey had proceeded without any incident until at last they had reached this place, at the very northern tip of the Caledonian coast and there was no more land to hug. With a sigh, Marcus wrenched his eyes away from Alexandros and turned to gaze at the land. He was clad in his heavy Dacian, winter coat, over which he was wearing a black Paenula cloak, a poncho, with a hood pulled up over his thick, red hair. The Paenula he'd found, was fairly waterproof and kept the biting wind at bay during the long hours he'd stood holding the tiller and learning how to steer the boat. His gladius hung from his belt in its protective brown leather sheath and on his feet he was wearing his hobnailed, army boots, thick socks, and over his tunic, woollen, leg wrappings had been fastened to his shins with string. Marcus reached up to scratch his beard and there was a sudden melancholy in his eyes, as he gazed at the distant coast. Somewhere along that rocky, mountainous shore was the Caledonian village where, twenty years ago, he had been kept prisoner, together with Emogene. Greer, the druid and Emogene's father, had kept him locked and chained up in a damp unhealthy dungeon, as he had waited for the appointed day to sacrifice him to his Gods and that would have been his fate, if Corbulo had not come to his rescue. And somewhere too, along that coast lay a sea cave filled with amber. The secret of the amber that had started   it all.

The black, ship's cat lay stretched out in its usual spot, on the roof of the deck house beside him, and seemed to be asleep. The cat was half feral and despite its cute appearance, it had a vicious streak. Nothing seemed to scare it but woe to the man who tried to touch it, as Cunomoltus had discovered on the first day at sea, when he'd been bitten, whilst trying to stroke the animal. Only Calista seemed capable of touching it without incurring a bloody injury.

Marcus's attention was drawn back to Alexandros and his wife. The log boat was leaving and its two occupants were paddling back towards the shore.

"Well?" Marcus cried out as he caught Alexandros's eye.

The captain shrugged as he and Cora headed for the deck-house below Marcus' feet.

"We are loading up with fresh water and some supplies, don't worry I negotiated a good price; they say they will be back here before dark," Alexandros replied. "And they don't know anything about land to the north. They say that this is where the land ends and that north of here, there is only the ocean."

"So we waste a whole day waiting here?" Marcus growled impatiently.

Alexandros halted and turned to look out to sea. "We could be here for several days," he called out in a cheerful voice. "We are not going anywhere if this wind continues. A northern western wind is no good. We will never be able to leave these shores. We are going to have to wait until the wind direction changes. The wind must come from the south or east before we can set out into the unknown. And the wind doesn't like to be hurried," he added, as he broke out into a short, deep booming laugh.

Marcus grimaced as Alexandros and his wife disappeared from view. At the bow Calista and Jodoc, the young druid, were standing close together, staring at the log boat as it moved up and down through the waves. Jodoc and his father had been a model of cooperation and had caused no problems since they had come on board and had promptly followed up on every command and order Alexandros had given them. Marcus allowed himself a small shake of his head. Calista and Jodoc had surprised everyone. Despite Cora's grim warning to them in the port of Londinium, not to touch her daughter, the two youngsters seemed to have formed a strong friendship, that was rapidly blossoming into romance, a romance that everyone on board could see, was real and powerful. Even Cora had decided not to intervene, although now and then Marcus had caught her muttering, that she had provisioned the ship for seven souls and not eight.

Looking bored, Marcus closed his eyes and rubbed his rugged, weather-beaten face as the wind tugged at his cloak. He opened his eyes as he heard someone clambering up the ladder towards him. It was Cunomoltus. His brother was clad in the same Paenula as he was wearing and the unhappiness and moodiness that he'd displayed on the first few days at sea had vanished. Catching sight of the ship's cat, Cunomoltus's face, however, darkened.

"Go on, fuck off, ugly beast," he growled, gesturing at the cat with his hand, only to be rewarded with a deep throated, hissing, warning, whine from the cat.

"I see you are making friends," Marcus said, as a little smile played at the corner of his mouth. "Alexandros says we must stay here until the wind changes. It could be a while."

"I heard," Cunomoltus muttered, as he came to stand beside Marcus. "So we wait."

"We wait," Marcus nodded.

For a while, the two of them were silent as they stared out across the choppy sea.

"Look at the birds," Cunomoltus exclaimed at last in a calm voice, as he pointed at the formations of migrating birds flying overhead, "They are all heading north, out into the ocean. Those traders in their log boat may say there is no land to the north," Cunomoltus added with a shrug, "but I think the birds may know something that we do not. Where to are they flying? It must mean that there is land out there, to the north."

Marcus was staring up at the birds in the sky with a sudden, impressed look. Then he nodded in agreement.

"You have been spending a lot of time with the captain," Marcus replied as he turned his back into the wind. "Everything alright?"

"I am learning about the sea and how the ship works," Cunomoltus replied, as he too turned his back into the strong breeze. "It takes my mind off matters and its actually quite interesting. Alexandros knows what he is talking about."

"He doesn't secretly drink does he?" Marcus growled, glancing at his brother.

Cunomoltus shook his head. "No, I haven't seen him touch a drop of wine since we left Londinium."

Marcus grunted in approval. Cunomoltus had somehow managed to master his fear and transfer it into an intense, obsessive interest in anything to do with the sea and the ship. It was his way of keeping panic at bay. But he could also see that Alexandros was becoming a little fed up by the continuous stream of questions.

"You need to talk to Caradoc," Cunomoltus said suddenly, turning to Marcus. "I overheard them talking the other day, him and his son. Caradoc has been across the ocean to the druid trading post before and I think he is planning something. There is going to be trouble."

***

Caradoc was sitting cross-legged in the hold of the ship beside the mysterious iron box, as Marcus clambered down the ladder. The druid was humming to himself as he patiently scratched letters into a thin piece of wood, with an iron tipped stylus. He paused and looked up as Marcus approached.

"Alexandros says we must wait for the wind to change," Marcus muttered, as he stared at the long lines of neat writing that covered the thin piece of wood on both sides.

"Then we wait," Caradoc replied, turning back to his work.

"What are you doing?" Marcus said, as he folded his arms across his chest.

"It's a diary, a report on our journey so far," Caradoc replied, without looking up. "I write down what I see and what I hear."

"I thought the druids wrote nothing down," Marcus said sharply, "I thought you only passed on knowledge through oral communication."

Caradoc paused in mid scratch. Then slowly, he looked up at Marcus.

"I don't know anything about the druids," Caradoc replied, with a sudden glint in his eye, "other than what they did to captured Roman soldiers. It must have been terrible for those legionaries and Batavians to have their hearts ripped from their bodies, whilst they were still alive, but that is what happens when you take away another man's land."

Marcus' face darkened. Slowly he took a step towards Caradoc. "There is no point in trying to hide who you are," Marcus growled. "I know who you are and I also know that you have been to the trading post across the ocean."

Caradoc shrugged and a little, cold smile appeared on his lips.

"And I know who you are Batavian, veteran of Rome," Caradoc replied in a steel tinted voice, "But my son and I have done nothing to offend anyone on this ship. We just want the same thing that you want, to cross the sea, alive."

"How large is this trading post, tell me what you know about it?" Marcus said.

Caradoc looked down at the wooden keel, as the ship creaked, groaned and rolled in the waves.

"It's a small community, only a dozen or so druids," he replied. "They live with the Hyperborean's in their tents and some have learned to speak the native language. They trade high quality iron weapons, tools and wine for gold and silver, which the Hyperborean's have in abundance."

"How come I have not heard about this place before" Marcus said quickly. "No one seems to know about this trading post. Hyperborea itself is more a myth than real."

Caradoc smiled.

"The druids keep the existence and location of the trading post a secret, only known to them and it is only their ships, sailing from the forbidden islands on the western coast of Hibernia, that make the journey." Caradoc sighed. "We would have gone with them but there is trouble amongst the tribes in Hibernia and the route is closed for the moment. So we came to Londinium in search of a ship."

"So how come you know about this place?" Marcus snapped. "How come you have been there, if only the druids know about it?"

Caradoc stopped abruptly as he realised that he had walked into a trap. For a moment, he said nothing, staring at the floor. Then he looked up and smiled again.

"The druids need men to crew their trading ships," he replied in a calm voice, "I was a sailor on one of these ships, that's how I came to cross the ocean."

"Well that's strange," Marcus growled, "for when Alexandros brought you onboard he said he didn't think you were sailors and he should know. You also have not asked for any payment or reward to make this crossing, which makes me suspicious. You do not look like a sailor. You didn't even know how to adjust the sails."

Caradoc smiled in embarrassment, shrugged and remained silent.

Marcus eyes narrowed angrily. Then abruptly he looked away. "In Londinium," he said sharply, "I only learned about the druids who lived in Hyperborea from a criminal who controlled the Reds, the gangs in the docks. He told me that there is much gold and silver in Hyperborea. He told me the druids have mountains of the stuff just waiting to be collected. That is why I am making this journey. We are going to cross the ocean to make ourselves filthy rich."

"I see," Caradoc frowned as his face darkened, "So Meryn told you that? You should know that Meryn was my friend and now he is dead, murdered by you and those scumbag Batavians. Oh, I know it was you. I saw what you did to the men inside the Gay Crab. Presumably you killed him to cover your tracks or is that just who you are, a killer?"

"He was your friend?" Marcus shot back.

"He was," Caradoc replied angrily, "I knew him well, but you won't find mountains of gold and silver in Hyperborea."

Marcus remained silent, as he turned to look away and sought to calm himself. The druids were annoying and hostile but he still needed them.

"Tell me what you know about the Hyperboreans?" he said at last, in a calmer voice. "Are they like us? Will we receive a warm welcome or will they try and kill us?"

Caradoc paused, as he too struggled to calm himself and contain his hostility.

"They are different," he said at last in a quiet voice. "They are more primitive. They do not have permanent homes, coins, roads or even horses and their ships are no more sophisticated than hollowed out tree trunks. They live in simple, wooden tents and hunt in the forests, lakes and rivers, which cover the whole land. They move about in small family groups from one camp to the next when the seasons change and they are split into hundreds and hundreds of different tribes, many which are constantly at war with each other."

Marcus remained silent as he stared down at the keel of the ship and digested what Caradoc had just said. Then slowly, he raised his head and fixed his eyes on the druid with a crafty look.

"So as you knew Meryn well," he said in a quiet thoughtful voice, "you must have known his wife, Emogene?"

Caradoc said nothing, as he stared at Marcus with a stupid expression and his mouth opened just slightly, but in his eyes, Marcus thought he glimpsed a brief look of recognition.

"I know of her," Caradoc muttered uneasily, "Emogene, is a druid. She went mad and left Meryn and his children. She crossed the ocean to the place where we are going to now. She has been there for some years."

"So you know Emogene?" Marcus said silkily. "You can recognise her. She knows you."

Caradoc looked Marcus straight in the eye with growing surprise and in that single moment, Marcus realised that the druid knew far more than he was telling him.

Caradoc's surprise turned to alarm.

"You are not making this journey for the gold and silver are you?" he exclaimed in growing alarm. "You tricked me. What do you really want? Why are you really making this voyage?"

Marcus stared at him and smiled.

"You are not interested in gold or silver, you are not even interested in Hyperborea," Caradoc growled, as his eyes widened in growing alarm. "You are going after Emogene. That is what this is all about, but why? What do you want from her?"

Marcus shrugged. "That's my business," he retorted.

***

Marcus was asleep on the hard wooden floor of the hold when a hand shook him. Instantly he was awake, a knife gleaming in his hand. Alexandros was standing over him, his face grim.

"The wind has changed," the captain growled, glancing at the knife with a worried look. "We should take advantage. It's time to head northwest into the unknown."

Chapter Thirty-Two – The Endless Sea

The Hermes groaned and creaked as the little ship pitched, rose and rolled through the waves and the swelling sea, sending very cold, salty spray flying across the deserted deck. It was night, the noise of the slapping waves striking the hull and the moan of the wind had deadened, and dulled Marcus' hearing. The others were down below in the hold, sleeping and resting whilst he stood beside Alexandros on the roof of the deckhouse as the captain held the tiller, steering the ship on a northwesterly course. The two men were silent, as in the dim, reddish light of the ships oil lantern; they stoically peered into the darkness beyond the rising and plunging bow. For two days they had followed the formations of migrating birds, and the southerly wind had blown them northwards and for two days and nights they had seen nothing but the endless grey and cold sea. They had however, made good progress, and Marcus had been humbled, by the vastness and raw power of the sea and the sheer enormity of the voyage he had decided to undertake. After their first day and night out of sight of land, Cunomoltus, despite his attempts to manage his fear, had panicked and Marcus and Alexandros, had been forced to tie him up in the hold until he came to his senses.

Above the mast and the taught, bulging, square sail, the stars lit up the night sky in a beautiful mosaic of tiny twinkling pinpoints of light. Marcus glanced across at Alexandros and noticed that the captain too, was staring up at the night sky.

"Is this how you navigate at night?" Marcus said as he adjusted the hood of his Paenula cloak. "You look at the stars?"

Alexandros nodded, as he looked up at the night sky. "We are lucky," he growled, "That we have a clear night so that we can follow the old Dog. Look, over there," Alexandros said, pointing at the constellation of Ursa Minor. "Cynosura burns brightly and the Dog will show us the way to the north, as she always does."

Marcus said nothing as he stared at the little bear in the night sky.

"Praise the seven stars of Cynosura, which vie with each other for true north and under whose guidance, the ships of Greece set sail across the seas," Alexandros muttered.

"How do you know which way is north?" Marcus replied.

Alexandros grunted and pointed at Ursa Minor. "Look, there, the brightest star, that is Polaris, the dog's tail. Now look at the Kochab and Pherkad. They are not as bright, but the twins circle the pole and, if we keep the ship's bow aimed at a spot between those two stars, then we can be certain that we are heading north."

Marcus nodded as he steadied himself on the moving deck and stared at the stars.

"How do we know how far we have come?" he exclaimed.

"Well there are no maps or charts for these waters. Some sailors will use an astrolabe. I like to use my fingers," Alexandros said gruffly. "It's quite simple. Take a specific hour. Stretch out your arm, squint, line up the sun and the horizon and then count how many fingers there are between the horizon and the sun. One finger less than before and you know that you are seventy miles or so closer to true north since your last measurement."

"So how far have we come?"

Alexandros shrugged, "Hard to say exactly, the movement of the ship makes it harder to take the measurement than if you were on land, and there is a powerful current which has been pushing us to north east, but I think we must have come north a hundred and fifty miles or so. The gods seem to favour us, for this wind is just what we need. Let's hope it lasts."

"And what happens when the skies are overcast?" Marcus said.

"Most sailors would be screwed," Alexandros growled with sudden pride, "That's why most don't like to sail beyond sight of land, but I am no ordinary captain. I have a couple of tricks that we can use if we cannot see the sun or the stars. Do not worry, Marcus, you hired the finest sea captain in the civilised world. They are going to be telling stories about us for hundreds of years to come when we get back."

"Let's hope so," Marcus replied.

For a while, the two men were silent as the Hermes ploughed on, up and down through the darkness and the cold, endless swelling waves smacked and surged past the side of the hull to vanish into the darkness.

"In all your time as a sailor," Marcus said at last, "You never heard about a land in the far west, across the ocean?"

Alexandros remained silent as he stared at the bow of the Hermes.

"You need a very good reason to enter onto the ocean," he replied. "And most sailors have no reason to do so but the Carthaginians knew something. I heard a few rumours. Several hundred years ago, the ancient Punic sailors claim to have discovered a new world in the far west but the only proof of these voyages was burnt and destroyed when the city of Carthage was sacked and captured by Rome. It is a shame. I would have liked to have seen those reports."

"My father", Marcus said, "says he saw ships out on the ocean off the west coast of Hibernia. He claims that the Hibernians had made the crossing to Hyperborea. He told me that he even saw one of these Hyperborean's. The man had feathers in his hair and the druids had fruit, the like of which he had never seen before. My father was convinced that the druids knew something about the land beyond the ocean."

Alexandros nodded grimly.

"I have no doubt that there is land out there, across the sea," he replied in a firm voice, "The only thing that has been lacking so far is someone with a reason and the balls to go and find it."

***

Marcus was standing alone on the roof of the deckhouse, holding the tiller when dawn finally came. To the east, the sun rose from the sea, a splendid orange ball of welcoming light and warmth. Marcus peered at it with red, exhausted, squinting eyes and slowly adjusted the Hermes' course to the northwest, just as Alexandros had taught him to do. The hood of his Paenula was pulled over his head and despite his thick clothing; he was soaked, freezing, exhausted, bored and stiff. Alexandros had handed him the tiller a few hours earlier, so that he could catch up on some sleep and now, only the black ship's cat, lying in her usual position on the roof beside the helmsman, was keeping him company. The animal was licking her paws and seemed oblivious to her surroundings.

Around him, visibility was good and in every direction, right up to the horizon, there was nothing but the swells of the cold, grey and dark green sea interspersed by the occasional, white tipped wave and to Marcus, standing at the tiller, every direction looked the same. It was becoming clear to him now, how easy it was, to become lost, and to lose your sense of direction and at night, it had been even worse. The Hermes was utterly alone, a small wooden shell on a vast, shifting, moving ocean and once again Marcus felt the humbling force of the ocean as he struggled to deal with the enormity of the voyage he'd begun. As he wearily stared out across the bleak, endless waves the ship rolled, rose and plunged and the rigging of the bulging main sail and the smaller supparum groaned, tightened and relaxed.

On the deck below, Caradoc was standing beside the main mast, steadying himself with one hand, as he stared out to sea. Marcus's face darkened. Since their last confrontation, the two of them had chosen to ignore each other, and for the past few day's, Marcus and he had not said a word to each other. Marcus sighed and turned to squint again at the rising sun. Then, from the corner of his eye, he caught sight of Cunomoltus, clambering gingerly up out of one of the forward hatchways that led down into the hold. His brother looked pale and unsteady on his feet, as he slowly made his way towards the deckhouse, across the moving, tilting deck. In his hand, he was clutching a bowl of what looked like soup. A grim expression appeared on Marcus's face as he watched Cunomoltus coming towards him. It was the first time his brother had dared leave the hold since his earlier panic attack. He was at last trying to confront his demons, he thought with sudden pity.

Suddenly Caradoc, standing beside the main mast, cried out in warning and pointed at something in the sea to starboard. His shout was followed moments later by a blast of water, that shot high up into the air and in amongst the waves, Marcus caught sight of a huge, silent, dark beast, sliding gracefully through the water before vanishing beneath the waves. On the deck below Marcus, Cunomoltus froze as he too, caught sight of the sea monster. Then the bowl of soup smashed into a thousand fragments as it hit the deck, followed moments later by Cunomoltus, who seemed to have fainted in shock. There was no time to rush to Cunomoltus' aid. Marcus's eyes widened in horror, as close by, the huge dark animal rose up out of the depths before crashing back down into the swell and as it did so Marcus caught a glimpse of a dark, beady eye. Frantically he stared at the water into which the beast had vanished wondering, whether the beast was about to attack the ship, but as he stared at the foaming swells the beast did not reappear.

"What was that?" Marcus cried out in an alarmed voice, as Alexandros and his wife appeared on the deck below him.

"A monster from the deep," Alexandros snapped grimly as he grasped hold of Cunomoltus, who lay sprawled out on the deck. "It could be one of the guardians that protect the realm of the gods and come to see who we are. I think I will offer the gods a sacrifice today, for safe passage."

***

Marcus was woken by a loud shout, as blurry eyed, and disorientated, he stared up at the wooden deck above his head. He had been sleeping on the hard wooden floor in the port cargo compartment and it felt as if he had just fallen asleep. Wearily he staggered to his feet, feeling the stiffness in his muscles and turned towards the open hatchway that led up onto deck. Then he heard the shout again and his eyes widened in surprise as he recognised Jodoc's excited voice.

"Land, land, I can see land!" the young man shouted.

Quickly, Marcus clambered up the ladder and scrambled onto the deck. Jodoc was standing by the bow of the Hermes, pointing at something on the horizon, to the north. Marcus turned to see Alexandros at the tiller, and Cora and Calista staring at the horizon from the doorway of the deckhouse. The sun was already well advanced along its journey through the sky and around the ship, the sea was calm. Marcus made it to the side of the boat, blinked and peered in the direction in which Jodoc was pointing, and there, on the horizon was a faint smudge, a grey outline.

"That boy's eyes are better than mine," Alexandros muttered as Marcus came clambering up the ladder onto the deckhouse roof, "But he's right. That looks like land."

Marcus said nothing, as he turned to peer at the horizon, his chest heaving from exertion and excitement.

"I am going to head for the land," Alexandros growled, "and you had better fetch Caradoc, he claims to know the way after all."

There was however no need, for moments later, Caradoc came clambering up the ladder.

"Could it be Thule, the islands that Phytheas wrote about?" Marcus remarked, as all three men peered at the horizon.

"Maybe," Alexandros muttered. "Who knows? But this must be the place where all these birds are migrating to. We should be making a map of this, Cora," Alexandros bellowed, as he leaned forwards to look down at the deck. "Make sure you draw the coastline as we get closer."

From the cabin, there was no reply.

"The druids sail north, northwest from Hibernia until they reach the land of fire and ice," Caradoc said in a quiet, confident voice. "Then they turn due west until they sight mountains of floating ice."

"Well, is this the land of fire and ice?" Alexandros growled.

"I don't know. We are still too far out from the shore." Caradoc frowned. "But it seems unlikely. I don't think we have come far enough north. The druids say that it is twelve to fourteen days sailing from Hibernia to the land of fire and ice and that's with a favourable wind and we have only done three days."

"I am going to head towards the shore until we are certain," Alexandros growled as he turned to give Caradoc a quizzical glance. "What do you mean anyway, when you talk about a land of fire and ice?"

"You will see what I mean when we get there," the druid replied.

***

Spellbound, Marcus stood at the prow of the ship, holding on to the mast of the small foresail, as he stared at the strange coastline now barely half a mile away. The rocky cliffs rose abruptly out of the sea like stone giants, hundreds of yards high, making the Hermes look tiny and insignificant as she sailed past, Around the crags, thousands of birds circled, dived and rose, filling the sky with their loud, high-pitched shrieks, squawks and cries. The sight was magnificent and on board the Hermes no one said a word, as all of them stared at the spectacular cliffs. The green, barren land was treeless, much like the northern coast of Caledonia, with patches of snow and there was no sign of people. At the base of the cliffs, the waves surged relentlessly into the land with a dull, booming noise, sending sea water crashing and flying up into the air. Marcus grunted. The only disappointment was the coastline they had spotted seemed to be made up of a cluster of small islands and the cliffs made it impossible to land.

Abruptly Marcus tore himself away from his position and strode over to the deckhouse, where the others had gathered to stare at the strange and wondrous sight.

"Well, is this the land of fire and ice?" he said, turning to Caradoc.

The druid shook his head. "No," he muttered, "this is not it. We must keep heading north west."

Marcus glanced up at Alexandros, who was standing on the roof of the cabin, holding the tiller, but the captain had already overheard the conversation. Carefully Alexandros turned to look up at the sky.

"The wind has changed; its strong and its coming from the east, but this damned sea current is trying to push us the other way, towards the north east," Alexandros called out. "If we head due west and lose the current however, we should fly across the sea. Then maybe later we can turn north."

The captain shrugged and glanced at Marcus with a questioning look.

"Alright, let's do it, let's go with the wind," Marcus replied, "We will head due west."

***

Marcus was eating his midday meal of bread and cheese in the port cargo hold when Cunomoltus' head appeared upside down in the hatchway.

"Alexandros says you should come up on deck right away," Cunomoltus muttered in a miserable-sounding voice.

"It's not my watch yet," Marcus growled irritably.

"I think it's something else," Cunomoltus replied, as his head vanished from view.

Annoyed at having his lunch disturbed Marcus clambered up the ladder and onto the pitching and rolling deck. Jodoc and Caradoc were sitting together beside the mast repairing a tear to the fore-sail that lay spread out on the deck. They gave him a quick, disinterested glance, before returning to their work.

Around them the endless grey sea stretched from horizon to horizon. The visibility however had deteriorated and the waves and swells were more powerful than before; playing with the flimsy little ship as if she was a toy. Marcus looked up at the sky but there were no birds to be seen. Wearily he climbed up onto the deck of the cabin.

"What is it?" he said.

Alexandros had both his hands on the tiller and he was staring straight ahead. Any residual annoyance, Marcus may have felt at being disturbed, evaporated instantly, as he caught the look on the captain's face. Alexandros looked worried.

"Trouble," Alexandros said grimly.

Marcus said nothing as he waited for Alexandros to continue. Then, as he turned to look in the same direction as the captain was staring, he suddenly didn't need an explanation. Directly ahead the sky was filled with thick, dark and ominous clouds that stretched away across the whole horizon.

"Storm coming," Alexandros muttered unhappily.

Marcus said nothing as he stared at the approaching weather front. The others, down on the deck below, had not yet seen it.

"What do we do?" Marcus said, taking a deep breath.

"Normally we would head for land and seek shelter until it passes," Alexandros replied in a worried voice, "But those islands we saw are two day's sail to the east, far behind us. We will never make them before the storm hits us."

"How long do we have before we are in it?"

Alexandros shrugged, "A few hours perhaps. The wind direction has changed. It's now coming from the south west. The monster is charging towards us. We are not going to be able to escape it."

"The storm is approaching from the south west," Marcus growled, gesturing at the storm clouds," if we turn and run before the wind, it should drive us north and east. It's not ideal, but we do need a northern course. What other choice do we have? It doesn't look like we can go round it."

Alexandros sighed and for a moment he was silent.

"Yes, you are right. That is the safest thing to do. I have been caught up in storms before," he said unhappily, "in the middle sea and on voyages to India, but out here, Marcus, this ocean is the most powerful and savage I have ever seen. The gods only know how ferocious this storm is going to be. This is something I have no experience of."

Marcus was staring at the storm clouds on the horizon. Then abruptly he turned to look at Alexandros with a little smile on his lips.

"We will run before the wind," Marcus said, as he made his decision, "Everything will be alright Alexandros. When the enemy is charging straight towards you, screaming your death, you must trust in your comrades and yourself and that is exactly what we are going to do. And if that is not good enough, then the gods can go kiss my arse, when I stand before them."

Chapter Thirty-Three – Beyond the North Wind

The dark storm clouds were nearly upon them and the sea was unsettled, as the swells and moaning wind grew in ferocity. Gusts of grey, wind-driven, rain streaked across the bleak, restless, surging waves, reducing visibility to a hundred yards. The waves came crashing and slamming into the Hermes and, now and then, a wave broke over the side of the ship sending green, icy cold sea-water cascading and flooding across the deck. It was evening and the light was fading, as the Hermes headed straight into the gathering night on a north-eastern course. Soaked, Marcus and Alexandros stood on the roof of the deck house as they stoically turned to look behind them, at the approaching storm that was about to overtake them. The sea water was colder than Marcus had ever thought possible. The square, main-sail had been furled and lashed to the deck to prevent it from being lost overboard, as had the forward sail, the supparum - leaving only the two small triangular top sails. On deck, everything that could move had already been stowed or taken down into the hold, where Alexandros had instructed the rest of the crew to take shelter. The deck cargo-hatches had been battened down, as had the door to the cabin below their feet and the black, ship's cat had abandoned its usual spot.

Marcus steadied himself on the railing that ran around the roof of the deckhouse, as Alexandros gripped the tiller. Both men had a sturdy rope, a lifeline tied around their waist, that ran down onto the deck and was attached to the main mast. "In case a wave knocks you overboard" Alexandros had explained in an unconvincing voice.

"Our best chance is to sail down-wind and try and out run her," Alexandros cried out, making himself heard above the moan and roar of the wind. "It's suicide trying to sail into this monster. The gods only know how long it will last, but it can't be helped. Once we are in the storm, we go where the storm wants us to go."

And with that, Alexandros reached out to a small jug, lashed to the railing, raised it to his lips and poured a long, stream of wine into his mouth.

"Go on! Today you can have some," Alexandros yelled at Marcus, as he thrust the jug at him. "It will fill your belly and will give you courage!"

Marcus took the jug without saying a word and emptied the contents into his throat and wiped his mouth with the back of his hand.

"When this is over and we are in calmer waters," Alexandros cried, "the first thing I will do is make an offering of gratitude to Poseidon. Do you hear that master of the ocean? Your faithful servant is going to give you something big, fat and precious, if you allow him and his ship to survive."

Marcus said nothing, as he steadied himself on the pitching and rolling deck.

"The Hermes," Alexandros yelled again, as if trying to reassure himself. "She is a good little ship, sturdy and reliable and she will take what she is given. She has never let me down before. There is just one golden rule when in a storm. Do not let one of the big breaking waves hit us from the side, for they can capsize us."

"That's good advice," Marcus muttered, "if we are able to see the waves."

***

The full force of the storm hit after it had grown dark. Marcus and Alexandros hung on grimly, as the Hermes was thrown about on the violent swells and waves, pitching up and down into foaming, white-crested, eighteen-foot waves that crashed and slammed over the prow and hull, flooding the deck. In the absolute darkness around them the wind howled and roared, blasting them with ice-cold, salty spray and rain, ripping at their clothes and hoods. It was beyond anything Marcus had ever experienced and he struggled to suppress a growing panic. Soon the rain became torrential, lashing their faces and soaking everything. The ship's lantern was the first thing to be torn away, vanishing like a dying flame into the ocean, as a wave went completely over the ship. All talk became impossible as Marcus's attention was needed to keep his footing and prevent him from being swept off his feet. The Hermes groaned and creaked under the onslaught and the two, small triangular top-sails strained and pulled at their moorings as the storm blew them onwards. On the main mast any loose ropes in the rigging were flapping around like mad. Resolutely the little ship ploughed on, cresting one wave after the other and, as she ran before the storm, the Hermes slid down the sides of the huge waves, accelerating as she rode them.

In the darkness it was impossible to see in which direction they were heading, but despite that, Alexandros, with a face like stone, seemed to be able to keep the ship running straight with the wind. Tiredness, cold, hunger and even fear seemed to fall away, as Marcus stubbornly entrenched himself on the roof of deck-house; whilst around him, nature's full fury was unleashed.

Dawn brought no respite. Silently Alexandros gestured for Marcus to take the tiller, as he staggered to one side and knelt down as if in prayer. The captain looked utterly exhausted and water was streaming down from his waterproof hood and Paenula, poncho, cloak. Marcus grasped hold of the helm and felt his fingers trembling from the cold. Angrily he shook himself as the bow of the Hermes rose steeply up an eighteen-foot wave before slamming back down into the sea. In the growing light the endless white, foaming, breaking waves and huge powerful swells looked utterly alien and terrifying. Visibility was poor and the dull, grey, rain-clouds covered the entire sky and the rain had not ceased. The south-western wind howled and whined as it played with the Hermes and, as he looked up at the top of the mast, Marcus noticed that one of the small top sails, was nothing more than torn   shreds of cloth.

As the ship climbed up the next steep wave, the forward cargo-hatch suddenly opened and Caradoc's face appeared. For a moment he looked disorientated. Then he caught sight of Marcus up on the deckhouse.

"We've got a leak," the druid bellowed, "The ship is taking on water."

Marcus grunted.

"How large is it?" he yelled.

"Small," Caradoc cried out, "but the water is steadily coming in."

"Find the leak and plug it as best as you can," Marcus roared in sudden irritation. "Use whatever you have got, but that leak needs to be fixed."

Caradoc vanished from view without saying anything and the hatch quickly slammed shut above him, as a wave with an overhanging crest came slamming into the side of the ship. Marcus glanced down at Alexandros, who was still kneeling on the roof. The captain gave him an exhausted, silent nod of approval.

***

There was no time for anxiety; all Marcus's concentration was needed to control the ship. At his side, Alexandros seemed too exhausted to move and he crouched on the floor holding, on to the balustrade with both hands, his face bowed and turned to the deck. Stubbornly Marcus clutched the tiller and stared at the grey, windswept ocean beyond the bow of the Hermes. His face looked pale and his body was soaked and frozen to the bone; his eye lids red and swollen from lack of sleep and his fingers unable to stop trembling from the cold. The storm was showing no signs of abating and the struggle was turning into an endurance test. Visibility was down to fifty yards and there was no chance of choosing a course or checking their position. The storm was blowing them before it, like a sheep-dog driving sheep and they had no choice but to go with it.

An hour passed and then another. Gusts of wind tore at the remaining top sail and plucked at Marcus's clothes, as he stubbornly refused to let go of the tiller. The rain pounded the deck and the waves slammed into the ship as the Hermes climbed, crested and slid down the huge swells in endless repetition.

Towards the bow, the port cargo hatch was suddenly flung open and Jodoc's youthful face appeared. He looked pale and alarmed as his eyes adjusted to the daylight.

"We're still taking on water," he roared as he caught sight of Marcus, "But we have managed to slow the leak. We need to find land Marcus, as soon as possible. It's a complete mess down here."

Marcus said nothing as Jodoc vanished and the hatch slammed shut.

At dusk, Alexandros silently gestured for Marcus to hand him the tiller but defiantly Marcus shook his head. It was as if he had become glued to his position and, if he left it now he knew he would collapse. Alexandros was too weary to argue, as he slumped back onto the deck and closed his eyes while the Hermes pitched and rolled in the waves. Grimly Marcus kept his eyes fixed on the sea beyond the bow. He was not going to give up now. He was going to see this through to the end.

Darkness closed in around the Hermes and still the storm did not let them go. In the complete and utter dark, Marcus swiftly lost his sense of direction and only the force of the wind on his back told him in which direction to keep the bow. Up ahead, it became impossible to see where they were going and if the storm was driving them onto a shore, they would only see the danger when it was far too late.

It was sometime in the early hours, when Marcus's eyes widened in horror as he heard the distinctive cracking snap and thud of something breaking and hitting the deck. Wildly he peered into the darkness. Had the main mast broken? Had they struck something? It was impossible to tell. The Hermes felt heavy and sluggish as she surged on through the swelling sea.

With the approach of dawn, the storm finally began to slacken and the wind began to die away. Marcus swayed on his feet, as if he was drunk and half asleep, as he stared at the horizon with a stoic, exhausted expression. Beside him, Alexandros stirred and dragged himself up onto his feet and turned to peer at the sun, rising in the east. The captain said nothing, as he slowly rubbed his cheeks and then lowered his hood from over his head. The rain had stopped and. as it grew lighter, the visibility improved. At the bow of the Hermes the foremast had snapped in two and the wreckage of the rigging lay wedged and scattered across the deck.

As the swells and waves started to calm, the forward cargo hatch opened and Jodoc scrambled onto the deck. Marcus watched him as he staggered towards the deck house.

"Any idea where we are?" the young man cried out, as he looked around him.

Marcus blinked as if he had suddenly woken up.

"See for yourself," Marcus shouted back suddenly and defiantly, gesturing at the ocean, "We have sailed beyond the north wind."

Jodoc said nothing, as he sat down slowly on the deck.

"Look," Alexandros cried suddenly in an excited voice, as he raised and pointed at something on the western horizon.

Marcus turned to stare in the direction Alexandros was pointing and there just visible on the western horizon was a towering column of black smoke.

"What is it?" he muttered.

Alexandros shook his head. "I don't know, but where there is smoke there must also be land. Come on, let's find out."

***

It was late in the afternoon, when the gentle, north-westerly wind finally died away and the wind direction began to change to a more easterly one.

"Get them up out of the hold, young man," Alexandros bellowed, "I want the main-sail unfurled right away. Come on, move it."

Marcus swayed on his feet, as the Hermes slowly changed course and began to head towards the distant column of smoke. The main-sail bulged in the fresh, easterly breeze and the ship started to make good progress. On the deck, below Caradoc, Cora and Calista, sat and lay stretched out in the sunlight, too exhausted to do anything but rest. Alexandros turned to Marcus and gave him a quick, concerned glance before suddenly reaching out to grip his shoulder, with a wide grin.

"We did it," he hissed, in fierce, relieved, delight, "Thirty-nine hours without rest, lashed to the helm. You are a true sailor Marcus and you are right, we have sailed beyond the north wind."

"You said you would make an offering to Poseidon," Marcus murmured as he struggled to stay awake, "Now is the time to keep your end of the bargain."

"So I did," Alexandros muttered hastily, "So I did," he said as he quickly fished into a pocket and produced a single golden coin, which he held up to the light, before muttering a short prayer and flinging the coin into the ocean.

"You are a stingy bastard, aren't you," Marcus growled through half closed eyes.

Alexandros shrugged, grinned and then threw back his head and boomed with laughter.

As they drew closer to the huge, column of smoke hanging in the air, Marcus grunted as he caught the faint outline of land. Alexandros too, had seen it and cried out in relief, shouting the news down onto the deck.

"The smoke," Marcus said, in a tight exhausted voice - "it reminds me of something I read about the destruction of Pompei in Italia. The reports from that devastation say the mountain blew up and covered the town in red, hot, ash and stones. Could this be something similar?"

Alexandros's eyes widened with sudden realization.

"It's a volcano. You mean that smoke over there, is from a volcano?"

Marcus nodded. "What else can produce such a column of smoke?"

Alexandros turned to stare at the column of dark smoke, that hung in the air several miles high and didn't seem to be going away and as, they drew closer to the rocky coast, they caught sight of barren, snow covered mountains.

"The land of fire and ice," Alexandros exclaimed suddenly. "That makes sense. This must be the land that the druids spoke about. This must be it."

Chapter Thirty-Four – In the Land of Fire and Ice

At the base of the steep slope and the start of the scrub forest, Marcus paused and turned to look back at the Hermes, which lay anchored close to the shore. The broad, black, volcanic-beach in between him and the ship was flat and deserted but punctuated, here and there, by tall, rugged and isolated rock-stacks that formed strange shapes as they marched out to sea. It was around noon and, in the overcast sky, it was impossible to see the sun, but at least it wasn't raining today. Unlike the past six days they had spent at this anchorage. Up ahead, Cunomoltus and Jodoc were disappearing into the light forest, clutching wooden poles and a dozen or so watertight skins and, with a grunt Marcus set off after them. Above the scrub forest the green, heavily-forested hills rose steeply until they petered out into willow-tundra at their peaks. Patches of snow covered the higher elevations and, to the east the ominous pawl of black-ash and dust continued to hang in the air, several miles high. Marcus slowly shook his head, as he picked his way through the trees and stared at the incredible sight. The smoke they had thought they'd seen out on the ocean, was in fact ash-clouds and Marcus had overheard Alexandros muttering darkly about demons, that lived within the mountain and who didn't like strangers coming into their realm.

The Hermes had suffered significant damage during the storm and they had spent the past few days resting and repairing the ship. The hold of the boat had been a scene of complete chaos when Marcus had gone down to inspect the damage. Several amphorae, containing the ships stores had been smashed to pieces and they had lost half their supply of fresh, drinking-water. The bottom of the vessel had been submerged in a few inches of sea water and it had taken Alexandros three days to locate the leak, fix it and pump the water from the hold. Cautiously, Marcus glanced at Jodoc, who was leading them through the forest. He'd left Alexandros and Caradoc behind on the Hermes, where they were trying to repair the snapped and broken foremast, whilst the women tended to the torn sails and fished. But since their first exploration of the coast, a few days ago, he'd insisted that the young man accompany him, for he didn't want both father and son to remain together on the ship. The risk that they may do something or choose to abandon him on this coast was too great.

Soon the slope of the hill steepened and the scrub forest gave way to birch trees. The forest around them was silent and, since their landing, they had not seen a single person or animal except for the thousands and thousands of sea-birds that inhabited the nearby sea-cliffs. The coast they had landed on seemed uninhabited. The damp slope was littered with tumbled rocks and huge moss-covered boulders, but in the distance he could hear the roar of the waterfall. As it hove into view, Marcus paused to look up at the splendid, impressive sight. The white-water cascaded over a steep rocky ledge, hurtling down into a pool some twenty yards below. Cunomoltus and Jodoc were already clambering down the rocky path towards the pool, balancing the wooden poles and water skins over their shoulders. Jodoc was the first to reach the pool and with a happy youthful cry, he hastily stripped himself naked and taking a short run, he plunged into the water. He surfaced nearly immediately, gasping in shock at the cold. Cunomoltus and Marcus said nothing as they reached the water's edge and lowered their gear to the ground. Marcus got down onto his knees, laid Alexandros's bow and quiver, filled with arrows, on the rocks and quickly thrust his whole head into the pool as he ran his hands through his red hair and across his beard. Then he sat back up with a start, sending water droplets flying in every direction. At his side Cunomoltus had begun to fill up the watertight skins and, as each one was filled, he slid it onto the wooden pole like a fish hanging out to dry. The roar of the waterfall was deafening and, as Marcus and Cunomoltus busied themselves with filling the skins, Jodoc swam towards the spot where the water tumbled into the pool from the ledge twenty yards above, and as he did so, he raised both his arms and cried out in delight, making a great whooping noise. He was oblivious to the little glance that passed between Marcus and his brother.

When the water pouches were all filled, Marcus rose stiffly to his feet.

"Get dressed," he called out to Jodoc, who was splashing around in the pool, "We're going to take a look around in the forest. Maybe we will find something we can hunt. Then Cora can give us a feast tonight."

Obediently Jodoc did as he was told and, leaving the water-skins behind at the edge of the pool, the three of them started off into the forest. Carefully Marcus reached for Alexandros's bow and notched an arrow. Amongst the trees nothing seemed to move, apart from a few birds high up in the branches and, after half an hour of aimless wandering, disappointment started to set in.

"There is nothing here," Cunomoltus growled as he paused to stare at the trees around him. "No people, no game, nothing."

"Maybe the game is further inland," Jodoc replied.

"We'll keep looking for another hour," Marcus said, "Then we will head back."

It was a few a minutes later, when something suddenly moved in amongst the trees and Marcus came face to face with a small, fox-like creature, except that it looked unlike any fox he had ever seen. Motionless, the animal stared at the intruders. It's pure white fur and tail made it look like a cat. Then, with a sharp frustrated cry, Cunomoltus drew his knife from his belt and lunged at the Arctic fox. But the beast was way too fast for him and leapt away, before streaking off through the forest. Marcus raised his bow and released his arrow, but the arrow flew wide. Jodoc however was already sprinting after the animal, yelling and brandishing his knife. Marcus and Cunomoltus followed, dashing through the trees, but with little hope of the catching the animal and, after a while they came to a panting halt beside Jodoc who stood at the edge of a pond, staring at the rippling, steaming water!

"Look at the steam," the young man said with a frown, "The water is actually hot. Have you ever seen anything like that before?"

The three of them said nothing, as they turned to look at the steam rising from the water. Then gingerly Cunomoltus got down on his knees, stretched out his hand and carefully dipped his fingers into the water and, as he did so, he turned to look at Marcus in astonishment.

"He's right; the water is hot," Cunomoltus exclaimed.

He was just about to say something else when the center of the small lake suddenly erupted and a column of steaming, hissing water shot upwards, fully sixty feet into the air only to collapse and fall back into the lake.

The three of them cried out in shock and stumbled backwards in alarm, as seconds later another jet of water shot up high into the sky.

"What a strange place this is" Cunomoltus shouted, as he recovered from his shock. "No people, no game worth catching, pools of boiling mud, mountains that spew ash into the sky and now this; hot springs that blow water upwards, just like that sea monster we saw out on the ocean. If this is the land where the gods live, then they are welcome to it."

"I like it," Jodoc replied, staring at the geyser with a curious expression. "The Land of Fire and Ice - it's a good name."

"So maybe now is a good time to tell us what you and your father are up to?" Marcus growled as he came towards Jodoc, with an angry gleam in his eyes. "My brother here says that he overheard you on the ship, you are planning something. I want to know what it is you think you are going to be doing and I want to know right now."

"What do you mean?" Jodoc frowned, taking a step back towards the lake.

"You heard me," Marcus snapped as he advanced towards the young man, "I know who you are and I really do not like druids. Now, you either tell us what you know, or else we are going to leave you here and tell your father that you simply vanished off inland."

"What?" Jodoc stammered, as he glanced quickly at Cunomoltus, who was circling around cutting off his line of retreat. "We were just talking."

"About what?" Marcus roared angrily, as he stepped forwards and grasped hold of Jodoc's neck with his right hand.

"We were talking," Jodoc gasped as his face went red. "The druids at the trading post," he spluttered. "They don't want Romans coming there and making contact with the Hyperboreans. They have forbidden it. The druids alone control the trade. My father says that they want to keep the place a secret. They will kill anyone who is not allowed to come ashore. They will never let you land, Roman. You are sailing to a certain death."

Marcus let go of the boy's throat and Jodoc staggered backwards.

"So you and your father were happy to let us sail straight into certain death," Marcus roared. "You didn't bother about warning us? No doubt you thought that you could sail across the ocean without having to tell us your dirty, little secret until we reached our destination and it became too late for us."

"You fucking weasel," Cunomoltus cried out in sudden rage, as he kicked Jodoc in the legs from behind - sending the young man tumbling onto the ground. Cunomoltus was about to kick him again, but Marcus held up his hand.

On the ground, Jodoc groaned but said nothing as he looked down at the rocks.

"What is in the iron box that you brought onboard?" Marcus snapped.

Jodoc raised his head and looked up at him and there was a sudden defiance in the young druid's eyes.

"That I cannot tell you," he hissed, "Do what you like with me, but I will not tell you anything. Like my father said, it is none of your business."

***

As the three of them emerged from the scrub forest and set off across the black, volcanic beach towards the Hermes, the earth suddenly seemed to tremble and sway under Marcus's feet. The sensation did not last long, but it was enough to make him go pale. In front of him, Jodoc and Cunomoltus came to an alarmed unsteady halt, as they carefully balanced the wooden poles across their backs, from which the water skins hung. Slowly they turned to stare in the direction of the column of ash hanging in the sky.

"Now the very earth trembles," Cunomoltus exclaimed shaking his head, "the sooner we leave this strange land the better."

Marcus said nothing, as the three of them proceeded on across the black beach towards the Hermes. As they waded out into the surf, Marcus caught sight of Alexandros standing at the prow. The captain had raised his arm in the air. A mooring rope had been strung between the ship and the beach and the long and narrow raft made of planks ferried them across the short stretch of water to the side of the ship. As the precious fresh water-skins were hoisted aboard, Marcus clambered up the rope netting and over the side of the hull.

"Everything alright, you were gone a long time?" Alexandros said, as he eyed Marcus warily. Marcus nodded as he glanced in Caradoc's direction. The druid however, did not seem to notice the annoyed, angry look that Marcus gave him.

"Well we managed to repair the foremast," Alexandros said, taking a deep sigh, "It's not perfect but it should hold for a while."

"Then we are ready to sail," Marcus replied, turning to look at the bow.

"Yes and no," Alexandros said, "The ship has been repaired but if we want to head west, then the wind is not favourable. We are going to have to wait until the wind direction changes."

"So we wait," Marcus growled.

Alexandros nodded, "I'm afraid so."

"From the Land of Fire and Ice we sail due west, until we sight the floating mountains of ice," Caradoc said, as he came towards Marcus and Alexandros. "After that we sail towards the south west until we sight land."

"You mean Hyperborea?" Alexandros, said, turning to the druid.

"Yes," Caradoc nodded as he carefully glanced at Marcus, "Hyperborea is the name you Romans have given it, but the name should apply to all the land beyond the known world. We make no distinction. It's a whole new world."

"And when we reach the trading post," Marcus growled, "what will we do then? Will you know what to look for?"

"Yes," Caradoc replied, "I will recognize the native village, when I see it. The people who live there are called the Penawapskewi.

The trading post is on a promontory that juts out into the ocean. There is a good beach where we can land. Once I see it, I will guide us in."

"I am sure you will," Marcus said, in a cold, bitter voice. He was about to say something else when the calm was suddenly shattered by an enormous, rumbling, cracking, explosion that seemed to shake the ship. Marcus turned to stare in the direction of the ash cloud and gasped. Along the shore, many miles away a plume of smoke and debris was hurtling upwards, as the entire top of a mountain seemed to have vanished in a billowing dust cloud.

"Poseidon's left ball!" Alexandros cried out in shock, as he too, stared at the spectacular explosion, "Have you ever seen anything like that boys? I think that is a sign from the gods, telling us that they want us to leave."

Chapter Thirty-Five – The Divided Crew

The Hermes bobbed up and down on the choppy swells as the easterly wind drove them further out into the ocean. It was late in the afternoon and it was Marcus' watch and he stood clutching the tiller on the top of the deckhouse and turned to look behind him at the receding coastline. The land of fire and ice was behind them and the dull sky was overcast, making it hard to spot the sun. For a day and a night, after leaving their anchorage, they had proceeded westwards, hugging the coast. The volcanic eruption had continued to cover everything in a fine layer of dust and ash that had gone on almost non-stop and the crew had been constantly busy, cleaning the decks. At the bow of the ship Caradoc and Jodoc were conversing in low voices. Marcus glared at them with barely concealed hostility. The two men were too far away for Marcus to hear what they were saying. But ever since Jodoc's reluctant revelation, that the druids would kill them, if they knew who they were and tried to land in Hyperborea, the tension between him and them had been rising. It had manifested itself in silent, hostile glances, muttered curses and a growing reluctance to talk to each other. Marcus and Cunomoltus had started to carry their swords and knives with them and, on occasions Marcus had caught Jodoc watching him with a bitter, aggressive look. Calista too had started to give Marcus worried, nervous glances, as if the growing divide and tension was forcing the crew to silently choose sides.

The black, ship's cat lay in its usual position, its head resting on its paws and at Marcus's side, Cunomoltus was sitting on the deck, his back resting against the railing, as he sharpened his knife on a stone he had picked up from the land of fire and ice. He looked bored.

"So what are we going to do when we reach this trading post" Cunomoltus muttered as he laid down his knife and glanced in the druid's direction. "If Caradoc is telling the truth and there are a dozen or so druids at this place, together with hundreds of natives, then we won't stand a chance at making land fall. They will slaughter us."

Marcus's eyes were fixed on Caradoc and his son. Then slowly he shifted the weight on his feet and sighed.

"I don't know," he muttered. "I don't have a plan."

***

Dawn found the Hermes utterly alone and becalmed on the ocean, wallowing in the gentle swell. The wind had slackened until it was nearly still, and against the mast, the lackluster; red square sail flapped and billowed as the ship drifted aimlessly and without power. Marcus stood beside the door to the deckhouse as he looked up at the heavily overcast sky and from inside the cabin, he could hear the two women talking to each other in raised, annoyed and argumentative voices as they prepared breakfast. Earlier, Cora had informed them, that certain supplies were running low and in response Cunomoltus had joked that they should eat the cat, but his comments had sent Calista into a fuming rage.

"What should we do?" Marcus said, turning to look up at Alexandros, who was standing at the tiller.

The captain shrugged. "What can we do" the Greek sailor replied sourly, "There is no wind. We will just have to wait until it returns."

Marcus grunted and turned his attention back to the sea. Visibility was poor and it was impossible to say with any accuracy where the sun was in the sky, but it was not raining and there was no sign of a storm building.

He had just finished eating his cold porridge, when standing beside the edge of the vessel, a spout of water shot high up into the sky and an enormous black beast emerged from the depths, before plunging back down into the swell. Marcus stared at it in wonder as the sea monster resurfaced, before sinking below the waves, its giant tail fin the last bit to disappear. It looked like the same beast that they had encountered earlier on in their voyage. A few yards away, Cunomoltus's face went pale and he reached out to steady himself against the side of the ship but, as he stared at the whale, he managed to stay on his feet.

"See, it's not a demon from the depths," Marcus called out to his brother. "It's just an animal, coming to see who we are."

Cunomoltus did not reply as he stared at the foaming disturbed water, into which the beast had vanished.

The hours followed one after the other and still the wind did not come. The crew sat around in pensive, bored silence, scattered across the deck, cabin and cargo hold and there was little conversation, as the ship bobbed up and down, slowly drifting with the current. Around them the ocean stretched away, a desolate, watery wilderness that vanished from view into the dull, grey, overcast sky.

Wearily Marcus clambered up the ladder and onto the deckhouse roof, where Alexandros stood clutching the tiller. The captain gave him a cautious glance and Marcus noticed a small jug of wine at the man's feet.

"When the wind returns," Marcus said, looking up at the sky, "how will we know from which direction it is coming? In this weather, I can't see the sun. We need to head due west."

Alexandros nodded and reached for the jug of wine at his feet.

"I told you before," he said gruffly, "I have a few tricks that I can employ. Have some faith in your captain."

"What tricks?" Marcus replied, glancing at the jug of wine in disapproval.

"I will use the sunstone," Alexandros muttered, as he took a swig from the jug and burped, "It will allow me to see the position of the sun in the sky, even when it is overcast like it is today."

"What's a sunstone" Marcus frowned.

"It's a sort of crystal stone," Alexandros growled, "You hold it up to the sky and move it around until one part shines brighter than the other and from that you can tell the position of the sun, even when everything is overcast. I got it from a German in Carthage, years ago."

"And it works?"

"Of course it works," Alexandros snapped, "I wouldn't be telling you about it otherwise. I will give you a demonstration later."

Marcus was silent as he turned to look out across the ocean. Then, slowly he bent down, picked up the small jug of wine and flung it overboard.

"I said that there would be no drinking whilst we are at sea," he growled in an annoyed voice, as he started to climb down the ladder onto the deck below.

***

Towards dusk the wind finally began to pick up, but the weather remained overcast and, as the gloom deepened, there was no sign of the moon or the stars. Marcus, clutching the strange, crystal-like sunstone in his hand, stood beside Alexandros at the tiller on the deckhouse, as the Hermes surged across the waves; her square sail and rigging bulging in the cold, north-eastern breeze. The two of them had not said a word to each other since the captain had showed Marcus, much to his amazement, how the sunstone was able to determine the position of the sun on a cloudy day. Alexandros however, was in a bad mood as he stared up at the sky, searching in vain for the stars.

"These mountains of floating ice that Caradoc spoke about," Marcus muttered at last, as he steadied himself on the tilting, creaking deck, "they sound dangerous. If we were to hit one of them, it could surely sink the ship. Should we not post a permanent watch up in the mast or on the bow? We have a spare lantern which will provide us with some light."

"Then do it," Alexandros growled, in an unhelpful voice.

"Alright," Marcus grunted, "Cunomoltus will take the first watch, followed by the others at regular intervals. Everyone will do their bit."

"Good," Alexandros snapped in a sharp voice. "But I can't guarantee we are going in the right direction. Without the stars to guide me, we could be heading anywhere. When it grows light again I will release a raven."

"You mean those birds you keep in a cage, in the cargo hold?"

Alexandros nodded, with a gloomy look, "Another one of my tricks," he said sourly. "I starve the birds and then, when I need to know in which direction land is, I release them and carefully watch the direction in which they fly. The birds will immediately head for land and all we have to do is follow them."

"What happens if they don't fly anywhere?" Marcus replied.

"Then we are still too far out and you have wasted a raven, for you will never catch it again," Alexandros snapped unhappily.

***

That night the sea remained calm, as they headed westwards into the darkness with a steady wind at their backs. Marcus was alone at the tiller, as the bow of the Hermes plunged and rose through the swells and waves. Before leaving his watch Alexandros had rigged the spare lantern to the foremast and its dim, reddish glow looked puny and insignificant as it gently swayed to and fro, in the utter and complete darkness that surrounded them. The noise of the swells and waves striking the ship and the gentle moaning of the easterly wind in the sails, was the only noise that filled the night. Somewhere near the bow, Cunomoltus had taken the first iceberg watch and even though he would be able to hardly see anything, it made Marcus feel better knowing he was there.

Slowly the hours passed and one by one the crew came up on deck to take their turn on ice watch, but nothing was sighted and, as the darkness faded and the dawn light started to grow, there was no sign of any mountains of floating ice. Wearily, Marcus clutched the tiller, keeping the wind in the sails as the Hermes ploughed on through the endless waves. The movement of the ship had become so familiar now, that he hardly noticed it anymore. Suddenly he felt something brush against his shin and, as he looked down, he saw that it was the black cat. The animal was rubbing itself against his leg as it looked up at him, opening its mouth in a silent meow.

Cunomoltus came clambering up the ladder and silently handed Marcus a cup of water, a small, smoked and dried fish and some stale bread covered in olive oil. For a while the two of them were silent, as Marcus munched on his breakfast and peered out across the vast ocean with red-rimmed, tired looking eyes.

"I want to apologize," Cunomoltus said suddenly, turning towards Marcus with a sincere look, "about my recent behaviour and lack of courage earlier on in the voyage. I let you down and I made a fool of myself. It won't happen again. But by all the gods, Marcus, the things I have seen and witnessed on this journey so far: I would never have experienced anything like this, if I hadn't set out to find you. So thank you. These past few weeks have been most extraordinary."

Marcus nodded, as he broke off a little piece of fish, stooped and fed it to the cat who was brushing up against his legs.

"We need to stick together," Marcus replied, "and I need you to stay sharp. For the moment we all need each other on this ship, but when we reach the trading post all that will change. The druids won't care if we are killed. Once we reach our destination they will have the advantage. They may even attack us, so we need to be on guard."

"Calista is with the druids," Cunomoltus growled, "but I am not sure about Alexandros and Cora. They don't seem to care and Alexandros has started to drink again. I can smell it on his breath."

Marcus nodded again as he reached down to ruffle the head of the black, ship's cat.

"Well, we have made one ally here," he said with a gentle smile, as he looked down at the purring beast.

***

Around noon Alexandros called out to Marcus to take over the tiller, as he scrambled down the ladder and vanished down one of the forward cargo hatches. A few moments later he reappeared, carrying the little, iron cage containing the three ravens. Marcus clutching the tiller, watched him, as the captain set the cage down beside the main mast, opened it and grabbed hold of one of the birds with both hands. Around him, the crew paused to look at what he was doing. Marcus frowned as for a moment it seemed as if Alexandros was saying something to the black raven cooped up in his hands. Then, with a dramatic gesture, the captain raised his arms and released the bird. The raven sprang into the air, fluttered around wildly and then soared up into the sky, circled the ship a couple of times and then flew away towards the east. On the deck Alexandros's face darkened as he watched the raven vanish from view. The captain was cursing when he came climbing up the ladder onto the deckhouse roof.

"Fucking bird is flying back to the land of fire and ice," Alexandros growled, as he took the tiller from Marcus, "We have wasted a bird."

"We should release another, just before it goes dark," Marcus said.

"They're my birds," Alexandros snapped, "and I will decide when we release them."

"And we hired you to take us across the ocean," Cunomoltus said sharply, "So you will remember for whom you are working."

The captain gave Cunomoltus a dark, annoyed glance but said nothing and Marcus gestured at Cunomoltus to leave the man alone.

It was late in the afternoon when the sea mist appeared. Marcus stood at the bow of the ship on iceberg watch, as the Hermes bobbed up and down in the swell. The fog closed in rapidly and soon visibility was down to fifty yards. In the eerie, damp air the wind seemed to slacken and the Hermes slid along, like a ghost, silently moving across the waves. Soon the mist thickened and visibility became twenty yards. The sea was calm and the noise of the wind seemed to fade away, as a strange, deathly silence took over, that seemed to affect everyone on board. Marcus glanced back at his brother, who was resting against the main mast. Cunomoltus grinned as he gestured at the fog.

"Have you ever seen anything like this before" he called out.

After a while the visibility started to improve and Marcus was rubbing his tired eyes with his hand, when to port, a hundred yards away, a huge iceberg slowly loomed up out of the mist. Marcus mouth fell open in shock and, for a moment he stood frozen to the deck unable to act. The pure-white mountain of ice was enormous, several hundred feet high, as its edges disappeared off into the fog.

"Ice, Ice, to port," he yelled as he found his voice and turned in the direction of the deck house.

Alexandros, standing at the tiller, had also seen the iceberg and was already frantically maneuvering the Hermes away from the danger. Slowly, ever so slowly, the ship started to change course as the iceberg drew closer. Anxiously, Marcus stared up at the floating mountain as the ice towered above the flimsy, brown wooden boat. Then they were past it and moving away and, as they did, he heaved a great sigh of relief. As they sailed away,Marcus turned to look back at the floating monster with wide disbelieving eyes. He had been expecting small chunks of ice, not huge monsters like this, and now that they were clear of it, the mountain of pure- white ice was a truly stunning sight.

As the visibility improved and the mist faded, Marcus spotted more white icebergs wallowing in the dark sea. The crew was silent as everyone came up on deck to stare at the strange, majestic, white shapes drifting in the calm sea and, as they stared at the fantastic sight, Marcus suddenly noticed a lone, white bear, trapped on one of the ice flows. The silent polar bear, marooned on top of the berg, stared across at the Hermes, as they sailed past. The scattered mountains of ice all seemed to be drifting south on the current but, on the horizon, there was still no sign of land.

As his iceberg watch came to an end, Marcus clambered up onto the roof of the deckhouse and took over the tiller from Alexandros. Night was approaching and in the crystal-clear and cold evening sky, the first of the stars had already appeared.

"Time to release that raven, captain," Marcus said as he laid a hand on Alexandros's shoulder. "And I want two people on iceberg watch tonight. You've seen the size of those monsters. I don't want to hit one of them."

"Alright," Alexandros growled, as he slipped free from Marcus's grasp and descended down onto the deck. A few moments later, he re-appeared with the birdcage and grasping hold of a raven, he quickly flung it up into the air. As the bird fluttered about around the ship, all eyes turned to watch it. Then, with a high-pitched shriek, the raven flew upwards and turned west towards the setting sun.

"That way," Alexandros cried pointing to the west, "Hyperborea is that way."

Chapter Thirty-Six – The Secret of the Iron Box

The coast of Greenland looked stunning. Dark, treeless mountains, covered in snow patches, rose almost vertically up from the sea. Along the fjords that cut into the land, huge glaciers seemed to have discharged large blocks of their ice into the placid, ghostly blue ocean. Hundreds of floating pieces of pure-white ice clogged the coast and fjords, forming a barrier to any ship that wished to try to make landfall. Slowly the Hermes crept south through the calm, quiet Arctic waters, like a thief stealing through a deserted palace. The May sun hung high above the horizon and in the bright afternoon light, Marcus could see for miles. Along the side of the ship, the alien, yet utterly beautiful landscape had silenced the entire crew, as they all stared in wonder at the majestic, ice bound land. There was no sign of human habitation, no smoke or ships; just a deadly silence and the enormous white ice sheets floating in the still, blue water.

A strong ocean current seemed to be pushing the ship south and as Marcus started his watch at the tiller, a huge iceberg, the size of the new Forum in Londinium, slowly rolled over in the blue water sending a large tidal wave surging towards the Hermes. Reacting quickly, Marcus turned the ship's bow into the wave and, as the wave struck, the ship rose up at a crazy angle, almost out of the water, before slapping back down into the sea with a crash. Amongst the ice flows a troop of strange, streamlined animals with grey fur, whiskers and four limbs ending in flippers, lay resting on the ice. Close by, Marcus suddenly caught sight of a Narwhal, its long, straight tusk protruding from the water. Marcus shook his head in amazement as Cunomoltus clambered up onto the roof and turned to stare at the desolate, ice covered coast. On the deck below, Caradoc had found himself a spot beside the main mast and was busy writing his journal, scratching the words onto thin sheaves of wood pausing now and then to stare at the land and the sea. There was however no sign of Alexandros or his wife and Marcus had begun to wonder whether the captain was avoiding him on purpose.

Suddenly as he stood staring out across the ice flows Cunomoltus said very seriously, "The voices in my head spoke to me again yesterday. They are telling me that I should stick close to you, Marcus. They told me to watch your back. So that is what I am going to do."

Marcus glanced at the knife stuffed into Cunomoltus's belt, which was just visible under his Paenula. Then he nodded. The growing divide amongst the crew and the prospect of being attacked and killed, the moment they came ashore in Hyperborea was bringing him and Cunomoltus closer together and Marcus had, for the first time, felt some genuine affection for him.

"I have a plan for when we reach the trading post," Marcus said, lowering his voice and turning to Cunomoltus. "But first we are going to find out what is inside that precious iron box, the druids guard so fiercely. That box contains the reason why they are making this journey. You were right. So here is what we are going to do. I will distract both the druids long enough for you to slip into their cargo hold and take the box. When you come back up on deck with it, I want you to threaten to throw it overboard, unless they tell us what is inside."

Cunomoltus stood looking down at the deck as he listened. Then slowly he looked up at Marcus and a broad, delighted grin cracked across his lips.

"When?" he hissed.

"Tomorrow morning. Just after Alexandros has taken the tiller," Marcus growled, as he turned to stare at Caradoc, sitting beside the main mast.

***

Alexandros was unusually quiet as he took over the tiller at first light, which felt like it was in the middle of the night. To starboard the bleak, desolate, snow-covered mountains and fjords stretched away south to the horizon and the majestic, floating ice was everywhere. The Hermes had made good progress throughout the very short night, helped by the strong, coastal current, as the ship had sailed southwards along the coast. Now at dawn, the clear Arctic air was silent, the sea calm and placid and the views amazing. Marcus said nothing, as he climbed down onto the deck and made eye-contact with Cunomoltus. Jodoc was up at the bow, watching out for icebergs but there was no sign of Caradoc.

"Where is your father" Marcus called out, as he strode towards Jodoc. "I need to speak to both of you right now."

"He's down in the hold, resting," Jodoc replied in a sour voice, without bothering to look round.

"Go and fetch him," Marcus snapped, "I will take over your watch until you are both here. It's urgent."

Reluctantly, Jodoc turned round and glared at Marcus. Then without a word, he brushed past Marcus and vanished down the port cargo hatch. Marcus glanced at Cunomoltus, who was lounging around beside the deckhouse, pretending to be interested in the black ship's cat. When the two druids reappeared, Caradoc looked tired and annoyed.

"What do you want? What is so urgent that you disturb my sleep?" Caradoc growled, as Marcus retreated to the prow of the ship, drawing the two men after him. Marcus said nothing as he saw Cunomoltus silently cross the deck behind the druids backs and vanish down into the hold.

"When we reach the trading post," Marcus said glaring, at the two druids. "I want you both to vouch for me and my brother. I want you to go ashore and talk to the druids and convince them not to attack and kill us."

289

Caradoc's eyes narrowed and his face darkened.

"The druids do not compromise," Caradoc said sharply, "Their laws are clear, but yes maybe they will listen to me if I speak to them. They know me and I am trusted, but if I do this for you, then I want something in return."

"What's that?" Marcus replied, raising his eyebrows.

"You give up on this feud that you seem to have with Emogene," Caradoc snapped, raising his chin, "You leave her alone and you sail home at the first opportunity."

Marcus paused, as he seemed to consider the offer. Then behind the druids, Cunomoltus's head popped up from the hatchway. His brother gave him a quick disappointed shake of his head, before clambering up onto deck without the iron box. Marcus frowned and turned to look down at the deck.

"I can't make that promise," he said, "Emogene has something that means the world to me and I am not leaving until I have it."

"Whatever," Caradoc growled, shaking his head in sudden boredom, as he turned and headed back towards the cargo hatch.

Idly, Marcus strolled over to the side of the ship and stared out across the sea as Cunomoltus came to stand beside him.

"What happened" Marcus muttered.

"They have chained the damned box to a bulkhead with an iron chain," Cunomoltus hissed. "The only way you are going to break that, is with a hammer and chisel, but everyone is going to hear the noise and it's going to take a while."

"Alexandros keeps an axe in the deck house," Marcus murmured. "This afternoon before I take my watch on the deckhouse we will try again."

290

"But the noise," Cunomoltus whispered, "It's going to loud. They will hear me."

"Don't worry," Marcus muttered, "I will handle them. Just get the axe and break the chain and stick to the plan."

***

It was nearly dusk, the Hermes bobbed up and down on the gentle swell as the current and gentle wind pushed them southwards. The red, square main-sail looked oddly out of place in this bleak, white, grey and dark-blue world. The torrent of broken pieces of sea ice that littered the calm, quiet waters seemed to be following them and, now and then, Marcus caught a glimpse of green patches on the distant mountains. On the deck below, Cora was watching the rugged, desolate coast as she drew a map, inset with drawings of the beautiful and exotic animals, fjords and icebergs she had seen. Beside her, Caradoc was busy writing notes into his diary. Cunomoltus was on ice-watch at the bow of the ship and there was no sign of the young lovers, Jodoc and Calista. Marcus turned to glance at Alexandros who was holding the tiller but the captain seemed in no mood to have a conversation. Up ahead, the coastline seemed to peter out into a ragged, messy headland that jutted out into the ocean and, as they slowly made their way along the coast, Marcus could see that the land was deeply indented, by numerous fjords and steep-sided valleys and broken up into small, low-lying islands, rocks, inlets and sea ice. Beyond the tip of the last island, the coast seemed to turn away in a northwesterly direction and, to the south there was nothing but the open sea.

"Caradoc says we must head south-west until we sight Hyperborea," Alexandros said suddenly in a stoic voice, as he gazed southwards. "He says that the journey south will be difficult. There are strong, sea currents and it is likely we shall encounter storms and more sea-ice. When we reach Hyperborea, he says that we should follow the coast south until we come to a bay, from which a wide river leads inland. The trading post is located on a headland, jutting out into the sea. Caradoc says he will recognize it and show us where to land."

"Seems like you have been spending some time with him," Marcus replied.

"He says he knows the way," Alexandros grunted, "and he has interesting stories to tell. There is no harm in listening to that."

Marcus remained silent as he watched Cunomoltus and Caradoc swap places at the bow, as Cunomoltus' ice-watch shift ended. The two men passed each other in silence and without a glance. As he reached the deckhouse, Cunomoltus slipped inside and when he finally reappeared, he caught Marcus's eye and nodded, clutching something under his cloak. Leaving Alexandros at the tiller, Marcus descended onto the deck and moved towards the opened, cargo hatch, calling out for Jodoc to come up onto deck. At the bow, Caradoc turned to see what was going on, but he did not leave his post.

When Jodoc finally appeared, he looked annoyed. Marcus beckoned him to follow, as he made his way forwards to where Caradoc was staring out across the sea. When he had both men with him at the prow of the ship, Marcus scratched his beard and calmly turned to Caradoc.

"I have another proposal for you," he said sharply, "When we reach the trading post you will go ashore and reason with the druids. You will arrange that we can land without being attacked and, in exchange I promise you that, after I have retrieved what belongs to me, I will not kill Emogene."

Caradoc's lips curled in contempt.

"That's not much of a trade," he growled, "For if the druids do not permit you to land, then you won't be getting anywhere near Emogene anyway."

"There is an alternative," Marcus said, as a cold, little smile appeared on his lips and he took a step backwards.

Caradoc was about to say something, when a dull metallic banging noise rang out. It was quickly followed by another and then another. Startled, the druids turned to stare in the direction from which the noise was coming. Down in the cargo hold the hammering noise continued, rising in intensity, as blow followed blow in rapid succession. At the bow, Caradoc's face suddenly went pale and he whipped round to stare at Marcus.

"What do you think you are doing" he cried out in alarm.

At his side Jodoc's eyes widened, as he realised what was going on.

"They are going after the iron box," he cried out as impulsively he rushed towards the cargo hatch but Marcus had been anticipating the move and as the young man moved forwards, the pommel of Marcus's sword punched into Jodoc's face, sending him staggering backwards with a howl. Blood came pouring out of his nose as Marcus flipped his sword over and raised it menacingly into the air.

"The alternative," he cried raising his voice, "is that I cut both your throats here and now and feed your corpses to the monsters of the sea. Either way, we are going to land in Hyperborea without any trouble. Am I making myself clear?"

Down in the cargo hold the metallic hammering continued. Then abruptly it ended. Silence descended across the Hermes and the only noise was the smacking of the waves against the bow. Clutching his forehead with one hand, Jodoc drew a knife from his belt with his other hand, but before he could make a move, Caradoc laid a restraining hand on his son's shoulder.

"No, son, put it away," the older man muttered. "This man is a killer."

Marcus looked deadly serious, as he calmly watched the two men cornered against the bow. Behind him, he sensed movement and, risking a quick glance over his shoulder, he saw Cunomoltus coming up from the hold, clutching the small, iron box in his hands. His brother gave him a quick, triumphant nod.

"I want to know what is inside that box." Marcus growled, turning to the druids, "and if you refuse to tell me, then Cunonmaltus will throw it overboard. He's rather accident prone, my brother, so if you value the box, then you had better start talking right now."

As if to re-enforce the message, Cunomoltus staggered across to the edge of the ship and raised the box up into the air. At the bow, Jodoc howled in a sudden mixture of rage and helplessness, as he clutched his blood soaked face. At his side, his father looked pale.

"It's a book;" Caradoc exclaimed suddenly, "The box contains a book. It is an account written by myself and it records seven hundred years of the history of the Briton tribes, from the time before the coming of Rome. It is unique, a treasure, a true gift, for there are only two such copies in existence. Please do not throw it overboard. I have spent years researching and writing it. It is my life's work."

"A book" Marcus frowned.

Caradoc nodded tensely, his eyes glued onto the iron box in Cunomoltus' hands.

"The book records, for the first time ever, in the written word, the history of my people. Everything is in there," Caradoc cried out, in a voice laden with growing emotion. "Seven hundred years of history, the entire collective memory of the druids. My son and I are taking it to the trading post in Hyperborea because it will be safe there. That is why the druids maintain the trading post. That is its main purpose. That's why the druids set off across the ocean and discovered Hyperborea. The land beyond the sea is a refuge; a safe haven, far away from the greedy, destructive clutches of Rome. That is why you will not be welcome. That is why the druids will kill you when they find out who you are. They don't want you there and there is nothing you can do about it, Roman."

"What's this," a deep voice suddenly boomed from the roof of the deckhouse. "Are you saying that you already know that I and my ship are going to get a hostile reception when we reach our destination and you didn't bother telling me" Alexandros roared in a furious voice.

Chapter Thirty-Seven – The Messenger of the gods

Alexandros shook his fist at the sky and a long, stream of curses escaped from his mouth as the Hermes wallowed ungraciously in the swell, its red, square sail flapping uselessly in the breeze. For several days the little ship had tried to head south-west and, on each occasion the contrary winds and a powerful sea-current had driven them back and further to the north.

"The gods don't want us to sail any further," Alexandros cried out angrily, his face filled with disgust, as he clutched the tiller. Marcus stood beside him, looking patient as he idly studied the crystal, sunstone in his hand. Around them the swells and waves stretched to the horizon, an alien, watery-world that had become a familiar view. At the bow, Cunomoltus was watching out for floating ice and there was no sign of the two druids. Caradoc and Jodoc had stopped talking to anyone and had started taking their meals separately from the crew, after the confrontation over the iron box. The confrontation and Caradoc's admission, that he knew about the danger the ship would face upon arrival, had firmly brought Alexandros and Cora over into Marcus' camp. Alexandros' rage had lasted two days, in which time he'd had to be restrained from throwing Caradoc overboard. Only Calista, his daughter had not seemed to waver in her affections for Jodoc.

With a weary sigh Marcus turned his attention towards the forward cargo-hatch. He had decided to keep hold of the iron box as insurance, a negotiating tool. It clearly meant something to Caradoc.

"The wind will change, we just need to be patient," Marcus said, in a quiet voice. "Like you said once, it doesn't like to be hurried."

Alexandros shook his head and muttered something under his breath.

"We can't wallow out here forever, Cora says that the supplies are running low. We need to find land soon or give up and go home."

"We're not going back until I have what I came for," Marcus said.

"I know, I know," Alexandros replied wearily, "But I don't intend to die out here and if we have nothing to eat and drink, we die."

"Our luck will change," Marcus said, turning to glance at the captain and giving him a little, encouraging smile.

"Why don't you ask that arsehole" Alexandros growled, gesturing at Caradoc who was clambering up out of the hold. "He seems to know everything."

Marcus glanced at Caradoc. For a moment, the druid stood looking around him. Then slowly his head turned and his eyes fixed onto Marcus.

"You and I need to talk," the druid called out, as he advanced towards the deckhouse.

"He wants to talk," Alexandros sneered. "Now he wants to talk."

Without saying a word, Marcus climbed down onto the deck and turned to face Caradoc. The druid seemed to have aged overnight and one of his hands was trembling, yet there was still determination and strength in his eyes.

"What is it?" Marcus growled.

Caradoc took his time in answering.

"I knew who you were from the first moment I saw you, Roman," Caradoc hissed. "I spent most of my life fighting and hiding from men like you. You are the slave-master of Rome, sent to enslave us. You think you are a free man, you think you are

297

spreading a civilisation, but you are just a puppet for the forces that have always governed this world."

"Is that it," Marcus said calmly. "Are you just going to stand here and insult me?"

"No," Caradoc said shaking his head, "I came here because I know you are going to kill me before this journey is done. That's what you do. You are a killer. You think I am going to betray you to the druids and maybe I will. So it makes sense to kill me when you no longer need me."

"It has crossed my mind," Marcus replied.

Caradoc looked down at the deck. "Then I must make this appeal to you," he said in a quiet voice; "if you can find the wisdom and love in your heart; if such a thing is possible. Do with me what you like, but spare my son. Jodoc is still young, he is impulsive, but he has a good heart."

Caradoc looked up at Marcus and there was a sudden fanatical, gleam in his eyes. "The book must survive at all costs," he gasped. "There is nothing more important than this. Rome has conquered. The druids are few in number now and if they die then the history of the Briton tribes, before the time of Rome, dies with them. That is why I wrote it down. This is my life's work. Don't let this happen, I beg you. Don't leave the history of my people to be written by Romans. If we forget who we were, we lose everything."

Marcus was staring at Caradoc with a hard look and, for a long moment he said nothing. Then he stirred.

"Nothing will happen to your book, as long as you co-operate," he growled. "But betray me or this ship and it will go overboard together with your bodies."

***

"Reduce sail and tie yourself on," Alexandros shouted at Marcus, as he cast an anxious glance at the sea. On the horizon the dark storm clouds were drawing closer and the swells and waves were growing in strength and height, playing and tossing the little ship around, as if she were mere flotsam. It was morning and the Hermes was drifting south after having finally broken out of the strong sea current, that was trying to drag them north. The moment of joy, once they'd realised they had finally managed to get away, had been short-lived as they had sighted the rapidly approaching storm bearing down on them from the north.

Marcus grimaced as he fastened his safety rope around the mast and then hurried over the wildly-pitching and slanting deck, towards the cabin. Cora was watching him from the doorway of the deckhouse, steadying herself against the doorway. She gave him an unhappy look.

"The good news is that the monster is coming at us from the north," Alexandros yelled, above the howl and shriek of the wind. "We will run before her, like we did the last time."

Marcus said nothing as he pulled the hood of his Paenula over his head and checked the rope, tied around his waist.

At the bow, the ship plunged down a huge wave, before rising up the next and Marcus had to make a grab for the railing to steady himself. On the mast in front of them, the main sail had been furled and only the small, top sails were straining in the wind and above them, at the very top of the mast, the flag carrying the face of Hermes, was fluttering madly in the wind. Marcus stared at it, as the ship went surging over the waves, sending white, salty spray and seawater flying and racing over the deck.

"Gods, she is a wild one," Alexandros shouted, as he stood looking behind him. "Look at those clouds. The gods don't want us here, Marcus. I think I have got the message."

"Hermes is the messenger of the gods," Marcus shouted, "They will let us pass. We are going to make it."

From the rapidly, darkening sky, the rain found the Hermes and came hurtling down, striking and plastering the ship and the ocean alike, with rain drops that jumped back up into the air. Marcus took a deep breath, as he turned to stare at the raging, boiling sea around him. The visibility was reducing rapidly and the swells were starting to become frightening, as they grew in size and power. On the deck below them, everything that could move had been taken below and the two, forward hatches had been sealed, so as to prevent sea-water from getting into the hold.

Marcus grimaced as a wave struck the stern of the ship, drenching him and Alexandros with icy-cold seawater.

"Remember to keep her bow in line with the waves," Alexandros roared. "If we are hit broadside by one of those monsters, they will capsize the ship."

Marcus needed no reminding as he peered at the worsening weather. There was no chance of finding a coast along which to shelter. They were all alone in the midst of the ocean, with no possibility of rescue if things went wrong. All they could do was try and ride out the storm and hope for the best. Wrenching his eyes from the clouds, Marcus glanced at Alexandros. The captain stood holding the tiller, a hard, determined look plastered across his face, as he focussed all his concentration on the ship and the heaving, surging ocean.

"She is a good ship and she has a fine captain," Marcus cried out, trying to sound encouraging.

"There is no better ship than the Hermes," Alexandros yelled in a voice suddenly filled with fierce pride. "She will see us through this. And if we don't make it, then what a ride, Marcus, what a ride we've had. I would not miss this moment for the world."

The wind came shrieking and howling, whipping up the waves and sending spray flying across the deck. Marcus tightened the hood of his dark, waterproof Paenula over his head, as the Hermes lurched up a steep, white-crested wave before plunging back down into the swell.

"Is this all you have got, Poseidon," Alexandros roared, as if he had gone mad. "Is this all you can throw against us?"

Marcus glanced quickly at the captain and then reached up and grasped his shoulder. There was a madness blazing from Alexandros's eyes.

"That's enough," he cried in alarm, "There is no need to antagonise the gods."

Another wave struck the ship, sending a sheet of water hurtling right over the deckhouse and nearly knocking both men off their feet. Alexandros was laughing now. Then he started shouting at the storm clouds in his native Greek. Marcus gasped as the entire bow of the Hermes disappeared into a wave, before reappearing as the ship rose up at a steep angle. There was no time to check on Alexandros, for all Marcus' attention was needed to just keep standing on the wildly- slanting and moving deck.

Onwards into the storm the little ship plunged and, as the hours started to pass, the weather and seas around them only seemed to grow in ferocity. It was late in the afternoon when a flash of lightning rent the sky, followed moments later by a deep rolling crack of thunder that was clearly audible above the shrieking, moaning wind and the crash of breaking waves. Marcus's face went pale, as he stared at the spot where he'd seen the lightning vanish into the ocean. Then close by, another strike forked through the sky, stabbing the ocean with deadly, pinpoint accuracy; its intense, bright light vanishing in an instant. The lightning was followed nearly instantaneously by another, huge crack of thunder. Marcus raised his head to look up at the ferocious rain pelting the ship and the ocean, as he silently cursed Alexandros for bringing upon them the wrath of the ocean spirits.

The next moment there was a very loud bang, followed by a tearing, shattering noise and from the mast, long shards and splinters of wood went hurtling in every direction. Beside Marcus, Alexandros screamed out in pain, let go of the tiller and fell down onto the roof, clutching his face with both hands. For an instant, Marcus stood stunned, unable to act. At his feet Alexandros was thrashing about on the deck as blood seeped out through his fingers. With a mighty effort, Marcus lunged forwards and clasped hold of the tiller, his eyes widening in horror, as he caught sight of the scene amidships. The lightning strike had struck the top of the mast, nearly splitting it in half and despite the heavy rain, the rigging was on fire.

"My eye," Alexandros screamed, "my eye, I can't see, I can't see."

There was however no time to tend to the captain. Marcus's fingers trembled as he stared at the mast and the hissing, leaping flames, struggling for life.

"Fire, fire," he roared, at the top of his voice, "Cunomoltus get up on deck. The ship is on fire."

There was no question of leaving the tiller. The Hermes was being roughly thrown about and the swells had become truly frightening.

For a moment nothing happened. Then one of the forward cargo hatches opened and a face appeared. It was Caradoc. Catching sight of the burning rigging, the druid did not hesitate. Valiantly, he heaved himself up onto the rolling and moving deck and began to crawl on all fours towards the mast and, as he did so he tore his cloak from his back. Marcus stared at him, as he made it to the mast, clutched hold of it, raised himself unsteadily up onto his feet and threw his cloak over the small, blue leaping flames that were biting into the rigging. Together with the pounding rain and wind, the flames were quickly extinguished and, as the last of them were put out, Caradoc turned to stare at Marcus, giving him a little nod. Marcus was able to raise his left hand before a huge, foaming rogue wave came slamming over the side of the Hermes taking Caradoc with it. Marcus cried out in horror. One moment the druid had been standing on the deck, the next moment he had vanished. Frantically Marcus turned to search the heaving swells and waves, but there was no sign of the druid. Caradoc had gone, washed clean overboard.

At his feet, Alexandros was groaning and howling in pain, as he clutched his face. Marcus stared around him in growing terror and tried not to think about what had just happened to Caradoc. Then, towards the bow, the other cargo hatch opened and Cunomoltus came slithering on his belly across the streaming, water-drenched deck towards the deck cabin.

"Alexandros is hurt," Marcus screamed. "Get him inside the cabin. He's can't see. He has been hit in the face by wood splinters."

"What happened?" Cunomoltus yelled, his face pale with fear. "I heard a loud bang."

"We were hit by lightning," Marcus roared. "Caradoc put out the fire but then a wave took him. He went overboard. He's dead."

Cunomoltus said nothing as he gave the ocean a terrified glance.

"Get Alexandros into the deckhouse," Marcus screamed, above the din of the wind and waves and thunder. "Cora will look after him. Once you have done that you come right back up here. I am going to need you, brother."

"I know," Cunomoltus yelled back, with a strange glint in his eyes, "I told you that you would need me before the end."

Chapter Thirty-Eight – The First People

The Hermes bobbed up and down in the calm sea. It was noon and the clear-blue June sky was cloudless. Marcus and Cunomoltus stood on the roof of the deckhouse, staring at the coastline, a half mile away. The monotony of the low rocky coast was broken by numerous, small islands, rocks, white sandy-beaches and inlets and, further inland, the country was covered in vast forests of dark, green pine trees.

"Is that it?" Cunomoltus muttered as he peered at the coast, "Do you think that is Hyperborea?"

Marcus did not immediately reply, as he studied the land.

"Caradoc said that all the land beyond the known world could be called Hyperborea," he said at last, "So I suppose yes; this is Hyperborea."

"So we made it," Cunomoltus exclaimed, turning to Marcus with an emotional, excited look. "We did it, Marcus. We crossed the ocean and sailed beyond the north wind. We took everything the gods could throw at us and we survived."

"We did," Marcus nodded grimly, "We have sailed beyond the north wind. But our journey is not over yet. Without Caradoc to show us the way, we are going to have to find this trading post ourselves. And then we are going to have to find Emogene and take back Corbulo's ashes and get home."

"Shouldn't be too hard," Cunomoltus said confidently. "How did Caradoc describe it? We should follow the coast south, until we come to a wide bay and the mouth of a river. The druid's camp is on a promontory, jutting out into the sea. That's what I remember him telling us."

"Meryn said the trading post was located amongst the people of the rocky river," Marcus frowned. "He called the people who lived there, Penawapskewi."

The two of them fell silent as they stared across the placid sea at the heavily forested coast. The storm had lasted for seven days and when at dawn on the seventh day, it had finally receded, they had found themselves off a low rocky coast. The storm however, had nearly wrecked the little ship. The lightning strike had weakened the mast and damaged the rigging and another leak had appeared in the hold, that had taken them two desperate days to plug. The Hermes looked battered and in a bad state of disrepair, as she slowly drifted southwards along the coast and, as she did, Marcus sighed, as he wondered wherever the faithful little ship would be seaworthy enough to be able to make the journey back home.

On the main deck Alexandros stood staring at the coast, clutching the side of the hull. Cora had managed to stem the loss of blood, but the Captain had lost an eye to the wood splinters and shards that had struck him and now his eye, was covered by a black, eye-patch. At the bow Jodoc and Calista too, were staring at the forested coastline. The young man had taken his father's loss badly, retreating into a world of grieving solitude, which only Calista seemed able to enter with any success. But now and then Marcus had caught Jodoc silently staring at him, with a murderous, hatred in his eyes.

***

Slowly the Hermes crept south along the coast, a stranger in an unknown world full of unexpected and amazing beauty. Out to sea, the huge icebergs drifted in the waves, their strange and bizarre shapes unexplainable. In the skies formations of V shaped birds were streaking across the waves. Pensively, Marcus stared at the rocky, deserted coast and the dark, thick and endless conifer forest that stretched away to the horizon. He wondered whether he was the first Roman to have ever seen this land. He was still thinking about it late in the afternoon, when Cunomoltus, on watch at the bow of the ship, cried out a warning and pointed at something in the water. Marcus, clutching the tiller, craned his neck to get a better view of what his brother was pointing at. Then his eyes widened in shock. Slicing towards them through the waves, were two canoes.

"Father," Calista shouted, as she too caught sight of the approaching canoes and rushed to the side of the ship. She was joined moments later by the rest of the crew. The four men, two to a canoe, were paddling straight towards the Hermes and as they drew closer Marcus could see them clearly. The natives were clad in long, brown and finely-decorated buckskins; their legs covered in Caribou-hide pants and their long, coal-black hair was tied into a knot at the back. Their swarthy, oriental looking faces, were staring at the Hermes, as they powered themselves towards the little Roman ship.

"Alexandros, take the tiller," Marcus cried out. The captain hastily climbed up onto the roof without saying a word, as Marcus slipped down the ladder and hastened towards the side of the ship. When the newcomers were half a dozen yards away they stopped paddling and silently stared up at the people on the Hermes, as their primitive-looking wooden canoes bobbed up and down in the waves. For a long moment, no one said a word as Marcus stared at the natives in astonishment and they stared back at him. Then, in the canoe, the oldest looking man amongst the four, raised a long bone-headed harpoon above his head and cried out something in a language that no one on board understood or had ever heard before. When there was no response, the man raised his harpoon and shouted at them again.

"Throw the netting over the side," Marcus growled turning to Cunomoltus. "Let them come on board."

"Is that a good idea" Cunomoltus replied, as he stared at the natives with an alarmed, worried look. "Something tells me they are not going to understand a word of what we say and they are armed."

"Just do it," Marcus said sharply.

The four men in the canoes remained silent, as the netting rolled down the side of the hull and splashed into the sea.

"Come on board," Marcus cried out to the men in the canoes, gesturing at the older man with the bone harpoon. "Come on. Climb up."

In their canoes the natives did not react, as they looked up at the faces peering down at them. Then, as Marcus beckoned to them with his hand, the older man called out to his friends and with a cautious dip of his oar, he approached the side of the ship and grasped hold of the netting. The other canoe however held back, their occupants seemingly torn between an intense curiosity and fear. Marcus could see that they were armed with bonehead harpoons with handles made of antler and, lying at the bottom of the second canoe, was a dead seal and a stone axe. As the older man clambered up and over the side of the hull, silence descended across the ship, as the crew of the Hermes slowly retreated, their faces tense, fascinated and fearful. Marcus however, stood his ground as the Hyperborean found his feet on the gently swaying deck and turned to look around him with wide, astonished eyes. The man was tall, pale, and around his neck he was wearing a fine bone-necklace with strange shaped engravings and on his feet he was clad in boots made of Caribou skin. A wooden war-club with a ball-like ending was strapped across his back.

No one spoke as the Hyperborean looked around at the ship and the crew, his eyes and mouth gaping in astonishment. The man lowered his nose to the wooden hull and sniffed a few times, before slowly turning to stare at Marcus, with dark, penetrating eyes. Marcus did not move, as the man cautiously reached out to touch his beard and then his red hair. Then the native backed away and shouted something to his friends down in the water, in an excited, tense sounding voice. From his belt Marcus, carefully pulled free a Roman-army Pugio knife and held it up for the man to see, before offering it to him. The native stared at the steel weapon in silence before gingerly reaching out and taking it from Marcus's outstretched hand and, as he did so, Marcus had the impression that the man had never seen a metal knife before in his life. Cautiously the Hyperborean ran the sharp point across his hand and then raised it to his nose and sniffed. On the deck of the Hermes no one moved, as every eye focussed on the strange, historic encounter taking place. Marcus was just about to speak when the native, with surprising speed, caught hold of Marcus's hand and nicked his hand with the knife. As the blood welled up from the wound Marcus cried out in shock and pulled his hand free and in response the Hyperborean took a quick step back in alarm. Marcus grimaced as he looked down at his bloody hand, but the small wound was not deep.

"What did he do that for" Cunomoltus growled tensely.

Marcus looked up at the native. The man was staring at the blood welling up from the wound.

"I think he is trying to find out whether we are gods or mere mortals," he growled. "And I think he has his answer."

The Hyperborean had turned away from Marcus and was staring at the rest of the crew, who had formed a semi-circle around him. Then, catching sight of Calista, he cocked his head to one side and slowly advanced towards her and, as he did so, the girl started to back away nervously.

"Stay where you are," Marcus called out to her in a sharp voice. "It will be alright."

Calista was staring at the native with large fear-filled eyes but she did as Marcus had said and, as the Hyperborean came up to her, he reached out and ran his fingers through her hair and across her cheeks. Then he reached out and grasped hold of her breasts. The movement was too much for Calista and she squealed and staggered away backwards. The Hyperborean however did not seem to notice her reaction, for swiftly he turned round, opened his mouth, revealing a couple of rotten yellow teeth and started to laugh. His laughter drifted away across the placid sea as he made it to the edge of the ship and gestured at his friends, crying out to them in a language, that to the crew, was completely alien and unintelligible. Swiftly Marcus took a step forwards and, before the man could react, he had snatched the Pugio from him. Startled, the Hyperborean stumbled backwards as his laughter was abruptly replaced with a look of alarm.

Marcus fixed his eyes on the stranger, his face grim but not aggressive, as he held up the Roman army knife.

"We will trade," he said slowly in a clear voice, "We need food and drinking water. If you can bring this to us I will give you this knife."

The Hyperborean was staring at him with a nervous, watchful expression but it was clear he had not understood a word of what Marcus had just said. Patiently Marcus pointed at himself and then his mouth as he started to munch on imaginary food and drink imaginary water before offering the knife to the native. On the second attempt the man seemed to understand, for a flush of sudden excitement appeared on his cheeks, as he called out something to the men in the canoes.

"I think we are finally getting somewhere," Marcus said, as the man nodded at him, his face cracking into an eager smile.

"Don't give him the knife before he has brought us those supplies," Cunomoltus called out in warning.

"Have you seen their boats and weapons," Marcus replied. "Stone tools and weapons made of bone. If these men are warriors then they have no proper shields, no body armour and no steel weapons. Caradoc was right. They look rather primitive. But they clearly do like the look of our knives and swords. If Emperor Trajan were to decide to ship the Twentieth Legion across the ocean, they should have no trouble in conquering these people."

"Don't scare him away," Cora suddenly frowned. "We need food and water. Our supplies are very low, especially fresh water. Make the trade."

The native was peering at Marcus with his dark, curious eyes. Then he called out to his friends in the canoes before untying and taking something from a small leather pouch that hung around his waist. Stretching out his hand towards Marcus, he opened his fingers to reveal a small piece of brittle, Chert stone. Marcus frowned as he stared at the stone in the Hyperborean's hand. Then slowly, so as not to startle the man, he took it and held up in the air, examining it carefully.

"What is it" Cunomoltus called out.

Marcus was silent for a moment as he studied the stone.

"I think he is offering us this stone in exchange for the knife," he replied. "The stone must be a precious commodity. Maybe they make their tools and weapons from this stone."

"Maybe he is having a laugh," Cunomoltus snapped unhappily. "Anyway we need supplies not stones. We can't eat stones."

Abruptly Marcus handed the stone back to the man and shook his head.

"Penawapskewi," Marcus exclaimed pointing at the Hyperborean. "Penawapskewi?"

The name seemed to mean nothing to the Hyperborean but from the expression on his face Marcus could see that he had understood, that the words had meant a question, for swiftly the man replied spitting out something in his own language. A wry little smile appeared at the corner of Marcus' lips as he stared at the native and in response the Hyperborean's face slowly cracked into a grin.

"I think we shall call them, the first people," Marcus called out, "As they are the first people we have met in this new world."

310

Chapter Thirty-Nine – The Home of the gods

Marcus stood alone holding the tiller as he slowly navigated through the sea straights. It was morning and above him the clear, blue sky stretched away to the horizon. A single, sea bird hovered high above the ship, its graceful white wings spread wide, as it peered down at the Hermes with sharp, curious eyes. A strong, fresh wind was propelling the ship southwards through the straights and the Hermes's main, red, square-sail and foresail bulged outwards, powering the little Roman ship through the water. At its usual spot, beside the helmsman, the black ship's cat lay stretched out on deck, enjoying the warm sunshine. Marcus peered ahead at the point where the land funnelled inwards to form a narrow sea-straight maybe ten miles across. Apart from the white chunks of drifting sea-ice, the passage ahead looked easy enough, but if he'd learnt anything in these past few weeks, it was to never underestimate the ocean and mother nature. To port and starboard the low rocky coast was interspersed with small islets, sandy deserted beaches and lone rocks. Further inland the dark, green conifer-forests stretched away into the distance.

On the deck below, Alexandros was staring at the coastline. He'd been unusually quiet since losing his eye in the thunder storm, but now he turned to look up at Marcus with sudden excitement, as he pointed ahead at the straights.

"When you pass through the Pillars of Hercules," Alexandros cried out, his good eye shining with sudden passion, "I tell you, you will feel Hercules himself watching you. The pillars are the gateway to a different world. Maybe these straights up ahead are the same. Maybe we are about to sail into a new world. Maybe, beyond, we are going to find the home of the gods, Marcus"

"You had better clean yourself up in that case," Marcus responded with a good natured smile. "If we are about to meet the gods, then you look like shit."

Alexandros turned away, shaking his head in silent disgust and Marcus turned his attention back to the sea and the icebergs, that seemed to be accompanying the Hermes south. The trade with the Hyperboreans had gone well and the natives had returned to the ship that same day, and a vast quantity of seal and Caribou meat had been exchanged for one steel Roman army Pugio knife. That night Cora and Calista had cooked up a fantastic stew and the whole crew had feasted, stuffing themselves silly, as they'd enjoyed their first taste of meat in weeks. The feast had lifted their morale and the next day even Jodoc had even managed to say a few words.

"We need to put into land soon," Alexandros called out, without turning to look at Marcus. "I am worried about the mast. That lightning strike has damaged it and the temporary repairs we have made to the hull also need looking at."

The smile on Marcus's face faded away as he studied the sea ahead.

"We should keep going," he replied. "We can make repairs when we reach our destination."

"That could take weeks," Alexandros cried out in an annoyed voice. "And we don't know what reception we are going to receive when we get there. Besides you don't even know where this trading post is. We lost the only man who did."

Marcus glanced at the coast. "We will find it," he growled. "We will keep heading south along the coast until then. We know what to look for and we know the name of the Hyperborean tribe, in whose territory the druids have made their home. Sooner or later some of these natives are going to recognise the name and show us the way."

"And how are they going to do that, when we can't understand a fucking word they say," Alexandros snapped.

"We are going to listen and keep our eyes open," Marcus cried out. "I got us the meat didn't I? These Hyperborean's seem happy to trade with us. It's a good sign. The next time we trade, we will not be trading for meat but for information. Pale faced men like us and the druids will stand out here. Somewhere, someone will know about this trading post."

Alexandros was silent, as he digested what Marcus had just said. Then he turned round to look up at him and slowly adjusted his black eye patch.

"The women want to go ashore," he growled, "We have been stuck on this ship for weeks Marcus. All of us want to spend a night ashore on solid ground. Just one night and we need to make these repairs. The ship is in a poor state. You know this."

Under his breath Marcus growled in frustration.

"Alright, we will keep an eye open for a suitable landing spot," he replied. "The land to port looks more promising."

**

The white, sandy beach looked deserted as Marcus, Cunomoltus and Jodoc waded ashore. Marcus was holding an axe and a coil of rope was slung over his shoulder and Cunomoltus was armed with a bow and a quiver, that were strapped to his back. As they stumbled ashore, Marcus paused to look around as Cunomoltus sank down onto his knees in the sand, grasped hold of the earth with both hands and held it up, allowing the grains of sand to slowly slip through his fingers. Inland, the thick conifer forest stretched away to a line of distant hills and there was no sign of human habitation. The forest looked dark and uninviting. Jodoc was staring moodily at the trees as he clutched his axe and Marcus gave him a wary glance. Out in the small bay, the Hermes lay at anchor, her sails furled and Marcus could see Alexandros, pottering about on the roof of the deckhouse.

"Come on we need a good tree," Marcus said turning to his companions, "Jodoc, you and I will cut it down. Cunomoltus, you will stand guard. Keep your eyes open. We are strangers in this land. The gods only know what is lurking in those forests. Maybe we will even run into Hermes himself," Marcus added with a little smile, as he tried to lighten the atmosphere.

Cunomoltus and Jodoc did not seem to appreciate the attempt and they remained silent, as the three of them started out towards the forest. As they advanced across the beach, Cunomoltus however reached out for his bow and strung an arrow, as he peered nervously at the tree line.

The forest air was cool and shady and amongst the trees, it was quiet and nothing moved. As they pushed on deeper into the woodland, the trees reminded Marcus of the forests he had seen in Caledonia. When he judged they had come far enough, he raised his fist in the air and turned to examine the trees.

"This one will do," he said at last, as he placed his left hand against a sturdy-looking trunk. "Alexandros said the new mast should be tall and strong. We'll cut it down and drag it back to the beach."

The rhythmic thud of an axe striking into wood echoed away through the forest as Marcus and Jodoc took turns at swinging their axes at the tree. Lightly-coloured wood chippings lay scattered across the forest floor and Marcus was sweating from the effort. A little way off, Cunomoltus stood clutching his drawn bow as he warily scanned the trees.

"I am sorry for your loss," Marcus said with a grunt, glancing at Jodoc as he freed his axe head from the groove they had cut into the trunk. "But I did not kill him. His death was an accident. The waves washed him overboard."

Jodoc said nothing, as he stepped up for his turn to strike the tree. His axe struck the trunk with a fierce, vicious thud.

"Listen," Marcus growled as he swung his axe into the groove. "I know you hate me and you blame me for your father's death, but you are going to have to put that all aside. You are going to have to embrace the truth. We all need to work together. The ship needs a united crew and we need a friendly reception from the druids, if this voyage is to be a success. If you can do that; if you can make that happen, then I promise you, that I will give you back the iron box and allow you to go your own way, after we reach the trading post."

Jodoc's axe thudded into the trunk, making the tree sway and creak.

"Without my father and I, how will you crew your ship on the return voyage" Jodoc hissed.

Marcus slammed his axe into the trunk and looked up to see tree top wobble dangerously.

"I will find a way," Marcus said confidently.

"You will give me back my father's book?" Jodoc snapped.

Marcus nodded. "I will, if you don't cause trouble for us with the druids."

There was no more time to discuss the matter as, with a long cracking groan, the tree started to topple over into the forest. Marcus cried out a warning to Cunomoltus as the three of them sprang away and the tree came crashing to the ground snapping branches in the process.

Marcus and Jodoc had just fastened the rope to the end of the tree and were preparing to start hauling it away, when Cunomoltus cried out in alarm. Marcus whipped round and stared in the direction in which Cunomoltus was pointing. Amongst the shady, cool forest, he could see nothing. Then, from behind a tree, he caught a sudden movement. A red-painted face appeared and then slowly a man stepped away from the cover. The native was clutching a stone axe and his face and buckskins were painted and decorated with red ochre. Marcus grunted in astonishment. Then amongst the trees, two more men and a boy appeared, similarly dressed with their faces painted red. The hunting party were armed with short stone knives and one of them was holding a bone-headed hunting spear. All four hunters looked nervous as they stared at Marcus and his companions with tense, wide-eyed astonishment.

"No one move," Marcus called out in a tight, tense voice, as his hand dropped to the pommel of his gladius that hung from his belt. "Don't do anything to provoke them."

The forest grew silent as the strange, unexpected standoff continued. Then the Hyperborean's started to nervously inch forwards and the man carrying the spear raised the weapon above his head and into an aggressive throwing position. The native closest to Marcus suddenly cried out in a strange sounding, unintelligible language and raised his stone axe threateningly, gesturing at Marcus and his companions. The men's red-painted faces and strange apparel were like nothing Marcus had ever encountered before and for a moment, he could do nothing, but stand his ground. Close by, Jodoc had pulled his knife from his belt and was staring nervously from one hunter to the next.

Then, with a high-pitched shriek, the native holding the stone axe lunged towards Jodoc. The boy yelled in terror as the stone axe came swooping down, aimed at his head, but somehow Jodoc managed to grasp hold of the native's arm and the two of them went tumbling onto the forest floor in a desperate flurry of snarling, grappling arms and legs. The native clutching the raised spear, never managed to release it, for a split second later, Cunomoltus arrow punched straight through his neck, sending a jet of blood spurting into the air. The man was dead before his body crumpled to the ground. With a well-practised movement, Marcus pulled his gladius from its brown leather sheath and charged towards the remaining hunter and the boy, roaring a furious battle cry. The fierce shouting and the unexpected charge were enough to send the two Hyperborean's fleeing into the wood.

As Marcus wheeled round to come to Jodoc's aid, he saw the young man gasping, bleeding and rolling over the ground in a desperate, vicious fight for survival. Cunomoltus however, was the first to reach him. He dropped his bow, caught hold of the natives long black hair and swiftly sank his knife into the man's head, with a sickening crunch. Jodoc screamed as his face was splattered with the dead man's blood and frantically he struggled free and rolled away from the corpse. Cunomoltus stood staring at the dead native, his chest heaving from exertion, his hand clutching his bloodied knife.

Marcus was breathing heavily as he stared at the carnage. The forest around him had fallen eerily silent. Then he caught Cunomoltus' eye and gave him a little appreciative nod, which Cunomoltus silently returned. Jodoc, bleeding from a cut to his head and looking shaken, was sitting on the ground, his legs drawn up under him, as he stared wide-eyed at the dead man who had just tried to kill him.

"Why did they attack us" Cunomoltus blurted out.

Marcus shook his head.

"Fuck knows," he replied, "But we need to get back to the ship right now. Leave the tree. Those hunters may come back."

Cunomoltus nodded in agreement and Marcus was about to heave Jodoc up onto his feet, when something on the corpse of the red-painted man, who had been stabbed in the head, caught his eye. Frowning he stooped and reached down and pulled free a leather cord from around the native's neck. The cord was adorned with animal teeth, worked antler-bone fragments, coloured stones and a single, small and round bronze coin.

"What is it?" Cunomoltus exclaimed as Marcus held the bronze coin up in the air to get a closer inspection.

For a long moment, Marcus did not reply. Then a flush appeared across his cheeks and he slowly shook his head in disbelief.

"Well, would you believe it," he exclaimed in surprise. "The coin is Roman and is showing the face of Emperor Vespasian. These natives must have gotten it from the trading post. We must be close."

Chapter Forty – The Language of the World

Marcus watched the large bird circling the ship, as the Hermes surged southwards through the choppy sea, her red sail billowing in the wind and her proud pennant fluttering high up in the mast. It was dawn and several days had passed since their violent encounter with the red-painted natives. The Hermes had left that coast the same day and after a short dash across the open sea they had sighted land again. Now, a mile to starboard, they were hugging another rocky coastline, one of heavily wooded, rolling hills and dozens of small barren islands. Bored, Marcus squinted up at the bird, as he stood beside Alexandros, who was holding the tiller. But the bird was too far away for him to make out any distinctive features. At the bow, Jodoc slouched against the side of the boat, keeping an eye open for icebergs, even though they had not seen one for some time now, and the likelihood that they would, was decreasing rapidly, the further south they went.

Alexandros scratched at his black, eye patch as he stared stoically and silently at the sea ahead. The crew had become silent and withdrawn and for the past couple of days no one had seemed interested in talking. They were all weary Marcus thought, as he caught sight of Cora standing beside the mast, staring at the distant land. Morale on board, raised by the supply of fresh meat, had plummeted again after the violent encounter with the red-painted natives and Marcus had realised that the crew were growing exhausted after such a long time at sea. They needed a proper rest on land and a break from the constant danger. They needed to find this trading post and they needed to find it quickly. Marcus sighed and turned his attention back to the bird, as it seemed to draw closer. As he watched it descend in a slow, graceful circular dive, the creature suddenly shot forwards and alighted on the top of the mast, and as it did, a sudden flush appeared on Marcus's cheeks. The strange bird with its sharp eyes, brown wings, white head and tail and curved beak was peering down at the people on the deck of the Hermes.

"See that," Marcus cried out in an excited voice, as he pointed at the bird, sitting on top of the mast. "It's an eagle. I am sure of it, it's an eagle."

Alexandros glanced up at the mast.

"Well if it is, then it's like no eagle that I have ever seen before," he muttered in a disinterested voice.

Marcus's eyes however, gleamed excitedly, "You don't understand," he called out, as he studied the bird, "This is a good sign. The eagle is the sacred creature of the legions and of Rome. If an eagle chooses to land on the Hermes, then it can only mean that the gods approve of our voyage. My father would have gone down on his knees, if he had been here to see this. This is a sign."

"A sign?" Alexandros growled.

"A sign that our journey is nearing its end," Marcus nodded as he peered up at the bald headed eagle, perched on the top of the mast. "It must be."

A little smile appeared on Alexandros' lips as he took another look at the bird.

"Not everyone is so happy to see your Roman eagle," he said gesturing at the black ship's cat, who was staring up at the bird in alarm, it's ears flattened against its head and its mouth making a silent, hissing noise.

Alexandros shook his head and called out to Cora in his native Greek, which Marcus could not understand, but the captain's comment brought a smile onto his wife's lips and from the doorway of the deckhouse Calista burst out laughing.

***

"It's a bay and there is a river, but there is no headland and I can't see any camp or settlement," Cunomoltus called out, in a

320

disappointed voice as he stared at the coast, holding up his hand to shield his eyes from the sun. It was late in the afternoon and all day the crew had been watching the coast, searching to no avail for a location that fitted the one that Caradoc had given them. Marcus sighed in disappointment, clambered down onto the deck, and came and stood beside his brother.

"Keep searching," he muttered. "We are close. I know we are. Caradoc said the headland had a good beach."

"What else is there to do," Cunomoltus growled moodily.

Marcus raised his hand and gripped Cunomoltus' shoulder. Then he turned towards Alexandros and Calista, who were standing by the tiller on the roof of the deckhouse.

"Listen," Marcus cried out in a loud voice. "The first person to spot this trading post will be rewarded with five Denarii in gold. Do you hear me? Five Denarii for the first person who sees our destination, but if you claim the prize and it turns out to be false then you will be disqualified. Keep your eyes open. We are close. We are not far away now."

"That's what you said yesterday and the day before," Jodoc muttered, as he strode towards the bow.

The crew remained silent and Marcus turned his attention back to the coast. The heavily-forested rolling hills, small inlets and rugged-rocks and islands looked beautiful, but he could not enjoy the scenery. Impatiently he tapped the remaining fingers of his left hand against his thigh. Then he turned towards Alexandros who was at the tiller.

"Take the ship closer inshore, we're too far out," he called out.

Alexandros frowned. "I don't like those rocks," he cried, "We don't know these waters and if we get any closer to the shore, we may run aground or strike one of those rocks. It's not only the rocks you can see, that you should worry about. There are also the underwater obstacles. I don't like it, Marcus."

"We need to get a closer view of the shore," Marcus replied stubbornly. "We're too far out to see what is going on. Just do it."

Alexandros shook his head in disapproval, as reluctantly he began to turn the ship towards the shore.

It was early evening when Marcus suddenly caught sight of smoke, rising into the air in a long thin, black column. Rushing to the side of the ship, he peered at the smoke, searching the rocky coast. Cunomoltus and Cora swiftly joined him and for a long moment everyone on board remained silent, as they eagerly stared at the thick, green forest that covered the land.

"What do you think it is?" Cora muttered, as she gripped the edge of the ship with both hands.

"There is no wide bay and I can't see any river," Cunomoltus grumbled. "Wherever the smoke is coming from, it is not the trading post."

As the Hermes headed along the coast towards the column of smoke, Marcus peered at the shore, straining to take in every detail. Then, as they passed a small rocky island, he caught sight of a white, sandy beach. The column of smoke was rising from a fire on the beach and close by, six birch-bark canoes lay drawn up on the sand. A group of Hyperborean's had gathered around the fire. They were too far away to make out any distinctive features.

"Look," he cried pointing at the men and canoes.

The others had already seen the natives and were staring at them in tense, worried fascination.

"Heave to!" Marcus cried out, turning to Alexandros. "Get those sails furled."

"What are you doing" Cunomoltus exclaimed turning towards Marcus with an alarmed look.

On the beach, the men had spotted the Hermes and were coming towards the water's edge. Marcus did not reply to Cunomoltus's question, as he turned to stare at the natives. Then he ran his hand across his face and glanced quickly at Alexandros. However, the captain was already bringing the ship into the wind and the sails were flapping about, as the Hermes lost speed and direction.

"What are you doing?" Cunomoltus blurted out.

"I am going to speak with them," Marcus growled. "I am going to find out where this druid, trading post is."

"That's insane," Cunomoltus gasped in surprise, "Have you forgotten the reception we got from those red-painted devils? If these Hyperborean's are hostile, they are going to kill you. There are fifteen of them and they look armed."

"Nevertheless I am doing this," Marcus snapped, as he lowered the hood of his Paenula.

"How will you communicate with them?" Cora said quickly, "You cannot understand anything that they say and you don't speak their language."

"Jodoc fetch the amphora of wine, the large one, and bring it here," Marcus called out to the youth, as he ignored Cora. "Be careful not to drop it."

"It's heavy," Jodoc growled in protest.

"Just do it," Marcus shouted.

"What are you doing" Cunomoltus snapped unhappily, as he grasped hold of Marcus's shoulder.

Marcus turned to his brother with a grim, determined expression.

"I may not be able to speak to them but there are other ways of communication. In the army, we used flags and signal fires. With those natives over there on the beach, I am going to use wine. I am going to get them pissed."

Cunomoltus let go of his brother's shoulder and stared at Marcus in surprise.

"Then I am coming with you," Cunomoltus said at last, giving Marcus a short grim affirmative nod.

"I thought you said that would be insane," Marcus replied sharply.

"Shut up," Cunomoltus retorted.

***

Marcus was the first to slip over the side of the narrow raft and into the water, clutching a leather sack over his shoulder. A small, simple wooden-cup hung from a cord around his neck. Swiftly he was followed by Jodoc, holding the heavy, thirty litres, wide-handled, half-a-yard-long, ceramic amphora with both hands. Finally came Cunomoltus, who held onto the long raft, which had brought them to the beach from the ship. The gentle waves came up to his waist and it was freezing cold even for June. Marcus found his footing on the rocky, uneven seabed and paused to study the natives, standing on the beach a dozen paces away. The Hyperborean's were clad in brown, animal-hides and boots and were staring at him in alarm and wonder. They were carrying an assortment of stone axes, knives, bows and bone-handle harpoons and around their necks, they were adorned with a fantastic array of strange, carved bone and stone amulets. Their flat, oriental faces and jet-black hair, reminded Marcus of the first people they had encountered and amongst them, he suddenly noticed a man wearing a beautiful, feathered headdress.

"They must be a different tribe to the ones we saw before," Marcus said in a tight tense voice. "These men don't seem to have painted their faces red."

"They don't look very happy to see us," Cunomoltus said tersely.

Marcus grunted and started to wade towards the shore and the waiting men and as he did so, two of the natives quickly raised their bows in a threatening manner and pointed their weapons at him. On the beach, another of the Hyperborean's raised his harpoon in the air and yelled something at Marcus as he took a threatening step forwards before retreating. Undeterred Marcus made it onto the dry sand and when he was a few yards from the natives, he halted.

"Penawapskewi," he called out, looking at the Hyperborean's. "Penawapskewi?"

There was no response from the Hyperborean's as they nervously eyed Marcus and his companions. Silently Marcus gestured for Jodoc to place the amphora of wine in the sand in front of the natives. Then slowly, showing the men what he was doing, he pulled another Roman army Pugio knife from his belt and laid it in the sand beside the amphora. Working slowly, he opened the leather sack he was carrying and took out one of Cora's spare, iron, cooking-pots and the Roman army-helmet he had brought along specifically for this sort of occasion. The natives looked on in silence, as Marcus laid out the items in the sand, staring at him and the objects in growing astonishment. When he was finished, Marcus took a step back and gestured at the natives to come closer and examine the objects, lying in the white sand.

At first none of them moved. Then as Marcus beckoned to them again, the man with the fine feathered headdress pushed his way to the front and cautiously stooped and picked up the army knife, holding it up in the air with respect. The man had an old, wrinkled and wise-looking face and he seemed older than the other hunters. Then another hunter stepped forwards and gingerly picked up the cooking pot, lifting it up and sniffing at it, before biting it with his teeth. There was a small commotion as one of his fellow hunters snatched the pot from the man's hand, but a sharp cry from the man with the feathered-headdress, ended it, and the new possessor was allowed to keep the pot. But, when one of the Hyperborean's reached out to touch the amphora, Marcus took a quick step forwards, shook his head and raised his voice and the man backed away nervously.

Calmly, Marcus sat down in the sand and gestured for Cunomoltus and Jodoc to do the same and, as they did, the hunters seemed to relax slightly. Along the beach, the native's fire was still burning but the men seemed to have completely forgotten about it. Idly, Marcus turned to glance at the Hermes, which was riding at anchor a hundred yards from the shore. Alexandros and his family were watching them from the roof of the deckhouse.

When another hunter however, tried to touch the amphora, Marcus rose to his feet and boldly pushed the man away, before beckoning to the man with the feathered- headdress to come forward. The action caused a stir amongst the Hyperborean's and a few men cried out angrily in their unintelligible language, but again their leader silenced them. Marcus ignored the tumult and his eyes remained fixed on the native chief. Undoing the top of the amphora, he dipped the little wooden, cup inside and scooped up some dark red wine, showed it to the Hyperborean before raising the cup to his lips and downing it in one go.

"Drink some of the wine and pretend you enjoy it," Marcus muttered as he handed the small wooden cup to Cunomoltus.

"I do enjoy it," Cunomoltus replied, as he dipped the cup into the amphora.

Once his brother was finished, Marcus turned slowly to the native with the feathered headdress.

"Here, try some," Marcus said, as he offered the man the cup and gestured at the wine container.

Cautiously the old, wrinkle-faced chief took the cup and peered down into the amphora before dipping it into the liquid and raising it to his nose. Then quickly mimicking Marcus, he downed the contents in one single go.

"Good?" Marcus smiled broadly, as he looked at the man.

For a long moment the Hyperborean did not reply, as he looked down at the amphora. Then his mouth cracked into a toothless grin and he turned and called out something to his hunters.

"Look at this," Marcus said gesturing for the chief to come closer, as he held up the small, copper coin he had taken from the red-painted native.

"Penawapskewi," Marcus exclaimed, tapping the coin and straightening up to point around him in a wide circle. "Where can we find them?"

The chief however did not react in the way Marcus had been hoping. Carefully he took the coin from Marcus's hand, examined it closely, then pocketed it, and gestured at the wine.

"Don't get drunk," Marcus snapped in warning, as he quickly turned to Cunomoltus and Jodoc.

The natives had started to help themselves to the wine now and, as the wooden cup was passed around amongst them, the men began to relax.

***

It was growing dark and the deep-red sun was about to vanish beneath the distant mountains. On the beach the fire crackled and sent showers of sparks shooting up into the air. Marcus sat, staring silently into the sand, flanked by Cunomoltus and Jodoc, as around the fire, the natives talked amongst themselves in soft, quiet voices. Six of the Hyperborean's, one wearing a Roman army helmet, lay unconscious, spread eagled on the beach, completely intoxicated by too much wine. The native chief however, perhaps noticing that Marcus and his companions had not touched the wine, had refrained from drinking too much, and some of the older hunters had followed his example. The Hyperborean's had shared some of their kill with Marcus, a strange tasting meat that none of the Romans had ever seen before, but it had tasted good.

"What are we doing?" Cunomoltus hissed as he leaned towards Marcus. "Let's get back to the ship before they decide to kill and eat us."

Marcus shook his head as he stared absentmindedly into the sand. Across the fire from him, the chief, clad in his magnificent, feathered-headdress, was watching him in silence, his wrinkled, wise-looking face taking in every detail. Then suddenly he spoke in a sharp voice and the hunters around him fell silent. Marcus looked up and saw that the chief was holding up the copper Roman coin he'd taken from him. The coin gleamed in the fire light.

"Penawapskewi", the chief said, suddenly giving Marcus a little nod.

"What did he just say?" Marcus snapped as his eyes widened. But neither Jodoc or Cunomoltus were able to answer.

The chief slowly rose to his feet, as the fire sent another shower of sparks shooting upwards to die in the evening sky. Then he pointed at Marcus and said something that none of the Romans could understand. With a dismissive shake of his head the chief muttered something and beckoned for Marcus to come closer. As Marcus came around the fire, he saw that the man was crouching on the beach and rearranging the soft sand with the

Roman army knife. Puzzled, he looked down at what the Hyperborean was doing. The chief seemed to be drawing something in the sand with the knife. Then he reached out, picked up a stone and placed it on the sand, tapping it with the point of the iron knife.

"Penawapskewi," he said glancing up at Marcus.

For a moment no one spoke. Then Marcus felt a hot flush start to fill his cheeks.

"It's a map," he exclaimed, "He's drawing us a map. The stone is our destination. He's telling us where we can find the trading post."

"Penawapskewi," the man said again placing the copper Roman coin on top of the stone as he got to his feet.

Marcus peered down at the lines in the sand and the single stone as Cunomoltus and Jodoc joined him. Cunomoltus was the first to speak.

"If it is a map, then it is a very strange map," he said with a frown. "The bearings are all wrong."

"But it matches with what Caradoc told us," Marcus snapped, "Look, the stone is on a headland in a wide bay, into which flows a river."

Cunomoltus glanced at the native chief, who was watching them with an eager, amused expression.

Carefully, Marcus sat down on his haunches as he studied the sand. Then he reached out to gently touch the stone and, as he did so, he looked up at the man with the feathered-headdress.

"Is this where the sun sets," he muttered, tapping the stone and then pointing with his other hand at the deep, red ball of the sun that was about to vanish below the horizon.

For a moment the Hyperborean said nothing, as he peered down at the map and then looked in the direction in which Marcus was pointing. Finally, he seemed to understand, for he said something and nodded. Marcus turned to stare down at the sand in sudden excitement. Then, sharply he turned to look up at Cunomoltus with a triumphant grin.

"The map is right," he hissed in delight, "they just haven't drawn it like we would, with north at the top. They have drawn it from sunrise to sunset."

Chapter Forty-One

The Market of the Hyperboreans

Marcus remained silent as he stared at the headland. It was afternoon and he stood on the roof of the deckhouse, clutching the tiller. The Hermes's red-square sail billowed in the wind as the little Roman ship cut across Penobscot Bay. For hours the Hermes had been carefully and slowly picking its way around dozens of small, forested islands. The unending pounding by the ocean had created a coast, that was a beautiful, maze of secret winding-waterways, deep-inlets, small-bays, stony-beaches and treacherous-rocks. Now however, the waters were placid and along the low, ragged and rocky coast, the thick, green forest covered everything. It was quiet and warm and in the clear, blue sky a few birds were circling but Marcus was not watching the beautiful scenery or the animals. His eyes were fixed on the level terrace beside the sea, at the very end of the headland, and the Hibernian curragh that lay at anchored just off a sandy beach. The ship had a single mast and its hull looked like it had been made of animal hide. There was no one on board.

At Marcus's side, Alexandros was staring at the large native settlement, that covered the terrace beside the sea. The score of rounded, primitive looking Hyperborean shelters were clustered around a single, wooden longhouse, from which smoke was rising. Facing inland, there was what looked like a fortified palisade. Along the beach, a dozen or so birch bark canoes lay drawn up in the sand.

Slowly Alexandros turned to Marcus and silently the two exchanged an excited, triumphant glance. They had made it to the trading post. On the deck below them Cunomoltus, Calista, Jodoc and Cora were all standing at the side of the ship, as they peered at the native village in stunned, fascinated silence.

"You have earned the second part of your payment," Marcus said quietly.

Alexandros nodded but said nothing, as he stared at the native settlement and the distinctive Hibernian ship.

As the Hermes slowly sailed towards the beach and the rocky plateau, there was a sudden commotion in the village and a stream of Hyperborean's came running from their tents towards the water's edge to stare at the Roman ship and amongst them Marcus caught sight of semi-naked women and children. On the shore, the crowd of natives were pointing, whooping and shouting and, as Marcus stared at them, the first of the canoes were launched into the water and started to head towards the Hermes, their occupants paddling frantically through the calm, crystal-clear water.

"Heave to," Marcus cried out as he handed the tiller to Alexandros and slid down the ladder. On the deck, no one moved, as the crew stared at the rapidly approaching fleet of canoes.

"Heave to," Marcus shouted again in an annoyed voice and, as the crew finally responded to his order, Marcus caught Jodoc by his arm. There was a grim, warning look in Marcus's eye.

"You will remember our agreement," Marcus muttered, as he gripped the young man's arm, "Don't go causing trouble for us with the druids and keep your mouth shut or else that precious book of yours goes overboard, together with your dead body."

Sullenly Jodoc shook himself free and glared at Marcus.

"I remember," he growled, "Just keep your part of the deal like you promised."

Marcus watched the young man stride away, to help the others lower the sails. Then he turned towards the canoes that had nearly reached the Hermes. The natives were surrounding the Roman ship, whooping and crying out in excitement, as they stared up at him, but somehow they seemed to lack the same astonishment and wonder he'd seen on the faces of the first

Hyperborean's they'd met. It was as if these men had become used to seeing foreign ships appear from the direction of the ocean. As he studied the natives, half-expecting to see Emogene amongst the throng of strange faces, Marcus suddenly caught sight of a tall, ginger-bearded man, clad in a faded tunic similar to those worn in Britannia. The man looked different to the natives around him and, with a shock, Marcus realised the man must be a druid. The red- bearded man's eyes were fixed on Marcus and he did not look happy. As his canoe drew closer, Marcus slowly raised his hand in greeting.

"Who are you" the druid's deep powerful voice boomed across the placid water as he slowly stood up in the canoe and stared at Marcus. "Where have you come from?"

At the sound of the druid's voice, the rest of the Hermes's crew came to the side of the ship to stare at him. For a moment, Marcus was unable to reply. Then a broad smile appeared across his lips.

"You have no idea how good it is to hear a fellow Briton," he called out in reply." We have been at sea for a long time and the only people we have come across do not speak our language. My name is Ahern and this is my ship. We have come across the ocean from Londinium in search of this place."

"You have come from Londinium?" the druid bellowed, as his face grew concerned. "How can this be so? No one knows about this place. How did you know that we were here? How did you find us? What has brought you here?"

Marcus nodded cheerfully. "I am just a sailor and this is my ship and crew," he replied, "We were hired to undertake this voyage by a man called Caradoc, a druid like you. He told us about this place. He was coming here to give the druids a book, an important book that he has locked inside a metal box, but unfortunately, he died during our journey, washed overboard during a storm. However, we still have the book and we decided to continue and fulfil his mission, for that is what he paid us to do. He was a generous man."

"The book?" the druid cried, his eyes lighting up in surprise. "You know about Caradoc's book? You came all this way to give us his book?"

"Yes," Marcus replied, "Caradoc said it was his life's work. He said it was a written account of seven hundred years of the history of the Briton tribes from before the coming of Rome. He spent years compiling it. He said there were only two copies in existence. He called it a treasure. It was his life's work."

In the canoe, the druid was staring up at Marcus in silence, his shrewd, suspicious eyes boring into Marcus, trying to decipher him.

"You knew Caradoc" the druid called out suspiciously. "He is the one who hired you to come here? So describe him for me."

"Yes, he hired us, paid us in gold," Marcus nodded, "Bald fellow, about my age, carried a stick around and liked to spend his spare time recording things on wood with his pen. He was a scholar."

Down in the canoe, the druid was watching Marcus closely. Then the man's shoulders seemed to slump a little.

"So Caradoc is dead" the red-bearded man exclaimed, as he suddenly looked away, his voice filled with disappointment and a tinge of sadness.

"I'm afraid so," Marcus replied grimly.

The druid was silent for a few moments, as he digested the news. Then quickly he looked up at Marcus.

"No one has ever crossed the ocean without us knowing about it," the man cried out, "My name is Ail. I knew Caradoc, he was a friend and I know he would not have chosen to make the crossing in a Roman ship."

"Well, you are wrong about that," Marcus shrugged. "We're just sailors, hired to do a job. I work for anyone who pays me. Caradoc approached me in Londinium and told me that there was trouble in Hibernia and that the sea route was closed. That is why he came to Londinium and hired us. It is the truth. I swear it. Caradoc said he wanted to bring a copy of his book to this place, to keep it safe and far away from Roman hands. Once we have completed the task for which we were paid and repairs have been made to our ship, we will be keen to head home."

Ail peered up at Marcus in sudden irritation. Then his silent, suspicious gaze switched to the rest of the crew.

"So this is your crew?" the druid cried.

"That's right," Marcus replied. "There are six of us."

"I am coming on board to take a look," the druid growled, as he turned to the natives and said something to them in a language Marcus could not understand. In response, the Hyperborean's dipped their paddles into the water and propelled the canoe towards the side of the Hermes.

Marcus gave Cunomoltus a quick glance, before he turned and gestured for Jodoc to throw the netting over the side of the hull. As Ail clambered over the edge of the ship, the crew gathered around him in a loose, semi-circle, silent and watchful. Several natives followed the druid, climbing nimbly up the side of the hull and, as they reached the deck, they looked around in wonder.

"Have a look around," Marcus said, forcing a smile, as he opened his arms wide in welcome, "We have nothing to hide."

"I will," the red-bearded druid growled darkly. "And I want to see Caradoc's book."

As Ail and the natives swarmed over the Hermes, Marcus and the crew stood silently on the deck without moving, as they waited for the inspection to end and as he waited, Marcus glanced across at Cunomoltus and saw the same tension on his brother's face. Nervously Marcus's fingers played with the pommel of his sword. He was about to have to explain the weakest part of his story and if it all went wrong, they were going to have fight for their lives.

When at last, the druid came towards Marcus, he was scowling.

"Where is Caradoc's book?"

In response, Marcus gestured at Cunomoltus who, giving the druid a big, fake smile, silently undid his thick cloak to reveal the small, iron box strapped around his waist. From the corner of his eye, Marcus caught Jodoc's face darkening, as the young man suddenly realised where Marcus had hidden it all this time.

"Where is the key to the lock?" Ail snapped.

"Ah," Marcus exclaimed, "Well that's the problem. Caradoc had it on him when he went overboard. It is a sturdy, stubborn box. We cannot open it without possibly damaging the book inside."

"There is no spare key?"

"My friend here," Marcus said indicating Cunomoltus, "trained as a blacksmith. He is fashioning a new key, he just needs a few more days. The box needs to remain here though, until we can open it."

Ail was silent, as he stared at the iron box. Then he looked up at Cunomoltus who once again gave him a broad, fake smile.

"Alright," the druid growled, "do what you have to do. But you," he snapped turning to Marcus, "You will come with me and explain yourself to the Council. The rest of you will stay on board your ship, until we have decided what to do with you. You are forbidden from leaving or going ashore without our permission."

Hiding his relief, Marcus glanced quickly at Cunomoltus as the druid called out to the natives, speaking rapidly and confidently in their language. Then without saying a word, he followed the druid to the edge of the ship and awkwardly slipped his legs over the side and, as he started to clamber down into the waiting canoe, he felt a hundred eyes watching him.

"Do as the man says," he called out to Cunomoltus in a reassuring voice, as he lowered himself into the rocking canoe and steadied himself. "Everything will be alright."

As the natives started to paddle away towards the shore, the ginger-bearded druid sat down opposite Marcus and glared at him with a suspicious, watchful and unfriendly face.

"One word from me," Ail growled, "and these natives will tear you to pieces, set your ship on fire and hang your entrails from the nearest tree. So don't even think about starting any trouble."

***

In the arched entrances of their domed tents, Marcus could see children and women, wearing pointed hoods on their heads and clutching infants, peering out at him as, accompanied by the red-bearded druid and a loud throng of excited Hyperborean's, he strode through the native camp, towards the wooden, long house. The smell of smoking fish filled his nostrils and beside the native shelters, lay heaps of discarded shells. The Hyperborean's, clad in breechcloth and leather leggings and wearing Moccasins on their feet and clutching an array of stone and bone weapons, were making whooping noises and crying out to each other. Amongst them, Marcus suddenly caught sight of a number of mixed-race children. The primitive-looking conical, native shelters, constructed of arched saplings and with an outer cladding of birch-bark and brown, animal hides were arranged around the long house. Amongst the tents, Marcus caught sight of ceramic pots, hanging over cold, dead blackened, cooking fires and wooden racks, upon which freshly-caught fish had been hung up to dry. In between the shelters, an old man was repairing a canoe in which lay several fish traps and beside one of the wigwams, a woman was tending to a stack of beautifully decorated baskets. Tensely Marcus lowered his head and his right hand idly came to rest on the pommel of his sword. The decisive moment was fast approaching. If Emogene was here, if she had not died or returned to Britannia, he was likely to come face to face with her very soon. Would she remember him? Would she recognise him? Many years had passed since his last encounter with her, as a prisoner of war, during the Brigantian uprising and, although he was older now, his appearance had not changed that much since then. But there was nothing he could do about that. He would just have to stick to his plan.

The long-house was made of wooden logs and covered in bark, with an arc-shaped roof covered in branches with leaves and straw that stretched for some twenty-five yards. As the party approached, Marcus caught sight of three, bearded druids, standing beside the entrance. They were staring at him with hard, suspicious, unfriendly eyes. Without saying a word, they turned and one by one vanished through the hide-covered doorway and into the building. As Marcus stepped inside, he entered a dark, cool room. At the centre of the long-house, he could make out a dead fireplace and the only natural light came from the small, smoke-holes in the roof. Long, empty, wooden-benches stood arranged along the side of the walls and, in a corner was a large collection of ceramic, Roman amphorae, together with a small pile of Roman shovels, hammers, nails, spears, swords, knives and iron axes. At the far end of the long-house, clustered together under a flickering oil lamp that hung from the ceiling, the majestic druids, clad in their white, ceremonial-cloaks had gathered around a table. As Marcus approached he sensed a fierce, intimidating intelligence amongst the grand gathering. The druids, with their long beards, were staring at Marcus in solemn silence, their old, hard, faces, pensive and unhappy. There were thirteen of them and all of them were men.

As Ail led Marcus towards them, Marcus saw that the table was filled with a dozen wooden cups, several small ceramic jugs, and a single, polished white skull. The empty, eye-sockets seemed to be staring straight at him and as he caught sight of the skull Marcus froze, his feet suddenly unable to move, as a fierce, hot blush appeared on his cheeks. What had Fergus, his son told him? Emogene had turned Corbulo's skull into a drinking cup.

"How did you find us?" a man said suddenly, in a clear, authoritarian voice. "Who else knows about us? Are there other ships on their way here?"

One of the druids, an old stooping man with a white-beard had stood up and was pointing at Marcus with a gnarled stick, similar to the one Caradoc had brought on board the Hermes.

Marcus wrenched his eyes away from the gleaming white skull and turned to stare at the druid. The room fell silent as all waited for him to speak.

"No, it's just us," Marcus muttered, "No one else knows about this place. Only I and my crew."

Then carefully, Marcus repeated the story he had told Ail and when he was finished, the druids glanced at each other in contemplative, unhappy silence.

"No one comes here without our knowledge or permission," another of the druids said at last, speaking in a quiet, sullen voice, "so your arrival is a surprise and we do not like surprises. We do not like strangers coming here for they only cause trouble. The Council will need some time to decide what to do with you. Until then, you are forbidden from leaving and one of your crew will stay here in this house, as a gesture of good faith."

The room fell silent.

"You mean as a hostage" Marcus said, "I already told you. We are not here to cause trouble."

"As our guest," one of the druids replied coldly.

Marcus remained silent for a moment as he considered the druid's words. "May I propose in that case," he said carefully, "that my crew take turns in staying here in this house? We have had a long, exhausting voyage and they are all eager to spend some time on land. It is only fair that they all get a chance to go ashore."

"That is acceptable," the white-bearded druid said.

Marcus nodded in silent gratitude and took a deep breath. "There is however another matter, that I need to discuss with you lords," he said in a slow, clear voice. "In Londinium, I knew a man called Meryn. He asked me to pass on a message to his wife, Emogene. She is a druid. He said she crossed the ocean to this place, but unfortunately, I do not see her here amongst you. Can you tell me where I can find this woman?"

"What message" one of the bearded druids growled.

"It is of a private nature and I am to give her the message verbally," Marcus replied uncomfortably, "I was told to give it to her and her alone. Meryn, her husband, was very specific and I gave him my word that I would."

Around the table, the druids were silent as they glanced at each other.

"The woman you speak of is not here," the white-bearded man grunted in reply, as he peered at Marcus.

Marcus's shoulders sagged and quickly he looked down at the floor, as he silently cursed himself. The journey across the ocean had been a complete waste of time! Meryn had lied to him and he had believed the false information. He had risked his life for nothing. Fool!

"Emogene has gone inland to stay at another native camp," the druid continued. "She will return here at the end of the summer. She has gone to appease the thunder spirit who resides on Mount Katahdin."

Marcus blinked in surprise and in his chest; he could feel his heart pounding away.

"Then with your permission, I would like to go and find her," Marcus said, as he felt his mouth drying up. "I am honour bound to deliver my message and I cannot wait here until the end of summer, for I and my ship are keen to return home, before the winter storms make the crossing impossible."

Again, the druids glanced at each other.

"Why the rush?" one of the druids snapped suspiciously. "Why not stay here and wait for her to return. It would be easier. After such a long and perilous voyage, why are you so keen to leave?"

"Like I said," Marcus growled, turning calmly to look at the man who had spoken, "I and my crew were paid to come here. It's a job and I have a pregnant wife back in Britannia. I would like to be there when my child is born."

"We don't know you," one of the druids cried out, "Why would Meryn entrust you with a message to his wife? A message that you are not allowed to reveal. Why would he do that?"

Marcus shrugged. "Maybe you should ask him," he replied, "But I am telling the truth. I was paid to bring Caradoc here and pass on a message to Emogene and that is what I am going to do."

"You look like a soldier," another druid hissed, "and you carry a Roman sword. Now why would you have a Roman sword?"

"You have Roman swords over there," Marcus growled in an exasperated voice as he pointed at the corner, in which the trade goods lay piled up, "They are actually quite good, as I am sure these Hyperboreans will agree. Carrying a Roman sword does not make me a Roman and how many Romans have you met who have red- hair like mine?"

"Rome has many slaves who fight for her. Maybe you are one of them," a druid called out in an angry voice.

"No," Marcus retorted, "I am just doing what I was paid to do. We can go on debating this all day."

The room fell silent, as the druids considered what had been said and, as they did Marcus felt their intimidating eyes fixed on him, searching, probing and trying to see into his very soul.

"Alright," the white-bearded druid said at last, "once we have managed to retrieve Caradoc's book and on condition that one of your crew remains here, we shall allow you to go to meet Emogene and deliver your message. Your ship however, will stay here and one of us will accompany you as a guide, for you do not know the way or the natives, like we do."

Marcus remained silent as he considered the druid's words. "This mount Katahdin," he said at last, "How far away is it?"

"A hundred and fifty miles inland," Ail replied sharply. "The journey will be by canoe up the river. The mountain is a holy place for the natives."

Then the red-bearded druid turned to his colleagues. "If it pleases the Council I will accompany them. I know Emogene well and I know how to keep her calm. It will also give me a chance to check up on the native camps along the river and confirm whether the news that they are starving, is true. If they are starving, it may explain the recent hostility that we have encountered."

There was a murmur of approval from the assembled druids.

"I would like to leave as soon as possible," Marcus said. "And I will be accompanied by my brother and one of my crew. The others will stay here."

"Alright Ail," one of the druids called out, "It is agreed. Take two hunters with you and a couple of canoes." Then slowly the druid turned to Marcus. "You may leave as soon as you have managed to open the iron box and have given us Caradoc's book."

Marcus nodded in agreement.

"How long will the journey take" he muttered looking over at Ail.

"Six or seven days," the red-bearded druid replied sullenly, "We will be travelling upriver for most of the way."

"And as for your pregnant wife," a druid said in an angry voice, "You may not be there at her side when she gives birth. The Council has not yet said whether you will be allowed to go back to Britannia. Caradoc was unwise in hiring you and you were foolish in accepting his offer. We do not want the knowledge of our trading post to spread to others. We do not want others coming here. You and your ship's departure will depend on whether we feel we can trust you."

The long house fell silent, as Marcus sighed and looked away, feigning alarm.

"Well, let me know when you have made up your mind," Marcus replied in a sour voice.

Then he turned and pointed at the polished, white skull lying on the table.

"Why do you keep a skull on your table? Who did that head belong to?"

"What does it matter? Why are you so interested" a druid retorted, in a sharp suspicious voice.

"No reason," Marcus replied hastily.

"The skull belongs to one of our enemies, a Roman soldier," a druid growled. "Emogene brought it with her to use it as a drinking vessel. It reminds us that our enemies can be defeated. And one day soon, we will be able to return home, for the power of Rome will fade and her occupation of our land will end."

Marcus did not seem to hear the last part of the druid's words. He was staring at Corbulo's polished, white-skull as he struggled to contain a surge of raw emotion and prevent himself from throwing up.

Chapter Forty-Two – The Secrets of the Druids

It was night when Marcus slowly opened his eyes and stopped pretending that he was asleep. He lay on a rug made of animal fur, which lay on the earthen floor, alongside the wall of the long-house, and in the spacious room; he could hear the gentle snoring and the occasional cough coming from the druids. Silently he sat up and looked around at the sleeping bodies. The smell of wood-smoke clung to his clothes and the walls, but the fire at the centre of the room had died out hours ago. The druids seemed to have the hall for themselves, and even though there was a huge amount of space, none of the Hyperboreans had come inside to share the shelter. Close by, a glowing Hyperborean stone-lamp, filled with seal-oil hung from the ceiling beside the doorway and another faint glow of light was coming from a small room at the far end of the house. Marcus blinked as he waited for his eyes to adjust to the darkness. He had volunteered to be the first person to stay behind with the druids, but there had been no chance to tell the crew of the Hermes. As he waited, his head slowly turned in the direction of the table, around which the druids had gathered, when he had first spoken to them. The druids had left Corbulo's skull lying there, as if it were a mere utensil, just another drinking cup, to be used and discarded, when they were thirsty. Marcus steadied his breathing and for a moment, he could hear his heart thumping away.

Silently he rose to his feet and looked down at the nearest, sleeping man. He had learned that there were fifteen druids in all, some of whom had been living at the trading post for nearly all their lives. Carefully he began to pick his way across the floor and over the sleeping men, taking great care not to tread on anything. Corbulo's skull gleamed in the faint light. It was lying upside down, where the druids had left it on the table. Reaching out, Marcus grasped hold of it and as he did, he closed his eyes and his cheeks burned. Quickly he slipped the skull into a leather sack and turned to start retracing his steps towards the doorway, but as he did, he heard a sudden muffled noise coming from the small room, at the far end of the long-house. Torn by sudden indecision he hesitated. Then biting his lip, he crept past the cold fireplace towards the faint gleam of light. As he reached the doorway leading into the room, he paused as he heard voices talking quietly. Through a gap in the animal hides that covered the doorway, he saw two druids pouring over a table, upon which stood a strange, box-like machine with bronze, hand-cranks, dials and two concentric circular scales set into the front. The men were carefully adjusting one of the cranks on the front face of the machine and, as he stared at the mechanism, Marcus could make out words marking the outer and inner scales, but he was too far away to read them. Marcus frowned. The machine was like nothing he had ever seen before. What were the druids up to?

Silently he retreated from the room and turned towards the distant doorway. Whatever these men were up to, it was none of his business, and he had more important things to do. Carefully picking his way across the room, he made it to the doorway. A cool, refreshing breeze was gently moving the animal hides back and forth and for a moment he paused to listen, but the night remained quiet. Boldly Marcus pushed the skins aside and poked his head outside. In the native encampment, a few campfires were still glowing but in the peaceful darkness, nothing moved. The Hyperborean village seemed to be asleep. Marcus looked up to where he could just about see the dark, outline of the forest as it merged with the night sky. The heavens were covered by a fantastic and beautiful array of stars and a single full moon.

Slowly he turned to look at the large heap of discarded shells, which had been dumped beside the doorway into the long house. The natives, he had observed, had enjoyed eating shellfish and had thrown the left-over shells onto various rubbish dumps around their village. Marcus stepped forwards, pushed his hands into the heap of loose shells to make a space, before quickly stuffing the sack, containing the skul,l deep into the mound and covering it up again. Once the sack had been hidden, he looked up and paused to listen, but the night remained peaceful and quiet. Then, taking a final glance at the rubbish dump, he muttered a hasty apology to his father's spirit, before turning towards the door and slipping back into the long-house.

***

Jodoc looked unhappy as he strode purposefully across the deck towards Marcus. It was morning and the Hermes lay at anchor in the calm water. Alexandros was standing in the canoe, that had brought Marcus back to the ship, as he waited his turn to go ashore and take Marcus's place amongst the druids and Cora was sitting beside the mast making a drawing. She paused to look up, as Jodoc stormed past her.

"I want to go ashore," the young man cried out in an aggressive voice. "And I want to give the druids my father's work. You promised me that you would give me the book and let me go once we reached the trading post."

"No," Marcus replied sharply as he clambered over the side of the ship and landed on the deck. "Not yet. For now, you will stay here and so will your father's book."

"You promised," Jodoc snapped in an accusing voice, as he raised his hand and pointed at Marcus.

"When the time is right you may go," Marcus growled, fixing his eyes on the young man, "Until then you and the book, will stay here. Is that a problem?"

A light, blush appeared on Jodoc's cheeks and suddenly he seemed less sure of himself.

"My brother has killed men for less," Cunomoltus called out cheerfully, as he casually ambled up behind Jodoc. "So what's it going to be, arsehole?"

A bitter defeated look appeared on Jodoc's face and, with a snarl he turned and stomped away, vanishing down the ladder into the cargo hold.

Marcus caught Cunomoltus' eye and silently gestured for his brother to follow him to the poop deck at the stern. For a while Marcus stood clutching the side of the ship, as he wearily stared out across the water at the Hyperborean camp and quietly brought his brother up to date with what had happened with the druids. Beside him Cunomoltus, his elbows resting on the edge of the boat, listened in silence and, as he did so, he grew increasingly sombre. From the roof of the deck house, the black ship's cat was watching Marcus with half closed, contented eyes and close by two Hyperborean's were fishing from a canoe, tensely searching the clear water with their tripod harpoons.

"Do you really believe the skull is our father's" Cunomoltus said at last.

Marcus nodded.

"When the time comes, I will retrieve it," he muttered, "For now it should be safe. I hid it in a pile of sea shells. I don't think the druids have noticed it is missing yet. To them, it is just another ritual cup."

"Those bastards," Cunomoltus hissed, shaking his head in bewilderment, "Maybe tonight we should go ashore and kill them all in their sleep. Three of us would be able to manage that. This insult will not stand. We should avenge Corbulo! That's why we came here."

But Marcus shook his head.

"No," he replied firmly, "They have the natives on their side. If we tried to kill the druids, we would never get away from here alive, nor would we find Emogene. Alexandros needs time to repair the ship and we need everyone to be alive, if we are to make it back home."

348

"Then what?" Cunomoltus growled unhappily.

For a moment Marcus said nothing, as he stared at the native encampment.

"The druids have asked me to hand over Caradoc's book," he murmured at last, "Once they have the book they have agreed to let us go upriver to find Emogene. Ail is coming with us to act as a guide and no doubt to keep an eye on us. The druids say that Emogene has gone to appease the thunder spirit, who lives on a mountain. It sounds like it's a holy place. We will go along with it, until we have what we came for."

"If we hand them the book," Cunomoltus exclaimed in alarm, "Then what is there to stop Jodoc from telling the druids why we are really here? You saw him. He only cares about his father's work. He's itching to abandon us."

Marcus raised his hand to quieten his brother, as he hurriedly turned to look around, but there was no sign of Jodoc or Calista.

"I have thought about that," he said quietly, "We are going to give the book to the druids and you will continue to wear the iron box around your waist and make sure that Jodoc sees it. The druids will be satisfied and Jodoc will think we still have the book."

A sudden gleam appeared in Cunomoltus's eyes as he studied Marcus.

"I like it," Cunomoltus hissed, "Except what happens if the druids talk? What happens if Jodoc finds out that they already have his father's book? You are proposing a dangerous game Marcus. If it goes wrong, we're dead."

"He is not going to talk to the druids," Marcus replied sharply. "He is coming with us on the journey to the mountain. Then we only have to worry about Ail. The others will stay here.

Alexandros can be trusted to keep his mouth shut. We keep our friends close and our enemies closer."

"Clever," Cunomoltus muttered, as he looked away and took a deep breath. For a moment he was silent. Then he turned to Marcus.

"Why don't we just kill him," Cunomoltus muttered. "It would be simpler."

Marcus shook his head. "Maybe," he growled. "But I promised Caradoc. I said I would not harm his son."

"You and your sense of honour are going to get us all killed," Cunomoltus muttered darkly.

Marcus remained silent as he watched the Hyperborean camp. Then he raised his hand and rubbed his tired eyes.

"The druids were up to something last night," he said. "In the middle of the night, I saw two of them hunched over some kind of machine."

"What kind of machine?" Cunomoltus frowned.

Marcus shrugged.

"I don't know but the druids have secrets. How else can fifteen men, not even warriors, command such respect amongst these Hyperborean's? How did the druids manage to gain so much power and influence over these natives? It can't just be the trade goods that they provide."

Cunomoltus raised his eyebrows as he stared out across the water.

"I don't think they intend to ever let us leave," he murmured unhappily, "They are too afraid that news of their little colony is going to get out."

Marcus turned to give his brother a careful, thoughtful look. Then he laid a hand on Cunomoltus's shoulder.

"I could not have done this without you," Marcus muttered, "Stay cool brother, we must remain calm. The gods favour the bold but we are going to get only one chance to find Emogene and honour our father. So let's make it worthy of his name and memory, for his spirit is watching us and one day, maybe soon, you will meet him again and you will have to explain yourself. That much is certain."

"I hear you brother," Cunomoltus growled looking away, so that Marcus would not see the sombre mood that was weighing on him, lift and vanish. "But we need to act fast. Sooner or later the druids are going to learn why we are really here."

Chapter Forty-Three – The River Journey

"Why should I go with you?" Jodoc cried out in protest.

"Because that is how you will get your father's book back," Marcus retorted, as he stood facing the young man on the deck of the Hermes. It was morning and it was promising to be a hot day.

"You already promised me that," Jodoc snarled, "Why can't I just stay here? You don't need me on this journey. What do I care about this Emogene?"

Marcus shrugged, "nevertheless you are coming with us."

"You are a bully and a murderer," Jodoc snarled, "I am not your slave. What are you going to do if I refuse?"

Jodoc's head suddenly jerked backwards and a knife appeared, pressing against his exposed throat, as Cunomoltus came up behind him and caught hold of the young man.

"Now listen very carefully," Cunomoltus hissed, as he pressed the steel blade against Jodoc's flesh. "My brother over there is an honourable man. He keeps his word. I however am, not like my brother. I am the arsehole of the family. I spit on honour. I cheat, I kill and I steal and I don't give a fuck whether you or your precious book survive. I will not hesitate to slit your throat if I think you are going to cause trouble for us. So that is why you are coming with us. There is your reason. Now repeat after me. I will be happy to come with you Marcus."

Jodoc seemed to be having trouble breathing.

"I don't hear you," Cunomoltus hissed.

"I will be happy to come with you Marcus."

"That's better," Cunomoltus exclaimed cheerfully, as he withdrew his knife and gave Jodoc a push that sent him staggering across the deck.

"Pack your things and say goodbye to Calista," Marcus said, fixing Jodoc with a grim look. "We are leaving within the hour."

Jodoc said nothing, as he gave Cunomoltus a hateful look and stomped away towards the cargo hatch. Marcus caught his brother's eye and slowly shook his head.

"Corbulo would be proud of you," he muttered. "He would say you knew how to handle difficult situations."

"No," Cunomoltus replied with a serious face, "He would be proud of me because I protect your back."

"Maybe," Marcus said.

"You know that boy is going to be trouble, it's just a matter of time," Cunomoltus growled as he turned to look at the open hatch.

"I know," Marcus replied.

***

The clear, blue sky stretched away to the horizon and beneath it, the silent, vast forested land baked in the summer heat. Alexandros was standing on the roof of the deckhouse, looking at the coastline as Marcus clambered up the ladder towards him. The captain turned to give him a little nervous smile.

"So you are going upriver then," Alexandros said quietly, "You are determined to do what you came here to do."

Marcus nodded, as he turned to gaze at the Hyperborean settlement.

"If all goes well, we will return within fourteen or fifteen days," he replied quietly, "I want you to use that time to repair the ship and get her ready for going back to sea. But, be careful of the druids. They are suspicious. When I return we will be leaving right away."

"Whether the druids give us permission or not," Alexandros murmured.

"That's right," Marcus said, laying a hand on the captain's shoulder, "Here this is for you. The second part of your payment. You have earned it," he added, as he thrust a leather pouch into Alexandros's hand. "Whatever happens from now on, I know I chose well when I hired you."

Alexandros looked down at the bag of gold coins in his hand and, for a long moment he remained silent. Then quickly he slipped the bag under his cloak and rubbed his black eye patch.

"I did not accept this job for the money," he murmured, avoiding Marcus's gaze, "I came here to prove that a western route to the land of the Chin could be found and although I don't think this is the land of the Chin, I am now sure that the route is possible and when we get back, they are going to have to listen to me. No one is going to be able to ignore old drunken Alexandros any longer."

Marcus nodded, "Just don't tell the druids that. They are keen to keep the existence of their little colony a secret."

Alexandros turned to look at Marcus and, as he did, his rugged, weather beaten face seemed to soften.

"I will have the Hermes ready and waiting for when you return," he said quietly, "You can count on me."

***

The two canoes sliced through the calm, crystal-clear sea, one following the other and, as they rounded a rocky, forested promontory, Marcus turned to get a final glimpse of the Hermes, as she lay at anchor beside the Hyperborean village. Then she was gone. With a grunt, Marcus turned to look ahead. There was no going back now. The druids had Caradoc's book. He had given it to them that morning and now he was committed. At his feet, in the bottom of the narrow birch-bark canoe, lay Alexandros' bow and a quiver of arrows and a single leather bag containing some supplies and Corbulo's skull, carefully wrapped up and hidden in some spare clothes. Directly in front of him, Jodoc dug his paddle into the water in sullen, silent, resentment and behind him, Marcus could hear the Hyperborean guide doing the same. Up ahead, the second canoe containing Cunomoltus, Ail and a second Hyperborean guide, was powering through the water as it headed into a narrow, sea straight. In the summer heat Cunomoltus had stripped down to just one thin tunic and the empty iron box was slung over his back, in full view of Jodoc, as if done on purpose. Stoically Marcus bit his lip, as he dug his paddle into the water. The deception had to last. If Ail discovered the real reason why he wanted to find Emogene or Jodoc talked, then the whole journey would end in failure, for even if he managed to win a fight, he would have no idea where in this beautiful, vast and unknown land, he would be able to find Emogene. No, the fragile deception he'd woven had to last. There was no alternative.

Above him, the blue, warm, summer sky stretched away and the thick green, mysterious looking forests covered the land and hills. The Hyperborean canoe with its high curved bow, was surprisingly agile and light and, as they cut through the water, it suddenly reminded Marcus of the old, log boat in which he and Corbulo had escaped from Caledonia all those years ago. A little smile appeared on the corner of Marcus's lips. The gods were playing games with him. For now, instead of fleeing from Emogene, he was looking for her. Fate had come a full circle but soon the gods were going to have to declare their hand one way or the other. Soon they were going to have to choose sides.

***

The camp-fire flickered and crackled, sending a shower of glowing sparks shooting up into the dark sky. It was late in the evening and the six of them sat silently around the fire, stuffing their faces on freshly caught and cooked fish. Close by, the two canoes lay drawn up on the stony beach and along the wide, river-mouth the immense, trackless, pine forests and small, wooded islands were quiet and dark. In the Penobscot river the tide was out and the moon cast its pale light across the placid water. Ail was the first to break the silence as he threw a fish bone into the fire and turned to mutter something to the two Hyperborean guides, in a language Marcus could not understand. The natives however did, and as one of them replied Ail nodded and turned to stare sombrely at the camp-fire. Marcus glanced at Cunomoltus who was sitting beside Jodoc, the iron box tucked out of view under his cloak. His brother was doing a good job at keeping an eye on the young man, a fact that Jodoc seemed uncomfortably aware of.

"When you spoke at the Council about Emogene," Marcus said looking at Ail, "what did you mean when you said that you could keep her calm?"

Ail did not immediately reply, as he stared into the fire.

"How well do you know her" he snapped, looking up at Marcus.

Marcus shrugged. "I never met her," he muttered.

Abruptly Ail turned to stare into the darkness. "She is mad and she has become violent," he exclaimed. "She has a sickness of the heart. There is no cure and she likes to be on her own these days. She has become a hermit. The natives are terrified of her. They say that she is possessed by demons and maybe they are right."

"But you can reason with her, Marcus said quietly.

Ail nodded.

"Violent you say," Cunomoltus said, glancing at Ail, "What do you mean?"

"She killed a man," Ail muttered, "a native, soon after she first arrived. She has no fear of anyone or anything and she knows how to use a knife. She is dangerous. The natives claim that the bears in the forests do not dare go near her and that their dogs don't stop barking when she visits their camps."

"Sounds like a charming lady," Cunomoltus growled, as he licked his fingers.

"I hear she didn't like Roman's either," Marcus muttered, looking down at his boots.

"Who the fuck does" Ail snapped as he carefully examined a fish that was baking over the fire on a long, blackened stick.

"What will you do with my father's book?" Jodoc suddenly exclaimed, turning to Ail.

Marcus's head slowly turned and his eyes fixed upon the young man but it was too late to shut Jodoc up. At the young man's side Cunomoltus's hand innocently dropped down to his belt from which hung his sheathed sword. Ail frowned as he looked up at Jodoc from across the camp fire.

"Your father?" the druid exclaimed in a surprised sounding voice, "You are Caradoc's son?"

"I am," Jodoc muttered as a fleeting, painful expression flitted across Cunomoltus' face. "My name is Jodoc, I am his eldest son."

"Why did you not mention this before" Ail cried out. "Caradoc was my friend; he was one of us and that makes you one of us."

A hopeful, happy smile had appeared on Jodoc's face as he beamed at Ail. The young man's grin however faded quickly as he noticed Cunomoltus smiling at him.

Across the camp-fire the red-bearded druid was silent as he examined Jodoc. Then he shook his head in disbelief.

"Don't worry Jodoc. Your father's book will be kept safe. We will hide it in a place where no one will ever find it, without our knowledge. Is that not why he wanted to bring his work here?"

"It is," Jodoc muttered, looking suddenly uncomfortable.

"You and I should talk tomorrow," Ail nodded, "You father was a good man and I am sorry for your loss."

"There are only fifteen of you," Marcus interrupted with a frown as he turned to Ail, "How do you manage to maintain such power and influence over these Hyperboreans?"

"That's our business," Ail replied sharply, as his eyes lingered on Jodoc.

Marcus glanced idly at the two Hyperborean guides who were gorging themselves on fish. The two men gave no indication that they could understand a word of what was being said.

"So these natives never tried to attack you? We were attacked," Marcus added. "Red painted devils came out of the forest and tried to kill young Jodoc here and they would have succeeded if I hadn't saved his life."

"That's right," Cunomoltus interjected, giving Jodoc a broad smile, "You were a lucky bastard that day weren't you?"

Jodoc lowered his eyes to the ground.

With a sigh, Ail wrenched his eyes away from Jodoc and glared at Marcus from across the reddish, flickering fire.

"There has been trouble, I admit and it seems to be growing worse," Ail growled. "The natives are divided into two factions. Most of their chief's and clan elders favour us and are friendly but there is a section amongst the population who accuse us of being the bringers of death. They want us gone from their land. They are growing increasingly hostile."

"The bringers of death?" Marcus exclaimed with a frown.

Ail fixed his cold, hard eyes on Marcus.

"Disease," he hissed, "Some of the natives claim that we are killing them. They say that we have brought foreign diseases and illness amongst them, against which their medicine men are powerless to act. They say that wherever we go, we leave a trail of sick and dying in our wake."

Marcus was staring at Ail from across the fire, his rugged, bearded face a stoic mask.

"Well, is it true?" Marcus exclaimed, "have you brought disease with you?"

"Of course not," Ail snapped, turning to look away. "You have seen all of us. Do we look sick or diseased to you? We don't know why these natives make these claims or why they are dying."

From the corner of his eye, Marcus caught Cunomoltus watching him carefully.

"When I stayed the night in your house," Marcus said, gazing at Ail with a sudden thoughtful look, "I happened to see that you had some sort of machine. It had dials, lettering, scales and a bronze crank. I am not an educated man but I suspect this machine has something to do with how you maintain your position with the natives." A little smile appeared on Marcus's lips. "Well am I right?"

Ail looked unhappy as he glared into the fire. Then he turned and growled something to the two native guides and, without saying a word the men got up and vanished into the gathering darkness.

"The mechanism you saw is a Greek invention," Ail snarled, "It allows us to calculate the future position of the constellations, the moon and eclipses. Knowing these future astronomical positions means we can tell the natives exactly when the most opportune time is for them to plant their crops, conduct their religious rituals, move their camps and go out hunting."

"A Greek machine," Marcus muttered with perplexed look.

"It's the same mechanism that the Greeks use to calculate when to hold their Olympic games," Ail growled.

Chapter Forty-Four – A Vast, Rich but Empty Land

The afternoon was hot and Marcus could feel the sweat drenching the back of his tunic as he steadily dug his paddle into the water. Up ahead, Cunomoltus' canoe was pushing up river, the three occupants digging their paddles into the water in near-perfect rhythm and timing. Ail, his neck lathered in sweat, was sitting at the bow of the narrow canoe, his back turned to Marcus. On the river bank, the endless, dense, pine-tree forests stretched away as far as the eye could see. The towering, white pines were like nothing Marcus had seen before and in the distance he could see a line of mountains that never seemed to grow any closer. The river had narrowed substantially since they had left the wide, placid estuary behind. As it had grown increasingly wild, shallow and rocky, their progress had slowed and at times they had been forced to haul the canoes on foot over rapids and spectacular, torrential, gushing falls.

Noticing movement on the river-bank Marcus turned and saw a moose with huge antlers, standing dumbly amongst the trees at the water's edge staring at the canoes. Marcus grunted as he stared at the strange animal. The wild, rugged wilderness into which they were heading seemed to be a vast, rich but empty land teeming with fish and animals but very few people. They had only encountered one other native canoe heading downstream. To Marcus the people here seemed to live a highly isolated existence.

Tapping Ail on his shoulder Marcus raised his voice above the rushing torrent.

"These Hyperborean's," he cried out, "they seem never to have learned how to make bronze or iron tools. Why is that?"

Ail did not look round as he dug his paddle into the water.

"They live in harmony with nature and the spirits of the land," Ail replied in a loud voice. "Their stone weapons are sufficient to allow them to hunt and survive. They live like they have always lived since the earliest times. They had no need to develop iron tools. None of the tribes which we know about have developed iron or bronze weapons."

"A good trading opportunity," Marcus replied.

Ail shrugged.

"Yes, they do like our weapons and tools," the druid replied sourly. "We call the tribe who live around here the Penawapskewi, the people of the rocky river and this is their river. They move their camps when the season changes; during the summer they are camped along the sea; in winter they move inland. But this river is always very important to them. They say it is part of who they are as a people. They say that they are forever part of the river."

"What about this mountain, Katahdin," Marcus called out. "Why is it holy?"

"Because of the native god Paloma," Ail said. "The Thunder God lives on its summit. The natives believe it is he who causes thunder and bad weather and last winter the hunting was bad and food was scarce. Emogene has gone to the mountain to try and appease Paloma. The natives do not dare climb up to its summit so we do it for them."

Marcus sat back as he silently stared at the wild river and the thick, green forests that came up to the water's edge. Then he wiped the sweat from his brow and dug his oar resolutely into the river.

***

It was morning and the blue, summer sky stretched away across the forests. Slowly and carefully Marcus and his companions picked their way along the boulder-strewn river bank, holding their birch bark canoe over their heads. The boat was surprisingly light and over his shoulder, Marcus had slung his pack. Up ahead, Cunomoltus, Jodoc and one of the Hyperborean guides were disappearing through the trees, carrying their boat. Cunomoltus had Alexandros' bow and quiver strapped across his back. Through the trees to his left, Marcus could hear the Penobscot river. The water had become a foaming and thundering, white torrent as it coursed around and splashed over the rocks of yet another, debris strewn rapid. As the small party bypassed the obstacle and re-joined the river a little way upstream, one of the Hyperborean guides cried out and pointed at the rapids. There flying and leaping through the air, Marcus suddenly caught sight of dozens of salmon, as they forced themselves upstream on their long and difficult journey to their spawning grounds.

Lowering the canoe to the ground, Ail called out to the guides and quickly started off towards the boulder-strewn rapids, beckoning for the others to follow him.

"Fish, looks like we are eating fish again," Cunomoltus said sarcastically as he passed Marcus and headed on after Ail and the others.

When Marcus reached the riverbank above the rapids, the two Hyperborean's were already expertly and eagerly picking their way from rock to rock as they closed in on the section of the river where the salmon were hurtling through the air. Marcus shook his head in wonder, as one of the natives crouched on a large boulder and caught hold of a salmon as it leapt through the air. The roar of the raging river as it went over the rapids was deafening. Suddenly, as he stood watching the Hyperborean's trying to catch the salmon, Marcus noticed Jodoc talking to Ail in a hurried and animated manner. The noise from the river made it impossible to hear what he was saying but, as he watched, Ail suddenly looked troubled. Marcus's mood darkened and quickly he looked around and saw that Cunomoltus had also noticed the exchange. As he stood staring at the two men, caught by a horrible indecision, Ail turned to look in his direction as Jodoc's mouth continued to move. What was Jodoc telling him? Marcus was about to stride towards them, when a high-pitched scream of alarm from the river stopped him in his tracks. A dozen paces away a huge, brown bear had appeared from amongst the trees and was calmly ambling towards the salmon fishing ground.

In the river the two native guides were staring at the approaching bear in alarm and fear as they clutched their stone knives and raised their sharp, bone-headed harpoons above their heads. However, Cunomoltus was the first to react. Snatching his bow from his back, he raised it, strung an arrow and with deadly accuracy sent the projectile hurtling into the bear's exposed back. The blow sent the great animal crashing into the water. With surprising speed however, the bear emerged and leapt back onto the bank, and with the arrow still sticking into it, the beast swiftly vanished into the trees.

"Get back to the canoes now," Marcus yelled as he frantically gestured at the others to head back towards the spot where they had left the canoes.

***

The native camp stood in a clearing in the forest at the river's edge, a collection of small, domed tents and in, the midst of the settlement, smoke was rising up into the air. Slowly Ail steered the lead canoe towards the camp and, as he did, he silently gestured to one of the native guides. The man turned and called out softly to his colleague in Marcus's canoe. On the shore Marcus could see no one. The camp looked deserted. It was noon and on the embankment, four canoes lay pulled up out of the water and beyond them he suddenly caught sight of a small, domed hut that seemed to be set apart from the others. A single Hyperborean was sitting cross legged before the entrance, his eyes closed and his chin resting on his chest as if he was meditating. The entrance of the lodge had been blocked and covered with wood and branches. Silently the canoes drifted into the soft, muddy river-bank and cautiously Ail and the others slipped out into the water and swiftly hauled the canoe up onto the embankment.

"What's going on?" Marcus muttered, as he quietly joined Ail on the shore. The druid raised his hand in warning. The two native guides had stopped well short of the camp and were peering at the solitary Hyperborean sitting cross-legged on the ground.

"We should not go any further," Ail murmured.

Marcus was about to say something else, when he suddenly caught sight of the bodies lying scattered across the ground. In some of the domed tents the Hyperborean's lay half-in, half-out of the entrances to their homes, their arms outstretched clawing at the earth. It was as if, in their final moments, they had tried to crawl out into the daylight. Marcus grunted as he saw that the bodies looked wasted away and covered in evil, puss-filled sores. Beside the hut with the blocked entrance the solitary Hyperborean had not moved.

"So the reports were right," Ail growled as he stared at the ghastly scene, "They are dying from starvation. Another failed hunt. The gods are still angry."

Slowly Marcus turned to stare at Ail with an incredulous, angry look.

"This is not starvation," he hissed, "You know full well what this is. These people are dying from disease. I have seen those symptoms before. You don't want to admit it but, over there is why they call you the bringers of death. That's why some of the Hyperboreans are becoming hostile. You have brought disease with you to their land. Disease that they can't cope with."

"Are you calling me a liar," Ail growled turning to face Marcus. "Where could you possibly have seen these symptoms before. In the Roman army, on campaign perhaps?"

Marcus's hand dropped to the pommel of his sword as his face darkened.

"I am no Roman soldier," he snapped, "I told you who I am."

A contemptuous look appeared on Ail's face as he stared at Marcus, "Jodoc says you served in the Roman army. He says you are not who you claim to be."

"He is lying," Marcus growled. "He is saying these things because he is angry with me. He blames me for his father's death, but Caradoc died in an accident. I swear it. If I had murdered him, would I really have continued on with this voyage? Wouldn't I have just gone back home? You should not listen to Jodoc. The boy is being foolish."

Ail turned away to look at the young man and in that moment Marcus thought he saw a glimmer of uncertainty in the druid's eyes.

"When we return to the coast," Ail growled at last, "the others will need to hear about this. The Council will decide who to believe."

***

The large lake lay shrouded in the dawn mist. As he slowly dug his oar into the quiet, peaceful water, Marcus peered ahead into the fog. Ahead he could just about make out a heavily-wooded promontory and from somewhere amongst the steep, mountain slopes he could hear the roar of a waterfall. The tall, pine-tree forests covered the land fading away into the eerie white-misty vapours. Marcus twisted his neck to get a glimpse of the canoe carrying Jodoc, Cunomoltus and the Hyperborean guide, which was following on behind them. Jodoc was sitting in the front, the horrible-looking black eye that covered half his face, easily visible. Marcus turned back and thrust his oar into the water, so that the boy would not see his grim satisfaction. Sitting behind the boy, Cunomoltus dug his oar into the water in silence. The iron box was still strapped to his chest. Jodoc had haltingly explained that he had hit his head on a tree during the night when he'd gone to relieve himself, but Marcus was not sure whether Ail had truly believed the story. As he stared at Ail, who was sitting in front of him, Marcus bit his lip. Lately the druid seemed to have become withdrawn and his suspicion seemed to be growing for, now and then, Marcus had caught him staring at him with a hostile, worried look. But if Ail suspected something why was he still leading them towards Emogene? Why had he remained so calm? Or was he planning something?

"How far till we reach Emogene's camp" Marcus called out.

"We should be there by noon," Ail replied, as he dug his oar into the water.

Marcus nodded and looked down at his sheathed gladius that lay on top of his pack, in the bottom of the canoe. If Ail was planning something, then he would be ready but the druid had him at a disadvantage. He was in charge and for all Marcus knew he could be leading them straight into a trap, to a native camp where Ail would be easily able to overpower him and Cunomoltus. But there was nothing he could do about that. He would just have to endure the uncertainty and hope that his deception was still working.

As they paddled on across the long, twisting lake the mist slowly lifted and, as it did, one of the Hyperborean guides suddenly cried out and pointed at a mountain that had appeared, towering above the lake and the dense forests. The sheer granite and boulder-strewn upper slopes were devoid of trees and the horse-shoe shaped ridge line dominated the land, a mile high; its mighty peaks pointing at the sky in majestic and unconquerable silence.

"Mount Katahdin," Ail exclaimed, as he stared up at the mountain.

Marcus peered at the distant mountain in silence. To the north, dark clouds were gathering but above the mountain itself, the heavens were clear and blue. Behind him Marcus heard the Hyperborean guide muttering to himself in what sounded like a hurried prayer and, as he stared at the mountain, Marcus wondered what had driven Emogene to come here; so far from civilisation; so far from anything. What madness had driven her to this life of solitude?

The canoes scraped onto the stony beach and Ail was the first to leap out of the boat. He was swiftly followed by Marcus and the Hyperborean, who splashed into the shallow water and helped drag the canoe up onto the land. Stiffly Marcus straightened up and quickly looked around, as he fixed his sword to his belt. Trees covered the shore, but a little way inland, he could see a forest clearing. He swung his pack over his shoulder as the second canoe came sliding and scraping onto the small lakeside beach.

"Emogene's camp is over there," Ail said gesturing at the forest clearing. "She must be up on the mountain."

"How do you know," Marcus said guardedly.

"If she wasn't, she would be here to find out who we were," Ail growled, as he started off through the trees.

Marcus glanced at Cunomoltus, who gave him a quick, tense look before, clutching his bow, he followed Ail into the woods. With a grunt Marcus set off after him and, as he did so, he caught sight of Jodoc, his bruised and battered face contorted in sullen rage, giving him a look of pure, unbridled hatred.

Emogene's camp was a short walk through the trees and, as they approached Marcus saw a small, ring of blackened-stones, inside which lay the remnants of a dead fire. Close by, stood a single, small Hyperborean, domed tent made of birch- bark and branches and on a line between two trees, fish were hanging up to dry. An old discarded, broken-looking canoe lay in the grass alongside the hut. There was no sign of anyone. Marcus paused beside the dead fire as Ail pulled aside the animal fur,s that hung over the entrance to the hut and poked his head inside.

"She's not here," he said as he turned to look up at the mountain that towered above the campsite. "We will wait here until she returns from the mountain."

Marcus cleared his throat as he stood beside the dead fire.

"No," he said, "We shall go up the mountain. There is still enough time to find her."

"Why are you in such a hurry to find Emogene," Ail suddenly exclaimed turning to face Marcus with sudden irritation. "I said we will wait here for her. This is her camp. She will be back before nightfall. Why the rush?"

Before Marcus could reply however one of the Hyperborean guides spoke in an animated voice as he pointed up at Mount Katahdin.

"What's he saying" Cunomoltus growled, as he clutched his bow tensely.

"The guides do not want to go up the mountain," Ail retorted, "They say they are going to stay here. They fear Paloma. They say it is forbidden to climb the sacred mountain."

"Then let them stay here. We however will go on," Marcus growled.

"I know why they want to find Emogene," Jodoc suddenly blurted out, as he took a step forwards his hand clenched into a fist.

"They have come to kill her," Jodoc exclaimed. "That one over there," he cried pointing at Marcus, "he has some feud with her. He wants her dead. They threatened me. They threatened my father. They said that if I caused trouble for them they would kill me and destroy my father's book. That's why that one over there is carrying around the iron box with the book inside it."

The campsite fell silent.

Ail took a step forwards and frowned in confusion and, as the silence lengthened from the corner of his eye, Marcus caught sight of Cunomoltus wearily reaching for his sword that hung from his belt.

"What," Ail exclaimed, as his frown deepened. "What are you talking about? We already have the book. Marcus gave it to us before we departed up river. The Council already has it."

Jodoc's mouth opened and then closed again. Then slowly he turned to stare at Marcus, with wide, horror-filled eyes as realisation finally dawned.

"You lied to me," the young man hissed. "You made me believe that you still had my father's book. You were worried I was going to talk. Well fuck you, fuck both of you!"

Rapidly Jodoc turned towards Ail and cried out in a voice that was nearly hysterical.

"I am telling the truth. They are here to kill Emogene. It is they who hired the Hermes and its crew. This whole voyage was their idea all along. They have lied to you since the beginning. Now do something about it."

With a frustrated growl, Cunomoltus pulled his sword from its scabbard and came at Jodoc but before he could strike, Ail cried out and one of the Hyperborean guides caught Cunomoltus arm. Cursing, Marcus wrenched his sword free. Ail was fast but not fast enough and, as he pulled his knife from his belt, Marcus punched him in the face, with his left hand sending the druid staggering backwards into the side of the hut. There was no time to see what was happening to Cunomoltus. With a high pitched howl, Ail came at Marcus, the blade of his knife arching through the air aimed at Marcus's throat. With practised ease, Marcus evaded the clumsy blow and with a sickening, bone-cracking noise, he drove his sword straight into Ail's head. The man's blood and brains splattered onto Marcus's face as the red-bearded druid collapsed to the ground like a rag doll. Calmly wiping the mess from his face Marcus turned to face, Jodoc and the others. On the ground, Cunomoltus was grappling with one of the Hyperboreans, whilst the second man was limping away into the trees trailing a bleeding leg. Jodoc however, stood rooted to the ground, stunned by the speed and violence but, as he saw Marcus coming towards him, his eyes widened in terror and without a word he turned, and bolted for the trees.

Marcus face darkened, as Jodoc vanished amongst the trees. There was however no time to go after him. On the ground Cunomoltus, needed his help. His brother was bleeding from a cut to his shoulder, as he rolled over the ground in a vicious, snarling, life and death struggle with the Hyperborean. Swiftly Marcus caught hold of the native's hair and, yanking it backwards he slit the man's throat with his sword sending a stream of blood gushing and spurting onto Cunomoltus' face, neck and chest. Snarling, Cunomoltus rolled away from the corpse and staggered to his feet, panting, his chest heaving and his eyes filled with wild adrenaline-fuelled emotion.

"Jodoc's getting away," Marcus hissed, as he paused to catch his breath. "Bastard has made a run for it."

Without saying a word, Cunomoltus stooped to pick up his discarded bow and joined Marcus as the two of them ran towards the beach, where they had left the canoes. As they burst from the trees however, they caught sight of Jodoc and the Hyperborean guide paddling furiously out into the lake, pulling the second canoe with them. Quickly, Cunomoltus strung an arrow, raised his bow, took aim and released but, as the projectile shot through the air, it fell harmlessly short into the lake. Beside him Marcus growled in frustration. Jodoc was getting away and there was nothing he could do about it. Cunomoltus lowered his bow and sent a stream of foul curses out into the lake.

"Emogene has a canoe," Cunomoltus suddenly exclaimed, "I saw it. We could use that to go after them."

"If it floats," Marcus snapped, "It looked broken."

"We can't let that little shit get away," Cunomoltus gasped, as he turned to Marcus with an alarmed look, "If he reaches the druids before we do, he is going to tell them everything. Jodoc's going to raise the alarm and then we are never going to get home. We should go after him. He can't be allowed to reach the druids alive."

"I know, I know," Marcus said in a tight voice. Then slowly he turned to look at the mountain that loomed above the forests. "But we came here for Emogene," he said in a quieter voice, "We came here to carry out Corbulo's final instruction and that is what we should do. We should find her."

"But that little shit…"

"We will just have to take our chances," Marcus interrupted. "The longer we delay confronting Emogene, the more trouble we are likely to find ourselves in. No," Marcus said, giving his brother a grim look that brooked no discussion, "The time has come for us to finish this. So let's do it. Let's find her."

For a long moment, Cunomoltus remained silent as he stared moodily at the canoes, which were getting further and further away. Then with a weary sigh, he reached up and undid the cord that strapped the small iron box to his body and unceremoniously dumped the box into the water.

"No need to carry that piece of shit around anymore," he muttered.

Chapter Forty-Five

The Temple of the Hyperboreans

Marcus slung his pack over his shoulder and raised his hand above his eyes to shield them from the fierce sun, as he looked up at Mount Katahdin. On the barren, rocky, upper-slopes and ridges however, there was no sign of life and nothing moved. The mountain was giving him no clues as to Emogene's whereabouts. At his side Cunomoltus was cleaning his knife in the grass. They had dragged the two corpses, to the water's edge and pushed them out into the lake so that if Emogene did manage to slip past them and return to her camp, she would not know what had happened.

"We will head for that peak," Marcus growled, as he pointed at one of the mountain's peaks. "If we can't find her, we will move on to next peak and if that doesn't work then we'll come back down again and wait for her here."

"Would it not be better and easier if we waited for her to return to her camp?" Cunomoltus muttered. "The druid had a point."

"No, he didn't," Marcus snapped, as he started out towards the trees, "We are going to find her on the mountain. Who knows how long she spends up there. That camp fire over there has not been used for several days. We can't afford to waste precious time."

The two of them were silent as they picked their way through the forest. Amongst the pine trees nothing moved and in the hot noon sun they were soon sweating and reaching for their water pouches. The ground began to rise and, in amongst the trees, they started to come across huge boulders and rocks that had tumbled from the mountain a long, long time ago. As they steadily climbed up the lower slopes of the mountain the trees started to thin out, until at last they stood at the base of a steep, dangerous-looking slope filled with loose stones and gravel. The heat from the sun beat down on them as Marcus wiped the sweat from his forehead and looked up at the mountain peak, towering above them.

"There," he suddenly exclaimed in an excited voice, as he pointed up at a distant ridge; "smoke!"

Cunomoltus raised his hand above his eyes to block out the sun, as he turned to look in the direction in which Marcus was pointing. And there curling up into the clear, blue sky were puffs of brown smoke.

"Do you think it's her?" his brother said, as he rubbed the flesh wound on his shoulder with a grim, painful expression.

"Maybe," Marcus growled, "Who else could be up there? No Hyperborean dares to climb the mountain. Come on. Let's go."

As they started to clamber up the loose stones and gravel, Marcus found the going harder than he had expected. The loose stones made it treacherous to find his footing and, as he and Cunomoltus scrambled up the slope, they sent showers of stones, gravel and dust hurtling and clattering downwards. At last, after what seemed like an age, and with their aching bodies and tunics lathered and soaked in sweat, they made it onto firmer ground. Wearily Marcus paused to crouch beside a large jagged rock as he sought to catch his breath and pick the loose pebbles from his boots. Cunomoltus was leaning against a rock and peering at the smoke. His chest was heaving from the exertion.

"Half a mile up the ridge," he said with a grimace.

Marcus nodded as he tossed a pebble away and reached down to check his gladius. The blade was still stained with Ail's blood and brains.

"Marcus," Cunomoltus said, as he continued to peer at the distant smoke, "When this is all over I want to come and live on the farm at Vectis. Promise me that you will not turn me away."

Marcus frowned as he ran his finger carefully along the edge of his gladius. "You have proved yourself," he muttered, "I was wrong to doubt you. But when you first arrived on my farm you acted like a prick."

"I just did that to get you attention," Cunomoltus replied, as he studied the distant ridge, "and it worked."

"You are still a prick," Marcus muttered, as he sheathed his sword and turned to stare in the direction of the smoke.

"When I get back home," Cunomoltus said, as a little smile appeared on the corner of his mouth, "I am going to find myself a fat wife; one who knows how to look after a man and I am going to buy myself some dogs and start a new business. I may have not been accepted into the army but I am one hell of a good, dog-breeder. My dogs are going to be best-trained and raised animals in the province, in the Empire. When I get home I am going to be fucking famous."

"Let's go," Marcus said grimly, as he lifted his pack up over his shoulder and started up the rocky slope towards the smoke.

***

Emogene was sitting cross -egged beside the small fire. Her eyes were closed and at her side lay a small pile of sticks and branches. She had aged of course since he'd last seen her. Marcus recognised her straight away and for a moment he stood unable to move, a dozen paces away from her, as he was transported back to that day fifteen years ago, when he'd seen her slaughter Corbulo, slicing open his throat in one swift movement of her knife. Around him the mountain, the Temple of the Hyperborean's, was silent, as if the gods were holding their breath. Amongst the barren, waterless, grey stones, rocks and dust, nothing moved.

Suddenly as if she had become aware of his presence, Emogene opened her eyes and slowly turned to look at him.

Then with surprising speed she leapt to her feet and crouched like some kind of wild cat, agile, fast and dangerous. In her hands a knife glinted in the sunlight.

Without a word Marcus started towards her and when he was just a few paces from the fire, he paused.

Emogene looked like she had been out in the wilderness for a long time. She was clad in stained, torn, animal skins and on her feet she was wearing native moccasins. Her hair was long, uncombed and in places it had turned grey and her face was dirty and stained with dust and sweat and the smell of her unwashed body was overpowering. Around her neck on a leather cord hung a small, sealed canister. As Marcus approached she hissed at him and stared at him with a half savage, wild look. Then before Marcus could speak, she caught sight of his left hand and her eyes bulged in terror and she staggered backwards with a terrified howl and started muttering to herself; words that Marcus could not understand. Abruptly she sank down on her knees and raised her hand, as if to ward off an imaginary blow, her eyes widening in horror as she stared up at him.

"The man with two fingers," she rasped. "You are the man with two fingers. The one whom the spirits promised to send me. You have come to kill me. The spirits have sent you to kill me as punishment for my sins."

"You know who I am," Marcus's voice cut across the mountain slopes, "The feud between you and my family has lasted twenty years, but today it ends. You will give me back what belongs to me."

"Feud, feud," Emogene bared her teeth at Marcus in confusion. Then slowly she seemed to collect herself and as she calmed down, she crooked her head to one side like a bird and peered at Marcus intently.

"Do you not remember," Marcus said, as he stared at her, "All those years ago in Caledonia. The dungeon, the amber, my father Corbulo. You killed him. You murdered my father and stole his body and spirit and now I am here, to take back what is mine. I am his son. My name is Marcus and the gods are right, I am here to punish you for your sins."

For a long moment Emogene remained silent, her head crooked to one side as she stared at Marcus with wily, emotionless eyes.

"Yes I remember you," she suddenly hissed as her eyes glowed with sudden recognition, "Yes I know you, Roman. You have come for your father's remains. You have come for this canister of dust," she screeched holding up the sealed canister that hung from around her neck. "But he is mine. His spirit belongs to me. He keeps me company and you will not have him."

Marcus did not move, as he silently stared at the pouch containing his father's ashes.

Emogene suddenly shrieked with triumphant laughter. "You have come a long way Marcus, son of Corbulo," she screeched. "Such courage, such honour, such devotion and now you think you are going to free your father's spirit. You think you are going to take him home. Such love. But I am destined for hell, Roman. Everything that I loved was taken from me. I am cursed. Rome has cursed me and has turned me into the bringer of death, the destroyer of worlds. That's who I am. And you think I am going to release your father's spirit."

"My father and I did nothing to you," Marcus cried out, his face flushed with emotion, "We were never interested in the amber or you. My father came for me. He just wanted his son back and now I want him back. You did not have to desecrate his body. Only an evil spirit would do such a thing."

"What do you know about the spirit world," Emogene screeched, "I kept your father's ashes, because I made a promise to myself. Your father's closeness comforts me. I did not ask for my misfortune but, at every turn that I made I was punished and humiliated."

"You will give me back my father's ashes," Marcus cried out, "and if you do, I shall let you live."

A mocking, contemptuous look appeared on Emogene's face. "You think you are stronger than me," she retorted. "You think you are stronger than death. Nothing is stronger than the destroyer of worlds. Do you really think your love for your father and your family will be enough to impress me?"

Marcus was silent as he stared at Emogene, his eyes smouldering with emotion. Then, as he spoke, his voice seemed to change and his face mellowed.

"I feel sorry for you. Without something to love, we are nothing," he said, fixing his eyes on Emogene,"and the thing that I fear the most is not death, but not having lived when I had the chance. My father deserves to be granted his final wish. He travelled to the end of the world to rescue me and now I have done the same for him. This is who I am and I cannot change myself even if I wanted to, so you are going to have to either kill me or give me back his ashes."

Emogene's face seemed to contort as he spoke. Then, with a yell she launched herself at Marcus. The attack was so swift that he barely had time to react. As he desperately struggled to get a grip on her knife arm, Marcus staggered backwards against a boulder and cried out in pain, as the sharp rock dug into his side. Emogene was howling like a demon, her enraged body far stronger than he had ever dared imagine. As the two of them struggled with each other, Marcus raised his head and with a furious, heartfelt roar, he smashed his forehead into her face. The blow sent Emogene staggering backwards, with blood pouring down the side of her face. Marcus eyes bulged in fury and he spread his arms wide and suddenly he was no longer himself, but a savage, fighting beast, trained to kill with no fear at all. As he advanced towards her, a strange supernatural force seemed to take over and opening his mouth he roared as the pain, anger and bitterness of the past fifteen years came rolling out in a long verbal and violent cascade. Emogene shrank from him, her eyes bulging in sudden terror, her whole being shaking with horror and, as Marcus came towards her, she raised her hand in a futile effort to fend him off. Then with a startled cry, she tripped over a stone and tumbled backwards and instantly vanished from view. As Marcus reached the place where she had disappeared, he looked down the steep cliff over which she had fallen, and saw Emogene's body lying motionless on the rocks, a dozen yards below him. A dark, pool of blood was spreading out from under her smashed and broken body and her sightless eyes were staring straight up at the sky. For a long moment Marcus did not move as he stared at her. Then silently he turned and started to climb down towards her and, as he reached the corpse, he stooped and ripped the small canister from her neck. Hastily he opened it and silently gazed down at the ashes inside.

On the top of the ridge above him a face suddenly appeared. It was Cunomoltus. His brother was anxiously peering down at him.

"It's done," Marcus cried out. "We have what we came for."

Cunomoltus said nothing. Then he straightened up and sighed, as he turned to stare out across the vast, forested wilderness that stretched away to the horizon in every direction.

"Good. Now how are we going to get home," he called out.

Chapter Forty-Six – Last Man Standing

It was evening when Marcus and Cunomoltus finally made it back to the camp by the lake. In the west the sun had long ago vanished behind the mountains and in the cool June air, annoying mosquitoes were dancing around their sweat-soaked heads, necks and limbs. Marcus however, did not seem to notice them. The sealed canister containing Corbulo's ashes hung from a leather cord around his neck and over his shoulder, he had slung his pack whilst his Roman sword dangled from his belt. As the two of them emerged from the forest, Marcus headed straight towards the old canoe that lay beside the hut. Despite Cunomoltus's protestations, he had carried Emogene's body back up to mountain peak and there, at her fire site, he had burned her corpse and shown her spirit how it could find its way home. He had shown her honour, honour that she had denied him. Cunomoltus had not understood of course and he had berated Marcus for wasting precious time. Nevertheless, it had been the right thing to do for the endless cycle of violence, pain and madness could only end by such a forgiving gesture, and so he hoped it now had. However, Cunomoltus was right too. They needed to get home and the longer they delayed, the harder that was going to be.

"Jodoc has a full day's head start on us," Cunomoltus growled as if reading Marcus' mind.

Marcus did not reply as he dragged the old canoe away from the hut and turned to inspect it. The wood was rotten in places and there was only one paddle. He grunted as he ran his fingers along the bark.

"Only one way to find out whether it floats," he said, as he started to drag the canoe towards the lake. As he glanced round, he saw Cunomoltus snatching the dried fish from the line that hung between the trees and quickly thrusting them into his sack. His brother grinned as he saw him looking.

"I am so sick of fish. When this is all over I will not be eating fish for an entire year," Cunomoltus called out, as he hastened to catch up with Marcus.

"I am glad that you think we are going to get home alive," Marcus said grimly, as Cunomoltus stooped to lift up the other end of the canoe.

"That's something you taught me," Cunomoltus replied. "To have some confidence in yourself and not let fear overpower you. Isn't that what you are always going on about?"

Marcus grunted as he reached the lake and lowered the canoe into the placid water. Then he straightened up and stared out across the water. There was no sign of Jodoc or the two canoes and it was starting to grow dark. By his side, Cunomoltus was carefully pushing the canoe out into the water and to Marcus's relief, the flimsy craft seemed to float. Hastily the two of them waded out into the lake and clumsily clambered into the canoe. Marcus, sitting at the front, took the only paddle and started to move them away from the bank, as Cunomoltus tried to help by digging his hands into the water. The canoe groaned and wallowed and the bottom of the craft was already flooded with a thin layer of water.

"This rotten log isn't going to last very long," Cunomoltus, muttered glancing around the canoe with a worried look.

"It's not going to sink whilst I am sitting in it," Marcus growled.

As they steadily moved out into the lake, Marcus turned to give the mountain a final glance and there, still rising into the darkening sky, he could just about make out a thin column of smoke. For a moment, he paused and stared up at the barren, desolate peaks and then slowly his left hand reached up to the sealed canister around his neck. Corbulo had journeyed to the end of the world for him once. Despite the odds, his father had not given up on him and now he, Marcus had done the same for him. He had done what he had said he would do and somewhere his father and all his ancestors were watching. And, as he idly glanced up at the skies, he suddenly knew that Corbulo would be proud of him, even if he didn't make it back home and the realisation brought a look of grim satisfaction out onto his face.

"It will be dark soon, we'll need to make camp somewhere," Cunomoltus said, as they pushed on across the lake in their slowly leaking boat. "It will be impossible to find our way in the darkness and we need to rest. I am exhausted."

Marcus wrenched himself back to the present and dug his paddle into the water, as he turned to peer ahead at the distant shore. Despite the outward show of confidence, the odds of them getting away and back home were slim and growing smaller with every passing hour.

"We will rest when we get to the end of the lake and then start out again at dawn."

Behind him, Cunomoltus nodded silently as he wearily thrust his hands into the dark cold water.

***

It was dark by the time the canoe slid and grated across the rocks. Out in the placid lake, the pale light from the moon was reflected in the silent waters and over their heads, a vast mosaic of beautiful stars stretched away into infinity. Stiffly Marcus and Cunomoltus slipped over the side into the water and dragged the rotten canoe up onto the dark bank and, as they turned it on its side the water came gushing out. The night was silent except for their laboured, exhausted breathing.

"What a piece of shit," Cunomoltus growled as he wearily sank down against a tree and stared up at the stars. "That canoe is not going to last. Maybe we should consider walking down the river instead."

Marcus collapsed onto the ground, his back leaning against the canoe. Wearily he closed his eyes.

"No," he muttered, "The fastest way downstream is by canoe. If we walk, we will take far too long. The natives seem to use these rivers like we use roads back home and I can see why now."

"Does it really matter?" Cunomoltus grunted, "Jodoc is going to get back to the druids before us and warn them anyway. I should have killed that little shit when I had the chance."

Marcus opened his eyes and glanced in the direction of his brother and for a long moment he remained silent.

"Corbulo was wrong to have abandoned you," he said at last in a grave voice, "I can see that now. You are not so bad and for what it is worth, I am glad that you came looking for me. You now have a stake in the family's fortunes. I could not have made this journey without you and Corbulo's final request would not stand a chance of being fulfilled without your help."

In the darkness, Cunomoltus shifted his position and turned to glance in Marcus's direction.

"Now why would you say something like that," he said in a suspicious voice. "When you talk like that it means that you want something? So what is it?"

"I want a promise," Marcus said sharply, "I want a promise from you that if, in the coming days, you are the last man standing, you will take our father's ashes and try and make sure that they are buried on the spot where he instructed us to bury them. If you can do that then, I will know in my heart, that you are truly his son and my brother."

Chapter Forty-Seven

Hope and Despair at the Edge of the World

Marcus looked unhappy as he looked down at the canoe. The craft was not going to last very long on the rough, wild upper reaches of the river. It was dawn and a few yards away, Cunomoltus was munching on a dried fish, as he used his knife to shape a rough paddle from a tree branch. Along the edge of the lake, the thick, silent forest covered the mountain slopes and land, in an impenetrable dark green canopy. With a grim look, Marcus dropped his pack into the canoe and gestured at Cunomoltus to help him move the craft out into the water.

The river was narrow, twisting and strewn with raging white water rapids but in the fast flowing water, they made good progress and the canoe shot along in an exhilarating if challenging ride. It was morning when Marcus cried out and pointed at the upturned canoe, wedged in between two boulders in the midst of the river. As they swiftly hurtled towards it, Marcus tried to use his paddle to guide them towards the craft but the current was too strong and as they swept past, he saw that the back of the canoe had been broken in two and was half filled with water and debris.

"Could that be Jodoc's canoe?" Cunomoltus shouted from his seat behind Marcus, "He had both canoes when we last saw him."

Marcus shrugged. There was no way of knowing for all the Hyperborean canoes looked the same to him. Then, as they came shooting around a river bend, Marcus grunted and his eyes narrowed. On the stony shore just beyond the bend where the river water slowed, another canoe lay drawn up amongst the white stones and beside it lay a body.

Instinctively Marcus thrust his paddle into the river and guided the canoe into the calmer section of the river and towards the shore. There was no need to alert Cunomoltus, for he too had seen the body and was staring at it intently. The man lay face down on the ground and he was not moving. Marcus grunted as he noticed the knife sticking into the man's back. As the canoe came nosing into the bank, Marcus quickly swung his legs over the side, splashed into the river, and waded ashore pulling the canoe with him. Silently gesturing at Cunomoltus to watch the forest, he cautiously approached, knelt down in the sand and gingerly turned the man over, and as he did, Marcus swore. The dead man lying on the shore beside the canoe was the native guide who had escaped from Emogene's camp on the lake. There was no mistake as Marcus instantly recognised him.

"Looks like he died recently," Marcus called out in a quiet voice, as an anxious looking Cunomoltus crouched beside him, clutching his bow.

"Who could have done this?" Cunomoltus said in a low, cautious voice as he slowly strung an arrow to his bow and turned to look at the forest with a tense look.

"Jodoc," Marcus replied, as he looked down at the corpse, "It has to be Jodoc. Maybe they had a fight and Jodoc killed him. Ail said that hostility was growing amongst the Hyperboreans. Who knows? If the other canoe we saw in the river belongs to them then that means that both canoes are here and he must be on foot. He can't have gone far."

Silently Marcus gestured at Cunomoltus to move out and the two of them cautiously spread out across the riverbank, clutching their weapons, as they started towards the trees. Marcus was peering into the forest when a low whistle from Cunomoltus made him turn. Amongst the trees, his brother was silently beckoning to him.

"I found him," Cunomoltus called out in a tight voice, as Marcus came towards him. "He's over here."

Marcus stopped in his tracks as he caught sight of Jodoc. The young man lay face down on the ground, his arm stretched out, as if he had been trying to crawl away into the forest. Quietly Cunomoltus crouched down on his haunches and gingerly reached out to touch the body. Jodoc had been stabbed in the leg and there was another wound across his shoulder blade. A discarded stone knife lay just beyond the grasp of his fingers and he was not moving.

Quickly Marcus crouched beside his brother and reached out to feel for a pulse and as he did, he swore.

"He's still alive," Marcus muttered.

"What a shame," Cunomoltus replied darkly, as he picked up the stone knife, "Time to do what I should have done a long time ago."

But before he could do anything, Marcus caught hold of his brother's arm and shook his head.

"No, given time and treatment these wounds will heal," Marcus said quietly, "We need him alive."

"Why?" Cunomoltus blurted out angrily, unable to contain himself, "This little shit was going to betray us and warn the druids. He made his choice. He does not deserve to live."

"Maybe," Marcus growled, as he looked down at Jodoc, "But we do need him. If we are to get back home, the Hermes will need a crew and with Caradoc already gone, it will not be possible to make the journey. Even with Jodoc fit and on board, we are going to be fully stretched, sailing across the ocean. He is coming back home with us whether he likes it or not. We need him."

Cunomoltus opened his mouth, closed it and then opened it again with mounting frustration. Then his face darkened as he leaned towards Jodoc and spat onto the young man's exposed back.

"Well aren't you a lucky bastard," he hissed. "But if you do survive and we get back home, I am going to sort you out."

***

It was afternoon when Jodoc at last stirred and groaned. Supported by Marcus and Cunomoltus, the two of them dragged him downstream along the riverbank to where they had left Jodoc's canoe. They had abandoned the old, rotten boat beside the corpse of the dead native and had taken to the water in the newe, more seaworthy canoe until they had come to the falls and had been forced to carry the boat around them on foot. Out in the river, the huge boulder strewn falls were impassable and the roar of the river as it rushed past was deafening. As Jodoc groaned and stirred again, they carefully sat him down against a boulder at the water's edge and Marcus straightened up and folded his arms across his chest. On the ground, the young man slowly opened his eyes.

"Hello arsehole," Cunomoltus shouted, smiling, "remember us?"

Jodoc stared up at them in dazed confusion. Then slowly he reached out to touch the rough bandage, made from torn strips of his tunic, which Marcus had wrapped around his leg.

"Leave the bandage, I have cleaned your wounds as best as I can," Marcus cried out, as he reached down and pushed Jodoc's hand away from his leg. "What happened to you? We found the native dead beside your canoe. Did you kill him?"

Jodoc did not answer as weakly he turned to gaze at the roaring river. Then he seemed to recognise Marcus and Cunomoltus, for suddenly he shrank back against the rock in fright.

"What happened?" Marcus shouted above the roar of the river.

With a frightened look, Jodoc huddled against the rock, as he looked up at Marcus and Cunomoltus, his face pale, his lower lip trembling.

"The guide attacked me," he stammered at last, "I don't know why. One moment he was all right. The next he was coming at me with his knife. He stabbed me in the leg. He would have killed me if I had not gotten to him first. Maybe he blamed me for his friend's death. I just do not know. I couldn't talk to him."

Marcus exchanged a silent glance with Cunomoltus. Then he sighed and turned to look downstream at the raging white water.

"We're taking you back to the Hermes," Marcus called out, as he turned back to look at Jodoc. "You need to rest and let those wounds heal. It is going to take some time but you are going to be alright."

"You should leave me here," Jodoc blurted out in a voice filled with sudden despair, "I am done for. I am not going to make it. I cannot walk. I will just slow you down and your brother wants to kill me anyway."

"No," Marcus firmly shook his head, "You are going to live and my brother is not going to kill you, however much he would like to. You are going home with us. Your father's mission is accomplished. The druids have his book and there is no reason now for you to stay here. Your father would have agreed with me."

"Leave me," Jodoc groaned closing his eyes.

At his side, Cunomoltus stooped and slapped Jodoc hard across the face with the back of his hand. On the ground, the young man cried out in shock and pain.

"Listen, you little shit," Cunomoltus hissed, glaring down at him, "You are going to live and you are going home, so stop feeling sorry for yourself. That is now your task, to live, and if you do, we will all be very happy, including that pretty girl Calista waiting for you on the Hermes. So stop being a pathetic wimp and start doing what you are told to do."

"So what's the plan?" Cunomoltus muttered, glancing at Marcus as they pushed the canoe, containing the slumped, grimacing Jodoc into the river.

"That's simple," Marcus replied, "We continue heading downstream until we reach the sea. Then we make contact with Alexandros and the Hermes and sail away during the night. Alexandros will be prepared to leave when we arrive. He knows what to do."

"Let's hope it will be that simple," Cunomoltus said tersely.

***

It was late in the afternoon when Marcus woke with a strange sense of foreboding. Hurriedly he sat up and glanced around the campsite. Amongst the surrounding forest, all was quiet however, nothing moved, and yet something had disturbed him. Cunomoltus and Jodoc were both still asleep, curled up on the ground, and a few yards away, the canoe lay drawn up on the sand. The three of them were utterly exhausted from their long voyage down the river. Beyond the inlet, on the small rocky and forested island on which they had made camp, the wide, peaceful waters of beautiful Penobscot Bay glinted in the bright, afternoon light. Marcus had chosen the small island in the bay because it looked remote and because it was only a couple of miles from the druid trading post on the promontory, a perfect place on which to await nightfall and their next move.

Warily, Marcus rose to his feet and touched the pommel of his sword. What was wrong? Quickly he looked down and grunted in relief as he saw the small sealed canister hanging from around his neck. Then quietly he gave Cunomoltus a prod with his boot. His brother opened his eyes and hastily sat up and blinked with exhaustion.

"That late already," Cunomoltus murmured in a weary resigned voice. "I was just in the middle of a fantastic dream."

"Something is wrong," Marcus said quietly, as he scanned the trees, "Something has changed."

As he caught the look on Marcus's face, Cunomoltus's weariness instantly vanished and hastily he rose, stooping to grab hold of his bow and quiver.

"What is it?" Cunomoltus said warily.

Marcus sniffed, frowned and shook his head. "I don't know. It is just a feeling. Maybe it is nothing. Maybe lack of sleep and food is making me see things."

Cunomoltus peered at Marcus for a long moment. Then he sighed and strode across to the canoe and began to rummage around in his pack that lay on the bottom. Marcus turned to look at Jodoc as he heard him cough. Several days had passed since they had found him lying stabbed and unconscious on the river bank and despite Marcus's best efforts, the young man's wounds were not healing. Marcus bit his lip in frustration. Cora, onboard the Hermes had the required supplies. The wounds would heal if he had access to those basic medical supplies, but out here in the wilderness, all he had was fresh water and the linen from his tunic.

Cunomoltus handed him a smoked piece of fish and for a while the two of them were silent, as they hungrily munched on their frugal breakfast.

"That's the last bit of fish that we have, by the way," Cunomoltus said. "We're going to have to hunt or barter with the natives from now on."

Marcus did not reply, as suddenly he frowned, turned and set off into the trees towards the edge of the small island. Cunomoltus followed and he was just about to say something when he came to an abrupt halt. Marcus too, had come to a stop close to the water's edge and was staring northwards across the sea to where a towering column of black smoke was rising up into the pale, blue sky. The smoke was coming from the direction of the druid trading post.

"Shit," Cunomoltus hissed in alarm.

Marcus said nothing as he stared at the column of black smoke. The headland and the druid trading post were too far away for him to see whether the smoke was coming from there.

"Should we go and investigate," Cunomoltus growled, "That could be the Hermes on fire out there."

Marcus took a deep breath as he peered at the smoke. Then he shook his head.

"We will stick to the plan," he murmured, "If that is the Hermes, then there is nothing we can do about it anyway. We will head out tonight and approach in the fading light. That should provide us with some cover."

Then brusquely Marcus turned and started back to the camp.

Jodoc was awake as the two of them came striding into their little campsite. He raised his head, his face pale, soaked in sweat, and gave Marcus a weary, resigned look. Marcus ignored him as he started to pile his belongings into the canoe.

"What is it?" Jodoc croaked in a weak voice.

"Smoke. There is a column of black smoke coming from the direction of the trading post," Cunomoltus snapped in a nervous, tense voice. "You had better pray to every God you know, that the smoke is not coming from the Hermes, for if our ship is on fire, then we are not going to have any further need of you."

"Get some rest," Marcus growled, as he set off back into the forest, "I am going to see whether I can find us something to eat."

"Then you will need my bow," Cunomoltus snapped as he hurried after him.

***

The sea was calm as the canoe silently and cautiously slid through the water towards the low plateau and the deserted and ruined Hyperborean camp. Sitting in the front, Marcus slowly dug his paddle into the water, as he peered tensely at the promontory and the haze of black smoke that hung over the headland. The native camp had been destroyed. Parts of the landward facing palisade had collapsed and in the centre of the camp, the druid's longhouse had been reduced to a pile of blackened, smoking and burnt timber. Some of the Hyperborean tents were still standing but others had been torched and still smouldered. On the beach, the blackened, twisted wreckage of the Hibernian currach lay half in, half out of the water. As the canoe cautiously approached, Marcus turned to stare at an overturned canoe and close by, he suddenly caught sight of a Hyperborean corpse, floating face down in the water. There was no sign of the Hermes. Tensely Marcus craned his neck to get a glimpse of the coast further along but he could see nothing. The Hermes had gone.

As the canoe slowly bumped into the land, Marcus clambered out and took a few hesitant steps up the beach, before stopping to stare at the devastation. Plumes of smoke were still rising from the blackened, destroyed scar that had once been the native encampment. He could see no one about but in amongst the destruction he suddenly noticed corpses of men, women and children. The bodies lay scattered amongst the shelters and some had been burned; their ghastly-blackened bodies bloated and disfigured. Marcus turned to look over his shoulder, as he heard Cunomoltus wading ashore behind him.

"Jupiter's left ball," Cunomoltus hissed as he caught sight of the devastation. "What happened here? Who could have done this?"

Marcus did not reply. Then abruptly he turned and started to drag their canoe up onto the beach. Inside, Jodoc was staring in horror at the destroyed camp.

"Stay here," Marcus growled quietly, "We are going to try and find some food and water. Shout if you spot anything."

Jodoc remained silent as Marcus turned and set off up the beach towards the blackened, smouldering, ruined longhouse with Cunomoltus following close behind.

As they carefully picked their way through the chaos of blackened timber, burnt hides, collapsed shelters, bloated bodies and debris, Marcus became aware of a stench. By his side, Cunomoltus had raised his hand to his nose in an effort to muzzle the awful smell. Clouds of flies were dancing over the dead and in the darkening sky, the scavenger birds were circling.

"What are we going to do?" Cunomoltus hissed, in a voice that bordered on despair. "The Hermes has gone. They have left us."

Marcus said nothing as he came to a sudden halt. Part of the wall of the ruined longhouse was still standing and nailed to it, using foot long Roman, iron nails was the corpse of a druid. The man's tunic was torn, stained with dried blood and a Roman gladius had been thrust straight into his heart. Cunomoltus groaned in terror as he caught sight of the man. Silently Marcus strode on past the nailed corpse hanging from the wall and poked his head into the remains of the longhouse and, as he did, he saw another druid, lying spread eagled on the ground, his head completely severed from his body.

"Looks like they were attacked," he murmured as Cunomoltus came up to him. "Whoever did this was no friend of the druids."

"Who?" Cunomoltus said his voice trembling, "Who would do this?"

Marcus shrugged. "I don't know," he replied quietly, "But Ail said that the Hyperboreans were growing increasingly hostile. Maybe something happened to propel the natives to attack. Maybe another tribe did this. We will not know unless we find one of the druids alive and that looks unlikely."

"What are we going to do Marcus?" Cunomoltus said despairingly, "The Hermes is gone. We are stuck."

"Get a grip man," Marcus hissed irritably. "I don't have any answers for you. I do not know what we are going to do. First though, let's try and find some food and something to drink. Once we have eaten, we will decide on what to do."

Cunomoltus lowered his eyes and nodded silently as Marcus started to pick his way through the blackened, smouldering ruins of the longhouse. As he slowly moved through the debris, he suddenly grunted, stooped and pulled a brass box from out under a pile of burnt wood. As he wiped away the dust, he recognised the machine that the druids had used to forecast the position of the constellations.

"Four more of them over here," Cunomoltus called out.

Clutching the Greek mechanism, Marcus moved towards his brother. Cunomoltus sighed as he looked down at the corpses of four more druids. The men seemed to have put up a fight for broken and discarded weapons lay close by. The druids had been horribly mutilated and disfigured.

Carefully Marcus turned to look around at the devastation. The light was fading fast and darkness would soon be upon them.

"Maybe some of the druids and natives managed to escape into the forest," Cunomoltus murmured, looking hopeful as he stared at the corpses.

"Maybe," Marcus replied, "If so they may come back during the night. We will make our camp on the beach. No fire, and one of us will need to stay awake and on watch. If some of the druids have managed to escape, they may know how we can get home."

Cunomoltus nodded in agreement.

"The druids will not be coming back to Hyperborea again in a hurry," he said. "Not after they hear about this massacre."

***

Marcus was sitting on the rock trying to keep his eyes open as dawn finally came. Bleary eyed he turned his head towards the sun, feeling its welcoming warmth on his face. A few yards away beside the canoe, Cunomoltus and Jodoc were sleeping in the sand. They looked pale, bedraggled, wet, starving and exhausted but the worst thing Marcus thought, as he looked down at them, was that they were starting to give up. They were surrendering to despair. The short night had been miserable. It had rained and they had found nothing to eat amongst the destruction and only a little fresh water and no survivors had emerged from the forest.

What were they going to do now? Wearily Marcus looked down at the small sealed canister that hung around his neck. He did not know what to do. It was now likely that he would never be going home to fulfil his promise to his father and Corbulo would not after all, be buried together with his legionary comrades on the battlefield where he had faced the Barbarian Queen. The cruel Gods had been playing with him, encouraging him that he could complete his quest, only to snatch it away at the last moment. He should have known, he should have realised that the journey he had set out on, could only have one ending. But despite their precarious position, he had refused to show his despair to his companions. They were relying on him to find a solution and like any true leader; he had to show that he knew what he was doing, even when he did not.

As the light grew stronger and the sun rose higher in the clear blue sky Marcus stretched and rubbed his face and was about to waken his companions when a sudden movement amongst the ruined camp caught his eye. His eyes narrowed and instantly he was on alert. Had that been a man moving in between the burnt out shelters? In the morning sky, the scavenger birds suddenly rose up into the air, as if they had been disturbed and as they did Marcus blinked and his hand came to rest on the pommel of his sword. Then he groaned in dismay.

"Cunomoltus. Get up. Now," Marcus said in a tight voice.

On the beach below him, his brother stirred and opened his eyes.

"Cunomoltus. Now. We have company," Marcus snapped in a louder voice as he hastily stood up on the rock and drew his sword.

Without saying a word, Cunomoltus rolled over, grabbed hold of his bow, quiver, and staggered to his feet, his eyes blinking in confusion.

Marcus stood on the rock as he stared at the group of Hyperborean's, who were slowly advancing towards him across the blackened remains of the camp. Some of the men had dark, painted faces and others had feathers in their hair, and all were armed. They looked hostile and unfriendly as they approaching, forming a single loose line, as if they were hunting and were driving their prey towards a killing pit. And amongst them, Marcus suddenly caught sight of a native clutching a spear onto which the head of a bearded druid had been stuck.

"Get Jodoc into the canoe now," Marcus hissed, turning to his brother. "These men must be ones who attacked the camp. They have come back."

Cunomoltus groaned in pure terror as he caught sight of the impaled head on the spear. Then he turned and frantically began pushing the canoe out into the water. As Marcus stared at the Hyperboreans closing in on him, he heard Jodoc suddenly cry out, but there was no time to see what the young man wanted. Grimly he raised his sword and went into a crouch. There was no point trying to make a run for it, for the group of Hyperborean's had already cut them off from the land and, even if they managed to get out onto the sea, the natives would surely follow them in their own canoes. There was nowhere to go. No, he would have to fight but it would be a hopeless fight. There were just too many of them. He was going to die, right here on this stony beach.

Again Jodoc cried out, more frantic this time.

"Marcus, Marcus, look," now Cunomoltus was shouting as well.

Snatching a glance over his shoulder, Marcus turned to see what his companions were shouting about and, as he did, his eyes widened in surprise. Coming towards them across the calm sea, parallel to the land, was a little Roman ship with a billowing red square sail.

"It's the Hermes," Cunomoltus roared in an excited voice, "They have come back. Alexandros has come back for us. That big Greek bastard came back."

"Get into the canoe," Marcus yelled as he leapt down from the rock and caught hold of Jodoc and unceremoniously dumped him into the canoe. Frantically Cunomoltus pushed them further out into the sea and then, when he was waist deep in the water, he reached out with his arm and Marcus caught it and pulled him over the side and into the craft. On the shore, the Hyperborean's had come to a confused halt, as they stared out to sea at the ship with the red sail. Hurriedly Marcus and Cunomoltus started to paddle towards it, as Jodoc cried out in relief, coughing up some blood as he did so.

As they drew closer to the Hermes, Marcus looked up and caught sight of Alexandros standing at the tiller together with Cora and Calista. The captain's black eye patch was unmistakable and as Alexandros stared at the approaching canoe and recognised Marcus, he suddenly raised his hand in a fierce, silent and victorious salute. Down in the canoe Marcus raised his hand in joyous reply.

GLOSSARY

Aquae Sulis: Bath, UK

Aquilifer: Roman standard bearer carrying the Eagle standard of a Legion

Batavia: Area around the big rivers in the middle of The Netherlands

Brading: Site of a Roman villa in the south east of the Isle of Wight

Brigantes: A Celtic tribe living in the north of Britain

Camulodunum: Colchester, UK

Caestus: Leather and metal boxing glove

Centurion: Roman officer

Cohort: Roman military unit

Colonia Agrippina: Cologne, Germany

Contubernium: Eight-man Legionary barrack room/tent

Currach: Celtic boat

Dacia(n): The area in Romania where the Dacians lived

Decanus: Corporal

Decurion: Roman cavalry officer

Denarii: Roman money

Deva Victrix: Chester, UK

Eburacum: York, UK

Hyperborea – Veteran of Rome Series

Garum: Roman fermented fish sauce

Gaul: France

Gladius: Standard Roman army short sword

Hibernia: Ireland

Hispania: Spain

Hyperborea: Mythical land beyond the north wind

Imaginifer: Roman army standard bearer carrying an image of the emperor

Isca: Exeter, UK

Lares: Roman guardian deities

Luguvalium: Carlisle

Mona Insulis: Anglesey island, UK

Mons Graupius: The battlefield in Scotland where Agricola defeated the Caledonian confederation in AD 83

Munifex: Private (non-specialist) Roman Legionary

Noviomagus Reginorum: Chichester, UK

Optio: Roman officer, second in command of a Century

Pannonia: The Roman province in and around Hungary/Slovenia, Serbia, Croatia

Pilum: Roman Legionary spear

Prefect: Roman officer in command of an auxiliary Cohort or Magistrate

Hyperborea – Veteran of Rome Series

Principia: The HQ buildings in a Roman army camp/fortress

Pugio: Roman army dagger

Saturnalia: Roman festival in December

Tara: Seat of the High King of Hibernia, northwest of Dublin, Ireland

Tesserarius: Roman army watch/guard commander

Vebriacum: Charterhouse Roman town, Western England

Vectis: Isle of Wight, UK

Vexillatio: Temporary Roman army detachment

Author's Notes

The purpose of historical fiction novels, in my opinion, is to entertain and to bring alive, to the modern reader, the vanished worlds from the past. I love trying to do this and I hope this was your experience.

Hyperborea is a work of fiction. There is currently no evidence that the Romans or anyone else from the Roman Empire reached the North or South American continents but it is certainly possible that they could have made it, if they had tried. The Romans were already making long sea voyages from the Egyptian Red Sea ports to India and in 1970 Thor Heyerdahl proved with his Ra II expedition that an ancient Egyptian ship made of reeds could sail 6,100 kilometers from North Africa right across the Atlantic to Barbados. In 1976 Tim Severin on the St Brendan demonstrated that an ancient Irish currach, constructed using only ancient methods and materials, could have made the journey from Ireland to North America via Iceland. In 1934 a trawler fishing 250 kilometers west off the west coast of Ireland dredged up a 2nd century Roman pot from the seabed. The Romans are often portrayed as being reluctant, timid sailors and this may have been the case, but the Roman Empire included a large number of conquered and assimilated peoples who had a great and proud seafaring tradition. The Romans were not an inward looking people and would have built on the accumulated geographical knowledge and expertise of the peoples whom they conquered, to expand their own knowledge of the world. Thus the Romans were amongst the great explorers of the classical world, sending various maritime exploratory expeditions down the coasts of Africa and around the northern coast of Denmark and overland towards Uganda to find the source of the Nile. In Europe the Romans established the Amber Road to the Baltic coast and opened up trade with India and Hibernia whilst sending diplomatic missions to China.

The Atlantic Ocean would however have presented a formidable obstacle to the peoples of the Roman Empire. Its sheer vastness, the icy cold water and stormy weather would have acted as a major deterrent. If one had entered a harbour tavern in Roman London and had asked a sea captain if he had ever considered heading west out into the Atlantic, he would probably have thought you were mad. What possible reason would he have to go west, where there was nothing but dangerous stormy seas? That in essence is why the Romans did not cross the Atlantic. There was no known reason for them to do so.

To me however it is likely that at some point well before the Viking age, either a Carthaginian, Roman, Basque, Breton, Greek or Irish ship would have been accidentally blown, or sailed on purpose, across the Atlantic and would have therefore become the first European/Punic discoverers of the new world. There is no proof or archeological evidence to back this up of course but the lack of evidence doesn't mean it didn't happen. We may just not have found the archeological remains and the crew just never made it back to tell their story. For hundreds of year's people believed Columbus was the first to discover the new world only to be usurped by the Viking discoveries at L'Anse aux Meadows, Newfoundland, in the 1960's.

Hyperborea is a Greek myth and means the land beyond the north wind. Numerous ancient authors have tried to locate Hyperborea suggesting wide ranging places such as north of Bulgaria, the Ural Mountains, Scandinavia, France, the Arctic, Siberia or even Britain. Its existence or location will never be known. On my cover map I have labelled all the unknown land north and west of Europe as Hyperborea because to me Hyperborea represents the mysterious unknown of the classical world and not a single geographical and physical place just like Pindar, the ancient Greek Poet suggests. In my book the actual route that the Hermes takes is north from Scotland towards the Faroe Islands, onwards to Iceland, then west across the Denmark Straight to Greenland and then south-west along the Greenland coast and across the Labrador Sea to the Canadian coast. From their first encounter with the natives the Hermes then sailed south through the strait of Belle Isle and along the Newfoundland coast whose native Indians painted themselves red, hence the old fashioned term "Red Indians". Finally the Hermes sails along the eastern coast of Nova Scotia until finally turning west towards Penobscot Bay in Maine.

In researching this novel I am grateful to the sailors and travelers in my family for their enthusiasm, suggestions and for giving me guidance on how sailing ships work. The book, Through the Pillars of Herakles – Greco-Roman Exploration of the Atlantic by Duane W Roller, also provided a fascinating read.

William Kelso

May 2016, London

37667413R00236

Printed in Great Britain
by Amazon